ONI UMESHU MOJITO

High Table Hijinks Book Four

CHRISTOPHER JOHNS

MOUNTAINDALE
PRESS

This book has two dedications. One is to my family, my beloved Queen of Darkness, my little warrior prince, and my precious princess. All of you make my life so much more full.

The second, is to Kaz. You better rock the fuck out of this treatment, man. I need both of my Phone Gnomes and there's plenty of Sketti and Pie to go round, sister. Starfox out.

ACKNOWLEDGMENTS

I want to take a moment to thank all of my awesome readers, the real fans and the OG Axe Druid fans for giving this series a shot and for being who you are. Without all of you, my gladiator editors, badass betas and powerful patrons, none of this would be possible, or nearly as fun.

CATCHING BACK UP

Marcus' rough end to his service in the Marines caused quite the galactic stir when his magic was awakened and Galaxy, *the* first goddess in existence, was found to be inside him after having chosen him as her vessel. If that's not enough for you to need a drink, then let's add a bit more bite to the cocktail that is the story so far.

Marcus began working at the High Table to lay low and earn a wage, but when Jolly the werewolf took his imbibing a bit too far and attacked the poor bartender, well, that was the outing that Marcus needed to know that something wasn't right at this bar. Except, it was. The High Table prided itself on serving supernatural creatures, monsters, myths, legends, and gods around the world, protecting the innocent humans from their wrath and boredom one drink and karaoke night at a time and for quite some time, it had worked.

Entering from stage left was the first spot of trouble for Marcus, his newly-gained oni girlfriend and Arden, his co-bartender who happened to be a flame jinn, managed to find themselves with a new drug called 'Divinity.' This amplified supernatural beings' powers and allowed humans to see the world as it truly was. All while breaking their minds and making them slaves to their addictions, plus slowly eating them from the inside out, magically speaking. But that's neither here nor there.

Marcus and his friends, joined by a Warden-in-Training named Merlin, managed to end the production and distribution of the drug that could have taken the world by storm in a matter of months, rescued Marcus' estranged and kidnapped son from the assholes who took him, and then killed a lot of people.

Then, Marcus and the gang went to the world of monsters, Grestal, where they hunted for the long lost Huntsman's Mantle to give new life to the Wild Hunt. The group navigated the world as best they could, even managing to pick up a cheetah woman named Amabala along the way. She could open portals for them, but it took a lot of ingenuity, more than a little Warden dodging, and a whole hell of a lot of blood being shed before they managed to succeed where so many untold others failed.

The rebirth of the Wild Hunt immediately brought concern to the world of monsters. And though Marcus and his friends meant no harm to anyone outright, except a certain drug making dickhead who managed to stay alive by being out of the way when his people were taken down, that stigma made it a little awkward around the High Table at first. But their work wasn't over in the slightest.

Dealing with the changes going on in his son's life, discovering he had strange magic of his own while being coerced into assisting in investigating a string of murders in Cairo, Marcus and his friends were stretched to their limits to try to figure out what was going on and who they could trust. Using the power of his bonds with the rest of the Hunt, their wits, and some good-old-fashioned fuck-you attitude, they managed to figure out who was behind the murders and just what it was that was hiding in the temple prison Galaxy had been interred in.

Discovering he had Vorna blood in his veins, those born of a place called the Null where Galaxy was born, Marcus and his goddess partner were able to steal back slivers of her Dominion —her god-like power—so that they could fight these new foes and stop the murders and the most active hunt for Galaxy, but all it did was open a new can of worms for the world.

A new face has joined the race and someone is out there killing gods, two of them so far, and their suspect is so overpowered that they may as well be the final boss invading the second area of the game the group played, for all they could have done to them.

After some much needed talking about it, a little time off, and much recuperation, the group finds themselves closing on a *very* special date. But that's for Marcus to reveal.

CHAPTER ONE

"God damn it, Cassia, will you just talk to me already?" I threw my hands up, rolling my eyes at the oni woman as I followed her into the gym proper. She already stood across the room with her arms crossed, her preternatural speed on display once again. I'd spent the majority of the morning working out trying to get her attention with better and better gains, showing her I'd gotten stronger, but to no avail.

"You shouldn't have done it, man." Arden grunted as she passed me with her phone in hand, likely texting Masonai. "That was cold blooded, and she really didn't expect you to do her dirty like that."

A deep growl reverberated in my chest before I bellowed, "I didn't *know* that the drop was that fucking rare and that *my* getting it meant that R-N-Gesus was going to fuck you over, okay? I'll give it to you if it means you'll stop giving me the cold shoulder!" She looked at me with her sunglasses secured to her head by a strap so they couldn't slip off and have her gaze turn anyone into stone. No words, just glaring. "Cass, *come on*, it's been a week. Please?"

She sighed deeply and walked across the gym floor toward

me until she was within five feet. "You can't give items of that rarity away, Marcus. You use it."

"What can I do to get you to just forget this?" I raised an eyebrow and finally just pushed my hands out and shrugged. "Fuck it, fuck it. I'll help you grind that thing until my eyes fucking bleed so that you can get it. Will that help?"

She stared at me and muttered shyly, which was weird for an oni that could bench press a semi, but she had her adorable moments. "You mean that?" She stared at me and I recalled once more why, in part, I hated our power as her glasses reflected my face back at me. "It took us so long, though."

"What's sixty-seven more tries in the grand scheme of things if it means my girlfriend will at least acknowledge my existence again?" I may have sounded annoyed, though I was actually looking forward to gaming with her again after she had been ignoring my existence for that week because of my fuck up. Honestly, it wasn't even my fault but the damn drop rate was abysmally tiny, and you just had to get certain items in this game or there was no getting that certain piece of gear you wanted.

The last three months, while tense for a majority of the people we knew, had been some of the best since I had come to Columbus, Ohio. Tense was a bit of an understatement, as the supernatural world around the High Table had essentially gone into lockdown with the murder of a second god. Likely the one that we had tried to rescue from the Vorna but had lost to that mysterious man-creature thing.

No one went anywhere alone, and it wasn't uncommon to see larger groups of Wardens roaming the streets looking for the perpetrating being. Even angels and angelic beings could be seen in the sky if you looked hard enough.

The High Table started to act as a hostel of sorts to all kinds of deities, and business was booming, though there were some people who were truly and rightfully afraid about how things were going. It was just like being on deployment again, which in a weird way I had missed. Hours changed with the need, and we worked hard to ensure that our mission was taken care of, our patrons were safe, and so were my friends and loved ones.

Then there had been the Brownie incident. Seamus was *pissed* that I had forgotten to get him the snacks I had promised, and as such had refused to clean for anyone. Laundry had piled up and I'd had to spend more than a grand on various kinds of chocolate and more than three hundred dollars on Buckeyes for the little creature from Goumas to get him to forgive me. The angry glares from the residents and the staff had been almost as threatening as the creatures we'd been fighting recently.

Hell, I'd have preferred the fight to the Brownie being so mad at me.

Being cooped up for so long was part of what had started all of us going to Grestal to hunt and amass experience more often. If there was a way to stop the threat, then we would find it and be a part of the solution.

"Hey!" Keith called from the doorway. "Council member wants to see us."

"Just call him Yen, God damn it!" Cassia snarled at the werewolf who snickered and ducked back out of the doorway. "Why does he have to push everyone's buttons all the time?"

"Because he's Keith?" Arden raised a brow and snorted. "You're talking about the same guy who thought it would be hilarious to throw shit at a dwarf because he said lycanthropes were just furries who got their wish."

"Jayvali didn't mean that," I quipped and Cassia coughed and nearly doubled over trying not to laugh. "He was drunk and it took some time to work Keith out of his beard."

This had taken place last month on one of our breaks from training, when we'd been able to convince the dwarven armorer to come to the bar and have a drink with us. He'd just forgiven me for fucking up Thumper and was talking about making me another rifle when our booze started to get a little more potent. About an hour later, he and Keith were bickering over how lycans and furries were different.

It had taken about an hour to separate the two without hurting anyone or my chances at a new and improved rifle.

"We better go and see what Yenny wants." Cass collected herself and stood up to her full height before taking human form and stretching out. "Good workout today, by the way. Your butt's looking thicker."

I raised an eyebrow at the green-haired woman, her pigtails bobbing in the air as she strode beside me in her workout clothes. The way her shirt hung almost artfully off her shoulder made her look like she was some sort of model.

She glanced up at me, grinning. "You're forgiven, but I can't do this fight without you. So as long as you keep your word, we will fight together. Deal?"

"I hope you mean what I think you mean." I smiled down at her and she nodded, pulling her handheld system from her inventory. "Sweet."

"We will scrap too," she added.

"Come on!" Arden roared behind us, her sour expression making both of us laugh.

Cassia cast a glance back her way. "It's not our fault that Masonai wants to wait for a few dates before he puts out."

"I think it's classy," I offered in observance. "Shows he really cares about you."

"You two are insufferable," she griped and crossed her arms. "He's so... sweet. Ever since I asked him out, he's been different but the same. It's weird. No other man has been like this."

"Just means he was a good friend before too." I smiled, deciding I should make sure to invite him out for a drink some time to tease Arden.

She will flay you, Marcus, Galaxy warned, then purred, *I love it.*

I chuckled to myself as she continued her gaming upstairs in my room. *Sorry, research.* My correction saved me from her feigned ire. We walked through the entrance and were met by a rather large crowd made up of security, bar staff, those gods who had decided to stay in the rooms we offered, and a number of our regular patrons.

Uncle Yen stood on the bar and whistled sharply. While the crowd calmed itself, he then spoke to everyone. "Now, I know that the last three months in this sort of panicked state have been hard on all of us, and the Council and I, as well as the Warden Orders, have been working hard to figure out what—or who—is behind these attacks on the gods. I think I speak for all of us when I say that I'm glad that they seem to have stopped."

"You're damn right!" someone hollered and Uncle Yen grinned.

He held up a steadying hand and the murmur that had arisen from the outburst died back down. "We think it's been long enough that we've hidden behind these walls, so we're calling the lockdown off—you can go back to living your relatively normal lives—" People began to speak and the noise grew to new heights, so I whistled shrilly along with Uncle Yen to get the peace back so he could add, "With the understanding that it may still not be safe. Nothing is perfect, nothing is promised, but if you protect yourself, you're more likely to be safe. Still travel when someone knows you will be. Go in pairs if you can, and go directly if you can't. I don't want to have to worry about who I might have to bury if someone neglects to protect themselves, am I clear?"

Keith piped up loudly, "Yes, Councilman Yenasi!" Uncle Yen made a gesture as if asking for something and three loud smacks echoed around the room as Keith growled, "Damn it! I'm just teasing the man."

"Muzzle it, Keith. He doesn't like having been bullied into being on the Council," Cassia snarled, then turned back to my uncle to smile and offer a brief, "Sorry."

Uncle Yen just shook his head. "It's okay, Cass." He sighed and appeared to grapple with himself before saying, "Serving with the Council is hell. I hate it. I do. If I could tell them to stick it up their asses and walk away, I would—best believe that." He grinned as the crowd grew rowdy again and then after he raised his hands, quieted down a moment later for him to continue. "But I get to get in there and duke it out for all of you. To make sure that we work for *you* as we always should be. If my being forced to suffer those fools hiding behind their titles and machinations will serve all of you, then I will do it gladly."

He smiled at us, then pointed a finger at Keith and growled, "But don't think I won't grab a newspaper and beat your behind, son. Don't think it!"

Keith's eyes flew open wide and he held his hands up. "I ain't no pup pissin' on the carpet, I swear!" He winked at Uncle Yen and the crowd chuckled. Everyone cheered as Yen lowered himself from the bar and Keith howled, "First drink's on Yen!"

"And it's out of *his* pay!" Uncle Yen countered and the bar cheered again, Keith even joining in good-naturedly. Uncle Yen found us in the crowd and winked, then stopped and stared at me. "You're not going into Grestal again, are you?"

I shook my head. "Once in the last couple days is enough, considering how hard we've been hitting it, Uncle Yen."

"Well, all of you going over there to hunt is just... weird." He shivered and sighed again. "Though I suppose a lot of things are weird now, and I can't really blame you for trying to grow stronger however it is that you can."

I couldn't blame him for worrying about us either. We'd been smart about it all, hunting in safe areas along the outskirts of the Forest of Fel Tidings in Grestal, though that didn't always a safe hunt make. Still, in the months that everyone had been locked down, we had used that time to our advantage as often as we could. As soon as we clocked out for our time off, we were in Grestal killing anything we could get our weapons into, and we had gained another level to show for it.

If only the creatures there hadn't wised up and hid from us, we would have had more, Galaxy grumbled through my mind. *I still don't know why you insist on not letting me just eat Normies. They can be quite annoying to deal with.*

I rolled my eyes and ignored her, her chuckling dark and

understanding. She knew why she couldn't eat them as much as she complained.

I hadn't spent my earned points for months just to piss off Arden, and to push myself to fight smarter, and to really get a feel for our bonds. Every fight was so much more intense because I was learning things as we went, and with the bonds being more difficult to manipulate, Galaxy and I were certain that by the time I did spend my stat points, it would be easier to work with them.

I was hoping that was the case, because if it wasn't, I'd wasted three months and I had a cat to skin.

Threatening a goddess? Galaxy purred through my mind and I could almost *feel* her tail swatting me within. *Come say that to my face.*

I shook my head. *You got it, kitty, but later.*

"Talking to her again?" Uncle Yen looked toward the stairs and I nodded. "You better work on that bearing of yours, son, it's starting to be a tell."

He chuckled and went to walk away, but Arden stopped him. "Yen, we're going on vacation." That stopped him and he froze. "Yenasi."

He turned back to her and raised an eyebrow teasingly. "Yes?"

"We're going on *vacation*, remember?" The emphasis that she put on it made me grin.

He narrowed his gaze, then snapped his fingers. "Oh, that's right!"

"Yen!" Cassia yelped with horror, surprising me.

He grinned. "I'm teasing. Odd, though, that you're adding Marcus to this as well. Arden told me that this trip has been planned for quite some time, and that you've looking forward to this as friends."

My eyebrows shot up this time. "I'm sorry, was this supposed to just be a girls' trip? Do I need to stay behind?" I knew the answer would be no, and I knew why. Secrets to keep and whatnot.

Cassia waggled her hand flippantly, seeing as though her eyes were safely hidden behind her enchanted sunglasses. "We were planning to go separately before we became friends. Then it turned into a contest to see who could do the most when we got there. I have a lot saved for this trip specifically, and though I know that we need to put money in for a lair, this takes priority for me. Plus, I will be able to bring almost everything home with me in my inventory for *free!*"

She turned to me and grinned. "You coming along is two-fold, honey bear." Uncle Yen snickered at her newest moniker for me. "You get to meet my family, and you get to hold my bags. Of which there will be many."

I rolled my eyes and almost decided to spill the beans then and there, but she smiled at me and grasped my chin. "Come now, it'll be so much fun. And besides, I cannot *wait* to show you some of the cosplays I've been working on."

"You cosplay?" Uncle Yen and I both asked at the same time. I looked at him and he looked at me before we both pointed at each other and said, "You know what cosplay is?"

I stayed quiet while he cleared his throat and tried to appear dignified before finally giving up on it to reply, "I fell in love with the art when conventions first became a thing. It was sparse at first, real sparse, but there was some real heart to it. Nowadays, the heart is sparse but the cosplayers are all over, so I remain hopeful." Uncle Yen stared at her and narrowed his eyes. "Who were you thinking?"

"I'm not telling, but I'll have Marcus take photos while we're at the con."

"We're going to a convention?" I raised an eyebrow at her and she just grinned. "But I didn't sign up for anything online."

"Comiket is free," Arden stated as she joined us. "We'll be arriving a few days before the event so that we can relax and then we will come home a few days to a week after that. Our return flights are flexible."

Do you think Cassia will figure it out? Galaxy grunted and cursed at something on the other end where she was upstairs.

Not if we don't give anything away—Arden's been planning this trip for about six months and adding me in was annoying enough. They both deserve this going off without a hitch. I stared at the women as they babbled about their favorite cosplayers to each other, several members of the staff and patrons staring at them in surprise or amusement. *Her friend is doing something huge from what Arden will tell us, and that's important enough for Cassia to have to be there. So we keep our damned mouths shut.*

"Oh, that sounds cool." Uncle Yen rubbed his chin and cleared his throat. "And remind me again, when does your vacation start?"

"Tomorrow!" Cassia clapped and the man just rolled his eyes at her, but she stopped him before he could say another word. "I took care of security, and since all the extra bodies will be clearing out in the next few days, we can modify the schedule with this new one so that no one is overworked and my duties can be shared between my betas and Jolly."

"Jolly volunteered?" She shook her head at his words and he growled. "I'm not going to be paying him to sit on his ass."

"I'll sit on yours if you want, old man." Jolly growled at Uncle Yen from behind, making the smaller man flinch, much to the alpha's enjoyment. "What's wrong, wolf got your tongue?"

Uncle Yen snorted and rolled his eyes. "Not you, that's for damn sure. You ain't my type."

Jolly grinned. "There's the fire. Thought the Council would've been trying to extinguish it by now."

Uncle Yen shook his head. "They're damn sure trying. But I'm too feisty." He crossed his arms. "What do you want for helping out, Jolly?"

Jolly's one arm came up and he scratched his head. "I'm strong, but I don't wanna fight no more." He cleared his throat and nodded. "I wanted to interview your pups and offer them the throne."

Uncle Yen's mouth dropped open and I was pretty sure I heard Cassia's jaw hit the ground, but I couldn't be sure because I was more concerned for him. "You're a badass, Jolly. What do you mean you don't want to fight anymore?"

"I'm tired, man." Jolly grunted and waved at the bar. "I love this place, and I'll help out all I'm able, but I don't think I can take all the fighting required to keep the title anymore if someone wants to come in and take the pack."

My uncle took a deep breath and grasped Jolly's hand. "Okay. But you do it your way. I only have one request."

Jolly raised a brow. "What's that?"

"It better not be Keith."

Jolly growled with laughter along with the rest of us and we all came together for a drink.

CHAPTER TWO

"How are you still standing?" Galaxy snarled into the mic of her headset as she jabbed at buttons on the controller in her hands. "Dieeeeeee!"

The person she was fighting against somehow managed to block her combo completely and return with the cheesiest low kick button mash that I had ever seen, killing her character before she could recover and block properly.

She yowled in fury and sprang to her feet. "Marcus! We need to go and find this person right now!"

Cassia leaned closer to me as I stood next to her and muttered, "Is it bad that I kind of regret showing her fighting games like this?"

"No, I regret you doing it too." I blinked at the other third of our relationship and frowned. "We can't go kill them just because they play cheap."

"It was the shit talking that bothered me!" She scowled and took her headset off. "Humans can be so... vile when they want to be."

"We really can." I grinned at her and held my hands out so

she would come to me and give me a hug. She was grumpy. "Have you eaten?"

"I ordered food from Cyrus, but I forgot to go get it." A knock on the door startled all of us and I turned to open the door to Arden holding a Styrofoam food container. "Thanks Arden."

"Yeah, yeah." She huffed and walked inside, closing the door quickly. "I think Masonai wants to come over to my place tonight."

"Okay?" I stared at her and she kind of nudged her head forward a bit. "And? Details, woman!"

"God, you're starting to sound like Luci." Arden hissed and stilled. "Oh no."

"Oh yes, Ardent Flame." Lucifer chuckled from the hallway, his voice muffled behind the door. "You've brought the devil. Now, do I need to huff and puff, or can I just come in?"

Arden was too busy hanging her head in embarrassment to open the door, so Cass reached around her and opened it for him to come in and join us.

Galaxy and I stepped back and sat on the bed for the coming show. *Is it too late for popcorn?*

Galaxy! I chided softly but kind of wished I'd had some of the buttery goodness to watch the show with as well. Galaxy hit me on the forearm softly but continued to stare forward.

"So, what's the issue with Masonai?" Lucifer asked with little introduction needed, likely because he had been aware of the situation for a while, since Arden liked to talk to him regularly, as did Cassia.

Now that I thought about it, the girls spoke to him more about guy things than we spoke to each other about girl things. For us, it was mainly shows, booze, music, and maybe the odd vacation spot. We typically veered toward safer topics, but it didn't feel like an awkward friendship to me.

Sure, he wasn't a Marine, but he felt like a friend? Maybe we would need to address that properly.

"He wants to see me tonight and I leave for Japan tomorrow

night!" She threw up her hands and flopped onto the bed beside Galaxy and I. "I like him, and he's a good man for a Normy."

"Ouch." Lucifer grumbled at her and she sighed knowingly. "Masonai has been your friend for years, Arden. He's not just a Normy, he's the man you've been developing feelings for. What is it that you truly worry about with him coming over to your house tonight?"

"That I'm going to mess it up and lose a friend and valued gaming buddy because I'm jealous of the relationships around me." Her dejected face said it all, and I felt bad. Genuinely bad because of the love that I had been getting recently.

"Arden…" Cassia stared at her friend with her hands held out in front of her. "You don't have anything to be jealous of from us."

Arden just growled and shook her head. "It's not just you! Some of the patrons have been hooking up, and then there's Amabala and Merlin and—"

My eyes widened and I leaned forward in shock. "Shut the fuck up!" I looked around at their shocked faces and said, "Are you for real?"

They nodded and Arden explained, "For about a month now. Did you seriously not know?"

"No!" I roared and hopped to my feet to move, the news startling. Without really having the time or open mind to really dwell on it, the news had surprised me a great deal more than I liked. "I just thought that they were spending so much time together researching portals and how to make a permanent one."

"Is their relationship not okay?" Galaxy asked, knowing damn well how I felt, but for the sake of the others, I decided to stop pacing and articulate my thoughts.

"No, nothing like that. I'm surprised? Actually, I'm really happy and kind of weirdly proud of Merlin for that?" I blinked at the others as more than one set of eyebrows raised in surprise. "Not for anything weird like that, just that he could get her. She's a good lady, and having gotten to know her a bit better, she's really kind and sweet and observant. I think they're a great match. He's just so awkward sometimes, you know?"

"Painfully," Arden purred and grinned. "But you're right, they're a great match. Which is why I worry about Masonai. I like him a lot, and I don't know if it could be love or just jealousy pushing me toward him."

"I don't think you're the type to truly be jealous of anyone," Lucifer murmured thoughtfully and stared at her. "You're the one I go to for relationship advice, and now look at you."

Arden put her face in her hands and groaned, "I *knooow*."

"Be brave, dearest friend." Lucifer leaned down and patted her shoulder softly. "Masonai is a good man. If there is anything that happens tonight that you regret, you'll regret never knowing more. Trust me."

"How are you so silver-tongued?" Arden growled and threw her hands up in defeat.

Lucifer chuckled. "All I'm doing is repeating things that *you've* told *me*, Arden." He pulled her up into a hug and squeezed her before pushing her back to arm's length to look at her. "How long do you have before he comes over?"

"A few hours or so?" She shrugged.

"Then why don't we go and get you a nice new sundress that men find so fascinating these days and see if we can't tempt him, shall we?" Luci grinned like the cat about to eat the canary. "Would that give you a boost of confidence?"

"Maybe a little liquid courage on the way out?" She raised an eyebrow and Lucifer nodded sagely. She turned back to us and said, "See you later. I'll let you know how it goes."

"You want me to make your drink?" She shook her head at me, and I shrugged. "Have fun."

Galaxy called, "And send us photos of the dress too!" The door closed and she smiled. "She said she will."

"Weird to see her so affected by this." I stared at the door as Cassia joined us on the bed and put a hand on my thigh.

"If I had known you for years before asking you to fight, I would have been nervous as well." Cass squeezed softly and added, "Especially if our interests and 'normal' lives were so closely linked as theirs. They play almost every game together and when they *don't* play the same game together, they're still in a party chat talking to each other—they almost eat, breathe, and sleep gaming. I've seen their relationship and I think that, even as a human, he is strong for her in the way that she needs."

Galaxy blinked and looked at her as if she had been struck. "Wait."

Cassia nodded. "You heard that right." She smiled and reiterated, "I think he is strong the way that *she* needs. Not me. I know that she can defend herself and him, if pressed, and I am content with that for now."

"I am so proud of you," Galaxy whispered and leaned over me to give her a kiss on the cheek.

"You aren't the only one who has been doing some soul searching these last three months, Galaxy." Cassia grinned, her hand snatching her chin into her grasp so that she could kiss the other woman. "I've been thinking of a great many things, and I like the way things are, don't you?"

Galaxy nodded and replied, "I do, indeed. But you know what this night needs?"

"A shower, shower beer, nachos, cuddles, and anime?" I piped up and both women turned my way. "Okay, sorry. Shower, shower cocktails, *pizza*, cuddles, and anime."

They both grinned and Cassia said, "It's like he knows us."

"He just wants a scrap." Galaxy waggled her eyebrows playfully and I grunted as Cassia shoved me backward and growled, "Let's see about that."

———

I reached out and grabbed another slice of pizza as the protagonist on screen climbed back up to his feet while the villain monologued and droned on. So simple. Who let someone do that shit?

"I know, right?" Galaxy muttered and dipped her slice in some ranch before taking a bite. "Just kill him."

"It's anime, guys." Cassia sighed and turned to look toward us, but not directly at us with her glasses off. "It's shonen anime, too, so there's a lot of talk and a lot of fighting. Do you want to pick the next one?"

"Kind of?" I said with a smile. "There's one called 'My Love Story' that sounds like a lot of fun."

"You're such a romantic!" Cassia cried and slung a pillow backward toward me, hitting me in the face. "I want something with fighting, and power!"

"Dude is huge, so I think it's okay."

"Fine!" Galaxy grunted and whacked me with her own pillow. We watched some more of the episode before my phone rang. I looked at it and it was Luca's phone number.

I stepped into the bathroom. "Hello?"

"Marcus, so glad that I caught you!" Luca sounded exhausted. "I got your messages and wanted to let you know that Conellar is safe, and his magic has been behaving so far."

"Did you get my questions?"

"I did." His voice turned muffled momentarily and he came back. "Sorry, we are on the move for now and there are a lot of moving parts. Your questions, he retains the magic for a short period of time, then it seems to dissipate on its own, so if he were to take some of your ice magic and his power ate it, he would have your magic for a time of about half an hour now. Otherwise, his magic does what it wants to when it's... *hungry*?"

"That's concerning." I grumbled and shook my head, focusing on Connell. "How's he taking it?"

"Is it weird for a young child to be enamored with their magic one minute, then be repulsed by it based on how it consumes things that the child likes the next?" Luca chuckled to himself, but I said nothing, because I had no idea. "Forgive me, things have been tense. He seems fine, but when it eats, it eats anything it can. He worries now that it might try to consume one of us if we become complacent."

"That's not good," I muttered and tried to take a deeper breath to get a hold of myself. "You know, if you need me to, I can come and try to see if I can help figure it out. I told you it likely had something to do with my bloodline relation to a weird creature, right?"

"I recall, but there is nothing that you would be able to do other than give him one more thing to worry about." He must've been able to sense my discomfort, because he said, "Relax, Marcus. Our best are looking into this, and I have even called in a few favors to have some people search wider. We're going to make sure he's okay. For right now, we need you safe and keeping the fear in certain unsavory types."

"Someone you have in mind?" I raised an eyebrow at his tone.

"The Seelie have been on the move against my people for some reason. They claim that the Unseelie have been attacking them around the world and have begun to investigate and retaliate in kind." He said something away from the phone again, then came back. "Annoyingly enough, I truly do believe that it is the Unseelie doing it, but I cannot prove that they are our people."

I had an idea of who it could be, but my oath with him made it so that I couldn't interfere in his business without painting a target on the people I held dear and myself. "That's a really weird issue to have."

"It is." He sighed and remained quiet a second before saying, "I think we will need to be moving again soon. If we need you, I will call. Conellar wished for me to tell you he said, 'hey,' and that I pass on that he schooled me in training the other day."

"Did he?" I chuckled a little bit.

"No, but it never hurts to let a boy dream, does it?" Luca laughed and said, "Goodbye, Marcus. Have fun on your trip, and try not to worry over the boy. He is the tough sort."

"Thanks, Luca. Have a good one, and call me at the earliest sign of trouble."

"Of course, good luck."

The line went dead and I hung in the bathroom for a moment, trying to think of how to tell the others about what was going on and if I should talk to Zeke about this.

His war against the Seelie is starting to affect my son's safety, isn't it?

It could be, call him. Galaxy spoke clearly and concisely, but added, *Maybe don't accuse the man who could appear here and kill us without a second thought, though. I'd hate to piss him off for no reason, you know?*

Yeah. I unlocked my phone and pulled up his number, pressing talk. The phone rang a couple times and when the line picked up, I said, "Hey man, you busy?"

"I really prefer a handwritten message over talking on the phone, but nah—what's up, bud?"

"I just got off the phone with the prince of the Unseelie Fae. He said that the Seelie have been attacked by Fae claiming to be Unseelie?" The man on the other end of the line remained silent for too long and I asked, "I suspect they could be your Fae, and while I'm all about your people kicking their asses, it's starting to affect my son."

"I remember our agreement, Marcus." He sounded cool despite what I was saying. "I also have people watching over Connell, Aeslyn, and Luca as we speak. They're safe, I mean that. Anything happens, I'll step in and protect them because—to me—they're mine. I'm sorry that the Seelie are bothering them, but they've been a nuisance for far too long and it's time to end them."

"Are you going to war?" It was hard to keep my heart from pounding as I asked the question.

What I hadn't been expecting was for him to just laugh, and say, "War would mean that they stood a chance of winning, Marcus. I'm playing for keeps, and I'm going to wipe the floor with them so I get what I want. If you see any out there, let me know and I can come bop them for you, okay?"

I blinked and uttered, "Yeah, man. Sure."

"Seriously, bud, the boy is safe." He was quiet for a second then added, "I forgot about the shadows manipulating classes! Shit! When are you free?"

"I'm heading to Japan tomorrow for about a week or more, so there's really no time between now and then that I can meet up with you." I thought about it and asked, "I can call you when I come back?"

"Yeah, man, do that." He sounded like he was smiling. "Stay safe out there, okay? Oh, and watch yourself. Travel abroad can be weird enough, but I've heard of some supernatural creatures being *really* territorial."

"Really?" Then I remembered him almost killing us all for trespassing in his territory. Then there had been the Harpy pirates on the way to Cairo. "Yeah. Yeah, there are. But you've had dealings with some?"

"Yeah, I've run into a couple that think anything they see belongs to them." He sounded like a grin had spread across his face as he continued speaking. "They learned the hard way that isn't the case, but you'll be the one doing the trespassing there, so just be careful, yeah?"

I nodded. "Sure thing. Have a good one, and you be safe too."

"Count on it, brother. Later." He hung up and I just looked at the phone for a moment. He was pretty... him. I knew a lot of Marines who were the same way.

"Marcus, we have a problem!" Cassia bellowed and I opened the door and almost ran into her.

"What?" I looked around and she smiled, making me frown. "*What?*"

"We've run out of snacks." Galaxy smiled over at me, peeking from behind Cassia. "We've voted, and you're to go and get some."

I rolled my eyes. "Does that mean I'm borrowing Baby?"

Cassia, eyes safely hidden behind her glasses now, snorted. "Hardly."

I rolled my eyes and muttered to Mako, "Looks like we get to go to the store together, little fella."

His body, a shadowy figure made of mana that looked like a tattoo on my forearm, wriggled and tickled me a little bit as I stalked past Cassia to get to my shoes. "Text me what you want."

My phone vibrated as I finished speaking and just let my head fall forward. "Did I even have a chance of not going?"

"No." Cassia giggled and grabbed me from behind. "But if you get me what I want, we can always go again?"

I snorted and Galaxy laughed. "Okay, be back soon as I can."

"Fine, fine," Cassia said, looking like she was considering something. "Find what I want, and I'll let you choose what we watch before we go to bed, okay?"

I grinned back at her. "You're on." She laughed as I gave her a peck on the cheek and threw my zip up on over my t-shirt, heading out the door with my wallet in my inventory.

Through the crowded, boisterously noisy bar and all the people who tried to stop me for a drink, I finally made it out onto the street. The security eyed me with the line full of students—who wouldn't be getting in tonight, just like they didn't every other single night because this wasn't a normal bar—eyeing me as well. The former because they knew me and were curious, the latter because they were hopeful I might let them in.

"Yo. Be back in a bit, I'm on a snack run." I turned to leave, then paused and turned back. "You want anything, Sabbath?"

The hulking mass of muscle stepped out from the corner of the building and grinned at me. "A Twinkie, maybe? Or something with honey." He looked at the security by the door bouncing and said, "You want anything?"

"I'm good, bubba, thanks though." The bouncer there grinned and turned to a particularly pushy kid who tried to sneak past him, growling, "Ain't I tell you kids ain't allowed?"

The boy whined and walked away when the bigger men glared at him.

I snorted and took off at a run, calling the power of the

Mantle around myself before summoning Mako. With the power of the Mantle as a cloak, no Normies should be able to see us.

That made the trip to Target for some necessities, and then to a nearby gas station for the rest of the snacks that I couldn't find at the other store, easier.

"Man, no fucking way!" Someone shouted near me loud enough to grab my attention. I poked my head around the candy bar aisle and found myself staring at three people enraptured by a phone screen. I was mainly just glad it hadn't been a fight about to happen.

I'd have stepped in to help, but it would have taken some serious discipline not to kill one of them by accident. I scooped up enough sugar to give the two ladies diabetes and even managed to grab a few packets of Twinkies—one for me and the others for the mountainous Sabbath.

I walked back over to the pop section and just shoved bottle after bottle into the damn shopping basket I carried in my left hand so that Galaxy hopefully would be satisfied, especially if anything came up. This way she should at least be good. Cassia was a little more simple, she just liked things with peanuts and caramel, then salty things like chips too.

I referenced my phone and shrugged, knowing they'd been intentionally vague. I would still have plenty of time to binge some of the anime I wanted on the flight to Japan the following evening, so all was good. I also made sure to grab some snacks for Seamus. The brownie had been putting in overtime with our bloodied and soiled clothes whenever we returned to the Table after a fight, or whenever Arden's washing machine busted because of the use.

Because apparently a lot of monster blood is bad for a washer and dryer? Who would have thought of that? But that didn't bother Seamus. Oh, no. That brownie cleaned the shit out of almost anything we gave him and never uttered a single complaint.

So I got him some buckeyes, a few fudge pops, and a can of mocha Monster.

The last one I wasn't so sure about, but all the other monsters in my life loved caffeine so why not him?

I walked up to the counter while the small crowd there watched something over and over, speculating wildly. "Dude, there's no way that's not CGI or some shit."

It was hard to see over their shoulders and the screen was small so I just cleared my throat. "Sorry guys, but I have some very hungry people waiting on me."

"Oh, yeah, sorry, no problem, man." The clerk, a younger-looking kid in his late teens shooed his friends to the side of the counter and began to ring me up. He frowned and said, "Sure you're not having a party or something?"

"Just some late night cuddles." I grinned and he shook his head. I turned to the other two who were quiet and shyly watching. They didn't look out of the ordinary, so I lost interest pretty quickly.

I paid my hefty fee for the snacks and left the gas station as they came back together. "Dude, seriously, he lifts the car up and fucking tosses it. That's some comic-book shit."

"There's no way it's not some kind of trick, man, come on." The words faded a bit as they watched again. "See? Tail and all."

That got my attention, but other than trying to see what they were talking about myself and potentially looking weird, or drawing more attention to myself, I left it alone.

Walking around the side of the building toward a darkened street, I put the groceries into my inventory with a thought and summoned Mako and the Mantle once more to go home.

On my way, I watched for anything that could be a threat, though the sky and streets below were fairly empty. Which was nice for a change. As we closed in on the campus area, there was more activity, but nothing too far outside of the norm, and that was good considering we would be leaving.

Amabala and Merlin would be staying behind to research

and I guess spend more time together, which was good. If we needed them, Amabala could always just have Galaxy read one of our minds and give her all of the necessary information to get to Japan. A nice vacation and surprise for Cassia could be considered a godsend after everything we had been through in such a short time.

For a change, I was really looking forward to something like this—and the flight wasn't as daunting this time.

CHAPTER THREE

Arden was a no show for the morning when we were supposed to meet and have breakfast, so Cassia decided. "If she's not here in ten more minutes, we're going to her place."

"You can't just settle for calling her?" I raised an eyebrow at her over my coffee. The diner across the street from the Table had some of the best breakfast food, and their coffee wasn't the worst I'd ever had, either. Marines were known for putting terrible shit in their coffee. I'd even heard of some using Redbull in it, and that was just a terrible idea.

"No, what if she needs help hiding him for rejecting her?" she replied and took a bite of her sausage and gravy. She swallowed and grinned at my mock horror. "I like Masonai, but if he hurt her and she killed him, I would understand."

I shook my head. "Y'all are some damn savages." She laughed at that and Galaxy bit into a biscuit and moaned. "Good?"

"Grape jelly is *so* good." She purred and put yet another small packet on the biscuit. Could've been her third or fourth, who was counting? She stared at me pointedly. "You are, so stop counting."

I chuckled and took another sip of my coffee, looking out the window, my food already eaten, and another couple plates on the way. My appetite seemed so much more unreal with all the changes to myself.

Your magic is growing, and something about your Vorna blood makes you hungrier too. Especially after having stolen a dominion.

I nodded and my latest order arrived; several flapjacks, a bit of sausage biscuits and gravy slapped on a small plate over some scrambled eggs, and a couple slices of toast. It all looked divine as I lifted my fork in salute to our waitress. "Don't stuff yourself too full, okay?"

We laughed and Cassia just grinned. "He can put it all away. I'd invite you to watch, but it may nauseate you."

I rolled my eyes. "Thanks." Once she was gone, I shoved a couple more bites into my mouth and grunted; it was hot, but so damned good. I finished my bite and swallowed. "I'll be sure to leave a good tip, as this place is just so amazing. I still can't get over how good it is."

"Their whole business is here *because* of us." Cassia laughed and took another sip of her drink. "Did your uncle ever tell you the owner and he go way back? The idea was to build a place where all the staff could come and have a hot meal when our kitchens were closed."

"That was an intelligent business idea." Galaxy purred as she picked up the other half of her biscuit, scanning the table for more jelly and finding the grape all gone. I rolled my eyes and slid her the strawberry, and her eyes lit up. "Thank you."

I tossed my chin up as a reply and she slapped a couple of the little packets onto the biscuit and bit into it. Her eyes rolled up and I was a little worried she was going to cry out, but instead she whispered, "Oh, sweet strawberry. Where have you been all these millennia?"

"That's it, I'm calling her." Cassia growled and pulled her phone from her pocket just as it vibrated. She pressed the screen once and held the phone to her ear. "Dude, I was just about to call you."

She listened quietly for a moment then grunted, "On our way." She looked at us and stated, "Arden needs us, there's something that Masonai showed her that's concerning."

Galaxy's eyes widened. "Is he married?" She looked at Cassia and the oni just blinked at her, "I'm trying not to read your mind as much. Sorry. Let's get this to go?"

Cassia nodded and we hailed our waitress for to-go boxes and took off in her SUV for Arden's place.

Her house, nestled into Zeke's territory, was where the majority of us had been sleeping for the last three months when we weren't hunting in Grestal or at work.

Except for when we let Arden have some much needed privacy so she could see her man.

When we arrived at the house, the massiveness of it still got to me, even after the last few months of having been in and out of the place often.

There was another vehicle I didn't recognize in the drive and a motorcycle as well. I frowned at that and headed inside without knocking. Arden called out, "In the dining room."

We walked down the hall and hung a left into the large dining room where we found Arden, Amabala, Merlin, and Masonai waiting.

Arden wore a soft green crop top over some jean shorts that showed off her long, toned legs. The top went well with her flaming red hair. "Hey."

I nodded to her and said, "Yo." I looked over to Masonai. The dark-skinned man grinned back at me, his hair a little longer than when I had first met him, but it was still faded well from the bottom up. "Oh, sporting a low-regs cut? Ballsy for the Army little guy."

"This is serious, Marcus." Arden growled and Masonai poked her with a crooked finger. "What? It is."

"Doesn't mean I can't say hi before we get into it, damn." Masonai rolled his eyes and offered me his hand across the table. "How's it going, Marcus?"

"I guess not as good as I had thought?" I shrugged and he

just shook his head as I turned my gaze pointedly to the jinn on his left. "What's so important that it couldn't wait for pleasantries?"

"This?" She waved a hand at the wall behind me. I turned to find an image from a projector in the ceiling that I had somehow *never* noticed until now. Though we did eat the majority of our meals while drinking or gaming.

On the screen was a slightly blurry image of a person holding a car above their head like they were some kind of fucking superhero. It buffered for a second before playing, the person in the image throwing the car like it was no more than an inconvenience.

"It looks computer generated to me." I shrugged and turned back to them but Masonai shook his head. "What?"

"I took that video, Marcus." He breathed about the same time I did, and nodded. "My phone is shit and I need a new one, I know, but I've not had the money before. I think I will now."

Arden crossed her arms and lifted her chin. "Yes, you will."

I raised an eyebrow at that, then shook my head and leveled my gaze at Masonai. "You're sure you're not fucking with us? This isn't an elaborate-ass prank?"

He shook his head. "Soon as I took it, I had to get the hell out of there, and to someone I trusted. That was Arden." He looked up at her, confused. "Though I don't really know why you called the rest of them here."

She closed her eyes and Galaxy spoke to what I assumed was the rest of us, *She wants to know if it's okay to tell him.*

I sent a mental shrug, then looked at Merlin. *He says he has enough components for one last casting, but then he has to get more. Apparently getting components with Xehano gone is a bit more tiresome.*

Arden spoke softly and calmly as she motioned to the screen. "Because they, like me, can do those kinds of things." The man's face went from confused to hurt, then to angry. When he opened his mouth to speak, she held a finger up to his mouth and hushed him.

Arden held out her hand and with a soft squint of her eyes, her entire being exploded into flames, but not a thing around her was affected by it. Her hair ablaze and her body covered in barely-visible flames, her hand had a globule of water just above it. "Masonai, the world around you is so much more broad and unknown than you think."

He opened his mouth and closed it before he looked at the rest of us. "If this is some kind of projected image or some shit, you need to knock it the fuck off. I was serious with this video."

"And so is she," Merlin stated calmly, flexing his hand so that his staff and sword appeared. "This isn't some LARPing event, the only projection system in this room is pointed at the wall, and you're surrounded by supernatural beings."

"Please don't freak out." Cassia spoke in a low tone, but she remained in her human form, likely so that she didn't scare the hell out of him.

"Okay, magic tricks are cool and all, but I'm not going to sit here and be made a fool of." He stood up and made to leave, but I stood in front of him in an instant. I got there so fast that he bounced off me and back onto the ground with a solid thud. He'd hit his head on the floor pretty hard and looked to be unconscious.

"Marcus, what the fuck?" Arden snarled and moved around the table to attend to the man. "Did you have to use that spell?"

"No, but it was a way to prove that we are what we say we are." I scratched my head and couldn't keep myself from making the small poke at his service. "Not my fault the Army doesn't make something that can penetrate well. That's why the Marines are here."

"He penetrates perfectly fine, thank you." She growled, then realized what she said and the blush that crept over her face was only matched by the dawning of what she had said on our faces. "Wait. No—"

"Yes!" Cassia roared and startled all of us. Our gazes flew to her and she just stood there in the corner wriggling and writhing happily, no cares on her face as she said, "I knew it! I knew it, knew it, knew it."

She grinned at Arden, whose face had almost turned blue with how hot she was, and said, "Congratulations."

"Would you grow up?" Arden cried exasperatedly before swearing under her breath.

"I'm grown as hell." Cassia huffed and folded her arms under her chest. "I mean, you're the one getting embarrassed about a scrap."

Arden ignored her and looked at Merlin. "This is getting us nowhere, and we're going to lose him if he wakes back up with the memories of what just happened. Can you use that spell to make it so that us telling him this is easier on him?"

Merlin thought about it for a moment, grimacing and staring at the man who lay unconscious by the table. "I could, in theory, help ease the blow and it might make him a little more accepting."

I frowned. "I sense a 'but' coming."

Merlin nodded once. "But with his head injury just now, it could do more harm than good." He ran his hands through his mop of hair and sighed. "We could try to heal it with Cassia's magic, but there's no way to really know with the brain. He's a Normy. They're not as good at taking the weird with the normal stuff, Arden."

"Let's try the healing magic anyway." Cassia grunted as she knelt by the man, not really because it took any effort, but because she accidentally moved the heavy table when she bumped it. "Whoops. Sorry. Here we go."

She put a finger out and flicked Masonai in the center of the forehead. Arden slapped her in the back of the head and she muttered, "Hey!"

Masonai started awake and looked around blearily. "What happened? Why am I on the floor?"

"You were getting ready to—" Merlin started to explain, but Amabala put a hand on his chest and shook her head.

"You were going to get something to eat with us, and listen

to what it was that we had to tell you about that video." She smiled and he relaxed a little. "You have blood sugar issues? You got up so fast and when you tried to clear the table, you just keeled over. You okay?"

Why is she suddenly smoother than ice cream? I asked Galaxy and the woman just shrugged.

She's calming him pretty effectively. His heartbeat had been so erratic when he came to, and now it's slowing down. She's learned much in the time we've had here on Earth without someone actively trying to kill us.

"I don't think I do, no." He rubbed the spot that Cassia flicked and gave her a weird look. "Did you flick me?"

She smiled. "Yup. Had to make sure my buddy was safe."

He snorted and shook his head. As he looked around, I asked, "You okay? You weren't out for long but do you feel like you need medical attention?"

He shook his head. "Few minutes before I woke up are a little fuzzy, but there's no ringing or anything, and I can feel all my toes and fingers. I thought we were having an argument."

"We were," Merlin said, but this time when Amabala tried to stop him, he smiled and added, "You said you wanted to pick the place to eat and I got a little heated with you. I'm sorry."

Is this blatant lying doing anything for him?

It is, Galaxy answered. *Merlin plans to use the spell on him when he's absolutely certain that it will help and not be a danger to Masonai, his mental state and well-being, but it will take some time.*

Do they have it?

She nodded once after they walked past us and I waved goodbye. Once they were clear of us and out of the house, I sighed. "That was almost a disaster."

"Tell me about it." Cassia leaned up against the table. "I was wondering how he would take it, but the way she told him was wrong for people of this day and age."

"And you could have done better?" I was teasing, honestly, but her shaking her head to say no, surprised me. "What do you mean, 'no'?"

"No. I couldn't have." She grinned at me. "Jolly freaking out and attacking you worked to my benefit because of how attracted to you I was at the time. I got really lucky."

"Aww!" Masonai's voice behind me startled us both and I turned to find him standing in the doorway. "You two are so cute together. Have fun in Japan! Arden will be at the flight once she can make sure I'm okay. She promised to get me some manga, Cass, so don't let her forget to get it, okay?"

"You got it!" She smiled back nervously, the look on her face clearly wondering how long he had been there.

He smiled wider and turned around with Amabala in the doorway smiling at him while Galaxy explained, *About when she had said she was lucky Jolly attacked you. So we're good there. He's still a little out of it.*

I nodded and grunted. "Let's get the fuck out of here before they come back again."

Cassia nodded and I offered her my arm. She took it and asked, "Did you pack everything?"

"Yup!" I smiled as I walked toward the door.

"Mister Quacks?" She raised an eyebrow and I pulled him from my inventory with a flourish. "Oh, you're good."

"You can take him for a shower if you like," I offered innocently. "He likes to stand guard."

"Could use more security staff like him." Cassia snorted and we were on our way to relax at the Table before our flight later.

CHAPTER FOUR

The flight had been long, but it was first class so it wasn't unbearable, and true to my word, almost the entire flight there, I had helped Cassia—with the help of Arden and Galaxy—grind for the item I had unfairly 'stolen' from her. It took us nearly sixteen times in that same mission, against that same monster, to get the damn thing, and I was so glad for it to be done.

"Okay, and now we need to get the armor set that Arden needs." I rolled my eyes and turned my gaze to her as Cassia said, "That item is just a little less hard to get than the one that I needed."

I rolled my eyes again at her and she just snorted. "Come on, let's go again!"

The PA system dinged overhead, the pilot speaking casually. "Welcome, everyone, to the Land of the Rising Sun. It's been a pleasure to see all of you here, and thank you for such a nice flight. We'll be touching down at the Haneda Airport within another ten minutes or so, then we will get you all to the gate. Thank you for flying with us, and Nihon e yōkoso."

"Oh, his pronunciation is pretty good, he must fly here a

lot," Cassia observed politely as the plane quieted back down. She stared down at her game disappointedly and sighed. "Better save and get ready to go."

We both did as she had suggested and sat for a moment before the thought occurred to me that I had no idea how Masonai was. I leaned over and asked Arden, "So what happened when y'all went out to eat?"

"We watched him for a while and when he had this look of shocked horror come over his face, we kind of thought that he had been able to work through his fog of things." She sighed and watched the staff buckle themselves in for a second before adding, "Merlin followed him to the bathroom to 'make sure he was okay' then hit him with the old razzle dazzle and now he's been made much more receptive to the supernatural. Not to the point that he knows who and what we are, but that he has a more open mind than before."

"And are you dating?" Cassia asked suddenly with a grin almost splitting her face.

Arden's eyes widened and she blushed a bit. "Well, I'm not going to let just any man tup me, am I?"

That made Cass frown. "Why not? Strong men are fun to fight with."

I raised an eyebrow and she waved me off. "I'm a freak for what I've become with you and Galaxy, Marcus. Most oni aren't monogamous as it is. They find the strongest they can and fight with them. It's the best way to have the strongest offspring."

"Well, that's harsh." I grunted and Galaxy chuckled from where she sat across from us, earning her a look as well. "I suppose you're okay with the freak part?"

Galaxy purred, much to my surprise. "Why wouldn't I be?"

"Crowded plane?" Arden hissed and motioned broadly.

The goddess just shook her head and said, "Anyone listening in is in the wrong and deserves to be a little disgusted." She stared pointedly at the back of the seat in front of her before adding, "Cassia is right though. Her people prize strength over all else, and emotion is left in the back of the mind where children are concerned normally. So, the fact that she's chosen someone she feels is strong now to bind herself to is truly amazing."

Arden groaned. "Ugh, what is it with you people and your minds?"

"Just answer the question," Cassia said lightly.

"We are, though for right now we're taking things slow as far as the relationship is concerned." She blushed and threw her hands over her face as if to hide herself. "I was so excited I kind of jumped him and he went with it. It was his... first time."

"Oh my God!" Someone in front of us gasped and all of us just turned and stared, Arden nearly crying out from the embarrassment.

I found that strange due to how she had acted before around me. Never overtly sexual, sort of close to it, but never crossing a line? It was weird.

She was raised very traditionally jinn. They marry and have children. The fact that she's only married once, to a human who she mourned for centuries after his passing, and is now with another is surprising and odd for her. The goddess paused as we landed and sighed with relief before adding, *The fact that she had considered you was strange for her kind, but she wants to love again. We cannot begrudge her that.*

Would you consider adding Masonai to the fold? She shook her head and I gathered why. *He wouldn't survive it, would he?*

She shook her head and I left it at that. The look of sorrow on her face was enough to allow her to evade any further questions on the matter, at least for now.

About ten minutes of Cassia and Arden bickering back and forth like crazed children found us safely at the gate where the crew allowed us to collect our bags—small packs in the overhead bin just to keep up appearances that we were tourists. *We are, Marcus. This isn't a work trip. We're here to have fun and reunite Cassia with an old friend.*

I tried to relax a bit more, but it just felt a little stifling in the airport. American passengers got off the plane and hustled and bustled while a lot of the Japanese folks around us were quiet and respectful. With the size of the place, one might think that with the space there would be at least a dull roar, but instead it came from us.

"I'm gonna go get changed real fast, okay?" Cassia waved at us and we shrugged. I was wondering why she was going to go and change here, but it was her choice to do so.

About ten minutes later, a woman walked out of the bathroom that I didn't recognize but her aura was the exact same as Cassia's. She was a five-foot-three Japanese woman in her twenties like Cassia had been in her American form. It was odd to me that she would change in the first place, but when she looked at me, I could clearly see Cass in there.

Her hair was a vivid pink with green highlights that screamed main character from any anime, spiky and long at the same time. She winked at me. "Like it?"

"Am I about to die so that you can go and save the world?"

She snorted. "Hardly. Let's go get a drink!"

It was early back home, but here it was early afternoon, so we opted to go check into the hotel before grabbing food and drinks.

Even for someone wearing a Japanese form, Cassia got quite a few looks from all of the people we passed in the area before we found a taxi that would take us to our hotel. The city was beautiful, and there were folks everywhere.

"Ota City is a really nice place," Cassia observed as she stared out the window. "Much nicer than the last time I was here, but that's okay."

"It looks like a pretty bustling place," I stated as I watched her. She didn't look depressed or anything, but that wasn't to say that being back in her homeland wasn't a bit much for her after being away for so long.

"Yeah, it's the tech place of Japan, if their website is to be trusted," Arden added. "I guess a lot of companies have parts made here, or something. Hell, I'm pretty sure game companies like Bandai and Sega do. What was it when you were here, Cass?"

"A fishing village," Cass muttered, then looked back at us. "I appreciate the interest in our culture, and I want to discuss it, but let's just enjoy it first before we really get into the nuts and bolts of the history and people, okay?"

"Okay," I said to her and put a hand on her leg. She flexed her quad and smiled at me. "You alright?"

She nodded. "Just different is all." She sighed and her smile softened considerably. "The changes are just so... unreal. It's one thing to read about it and see it in anime, but to truly experience how life here has become so different from the era I grew up in is just intense."

Arden and I nodded, glad that there was a barrier between us and the driver that kept us from being overheard.

"So when do we meet your sister?" I asked and she looked over at me. "I'm a little nervous."

"We can worry about that later." She smiled and this time it was genuine. "We will be stopping at the Table here this evening for dinner, though. I hear that their sushi is some of the best and I have to have some."

I grinned. "You got it."

The ride there had been uneventful enough, though Cassia said that the driver had warned her about watching the streets at night for gang activity in the area, but Cass hadn't been worried. Why would we be?

Our hotel room was simply amazing and all thoughts of anything else were shoved out right away.

It could have qualified as more of an apartment to me, honestly. There was a small balcony that opened up to the city with two doors that slid to the side and then inward around a set of small tables in the dining area with a small kitchen as well.

"It has its own rice cooker!" Arden whispered happily as she explored the room just before Cassia and me.

We came in next, equally amazed at the anime-inspired rice cooker being available, and then there was the room.

"You both can have the master suite and I'll take the pull out couch." Arden had popped around the corner and surprised us both, then ran over to pull the couch out to make it a bed. It was easily as big as a full-size bed. "When did you want to head out, Cassia?"

"Soon as we drop our stuff off and shower should be fine." She walked a little further into the room and looked around. "Go ahead and take a shower, Arden. I need to talk to Marcus."

She made it sound like it was some kind of bad thing, and Arden just shrugged before going off to where the bathroom was and squealing, "It's so tiny!"

"That's the best kind." Cassia grunted, then grinned. "More intimate that way."

Arden huffed and went in to figure things out on her own before Cassia turned to me and nodded toward the bedroom.

I walked in, the bed easily taking most of the size away from the rest of the room. The walls weren't far from the outside of the bed at all. There was maybe a foot to a foot and a half of room to move that wasn't bed. But the sheets and the comforter were very nice.

"They gave us an actual mattress? I was hoping for a futon we could share, like my room." She shrugged to herself and sat on the bed, patting it. "Come sit, and Galaxy, you can join us."

I did as she asked and sat beside her so that she could speak to me. "My mother and my sister are a little weirded out by our whole situation." She grunted and huffed, "Galaxy!"

"Sorry!" She appeared in the doorway to the room and offered a contrite smile. "I've been exploring and I cannot tell you enough how nice this place is. Very cat friendly."

"A lot of people in Japan are. Get in here, we're having a serious talk." Galaxy made an O with her mouth and joined us on the bed, there being just enough room for all of us to sit with the two of us sitting on the edge. "Guess I won't be spreading out in my oni form."

"That's unfortunate," I grumbled, genuinely upset. Although her oni form could be intimidating, it was her, and I was still attracted to that real side of her too.

"Focus." Galaxy swatted my shoulder and grinned at me. *I agree, though.*

I rolled my eyes and Cassia sighed. "Mother and my sister don't fully approve of our relationship. They think I'm keeping you, and while that isn't unheard of among our kind, it's odd that I don't have more mates unless you're *really* strong."

"He is the Huntsman," Galaxy said as if that were the only explanation.

"They don't care." Cassia shrugged. "The last one fell and they know that Marcus is only 'just Touched' and to them, he has to be able to back up the power that would be required for him to keep *me*."

"I'm going to have to fight some people, aren't I." Not a question and she just nodded anyway, confirming what I had known the moment she said she was introducing me to her family.

Kenshi took great pleasure in beating my ass, though lately the fights weren't so one-sided and that was good, especially for not having spent any of my points from the level I had gained.

"They may test you themselves, or they might have someone test you. Either way, I need you to know this." She sighed and crossed her arms, looking at the bed before lifting her gaze and staring me in the eyes. "I love you. And Bubba Kenshi says that he approves, and his opinion is all that really matters to me."

My eyebrows rose and I fumbled with a response for a moment before lamely replying, "I love you too." I blinked and frowned. "Bubba Kenshi approves?"

"Yes." She nodded. "He says that you take to the Way of the Blade much easier now that you've been training with him more closely. Which leads me to my next point."

"I'm not giving up my guns." I grunted and crossed my arms before she could say it. I did it once and I regretted it. I wouldn't be without them again. Not after all the work Galaxy and I had put into making them what I was used to as the Huntsman.

"You don't have to give them all up, but I don't want you to carry openly." She held a hand up to stop me, interrupting. "I know that you're responsible and I understand that you are highly trained, but the people here only use them in the most basic situations. Hunting, sports, collecting, killing vermin— simple and basic things. Anything like you have and it would be outside what could be proven necessary. But that's not all."

She took a deep breath and said, "The majority of the people here, Normies, Touched, and even the supernatural creatures look down on those who use them for combat." She scratched her head. "They think using a gun to defend yourself is shameful, and the older beings will attack you outright if they think you without honor."

"Do they frown on magic too?" It was hard to keep the skepticism out of my tone and she shook her head. "So I can use magic to nuke someone, or appear behind someone and tear their head off, but a gun is frowned upon."

"I never said it wasn't silly." Cassia growled and some of her oni features began to bleed through, but she took a deep breath and let it go, her color returning to normal. "I'm just asking that you respect the rules here until someone is truly a threat, then you can use what you have available to you, okay?"

I grimaced. "Fine. We're here for fun anyway, and though I brought them for my comfort, I don't really expect to have to use them or anything like that."

She nodded her head once and sighed in relief. "Good." She brightened up considerably. "We can visit some of our master smiths and get you a katana if you like?"

I grinned. "Seriously?"

"I know you probably would never use it in an actual fight, but yeah." She grinned more broadly. "Kenshi will shit if you come home with one."

I laughed and she leaned forward, kissing me and pulling

Galaxy closer to us. "How about a quick practice scrap before our shower?"

"Practice?" I snorted and she growled as she grabbed me. "You were talking about the bed, weren't you?"

The oni's throat rumbled low as she said, "Hai."

CHAPTER FIVE

Showered and wearing a nice pair of black jeans and a crisp red button-up, short-sleeved shirt, I felt like a million bucks. From the looks I was getting, a lot of the people here were used to seeing my kind, and not all of the looks were happy.

"Did you have to dress like a schoolgirl?" Arden huffed for the fourth time at Cassia.

True to her statement, Cassia could have been the veritable school girl of any guy's dream, her hair up in pigtails now. It was a little disconcerting.

"Would you prefer a maid outfit?" Cass shot back. "I brought one."

"You did?" Galaxy gasped and stayed silent before she said, "You *did*."

Cass grinned and nodded once. "I wanted to come here dressed any damn way I please and I will."

We walked on, taking in some of the sights, the streets being so well kept and the crowds larger than they might usually be probably because of the upcoming con. After half an hour walking, we ended up in what could have been described as a dive bar that we had to knock on the back door of a restaurant to get into. The place was jumping, music of some kind of K-pop or J-pop band rattling the windows as we stepped through the main area where more than a few locals drank happily, likely enjoying being off work.

We worked our way to the back of the place and a massive man with a suit on put a hand out and spoke in a deep bass growl at Cassia in Japanese. She smiled and winked at him and he bowed before stepping aside and slapping his meaty palm against the door to his right two times.

The door opened and a refreshing scent of peach and herbs wafted through the doorway into our noses before we stepped through.

"Welcome to the High Table Tokyo Branch." Cassia smiled and spread her arms.

Just like outside, the music here was loud, but this sounded much more appropriate for an older clientele.

As I cast my gaze around while we walked into the bar proper, I noticed that there was a massive ring in the center of the room, almost like a pit that we were walking closer to.

Once we passed a certain point, the music changed and became much more hypnotic and club-like. "What the hell is going on?"

"For how surprisingly old school a lot of the Japanese supernatural beings are, they love to rave and club," Arden explained with a grin. She wore a green dress that looked like it could have been scales, either for a mermaid or a dragon, and it showed off plenty of leg. "So their High Table reflects that. They have all the same amenities we do, and more. They even have fighters come in and compete for their entertainment."

I just looked at her quizzically. "What? I have friends who have come here before and told me all about it. I'm a jinn, I get information from all over and not all of my gaming friends are Normies." My jaw almost dropped. "Plus there's a sort of informal directory of all the High Tables, so we can learn about them on our own time as staff. You should look into it. I really wanna see the fighters, though. Like, why is it so important?"

Before I could get a response in, a voice said just in front of us, "Our way of keeping the warrior spirit of our culture alive and youthful." The woman behind the bar dipped her head respectfully before looking up at us. "I am Hanazuki, and it is my honor to serve you this evening."

"You don't have to be so formal with us, Hanazuki-san." Cassia dipped her head in return. "I'm Cassia, head of security for the High Table Columbus Branch. This is my best friend Ardent Flame, and my boyfriend and girlfriend Marcus and Galaxy."

Hanazuki bowed to each of us in turn, fixing us with a bright smile afterward. "Then if there is no need for formality, let us dispense with the honorifics, Cassia."

"Thank God." I sighed and earned a look of concern from the woman. "I would have messed it up, Hanazuki, I am so sorry. I meant no disrespect, I just worry I'll make an ass of myself if I try too hard."

She covered her mouth and laughed, something that sounded like a summer breeze dancing through the leaves of a tree, but when she finished, she teasingly said, "Then you will practice with me, Marcus-san. So that you don't bring shame to Cassia."

All of the girls laughed at my expense and I just shook my head and acquiesced. "Very well. Thank you and please take care of me, Hanazuki-san."

She chuckled and looked at us all. "What can I get you to drink to start?"

"Sake!" Arden called and the woman behind the counter smiled and nodded once.

"I would like something fruity." Cassia surprised me and I think Hanazuki as well. "Do you have anything special in season?"

Hanazuki grinned. "Anything is in season on my shift. Do you like plum?"

Cassia nodded excitedly and I spoke up, "I think I'll have whatever she's having as well, please?"

"Please what, Marcus-san?"

My cheeks heated and I said, "Please, Hanazuki-san."

Her small smile returned as the girls laughed again and Galaxy said, "I would like a rum and coke, please."

Hanazuki went into the back and brought out a tray with several tools, like knives and scoops, that she placed on the counter then turned around and grabbed a couple bottles of sake from the counter behind her. "We serve our sake here at room temperature. However, if you prefer a chilled sake, we do have some. How would you prefer?"

"I'll start with this, thanks!" Arden took her bottle and looked at the smaller woman. "Gonna use those? I'm a bartender, Marcus as well, and we would love to see what you're making. Care to show us?"

"It would be my pleasure." She lifted her hand and closed her eyes, a branch of some sort dipping low to drop something into her hand and it surprised me, but it was a plum.

She cut the plum and pitted it, scooping the fruit into the glass she had picked out, muddling it with a small, simple, blunt press of sorts, like the ones we had in the bar back home. She then sprinkled some mint leaves into it before muddling it again, this time a bit more gently.

"Herbs like mint can be overpowering if you mistreat them, so a few gentle proddings in a sweet liquid helps truly bring the two tastes together." Hanazuki smiled as she poured in some crushed ice, half an ounce of simple syrup, one ounce each of freshly squeezed lime juice and sake. "Next, we have one and a half ounces of umeshu, or plum liquor that we make here at the High Table, and finally one ounce of white rum."

She poured it without the measurement and stirred it all out quickly before adding a lime to the drink and setting it in front of Cass. "I give you an Umeshu Mojito for the beautiful oni. Welcome home."

Cassia waited for mine to be made, which didn't take long with Hanazuki not having to exaggerate her movements and explain each step for us. She finished and placed mine in front of me. Cassia raised her glass and spoke cheerfully, "Here's to a wild time in Japan!"

Hanazuki raised her own glass with the four of us and said, "Kanpai!"

We drank and it was so sweet and delicious I almost didn't stop. I was never the best with plums, however this was great, and I would for sure be adding this to my arsenal.

Cassia must have felt the same, because she actually finished her drink before grinning at all of us. "Oh, that was fucking good." She looked around and grinned a little wider, scarily so. "Who wants to dance?"

I hadn't even noticed the dance floor some fifty feet to the left of the bar and there were people dancing there, with more folks coming in already even though it was only late afternoon and just barely closing in on the evening. But this trip was about Cass, so I'd dance if she wanted to.

The music carried us away to our own destination. Cassia and Arden danced close together before the oni woman grabbed my wrist and pulled me close so that she could grind herself against me to the beat thrumming through the air and into the floor. Hell, even Galaxy joined us, coming up behind me to rub her hands up and down Cassia's sides and back around me.

It was definitely a different sensation but not unpleasant in the slightest.

Finally, we decided that we were a little bit hungry and went to the bar to order some food and inquire about a booth.

"The booths are just over here to the right, and we will bring your food as soon as all of it is complete." Hanazuki bowed her head. "Will you be partaking in the fight this evening?"

"I can fight?" Cassia gasped excitedly, though deflated instantly when the other woman chuckled and shook her head. "Who's fighting?"

"It will be two sumo wrestlers." Hanazuki looked like she

was smitten as she said, "They are quite good, if I might say so."

"We would love to watch!" Arden laughed and lifted her third bottle of sake.

I grinned at her and had an Old Fashioned brought to the table with another random kind of cocktail that Hanazuki thought that I might enjoy. Cassia told her to bring a pitcher of that Mojito that she had made earlier and the woman raised her eyebrow.

"Weird that a Touched as powerful as her works here in the city and she's so nice," Arden observed.

"Very, but I ain't mad at her skill." Cassia took a sip of Arden's chilled sake and nodded. "Oh, that's pristine." She turned her head and called out, "Can we get some more chilled sake too, Hanazuki?"

"Yes!" Hanazuki called, another customer having come over and joined her, along with another bartender who looked to be starting his shift. While I didn't get much of an aura off of her, I got a major look at him and his aura was strange.

"She would have likely been put to work tending fields or the personal lands of a noble when I was here," Cassia observed almost to herself, then she turned and saw who I was staring at. "Oh, another yokai."

She stared at him a little longer, then decided something to herself, "He's not Night Parade strength, so he's not one of the major types of yokai. Likely Goblinoid of some type, but not. Could be a halfling?"

"Goro is a strong young man, please do not question his heritage to him." Hanazuki had joined us again as Cassia spoke and bowed politely. "He is favored by the owner here, and it is highly unlikely you will be allowed to return if you upset him."

"Ah, forgive us, Hanazuki-san." I bowed in return. "We meant no disrespect."

"I know, but there was a group of people who came to the High Table here and thought guessing his heritage was a good drinking game, forcing him to answer questions that made him uncomfortable." She sighed and shook her head. "Just classless, and since then, he's *very* sensitive about it."

"We understand." Cassia sat up straighter. "Thank you for warning us and letting us know about his preferences."

Hanazuki set the drinks down and bowed her head once more. "Your food should be coming out momentarily and then from there, our entertainment will begin. Thank you for your understanding and patience. Please let me know if you need anything else."

We smiled at her and she returned it with a soft one of her own, then went back to the bar.

"That was a near crisis averted." Galaxy smiled to herself as she sipped on her drink and closed her eyes. "Drinking like this feels good."

"Wait until you try some of the sushi I ordered." Cassia grinned.

While we waited, something wasn't sitting right with me, so I had to ask, "Is the Night Parade real?"

Cassia nodded as she sipped her drink. There was a tensing of her shoulders as I stared at her and she sighed contentedly as she put her drink down. "It is." She glanced at the man behind the bar for second, then turned back to me and spoke. "The Night Parade rules the seedier parts of Japanese crime and the black market. Most of the Yakuza that still operate are filled with lesser yokai just to keep them busy and from making too much trouble, but the Parade is... different."

"Can you tell us a little about it?" Galaxy sipped her own drink and her eyes lit up curiously. Likely due to the scent of food in the air from the booth near us as well.

"There are one hundred members made up of those strong enough to have fought their way into reality and to maintain their own forms." She scratched her head, her eyes drifting to a faraway place as she continued to explain. "They maintain peace within their domain by defending the lesser yokai who choose not to fight and keeping the others in Grestal. They even adopted the oni as yokai."

"Why would they do that?" I frowned at her. The way I'd learned it, oni had always been yokai and said as much.

"Yokai is a more generalized term for the supernatural in Japan than an actual moniker for any one specific kind of race, so most creatures of supernatural lineage are referred to that way." She tapped the table in thought. "As to why?"

She thought on it some more and just shrugged. "We're too strong not to be included."

Her response wasn't enough for me, because it felt like she was leaving out a lot, but I couldn't press as our food arrived carried by Goro himself.

Cassia had enough sushi to share, as did Arden, while I had some shrimp, fried rice, and an omelet with ketchup on it that said something I didn't understand in Japanese. Galaxy had a thick, juicy-looking burger with a hunk of pineapple on it and fries that looked tender and soft, the way we both loved them.

"Oh man." I grunted and looked at everything. "Think we can put it away?"

"Oh yeah." Cassia snarled happily until she caught a glance at my omelet. "Did you have them put that there?"

I shrugged. "I just asked for an omelet with ketchup, why?"

"It says 'hunt' on it." She frowned, then sighed. "Guess the jig is up and someone knows who and what we are."

"Doesn't matter." Arden grinned and popped a piece of sushi into her mouth, groaning. "Oh, that tuna is amazing. We're here on vacation. No saving the world. No kicking asses that don't earn it, just being nerds in the promised land."

"Whose ass have we kicked that *didn't* earn it?" I laughed and the rest of the table laughed as well.

An announcer spoke over the music and a small flat-screen popped up into the end of the table so that we could see the center of the ring in the floor that we had walked by.

A single referee stood in the center of the ring and spoke into a dropped mic on a cord, his voice clear as he spoke, his words being translated on the screen into English for those of us who didn't speak the native tongue. "Ladies, gentleman, gods, goddesses, and those with no gender or affiliation—welcome to tonight's Warrior Spirit!"

"That's a poor translation." Cassia grunted and explained, "It's really just a show of Warrior Spirit, or Warrior's Pride."

Arden chuckled. "How very anime."

Cassia laughed but the man spoke on and explained, "Tonight, we have two proud warriors whose very honor depends on this battle. Please join me in welcoming them to the ring with a round of applause!"

Everyone clapped. Even the people who had been on the dance floor earlier gathered around the fenced portion of the bar and watched with fingers wound between the links, calling and cheering as the wrestlers made their way into the ring.

Both of the men were built like traditional sumo wrestlers, neither of them having an aura of any sort that I could see through the screen, but I was just excited to see the sport itself so close.

Arden whistled. "Damn, there's hardly any lag on the action!" Hanazuki came over to refill our drinks for us and Arden asked, "How far behind is the TV from the event?"

She smiled. "Milliseconds, thanks to some rather clever gnomish technical engineering." She thought on it for a second longer then smiled. "And a fair bit of magic."

I nodded, glad for it since this was a first time nearly-live-view of the sport for me. Sumo wrestling was one of the oldest sports in Japanese history. They were the only people in the whole of Japan still allowed to sport the haircut of Samurai, though Cassia told me that some Kabuki actors had it as well.

To have that sort of tradition and honor appealed heavily to the Marine in me. Some of the traditions that we still followed to this day were set by those first brave warriors who started the Corps, and were what set us apart from the other branches of service. To know the sumo wrestlers still followed ancient traditions as well was just so cool to me.

The rules, according to the referee of the fight, would be simple; one would win by throwing, slapping, or shoving the other warrior out of the small red ring in the center of the pit, or putting them on any other body part that wasn't their feet. Once one of those things happened, then the fight would be over.

That was simple enough for me to follow and I liked the way that the fighters entered the ring with their faces masks of determination that sent chills down my spine. They went through their warm ups for a couple of minutes, seemingly paying no attention to their opponent before the referee appeared once more and called them out into the circle.

"Oh, this is going to be great." Cassia hissed and clapped a little as she leaned forward to watch. "Look at the muscle they have in their backs, chests, and shoulders! That's some serious power."

"You never talk about mine like that," I jokingly whined at her and she smacked my shoulder. "Hey."

"You can throw a car if you'd spend your damn points." She shook her head. "Noob."

"I'm just jealous of their rocking undies." Galaxy grinned and I snorted. "I think Marcus would look hot in that."

"I'd have to gain a lot of weight."

Cassia put a hand on my shoulder. "I'd be okay with a chonky Marcus. And they're called mawashi."

I laughed and almost missed the match entirely. The ref threw his arm down and after the wrestlers bowed to each other, they launched straight into it.

The one with the red mawashi slammed his open palm into his opponent's shoulder, then another palm into his chest before the two collided, both attempting to move the other's arms out of the way so that they could get the more advantageous position to try to throw the other.

But though red was the aggressor, blue had the patience to wait for the perfect time to strike. His hands shot under the other man's arms, his massive mitts grabbing his opponent's mawashi and *lifted* his bulky opponent off the ground. They grunted and pushed each other but in a fit of artful genius, blue turned his body slightly and pivoted perfectly, throwing his opponent.

The other, larger man lifted and fell onto his back to the thunderous cry of the crowd, cheers and clapping exploding all around them. Even in my seat watching the TV as I was, I wanted to clap and holler for them. That had been intense even though it lasted seconds.

That's what she said. Galaxy cackled as I scowled over at her. She snuck a piece of Cassia's sushi and groaned, giving herself away to the woman beside me, Cassia just shaking her head and pointing to a specific piece. "You want me to have that one?"

Cassia smiled. "Yeah, it's why I got the platter in the first place." Galaxy reached out with her fingers and went to grab it when Cassia smacked her hand loudly. "No! You're not a child, you'll grab it with chopsticks. Here, let me show you."

The oni spent about ten minutes helping Galaxy learn, and watching her fingers fumble the wooden sticks was simply entertainment that bordered on better than the fight that we'd just witnessed.

After she was comfortable with it, Cassia showed Galaxy the piece again and waited patiently while she fumbled with it. It was during the fumbling that I realized what the green stuff on the rice was and my eyes went wide.

I felt a hand on my thigh, Cassia's fingertips and nails grating slightly against the denim there as she distracted me. Galaxy growled to herself and focused in on the piece then lifted it cautiously, gasping that she was finally getting the hang of it.

She plopped the piece onto her outstretched tongue and pulled it back into her mouth, very much adopting a look one would associate with cats who ate the canaries. She chewed once and swallowed, confused as to why Cassia was laughing. "What?"

"Wasabi?" Arden gasped and Cassia nodded a couple times while Galaxy froze.

Tears sprang to Galaxy's eyes as she simply said, *"Help!"*

CHAPTER SIX

We helped the poor goddess then went back to our rooms for the night, Galaxy upset, but realizing that it was a joke.

"I'll get you back, Cassia," Galaxy swore, fanning her tongue. I knew for a fact that she was playing up the injury.

We laid down for the evening, really more tired than we thought and though she could have spent some time gaming by herself, Cassia chose to sleep with Galaxy and I as a way of appeasing the smaller woman. We woke up the next morning to the smell of brewed coffee, eggs, and the sweet scent of fruit.

I poked my head out of our room and found Arden sitting at one of the two tables, reading a manga and munching on some toast. She looked up and a smile spread over her face. "We have a cook here with us!"

I frowned and came around the corner to find a small woman in the kitchen, her hunched stature bent over the stove and the cooking food. She wore a more traditional style of Japanese dress and her hair was cut short on the side in a manner that almost reminded me of an 'I want the manager on a leash' style haircut. She looked nice, and luckily she hadn't seen me in just my boxers.

I woke the others up while I dressed for the day, a pair of loose shorts and a t-shirt all I really felt like wearing for the moment as I followed my nose to the source of the delicious food.

I walked out and spoke to the woman. "Ohio-go-zi-mas," I pronounced lamely.

Arden snorted at me, but the little old lady turned and the smile on her face was the brightest thing I could stand. She began chittering away at me happily and when she realized I didn't understand her, she switched to English almost as fluent as my own was. "You did very well, don't let Arden-chan belittle you for trying. Most people here would be delighted to know that you are at least making the respectful attempt to try to learn their language and put it to use instead of letting innate magic keep you afloat."

That last bit had been thrown at Arden with a heaping helping of venom that the woman just feigned looking hurt for. She sighed. "Tsuki, I'm sorry that not everyone is blessed with the ability to understand languages as swiftly as the jinn."

The woman, Tsuki, just waved at her, then turned back to me. "Please, call me Tsuki. You're so handsome—remind me of my grandson. Are you single?"

Arden spit out her coffee and hissed, "Tsuki!"

Cassia came out of the room wearing a loose, yellow sundress that fit her new form well, scratching her lower back and Arden shouted, "Surprise!"

Cassia lit up. "Little Tsuki!"

The small woman surprised me and ran around me to get to Cassia, who she jumped and hugged immediately. The oni just grinned and held her before putting her down and saying, "How is the family?"

"All of my grandchildren are grown and soon, I will ascend." She smiled at Cassia then turned to Arden. "I just had to see my friends one last time, and I have Arden to thank for this."

"Ascend?" Galaxy asked groggily as she came out of the

room wearing a black romper and a yellow jacket that accentuated her dark skin.

"Tsuki is the heir to the current luck dragon Shin Bai," Cassia explained, then came over to Arden and pulled her into a hug. "I don't know how you kept a surprise like this from me, but thank you. It's so nice to see Tsuki again."

Arden smirked and nodded to me and Galaxy. "I had a little help, but hon, I can see Marcus is still a few crayons short of the whole idea behind what she is."

I glared at her playfully, then my attention went back to Cassia as she continued to speak. "They can choose to ascend and take their ancestor's place, or rejoin the cycle and be reborn until they feel that they've lived a good enough life."

"Like from their perspective, or one that would be considered good by some cosmic force?" I asked out loud before I realized that it hadn't been just to Galaxy. "I am so sorry, Tsuki, I wasn't trying to be rude."

"Do not apologize for a curious mind." She smiled wider and went to the stove to grab food, Cassia joining her to assist in carrying it all over. "Please, come and sit for a meal with old Tsuki."

"You aren't that old, little Tsuki." Cassia shook her head at her and waited until she was seated to ask, "Did you want to explain, or did you want me to?"

"I can." Tsuki put a plate in front of us all and began to pour us tea and coffee before she sat with us and cleared her throat. "The luck dragon is a staple sort of demi-god who is tied to Japan, and though it is a known thing, much of our history and legend remains shrouded in mystery for good reason. Because if something were to happen that breaks the cycle of luck, the entire country could fall to the leader of the Night Parade."

"What's that?" Galaxy asked politely, I knew she knew from my memories but she wanted to hear the woman talk some more.

"The strongest of the yokai, the bad luck of Japan and her

people. Plus, they always have 'bound' muscle to help enforce their will," Tsuki explained, though she threw a cautious glance Cassia's way, but the oni only nodded. "Without the luck dragon to keep them from doing anything more than act like street thugs, they would quickly take Japan and their influence would likely spread to the rest of the world."

"Other supernatural creatures would be able to fend them off for a time, but that's not the point." Tsuki sighed as she continued. "I am the heir and I have lived a good, long life many times. It is time."

That gave me pause. "Many lives?"

"Dude, cycle of rebirth?" Arden whispered like I was dense. "Pay attention."

"It's a strange thing to think about even for those of us who are different, no need to be rude," Tsuki admonished the jinn who just rolled her eyes. "Did you just roll your eyes at me? Do I need to spank you?"

"Yes!" Galaxy roared, surprising us all, even Arden. "Sorry. I just think it would be funny."

"It would be, considering I'm thousands of years older than you." Arden crossed her arms and stared at the physically older woman. "Even with all your rebirths."

"So how did all of you meet?" Galaxy wondered as she scoured the table for something sweet, finding a small bottle of ketchup instead.

Cassia spoke first. "She was kidnapped and taken from her home in one of her previous lives, and when she arrived in America, I rescued her and sent her back home."

"I don't like the way you told that story—next!" Arden grinned as Tsuki did and the oni woman just looked on, embarrassed.

Tsuki splayed her hands out and began her tale. "All is as she said, but I will explain in detail—though for her sake, I won't gush as Arden would like." Arden swore swarthily and earned a glare from Tsuki that could have peeled paint off a wall. "I was stolen from my homeland one evening while on a stroll with my friend, the two of us having been young women at a time where they were highly valued by *traders* of that variety. We were forced to travel on a ship to what had been a growing new country. We were to be forced to work in mines, on railroads, and in other manners so that we could earn our way back home, but based on the rumors of those that they had used to lure some of the men onto the ship, that was unlikely to happen. They would never let us leave."

"The world was a different place back then, and all kinds of movement from one continent to another in hopes of a better life, or a more lavish one, were promised to those who came along with it," Cassia added because I had looked skeptical enough. "Sugar fields needed tending and there were people who felt that others were better suited to the work than themselves or those who should be paid a wage for it."

"Cass, she's telling a story." Arden grumbled softly. "We know how you feel about it, the good part's coming."

Tsuki took a sip of her tea and nodded to Cassia. "The night we were to make landfall, the shoreline was ablaze and as I could see from the ship where we were chained, oni wove through the burning homes and the place like death given wings."

She paused as if recalling the sight of it. "Our ship never made it to shore before one of the oni found us and attacked the ship, but only the crew was murdered. The oni who did it took us all aside and made us swear that if we told anyone of our survival, it was demons who were looking for revenge that did all the destruction. In addition, anyone who wanted to return home, could."

"And Tsuki wanted to." Cassia grunted, uncrossing her arms. "It's part of what made that whole experience so life changing. If she had died while away from Japan, she would have been lost to the cycle and never been reborn."

"And that would have been an issue for Shin Bai, as there are only so many reborn who can take his place. At the time, I was the only one." Tsuki heaved a sigh. "I've been so grateful that I have kept in touch with Cassia ever since then, even made friends with our fiery fury over here."

"I'm a jinn, *not* a fury."

"At least she didn't call you a furry." Cassia snickered and the room devolved into laughter. When we all calmed down, we ate and praised Tsuki for her wonderful cooking. She responded by joking about having perfected it over lifetimes of work. Cassia stared at the woman after wiping her mouth on a napkin and finally asked, "So when do you ascend?"

Tsuki smiled softly and ducked her head. "I would normally ascend with my family and friends, but there will be a storm in the next few days that I will ascend during, so I cannot afford to have my family there as a distraction."

"Why the storm?" My question brought about a grin from the older woman and she just winked at me. "Uh."

"She's teasing you." Cassia chuckled. "The storm is so that your ascension can't bring any crazier kind of misfortune, right?"

"The opposite," Tsuki explained. "This storm will be a bad one, with the potential to do much damage. I plan to ascend during the build-up and first wave of water to keep it from reaching all that it could become."

"Does your family know?" Arden sounded like she was sad, suddenly. As if the prospect of an old friend going away was a bad thing, despite what she was going to become. And it was in a lot of ways.

"Some of them, yes. Spreading this information is not something that is advised, seeing as though the Night Parade would gladly see me dead." She smiled, lifting her hand and wagging her pointer finger. "The heir's anonymity is what keeps them safe from the Parade, as we do not give away anything to hunt for. They have found some others by accident, but it was never really a threat as it is now that I am close to ascendance."

She grinned broadly, showing all of her teeth. "I have already found who my heir will likely be and I cannot wait to see who they become, but I will take that secret to the skies with me."

Galaxy frowned. "But if you're so important to the survival of your people, why is the Parade allowed to continue to exist?" Tsuki took a breath, but Galaxy added, "It seems like Shin Bai and all the Japanese people would be better off without them, right? Is it not a bit negligent for them to be allowed the reign they are?"

"Shin Bai keeps the yokai here in a sense that they cannot flee the presence of his luck," Tsuki explained carefully. "It forms a barrier of sorts that will eat the very souls of the true yokai who choose to try to leave. Even through the portals of Grestal, there can be no escape. The Luck Dragon's existence is a binding tether to the realm of Japan for all yokai. His direct issuance of justice would be an invitation for disaster as luck and misfortune would clash and cause chaos throughout Japan that would endanger all. The balance is maintained that way, and the Wardens here are adept at dealing with their antics if they overstep too much."

"Do you need someone to help you ascend?" I asked, seeing how worried Cassia had become, the set of her face giving her away even if I couldn't see her eyes. "Like a guard or something?"

"Since the last time I was kidnapped, I have enlisted a generational guard that has quite a few Touched among them and though this body is old, I have many, many years of practical training with magic and the martial arts since then." Tsuki smiled and bowed her head. "Your concern for me is appreciated, Marcus, but I will never be caught off guard again."

I nodded back to her and she turned to Cassia. "I know you cannot be there, my friend, as the Night Parade would see it as an invitation, but seeing you again after all these years has been wonderful."

"So, is the Night Parade actually hunting you?" Galaxy asked curiously. "And what happens to Shin Bai once his turn as the luck dragon is over?"

iefo

"He retires and rejoins the cycle as his body nourishes the land and his luck reinforces the barrier." Tsuki's explanation satisfied me, but I knew that Galaxy thought it was a waste and she would love to eat him and gain something from him. "After that, he and the next heir can decide when and who will ascend to replace me. The heirs have a way of finding each other."

"I see." Cassia smiled at the older looking woman and put a hand on her shoulder. "It was nice to see you again, little Tsuki, and I'm sorry that we can't be there for you. But I'll make sure that any of my old contacts in the Night Parade know that I'm here, and messing with you is a death sentence. If not from the Wild Hunt, then from me alone."

That made me pause. "You were... part of the Night Parade?"

Cassia nodded once and when I went to ask for more information, she shook her head and Galaxy spoke for her in my head, *Not now.*

Okay. But later for sure. "The Wild Hunt will be at your side should you need us. Get a hold of Cassia and we will come running."

"You keep strange company, Cassia." Tsuki snickered, staring at her friend. "To think that you would call yourselves the Wild Hunt."

"We are," Cassia said and looked at me. "Show her, please."

I nodded and focused myself, urging my Mantle to come to life, my practicing with it paying dividends.

The shadows around us deepened and sprang toward my body, building the Huntsman's armor as I sat in the chair, eating the food still.

Tsuki almost cried out when I glanced her way, likely the color change in my eyes. I swallowed my mouthful of food and cleared my throat, though it did nothing to the demonic edge in my tone that warbled my voice slightly. "It's okay, Tsuki, the Hunt means you no harm. We're friends now."

"I suppose having the boogeyman of the supernatural world as a friend would be good to most?" Tsuki stared at me for a moment, then turned to Cassia in near exasperation. "How do you find yourself entrenched in another group like this?"

Cassia shrugged, a little upset from what I could tell. "It's a skill, I guess."

"I should be on my way before my guard and children get worried." Tsuki stood up, giving Arden and Cassia a hug before looking at me and Galaxy. "Please, take good care of my friends."

I nodded. "We will."

She turned back to Cassia with a small smile. "May Amaterasu bless you a thousand times, and may luck go with you always."

She shimmered for a moment, then faded from sight and left us.

"How does she do that?" Galaxy asked softly and Cassia nodded once before Galaxy asked, "Care to explain this Night Parade business? Can I eat them?"

Cassia sighed, then offered her a smirk. "You very well may get the opportunity if they decide they want to try to kill Tsuki, but like I said, it would be a death sentence." She stood up and began to carry our plates to the dishwasher, loading them in quietly before she spoke again. "First, a little background. Oni weren't adopted by the Parade into being yokai like you would normally think. They were basically pulled in as muscle. The oni are the enforcers of the Night Parade; think mid-level mafia thugs that go out and break faces or protect the higher ups."

"Way to really mess with our view of it, but go on." I had to admit I was a little confused, but at least it was starting to make sense.

"Before I left Japan, I used to be a member of the Night Parade—not an enforcer or guard—an actual member. I was strong enough to earn my number." She glared at Arden, effectively stopping her from speaking. "My situation was pretty much like Jolly's, but it was the opposite for me. I wanted to take power, and when I took said power, it wasn't what I actually wanted. It was too much and there was no reward for it."

"So you left," Arden said. "Cass, why have you never told me this?"

"I never thought anyone would really recognize me, and telling you that would have done nothing but dredge up bad memories." She shook her head, turning around to face us while leaning up against the counter with her glasses shimmering in the light that filtered through the open window behind us. "Besides, saying it out loud to one person meant that someone could have overheard and told them where I had gone to."

"What, you think they would have come to find you?" I asked incredulously, but to my surprise, she nodded. "Why?"

"To kill me and bring honor back to the Parade." She grinned. "I'm the only one in thousands of years to successfully leave the Night Parade unscathed, but if they found out that I was still alive and close enough, they would come after me. Even Bubba Kenshi got hurt getting out."

That made me pause, because Kenshi was a fucking *monster*.

"So then why the fuck are we here? Had I known that, I would have just video-called Tsuki or something for you." Arden stood up and threw her hands out, then began to pace. "You literally just threw yourself onto their doorstep with a 'kick me, asshole' sign on your back."

"I'm part of the Hunt; I'm protected now." She shrugged, then added shyly, "And I was getting homesick."

She stared at us and said, "Seriously, Arden, you really did a very nice thing. Thank you." She rubbed her face and looked imploringly at the other woman. "Let's not let this ruin a nice trip, okay?"

I shook my head and Arden stared at her for a long moment before she said, "Go get dressed for a relaxing day of shopping, you two. We're on the prowl."

I snorted, not realizing that we would actually be doing that.

CHAPTER SEVEN

It was dark by the time we were back in the area of our hotel, the girls and I carrying a bag or so each of some stuff that we didn't really need to carry with how large Galaxy had made our inventories. Now we could store much more than before, and it was crazy how much it was, but even with that, it seemed like both women were striving to fill it in new and exciting ways.

Cassia had actually asked me to carry her bags like this because she thought it would be cute, so Arden took some photos to send back to Masonai, saying how lucky he was that he wasn't here to be a pack mule. That had earned a laugh from me as well.

We had stopped to get some takoyaki from a vendor on the side of the street three blocks from the place when Cassia and Arden both stilled and began to frown. The sounds of people screaming and fleeing from something drew our attention, and it wasn't until they were already on the move that I realized something was truly wrong.

We only had to go a block before someone screamed and the sound of gunfire and pinging metal on metal let us know we had reached the right area. Even with people hiding, there were some with phones pointed at the action. Unbelievable.

My aura sight kicked into overdrive as a massive man with muscles that would make you think 'Smash' came into view. There was no way this gigantic meatstick wasn't some kind of supernatural creature. The ones behind him, firing at the figures he was swinging at, were too. Their ears were pointed and their auras all glowed green.

"Those are Seelie," Arden growled, then began to move through the crowd, Galaxy taking over as her voice. *They're firing at those masked figures and into the crowd. We've got to get the people out of here.*

I heard Seelie and began to seethe. *You get them out of here. Cass, take care of the big guy. I'll get the gunners.*

I was about to cast Embodiment of Lightning when someone stepped from the shadows behind the gunners and swung twice, their heads falling to the ground as blood splattered their mask. The mask was wild and reminded me of the oni masks that people wore at festivals here, or at conventions.

Two more gunners left, so I cast the spell and used it to appear behind them and punched one in the spine as hard as I could before turning on the other and attacking him with the knife I pulled from my belt.

He'd had enough warning from my dropping his friend to turn and fire at me, but I had already pivoted to the side and used the momentum to swing my right arm around in a hammer fist. The bottom of my hand slammed into his chin and rocked him back on his heels, but he was still standing. I should've spent my points already, goddamn it.

Lament later—kill them now, Marcus. Galaxy huffed in my head. *There are too many witnesses and we don't have Merlin here or the supplies to keep people from remembering this.*

I grit my teeth and let out a breath before I attacked again, this time going for vital points with the blade. While he worried about what was in my right hand and blocked my strike, I took my left and cast Mana Blade toward his head and neck.

Mana burst from my fist and speared his head, splattering blood on the ground behind him. I turned and wrenched the blade from his body, turning to find the other elven man still laying on the ground, unable to move. "Galaxy, clean up the mess, please."

She stepped from my shadow as a cat. *Happily.*

The man tried to scream, but his cries were muffled by the cavernous maw that opened before him and began to swallow him bit by bit.

A chill ran down my spine and I whipped around with the Mana Blade raised to protect myself as the hulking elf barreled toward me. Cassia followed, battering him with her massive mace, but it did little more than bruise him.

"He's not taking much bludgeoning damage!" Cassia snarled and slammed the weapon into the side of his knee as he stopped to try to grab me. It crunched and buckled inward toward the center of his gravity and she smiled savagely. "There we go!"

Working together, she and I harried him until there was an opening where she could shove an earthen spike from her weapon into his open mouth as he bellowed in rage. The spike burst from the back of his skull and his body dropped a heartbeat later to both of us breathing moderately heavy. It had been too close of quarters for Cass to use her eyes to take our opponents out. Too much of a risk to everyone around us, especially since we didn't really know who they were.

The figures in the oni masks milled about us, seemingly uncertain as to what to make of us. The one that had killed the two elves stood in front of us and said in a husky, feminine voice, "Follow us."

They turned and began to walk away from us slowly at first, motioning to the others in a rather complicated set of hand signs.

"We aren't going anywhere with you." Cassia hissed and crossed her arms, standing where she was.

"The Wardens come, Sissy Cassia." The figure spoke over

their shoulder at her and began to walk again without another word as sirens blared in the distance and another odd feeling came over me.

"She knows you. Maybe we follow for now, and have Arden play overwatch?" I raised a brow at her and she grimaced.

Follow them. This guy was on a modified dose of what was in Columbus, Marcus, Cassia. If this shit is here, that means there's a bigger problem that could cut into our time here.

"Fine. Let's go." Cassia took off after the woman who had spoken to us as the other members of the group broke off and scattered.

As we moved along, the sound of sirens closed in on where we'd been and with how close some of the buildings were and how quiet it had been, it was almost deafening to hear.

Galaxy, as we move, will you help me allocate my points?

Yes, here is what you have so far.

Level 15

Stats

Brawn: 17

Dexterity: 15

Physique: 17

Mana: 30

Charisma: 21

Points to spend: 15

Spell Points to spend: 11

Spells Known

Wisp 2/6

Physical Buff 1/6

Bolt Havoc 1/8

Mana Blade*

Embodiment*

Inferno Haze 1/12

Hoarfrost*

Arcane Infusion

Icy Forge

Mentally, I could have fucking kicked myself because all

of this would have been great to have at almost any time, but as Kenshi would tell me when I complained, *"Loud grass get cut."*

I had no idea what he meant when he said that, but in this case, I knew it wouldn't do me any damn bit of good and only make me look like an ass, so I got busy.

I put four points into Charisma, putting it up to twenty five, five into Mana for thirty five, three into Brawn, two into Physique, and finally one into Dexterity. This left the other three stats at nineteen, twenty, and sixteen respectively.

I put four Spell Points into Wisp and instead of the normal one, this one just kind of fell flat. *Is that normal?*

Wisp is an original spell from me, so it's going to take a moment to scan through the spells you have to see how it should grow, since this is so far along in your leveling.

It took a moment before I had options presented to me that would replace the spell I had.

Cold Wisp – Summon a flame that burns with sub-zero temperatures as opposed to actual heat. 15 Mana.

Electrical Burn – Summon a flame with electricity coursing through it with a small chance to shock foes along with burning them. 15 Mana.

Enhanced Wisp – Summon a more powerful flame to use as you see fit. 15 Mana.

I liked the others, but there was just no way that I would get the same amount of utility as I needed with normal flame. Anything else, I could just use another kind of spell for. I chose Enhanced Wisp, resolving to still refer to it as Wisp when I used it anyway.

The other points I had could have easily gone anywhere, but I didn't have the time needed to sit and truly go through all the options I had. Having a broader range of spells could be useful, but specialization was a good thing too, when I had so many different abilities available with my bonds working the way they did.

I decided I would just dump them into Bolt Havoc later on if nothing else seemed appealing.

Blinking, I was back with Cassia and the mysterious figure that led us under an overpass and stopped, obviously looking for something before she stilled and stared at *something* on the wall that wasn't quite visible for some reason.

"Mana paint?" Galaxy asked with a soft gasp. "Is that graffitied on? What's that symbol?"

She looked back at us, her mask obstructing our view of her face. "It's not visible to the naked eye, nor any Normies, and it's informative." She looked back at us and then up to the symbol that looked like a square with a halo of some sort over it. "This means haven. Come."

She walked toward the wall, then raised a hand to touch the symbol before the wall melted away and allowed us entry into a tunnel.

The tunnel had more of the mysterious mana paint graffitied along the walls that let us see in better light. There were no holes in the walls that I could see, which gave me a bit more comfort, but I kept my hands at my sides and ready to call my weapons and spells into action should we need them.

We came to an intersection of roughhewn stone, and our guide turned us left and down into a set of tunnels that looked like an abandoned mine shaft or a fledgling underground rail station. Either way, the area was put together with enough pallets and items to be a small camp.

This was where we met more than a dozen other masked figures waiting for us. As soon as we were in the room, four of them jumped down from above us to block the exit and our escape.

"Bad move." I growled and dropped into a fighting stance, several of the figures mirroring me immediately as their bodies began to glow with their auras.

"Stop." Our guide grunted and took off her mask. A Japanese woman I didn't recognize stood there, but apparently Cassia did.

"Kimiko?" Cass stepped closer and the other woman raised her chin almost defiantly. "What are you doing?"

"Protecting our people and making a name for us," Kimiko answered before she sneered. "What are *you* doing in the middle of a fight with those Seelie drug runners?"

"I came home to see you and Mother, introduce you to Marcus and Galaxy. You know that already." Cassia stared at her in near disbelief before taking in the rest of the figures milling around. "Who are they, and why are you with them? We should leave so you can fill me in."

"They are the Phantomu, oni who are tired of living the way our ancestors did and the way people treat us now."

"Kimiko, no one lives that way anymore."

Kimiko roared, her skin turning a mottled shade of blue, "You know *nothing* of our plight, coward!"

"Coward?" Cassia returned and stood over her sister as her form began to grow monstrous and large.

"You fled the fury of the Night Parade instead of fighting them for your right to lead and left all of us behind!" Kimiko began to grow with her, but her clothes grew with the change somehow. "You were the one who could have changed everything for our people, but you fled."

There was an intensity to her words that made me flinch as she continued to speak. "We were the ones who had to fight them off, and they took their anger for you out on so many of our people because they wouldn't seek you out, and now we have to protect ourselves from both the Parade and invaders like these Seelie scum that are trying to peddle their drugs in our cities!"

The two of them looked like they were about to start swinging even before their forms had stopped growing.

I stepped around Cassia and tried to step between the two of them, saying, "We can help with that."

They looked at me and, in unison, told me to "Fuck off."

I just meandered back to where some of the other figures

stood and crossed my arms as both women began to move around each other. Cassia's clothes were gone, the only thing she had to protect her nudity was a pair of boxers that she liked to wear and that was it, but while it made me a little uncomfortable, the other figures around us didn't appear to be bothered about it at all.

They looked like they were about to start fighting, so I shouted, "Don't touch her glasses, she can turn you into stone with her eyes!"

That automatically made the oni woman facing off against Cassia still and growl, "Is he lying, Sissy Cassia?"

Cassia shook her head. "No. If you want to fight me because you feel you were wronged, that's fine. I will happily prove I am right, but do not attack my eyes." She grimaced as she explained, "I do not like that this has happened, as it feels weak to use without true need. I will tie my sunglasses on so that it's harder for them to come off, but if you don't want to be in serious mortal danger, don't touch them."

Kimiko stared at her as if deciding whether or not this was a good idea and finally decided, "Tie them." She stood back and crossed her arms. "I will not be placed in needless danger to prove you wrong."

"You shouldn't be fighting at all, but I'm just here twiddling my fucking thumbs." I went to lean up against the wall and two of the goons with her stepped forward to bar my path, one of them shoving me backward.

"Shut up, human," one of them grunted. "The only reason you aren't a streak on the ground is because we won't attack someone under Sissy Cassia's protection until Sissy Kimiko says so."

I blinked at them and turned my head so that I spoke over my left shoulder. "That so?" Kimiko nodded once and I shrugged. "Works for me. Step aside so I can have a sit down for the show."

"You'll go nowhere." The second one's slightly muffled voice hissed at me and I rolled my eyes.

"Behave, Marcus," Cassia called without sounding like she had bothered to look at me.

"Why don't we have our people fight if you think he can win?" Kimiko suggested, crossing her arms. "That way you don't have to worry about your precious glasses."

"Because no one fights for me." Cassia snarled and snatched up a sleeve from the floor where it had fallen when she had changed to tie her sunglasses tightly to her head and lowered herself into a position to attack her little sister.

"Fine!" Kimiko snarled and rushed the other woman.

I turned all the way around by this point, Galaxy interrupted the show by telling me, *Arden is outside, ready to attack if we need her.*

Okay. I'm not saying we could take all of them at once, but they seem pretty content to listen to Kimiko for now, so if any of them attack en masse, she can come in. For now, we wait.

She gave me an internal nod and I crossed my arms as the two women began to try to grapple with each other.

Cassia lurched backward and dragged Kimiko with her, and the smaller oni sailed through the air onto the ground with a thud. Cassia followed her and sat astride her to start raining down strike after strike on her little sister as the blue oni defended herself well. As Cassia readied her hands for another paired strike with her fists clenched, Kimiko bucked her hips and sent her sister over her while grabbing on and riding along.

She got into a guard and began to strike at any exposed opening that she could find, but Cassia just allowed her to find one that was too good to be true and grabbed her arm for an arm bar when Kimiko went for it.

There was no pulling and backing off to see if there would be any sort of withdrawal or a tap. Cassia pulled hard enough to snap the arm if Kimiko hadn't been flexing and fighting to keep it from breaking.

Kimiko whirled her body around, tossing her legs into the air and using them to leverage her body out of the grip while lifting her elder sister off the ground, only to slam her back down into it a heartbeat later.

Cassia let go of the arm and went for a leg sweep that Kimiko hopped over easily. What I wanted to know was why was she holding back.

She's still her little sister, Marcus, Galaxy explained. *If Connell had attacked you like this, would you be going full on to stop the fight?*

When the boy wants to come and try for the throne, he can come get his ass beat. I grunted like I had always thought if he'd ever searched me out to kick my ass. I'd have taken the beating and tried to convince him otherwise. *Yeah, okay, I get where she's coming from, but isn't that an insult to the oni?*

It is, which is why Kimiko is getting sloppier.

She was. Her fury looked to be mounting as she dished out blow after blow that had no rhyme or reason, and Cassia could tank them more effectively. The entire time they had been fighting, though, Cassia and Kimiko both had ignored the face of their opponent, as if they were trying to be fair about it all.

They fought for another few minutes before the action began to grow truly boring and I really just wanted to relax, or start looking for the Seelie myself.

I wonder if Qin Moira is here?

Do you think they would have put him here for some reason? I mean, the Fae aren't really native here. Galaxy paused to think on her statement a moment, then added, *Then again, oni aren't native to Columbus, so it could be an all over the world kind of thing.*

They could be hiding from Zeke and his crew. I shrugged and one of the oni behind me put a hand on my shoulder. I stilled and growled, "Can I help you?"

"Don't interfere." The one that touched me snarled, fingers digging into my shoulder in a way that—to me—seemed like it was supposed to either cause some kind of pain or make me think twice about whatever choices I was wrestling with.

I snorted and shrugged again, brushing his hand away with fingertips like you might brush dirt off your shoulder. "Not going to, Cassia has this on her own." I glanced over my shoulder again, annoyed. "But you both can damn sure stop touching me. I'm not the most angry person all the time, but that's pushing all the wrong buttons for me. Understand?"

"And what are you going to do about it?" The other shoved my shoulder from the other side, obviously trying to pick a fight.

Cassia said behave, Marcus. Galaxy sighed, then I could hear the tone of her voice shift to a more predatory one. *She never said* anything *about letting someone treat you like you're less than them. I don't think she wants you to kill any of them, though. So maybe no weapons or lethal spells?*

I snickered to myself as the one who hadn't shoved me grunted, "Something funny?"

I nodded, and told Galaxy, *Just make sure she knows they started it.*

Happily. Galaxy purred as I turned around and decked the one that had shoved me in the face so hard that his mask shattered just before he shot backward into the wall beside the tunnel entrance. To his credit, his friend didn't let that stand unpunished long.

He stepped forward and his fist landed in my tensed gut and it still felt like I was being slapped with a bag full of nickels. It lifted me off the ground momentarily and his other fist just missed my chin when I skidded backward, feeling something on my back that felt like a foot.

"The fuck are you idiots doing?" Cassia huffed and tossed Kimiko away from her for a heartbeat to see me. Then she grunted, "Oh. Okay."

She went back to her fight and so did I as the others around us had begun to gravitate toward my side of the room.

"If he attacks any more of you, kill him," Kimiko roared before launching herself at her sister.

"Kid gloves off." Cassia sighed as she clotheslined her sister, throwing a look at me. "Show them."

She means—

"I know what she means." I took a deep breath, breathing

past the pain of the punch to the gut and muttered, "Commence the Hunt."

The shadows in the room darkened rapidly and poured from where they were to both of us as our armor built and burst forth. My attackers froze and Cassia's sister Kimiko gasped in horror as she stared up at her older sister in the garb of the Hunt. "I hate that this happened, and I'm even angrier that you couldn't understand why I left the way I did."

Despite her fear, Kimiko responded in kind, "Oni do not recognize cowardice. If someone is a threat, we fight them and prevail or die. It is the oni way."

Many of the gathered members grunted with the saying, the agreement bolstering them somehow.

"The oni way also led to our being bullied and used by those who are strong enough to hold our leashes," Cassia insisted, throwing her hand out to the side. "How many of you have been viewed as nothing but mindless muscle and enforcers for some yokai gang, or supernatural being stronger than yourself? How many of you are treated like nothing more than that?"

The majority of them stayed quiet as Kimiko climbed to her feet to bar her sister's sight. "They answer only to me, now."

"And you will answer to whoever can prove they are stronger than you." Cassia snorted and crossed her arms. "You call me a coward for taking myself out of a power struggle that would have gotten you and mother killed if I had pressed further, but I call myself smarter than that."

"There is no reason to run if you can fight for yourself!" Kimiko screamed, tears fed by something deeper springing to her eyes now. She clenched her fists at her side and shouted again, "We would have stood with you! We would have fought for you and covered your back, but instead you followed Kenshi and ran away, leaving us alone for so many years!"

She's not mad because Cassia fled, or any of the other bullshit she's trying to sling, I thought to myself as the woman fought with herself and her emotions. *She's pissed because Cassia left them behind.*

It's hard to see what choices may affect when you were the one affected the most, Galaxy stated sagely. *I think that is why Cassia didn't beat her senseless to begin with.*

Makes sense, I grunted to her then sighed. "Hunt complete."

Our armor faded and my phone began to ring, text messages pouring through. I answered it and found a worried Merlin waiting for me. "What's going on? Are you okay?"

I frowned. "Yeah, just showing off. What happened to you, you alright?"

He shouted something that I couldn't make out and something crashed in the background.

"Merlin, what the fuck is going on?"

"Get off the phone, freak." One of the oni near me growled and tried to close the distance with me, only to earn a kick in the side of the head from Cassia.

The kick sent him flying as I snarled, "Merlin!"

"We're fine!" he bellowed back then shouted something again. "Honestly, we're babysitting Luci and his new friends. They saw the armor take us and freaked out, thought we were under attack, and started to defend the shit out of Luci's place. It wasn't pretty."

"Who is it?" Cassia asked me and I mouthed the boy mage's name. "Oh, where are they?"

"Luce's place?" I shrugged and she suddenly looked pissed. "What?"

"We haven't even been there and he gets to go?"

"They're babysitting Luci and some other people," I hissed back, and that only seemed to anger her more. "Who is it, Merlin?"

"Cassia, we need to go." Kimiko sighed. "Get him off the phone."

"We're okay. I'll call you back later after I get them calmed down." With that, he hung up and I turned to the others who were stepping toward me.

"The next one of you fuckers who tries to touch me is getting fucking nuked, I swear to God." It was hard to keep the rage out of my voice and it was Cassia smacking me that drew my ire next. "You get a pass, but they don't."

"No, asshole." She shoved me again, real indignation on her face. "Nuked, *really?*"

I frowned and Kimiko just crossed her arms and said, "Hiroshima? Nagasaki?"

Realization dawned on me and I almost concussed myself with the force my palm hit my forehead. "I am so sorry…"

Kimiko rolled her eyes and regarded her sister. "You fight with him?"

"He's strong." Cassia shrugged as if that said everything she needed to say, and I was somehow *hurt* and lost for words.

Am I being called stupid in an oni sort of way?

Very much so, but at least you're strong, right? Galaxy cackled after she said that, and I wanted to pick up one of the oni masks and hide my face.

One of the oni stepped forward and muttered something to Kimiko, then she sighed and looked at us. "This is not over, but you can come with us for now. Wardens have begun to come toward here and they search for us harder than they have in months."

"Let's go see mother, then," Cassia suggested and Kimiko stilled, prompting her elder sister to say, "What?"

"You won't like seeing her like this," she whispered, but when Cassia offered no further argument, neither did Kimiko, who just shrugged and said, "Come on, then."

CHAPTER EIGHT

Once we were out of a secondary entrance and into an alleyway behind a large building, sounds of sirens and raised voices flooded the air once again.

Kimiko turned toward us, frowning, then spoke to her people, "Hug the shadows and find out what is happening. Report back when you know."

Galaxy?

I'm already on it—I can *read your mind, you know.* She chuckled to herself and padded off as a cat toward where one of the oni had gone.

We began to move away from the noise when Kimiko got a call and answered the phone with a tense, "Moshi Moshi." She nodded and said, "Hai."

"She's going to watch them and report back?" Cassia tilted her head and Kimiko just glared at her. "I know, you hate when people eavesdrop."

"So don't do it," Kimiko hissed in return, then straightened. "Yes. Something with the Fae and the Wardens investigating us."

"That can't be good." I grunted.

It isn't, Galaxy hissed and returned to me, filling me in.

"The Seelie are blaming you and saying they were defending themselves from an attack. The Wardens are starting to believe them, based on some of the things you've been doing to get recognized." I told Kimiko, who stilled. "I have spies too."

As soon as I said that, Arden stepped out of the haze at the end of the alleyway and sighed as two oni stepped toward her. "I'm with your guests."

"She's one of ours," Cassia stated to support her friend and raised a hand to beckon her forward. "Okay, so what should we do, Marcus?"

"We need to get somewhere to hide and lay low until the Wardens stop searching for my people," Kimiko blurted before I could speak, prompting both Cassia and Arden to look from her, then pointedly to me.

"I can agree to that, but tonight, we need to find where they're holed up and take care of them." I stretched my shoulders a bit, already itching for a fight with all the bullshit the oni had been putting me through unknowingly. That made Kimiko still and drew my attention to her. "We've dealt with something like this before. We will take care of it."

"Not on our turf, you won't." She crossed her arms and stared at me, then turned to Cassia. "I cannot believe you're going to let some weak Gaijin speak that way. This is *our* land."

"And the people responsible for this kidnapped his son a little while back," Cassia stated with a shrug. "He's the Huntsman; we're the Wild Hunt. We know no boundaries."

Kimiko was so taken aback that she couldn't speak, so I offered an olive branch. "You can hunt with us, you know. We don't have to operate alone, and you can make sure that your people are safe."

She grunted and walked off, Cassia calling, "Don't be rude, Kimi." The other woman just stalked off while her older sister shook her head. "Little shit."

"She's just like you said she was." Arden smiled and

shrugged. "Guess I missed an almost fight? My armor almost gave me away to someone that was nearby."

"Yeah, something like that." Cassia grunted, then motioned that we should follow her sister.

We walked for a few minutes before she said, "Thank you." She looked over at me and my confusion. "For offering a place at our side to Kimiko. I know that you would prefer to handle this ourselves, but if you had decided to exclude her, she would have likely come just to spite you."

"I figured her for the type anyway." I smiled wryly to myself and she smacked my shoulder playfully. "She's your sister, Cass. I can't not try to get onto her good side."

"It's likely my mother who will be the one to worry about." Cassia huffed and began to walk a little faster.

"Why is that?"

Arden spoke up. "Cassia used to tell me all the time how old school she was." Cassia stayed quiet, contemplative while she walked on and Arden continued, "Like, she has no idea who her father is because he was too weak to keep her until Cass was born. Old school in the way that if someone can defeat you, you shouldn't be alive."

"She sounds so lovely." I smiled, more due to tension than anything else.

"She's a peach," Cassia called back. "Hurry the hell up."

———

We arrived at a more rural area that I hadn't thought would be this close to downtown, but Japan was known for making the space they had work. The houses here were still pretty close to each other but they had walls that separated them from each other and the streets with small gates keeping the public out. Just behind the majority of the homes stood a few apartment complexes that ranged in size from massive multi-story structures to some that only had two floors and a few balconies.

"Where are we headed?" I asked after a moment and Cassia seemed confused too. "What's wrong?"

"I can smell all of them, but her scent is weakest." She glanced over to her sister. "Why?"

Kimiko shook her head and nodded to one of the smaller apartment buildings nearest where we were, plain gray paint on the walls with a green roof and simple furniture outside on the small porch on the ground floor.

"Why aren't we going to the Onsen?" Cassia asked Kimiko and the younger oni just continued to walk until Cassia grabbed her. "Why are we here?"

"This is where mother is," was all she would say before walking to the front door.

Kimiko walked forward and produced a card with a magnet in the back, similar to one that Cassia had used to tease me when we were in Grestal. She made a face and it looked like she would need a new one after all.

We walked through the door and into the small receiving hallway and Kimiko grunted. "Uwabaki are inside the closet on the right if you need them. We don't really care if you wear them or not, but you will not wear shoes."

She didn't bother to put any on herself and walked off into the next room after the hallway, a soft voice greeting her. Cassia put on a pair of white slippers that had orange tips to them and then walked in as I took my shoes off.

The decorations in the home were pretty sparse, except for a few small trees here and there that weren't quite bonsai trees. The pots had muted and soothing colors. Furniture was scarce too, it seemed like this place was decorated this way for a reason.

The same soft voice greeted Cassia from across the room and I couldn't quite see who it was until she stepped to the side, but Arden stopped me from walking any further, Galaxy speaking for her, *Give them a second.*

I frowned, wondering why until I realized that they hadn't seen each other in some time.

The woman *looked* old, not quite frail, but the aura around her was so intense that I could see the oni woman for what she was as soon as she glanced our way. Outwardly, she was bent over a set of small pots with actual bonsai in them, with pruning shears and a small tin watering can that she held.

Her aura had other plans, though, and looked to face us and writhe with some intense emotion. She stood a foot taller than Cassia and Kimiko in their oni forms and her bulk made them look slim. She was massive, and her muscles moved as her aura observed. She had a massive horn, thicker than my forearm, coming out of the left side of her head at an angle. It curved slightly like a bull's, and that was all I could make out. I'd never seen one like this before and to be frank, it was more intimidating than I knew what to do with. Was that a testament to her strength or power?

She spoke again and suddenly the room felt inadequate for all of the energy that came off all three women in waves. Was another fight about to break out?

Cassia spoke to her mother and though I wanted her to, Galaxy didn't translate for me this time. This was their moment. We had to let them have it. Good or bad.

The older woman looked at me and sniffed once before her gaze flicked back to her daughter, her disinterest worrisome to me for some reason.

Not some reason, you're offended and wonder if she's questioning whether you're worthy of her daughter. Galaxy's interjection made me flinch and I just nodded once before suddenly feeling eyes on me.

"You feel the need to break into the conversations and musings of others, child?" The older-looking woman spoke to me now, but there was an edge of steel in her tone.

I shook my head. "Nope. Sometimes I talk back to the voices in my head. Need an expert opinion at times, and they don't like to be ignored."

Oh, you are such a shit, and she's likely about to smear you on the wall. Galaxy had no sooner said the words than a small watering can collided with my head with a thunk that instantly gave me a headache. *See?*

You're not fucking helping! I seethed back, my hand coming up to my head without a thought only for me to find that the shears she had in her other hand were now held close to my throat. I hadn't even seen her move and yet here she was staring at me coldly.

"You raise your hand to me in my home?" She sounded almost like she was offering someone cookies with how sweet her voice went.

This felt more and more like the drill instructors at Parris Island offering us sugar cookies, and I was not about to get my ass kicked and be covered in sand again. "No, ma'am. I simply wanted to feel the welt that you were so kind as to give me for speaking out of turn. I swear I meant you no disrespect."

She stared me in the eyes coldly, though her smile was still in place. "I don't like the weak."

"I'm not that, but I can understand how you might feel that way." I could feel blood trickling down my face though the wound healed in a matter of heartbeats thanks to my lycanthropic healing.

Cassia is begging me to tell you to shut up. She fears her mother will kill you. Or at least try to.

Is this a test? Do I fight back? She didn't respond to me and there was no time to wait.

Her mother growled at me softly, a rumble of the throat rather than the chest that Cassia and Kenshi were known for. "Who are you?"

I looked to Cass and the small woman in front of me actually grabbed my face and forced me to look at her.

Answer her! Galaxy's cry and Cassia's pleading face were enough.

"Marcus Bola, Marine, Huntsman, and Cassia's lover." Kimiko hid her face as I said that last part and Cassia's eyes nearly popped out from behind her glasses. "I've been fighting with Cassia for a few months now. She helped me rescue my son from the same people who are plaguing your city here."

"That is not my concern." The woman *did* let go of my face then, and turned her head slightly to look me over with one eye. As I was closer to her now, I could see that the other eye was milky and didn't track the same as the one on me now. "My concern is the strength of your arm and character if you are to be with her to produce stronger oni for the Night Parade's protection and glory."

"No," Cassia and Kimiko both snarled in unison, surprising each other. Cassia won out on who would speak next. "No one is having or producing anything!"

"And surely not for the Night Parade," Kimiko finished, crossing her arms obstinately as she spoke on. "All they do is force our kind to watch over their holdings, their deals, their people. Then send us out to bully and kill at their beck and call. We are dogs to them, nothing more. They've never cared about us and we're nothing more than fodder to them. To all of the other yokai."

The younger daughter shook her head and shook with fury barely contained as she spit, "And here you are, trying to force the role of protector of the Parade onto all of us. As the Fist of the Parade, or as our mother?"

"We are *warriors*, Kimiko," their mother spat, turning to regard her youngest daughter. "Warriors do not care for status, pomp, or the like. We thrive where the most combat is. We are the front line, and we are the *final* line for many. I am your mother always, but I have a duty to uphold our position as the protectors of the Night Parade."

She turned to regard Cassia. "What do you mean that there will not be more oni coming from you, Chiasa?" She was back to looking at me with a sneer. "If you are not strong enough for her to desire children, then you aren't strong enough to keep around."

With that, she took the shears and rammed them toward my stomach. I cast Embodiment of Lightning, stepping around her.

She didn't move, flinch, or anything as I stepped away, just kept stabbing forward until she realized I wasn't there.

I thought I'd gotten away from her but my stomach felt warm and it was a lot for me to be able to stand suddenly.

"Marcus!" Cassia launched herself toward me but her mother stood in front of her and slapped her hard enough that her head crashed through the wall, then her shoulders as well. Kimiko didn't give a shit about me and stood by, but I heard flesh against flesh and she cried out as she was thrown through the nearest glass pane behind her mother's bonsai.

Arden was next to me in an instant and moved me just in time to avoid another slash to the stomach. If she had wanted me to die swiftly, she would have killed me right away.

No, she wanted me to suffer for being too weak to fend her off.

I grunted and reached through my bond to Amabala, my consciousness only thinking of one thing—escape. Using Bond Thief, I took her Portal Creation from her and told Galaxy, *Get them all to me, now.*

On it. Shadows lengthened from me and Galaxy bolted forth from me in her massive big-cat form. She grabbed Cassia by the leg and yanked, pulling the unconscious woman from the wall with a couple heaves as Cassia's mom came for me and Arden again.

Arden was just able to keep her away from me, but even with the heat that she was building around her, the oni elder refused to back down, the only thing she seemed to care about were her small trees. The thought to burn some crossed my mind, but even as some of them caught fire from Arden just being too close to them, all the oni mother focused on was us.

Glass broke and Kimiko clambered back through the pane, knocking over one of the plants and grabbed Cassia from Galaxy, so Arden brought us over to her and I cast the spell. The portal opened to our room and Arden shoved both oni sisters through the portal as Galaxy padded through, then she smiled and said, "Let's get you safe for now."

I frowned and she shoved me through the portal as the shears left our attacker's hand toward the portal, like a too-big-throwing knife, as it closed and fire erupted in my right shoulder.

Arden wasn't with us in the room.

CHAPTER NINE

"Stay awake, Marcus, stay with me." Galaxy's worried voice flooded my right ear as hands moved over my back and stomach. "How is Cassia, Kimiko?"

"Who are you?" Kimiko returned confusedly. "Where did you come from?"

"That's not important. I'm with Marcus and Cassia. How is she?"

I fought to bring myself back to full consciousness, but Galaxy just touched my good shoulder and muttered, "No. Stay there for just a moment longer, I'll need to help focus your healing and it's not going to be easy."

"Who are you?" Kimiko sounded like she was coming more to terms with what was going on.

Galaxy raised her voice and snarled, "Hungry, so if you don't tell me how my girlfriend is, I will fucking eat you so I can heal them both."

"Arden." I managed to grunt as I opened one eye. Even with my healing, the pain was pretty bad.

"She's okay, she's just running interference." Galaxy focused on something, her eyes relaxing slightly. "She's on her way here. We will see her soon."

"Good." I hissed and tried to focus on the sources of pain; my stomach and shoulder burned.

"How many times did she stab you?" Galaxy muttered more to herself than to me, but I had to admit that I had no clue either. She'd looked *so* slow.

"Likely at least six times," Kimiko muttered from wherever she was. I still couldn't manage to open my eyes for very long and I wasn't going to look around. "She's fast and she's the one who trained Bubba Kenshi's master. The Way of the Blade is how she thinks. It's all she knows."

Flesh slapping flesh made Galaxy flinch as Kimiko growled, "Wake up. She didn't hit you that hard, Sissy."

Cassia bellowed a roar and must have hit her sister on reflex because Galaxy just snarled and howled, "Quit it, you two muscle-headed-idiots, before I start to get *really* mad." I opened my eyes just a bit to see her clenching her teeth. "Get your ass over here, Cassia, and help heal Marcus."

Cass grunted and there was a brief pause before I felt hands on my other, bad, shoulder. I hissed and then groaned as sweet relief surged through me. This was slightly different from the healing I was used to with her. Most likely from when she had leveled up, or something to that effect. I was too relieved to really care, outside appreciating her for being able to help soothe the pain.

"Why didn't you just tell me that mother was so deeply bound to the Night Parade, Kimiko?" Cassia's soft question surprised me, and I think her sister too, because the pause after that felt like it stretched forever. "Why not just tell me and save us both the heartache and potential loss?"

Kimiko was quiet a moment longer before she answered, fatigue in her tone. "Would you have believed me if I had said as much?" Then her voice hardened. "She only returned to them because you had left, and the void of losing two of her children was too much for her to bear on top of the dishonor.

She gave the magic Onsen to them, and the leader who took over after you fled took her eye, and then forced her to fight and fight until she was the strongest of all of us."

"But she hated the Parade." Cassia sounded confused. I was right there with her. None of this made a lick of sense to me.

"She hated losing you and Kenshi more." Kimiko sighed and shook her head. The pain fading almost fully from my body made it easier to look around. "They used her loss to take her mind, and now she's the one who protects the newest leader of the Parade. I had hoped seeing you might break her chains, but it only seems to have cemented it now. The Night Parade is up to something, and she won't tell me what."

"What if they really do plan on making a move on your friend's ascension?" Galaxy asked softly, a contemplative look on her face. "Tsuki said that she will be ascending soon, right? There was a calendar with several dates circled on the wall inside her house. What if the Night Parade is planning something?"

"Even as strong as they are, they can't hope to stand against Shin Bai, or even still Raijin," Cassia explained. Kimiko just watched her and Cass seemed to grow slightly uncomfortable with how her sister stared at her as she spoke. "Tsuki wouldn't say his name, because her doing so would summon his attention to her and make him mad, but he would send forces to protect her."

"What if the Night Parade had a supplier that could aid them in gaining the muscle they need to overpower her guard?" Kimiko asked with mounting concern in her tone. "The Night Parade's master would not be opposed to trickery to gain power; he's actually infamous for it. If he were to make a deal with the Seelie for that drug that they've been making and trying to sell on the streets here, then he would have the oni and other yokai take it so that they can overwhelm the opposition."

"Kill Tsuki and stop the ascent so that they take over," Cassia finished, her head falling into her hands. "I just wanted a vacation. How did all of this happen now? Of all times."

"Fate has other plans," Galaxy said sagely, but seemed to try to take a more pleasant approach as opposed to sounding reproachful. "Maybe this is some good luck rubbing off on you?"

My pocket began to buzz wildly as someone was calling. I was going to ignore it, but Galaxy pinched me. "Ow!"

"It's Merlin," she muttered and shooed me away.

I sighed and stood slowly before walking stiffly toward where our room was as I answered. "Yo."

"We are so up shit creek."

I frowned. "That's a hello for you. What's going on?"

"Someone's released more videos of supernatural creatures doing supernatural things." He paused and sighed. "I'm sending you some videos, but I can't get them to send to you as I'm talking to you. Watch them and call me back."

He hung up before I could say anything else and Arden joined me. "What's wrong?"

I shrugged and my phone buzzed once. "We're about to find out."

On the screen, she and I watched a man walking into a park and then shifting under the light of the full moon and running off into the woods beyond. He didn't look like anything I had seen in the Table, but I mean, how many types of shifters were out there?

"That's not good, but it can just be called CGI or some shit, right?" I grimaced and called Merlin back.

"Did you watch it?" The question caught me as soon as the call went through, making me nod, then I rolled my eyes. "I'm assuming you did. There are entire forums online dedicated to this right now. The Wardens and Phone Gnomes are attacking it and doing everything they can to try to get it down, but every time one video goes down, three more come back up."

"Okay, well, let them handle it. We've got a bit of a situation on our hands here as well, and we need you."

"Marcus, you don't get it—this shit could ruin us." I frowned and he continued hurriedly. "If the world finds out we exist, that means that there's going to be a shit ton of potential to start a war. Not to mention the more serious repercussions."

"There are more serious repercussions than war?" It was hard to keep the sarcasm out of my tone.

"Yes, asshole," Merlin snarled back. "Some of the more powerful supernatural beings, like gods, require faith in order to maintain their power."

"Okay. You would think that a little press would give them a little boost, right?"

"The kind of faith required is blind faith, Marcus." He sighed. Honestly, the kid sounded tired. "If Normies find out that gods exist, a holy war could break out *on top* of the racial war that could blow up the world, and the gods will be powerless to stop it."

"Is there any way that we can get ahead of this?" By now, Cassia and Galaxy wandered over to where Arden and I were standing, but Galaxy appeared distracted. *Listening in?*

Yes, I honestly thought this wouldn't be an issue at all. There seemed like so many different failsafes in place for this kind of thing.

"The Wardens are trying to find out where the video came from, and they're hunting down the original poster, but every time they think they got a hit on them, their global position changes." He seethed for a second and finally said, "We need the Hunt to help with this."

"We're kind of busy here too, man." I filled him in on the particulars and he listened without interrupting. Finally I finished, "If the Night Parade takes out the Luck Dragon, Japan is gone. And then they're free to really come at the rest of the world."

"I don't think that's quite the world-ending fiasco that you think it is." Merlin was careful in how he said it. "Sure, it's bad, but the Wardens there know how to fight the Night Parade."

Galaxy must have said something to Arden and Cassia, because the latter informed us, "If the Night Parade is released from Japan, then they can become even stronger, and will call even more yokai from Grestal to fill their ranks. So it won't just be the one hundred members of the current organization, it would be thousands, and they would all be free to go wherever the fuck they want. No one could fight that."

Galaxy added, "Not to mention they would all likely be on whatever drug the Seelie are peddling now."

I'd put Merlin on speaker by now and he groaned. "The Seelie are there?"

"Not just any Seelie—our boy Qin Moira." Arden huffed and crossed her arms before looking at me and Cass. "What do we do?"

I shook my head. "The Wild Hunt can't attack the internet." I closed my eyes and just shook my head again. "But we *can* make sure that we get on top of it. Kaz and Cornelius have my permission to call me with coordinates if they get them, so we can step in if we need to. If the perpetrator is found, the Hunt will bring them in, or at least put a stop to it. I want them on this as a priority."

"I put them on it already, they're the ones hunting the poster down, but the others are all in the way more than anything else." Merlin grunted. "They say this isn't really their area of expertise but they're gonna run this dog 'til it either hunts or drops. Whatever that means."

"What about us?" Amabala's voice came over the line and she sounded worried.

"You're best suited where you are." I frowned and scratched my head. "You and Merlin can get to us pretty much whenever you need to, and we're better off going at both of these things as hard as we can. Divide and conquer. We will find and crush the Seelie here so that we can clear up our schedule for the other situation."

Cassia gave me a pouting look, as did Arden. "Fate of the supernatural world, guys. Is cosplaying *that* important?"

Kimiko looked surprised. "You both cosplay?"

CHAPTER TEN

"Where is your guy, Kimi?" Cassia sighed as she finished looking over the wounds on my shoulder and back.

"He said he would be ten minutes. That's his code for an hour, shut up," Kimiko shot back venomously. The peace they had seemed to reach had begun to devolve after Cassia told her what her tastes in cosplay were, but honestly I couldn't care about it with everything going on and tuned them out.

I started to try to report the video wherever I could find it, knowing it likely wouldn't help, but it was what I could do. Who was trying to do this shit, and why? What was there to gain from this other than starting a world-wide shit show that could spell the end of an already-tenuous peace? Or at least Normy ignorance.

A sigh escaped my lips. *I was a Normy not too long ago. How far has my life gone that I can barely think of myself as human?*

You aren't, Galaxy stated pleasantly as she joined me. *Never really have been, had you?*

I shook my head, and as I was about to answer, someone knocked on the door.

Kimiko was closest and, with a nod from Cassia, opened the

door. She spoke to someone for a moment, then returned alone. "Room cleaner came around, she was curious if we needed help, but I turned her away for today."

"Thank you." Arden huffed and pulled out her Switch.

"If we have time to be gaming, we can be helping Kaz and Corn." I grunted, holding up my phone.

"We can." She sighed and put the game system back down. "I just want to calm down a bit. Cassia and Kimiko's mom is scary as shit and she's *fast*. She almost caught me."

"That had to have been scary." Cass grunted and stared at her. "How did you manage to get away?"

"I set the stove on fire and it started to melt." She shrugged. "She stopped to put it out—I just realized that I don't know your mother's name."

"It's Chiasa," Kimiko stated, then dipped her head at Cassia. "She gave her first born daughter her name to carry on her strength."

"It worked." I snorted, then frowned at her as Cassia looked away. "So why 'Cassia'?"

"It was close enough to my real name that responding to it was easier than making up something completely different." Cass spoke plainly, nodding to Kimiko. "Your father named you because he was strong enough to do so. I got stuck with the reminder that strength was all mother cared about. And this kind of proved that, didn't it?"

"If I had known she could stab me without hitting me, I would have gone in there ready for a fight." I had tried not to grumble, but I was feeling self-conscious.

Kimiko, Arden, and Cassia looked at me as if I suddenly wore a dunce cap. "Are you dumb?" Arden whispered hoarsely, then clarified, "You went into an oni home—to meet *Cassia's mother*—and you didn't go in ready for a fight?"

"Seems dumb, Cassia." Kimiko jabbed a thumb in my direction and the other oni woman just shook her head at my dismay.

The door rattled again with another knock and this time Cassia stood to go and get it.

She came back leading a teen boy who couldn't have been any more than sixteen or seventeen, by the looks of him. *Merlin's age.* Galaxy sighed and then I could see the aura around him. It was oni. But this one had no horn, and looked slim and lanky, like the boy standing in front of us, but just a bit taller.

Kimiko spoke in Japanese and the boy flinched. He looked at her and asked, "Can report in English? Need practice."

Kimiko raised a brow but raised a hand as if to give permission and the boy began, haltingly telling us, "Seelie working in river where house."

He frowned and Cassia spoke to him in Japanese. *She's telling him how to say it properly.* Then she actually said the word he meant and he bowed his head.

"Strong watch." He lifted his hands to mime people watching. "On roof, they watch street. Street watch take shipment. People. Students. Night Parade want come tonight."

"What do you mean they take shipments?" I asked, Cassia and Kimiko both asking questions in Japanese. "People and students? Are they kidnapping them?"

This time it was Kimiko who translated, because the boy just babbled in Japanese for a moment with a look of uncertainty and confusion on his face.

"The students come in and work on some portion of the floor of the warehouse, like packing and stuff," Kimiko explained with a frown. "Kind of like some warehouses are constantly moving their wares and stores to other places? Like that."

The boy spoke again and she added, "The people they take in are weaker yokai, Touched, and vagrants."

"The yokai and Touched must be where they're getting their mana from." Arden and I looked at each other, seemingly coming to the same agreement, then she added, "And I still owe them for hurting Soiphra. What do we do?"

"We don't have enough bodies to attack them on our own when they're both there, the Seelie and the yokai." I scratched my head and wracked my brain for a solution. If the yokai of the Parade were half as strong as Cassia's mom, we would be hurting.

"The Phantomu will attack them this evening." Kimiko stood up and nodded to the boy who stepped back as she looked at us. "We will attack them, and if someone happens to sneak in and do more damage how they see fit, then I cannot see anything wrong with this."

"That would be putting you in the crossfire between the Seelie, the Wild Hunt, and possibly Mother and the Night Parade," Cassia stated, worry clear on her features. "Are you sure you want to do this?"

"Mother has known that I will not forgive the Night Parade for their treatment of our people." Kimiko shrugged. "The oni will no longer be treated as mindless servants and enforcers. We are not lesser. We are equal, if not better than them."

She looked at Cassia and grunted. "I will fight the world to my dying breath to be free of the Night Parade for all of our people. Even if those people do not know they want it themselves."

"Can't argue with that," Arden hissed softly to me, and Cassia just shook her head.

Up to now, we'd had a smaller force than every other group of people we'd gone up against. Never really by choice, but more of necessity. Each time, it had been a mixed bag of wins and losses. Now though…?

"Three of us isn't enough to really safely go after the Seelie while they're distracted, especially not with the unknown at their potential advantage. If I have a choice, we need the assistance." I scratched my head, remembering the invitation of aid. "This may be one that we need to call Zeke in on."

"Why would we call him here?" Cassia frowned. "We can do this. I have a friend I will call to put her people on Tsuki, and then she will come and fight with us."

"He wants the Seelie just as bad as we do, and the guy is a

fucking monster," I retorted, then something hit me. "And we could possibly get his help back home too! He's a tool we can use to finish this faster so that Tsuki and her ascension happen, then we can be of use if they find out who's posting that damn video."

"Do you really think he will be able to get here in time?" Arden asked, concern on her face. "I mean, it's a last minute flight for sure."

"We don't know until we try." I pulled out my phone and called him. The phone rang for a bit, then went to voicemail. After it beeped, I spoke awkwardly, "Uh, hey man, Marcus here. We're in Japan and we have a bit of a Seelie problem, as well as some other things. We could use some help, you know, saving the supernatural world over here. Call me."

Kimiko raised an eyebrow. "You sounded pathetic."

"Your mother," I shot back and she just smiled. "What?"

"Almost killed you." She smiled a little wider. "You forgot to mention that part."

That gave me pause and I looked over to Cassia. "If your mother comes to whatever meeting this is tonight, she's going to try to kill me."

Cassia dipped her head once. "Yes."

"What about you two?" Arden's question made the two oni look at each other then back at her without another word. "She's going to try to kill you both, isn't she?"

"She might, if she feels like we're enough of a threat, but that's assuming she will be there." Kimiko shrugged as if it didn't matter, then looked uncomfortably at Cassia. "She only works for one person, and that's the master of the Night Parade. She will issue orders to the oni and the foot soldiers, but nothing more for anyone."

"Who is it?" Cassia tilted her head sideways and made sure her glasses stayed on her face as she waited for a response that didn't come. "Do you not know?"

Kimiko nodded. "No one knows. The new leader came in and tore the old Parade apart but left mother alone. He's only been in charge for a year or so, and operates in total secrecy." She ran her hands through her dark hair and grunted before sighing. "Only his inner circle knows who he is and outside of hearing his voice, someone would assume the leader was Mother or his second, Saizo."

"She probably only acts as his voice, like I know I can make decisions with Yenny's blessing without him needing to know until after my reports are in." Cassia grumbled thoughtfully. She stared at the ground for a long moment then looked to the newcomer. "Do you know what the set up will be?"

He looked to Kimiko, who answered for him. "The Night Parade is big on tradition, but they have evolved into a more... Yakuza style of things. They will likely invite their guests to drink with them somewhere nearby."

"Qin Moira is banned from the Table, as are all of his clan," I muttered back and sighed. "Which means that the High Table will be off limits to them for that reason."

"The Night Parade prefers not to go to the Table anyway." Kimiko shrugged and looked to her sister. "Mother hates that you work for them."

"She works for the Parade; she's no more honorable than I am." Cassia snorted, which made Kimiko cross her arms and stare at her with open distaste. "What? You know why I left, Kimiko. You've seen firsthand what being with the Parade has done to Mother. Can you truly think me honorless for leaving that all behind? Do you think *your* honor is more intact than my own by attacking your own people as they do what they're forced to do by their rulers? Normies and the like? By fighting against other people using us since before the dawn of mortal time, do you not degrade the honor of our people for setting boundaries and trying to defend them?"

"Can we drop the honorable bullshit and just agree that you both are doing what you feel is best for you and your situation?" Arden snarled and the oni boy flinched, flames wreathing his hands as he prepared for a fight and the jinn woman just shook her head at him. "You don't want to bring a lighter into a fight with napalm, kid."

She turned her gaze on Kimiko and Cassia as her hair began to flicker and shift, the flames of her flame jinn heritage leaking out as irritation mounted in her tone. "Stop making each other explain yourselves needlessly over and over. You've fought once, and you haven't stopped fighting since then. Do you have any idea what I would give to be able to have a spat with my sister?"

Kimiko looked offended, but Cassia appeared cowed and hung her head, muttering, "I'm sorry. I only turned her into stone to try to keep all of us safe."

"I'm not mad at you for that!" Arden snarled and her hair ignited fully, the reddish cast of it making her skin glow amber near her eyes. "I'm angry that you have your sister right there and all you can do is bicker. Don't you know what you have? Fuck! Just get over it already."

"It's not so simple as that…" Kimiko paused as if she was trying to find the words but they just didn't come to her in time.

"Do you love your sister?" Arden blurted and threw her hands out to her sides as she looked from Cass to Kimiko. "Do you?"

Cassia was the first to admit, "Yes. More than anything."

Kimiko looked shocked and embarrassed, but Cassia just sighed and said, "I'm honestly just jealous that you had the thought to unite the younger oni toward a cause for freedom from being used as muscle in this endless pissing match between light and dark, and all I did was get out when I had a chance to."

Kimiko looked away before she muttered so low I could barely catch it. "I was just trying to do something only *I* could do." She sighed and turned to look at Arden. "Bold of you to try to come into an oni argument. I've fought people for less."

Arden snorted and jerked a thumb at Cassia, but it looked weird the way she did it with her thumb going forward. "Your sister's been trying to beat my ass for years—if *she* can't take me, baby, I doubt you could. And I won't go easy on you, either."

Kimiko went stiff and Cassia roared with laughter until someone knocked on the door and startled all of us. Kimiko answered the door gruffly and promptly received—what could have only been—the dressing down of a lifetime from a small woman with a back scratcher in her fist that she leveled at the taller woman like it was a damned sword.

It was another three minutes of what could have been muttered threats or apologies to the old woman before the door closed and Kimiko returned to us with a sour expression.

I asked, "What?"

Kimiko looked up and announced, "She said that I woke her cat up, and then she kept asking me what I was going to do about it. I said, 'eat the cat' and then she got even more mad."

"Normies are protective of their food." Cassia chuckled and glanced at me and my shocked face. "We're joking."

"Yes, don't tell me you think all oni eat cats." Kimiko snorted and chuckled with her sister.

"It was a concern for a minute, but I have to admit that I'm a bit uneducated with your culture after all of this." I scratched my head and shrugged. "Thanks for taking the heat for us, and I'm glad that the bickering is over."

"Over?" Kimiko raised an eyebrow and smirked. "We've been playful for a while, not bickering."

Cassia sighed and rolled her eyes. "They don't know that, Kimi. Let's focus on what's to come and we can squabble later, okay?"

"After some sake?" Kimiko pressed and her older sister nodded, much to my surprise. "Yosh!"

"So, what will the Parade and the Seelie end up doing?" I asked again, then noted that Galaxy was quiet next to me watching all of this. *You okay?*

She flinched then nodded. *Yeah, just going through some of Cassia's memories of everything. Some things aren't adding up for her and she's worried. She's also not sure if her friends will be enough with her mom possibly batting for the home team, and that worries her more. We might be spread too thin on this, Marcus.*

It's the best we've got, Galaxy. I looked around the room at the people we had here. *I don't think one video is going to make the world lose its fucking mind the way they're treating it, but I'd rather have Merlin, Kaz, and Cornelius on it than all of us because we would likely just be in their way.*

That's hardly fair to say of all of us.

There was a loud crack from across the room and my gaze snapped to where Cassia and Kimiko had just punched each other. "I look away for two fucking seconds!"

CHAPTER ELEVEN

"You're sure this is where they will likely meet?" I tried to keep my voice low as Kimiko and I scouted a potential meeting spot.

"If this were the Yakuza proper?" She stared at the bath house in disgust and grunted. "No. But the Night Parade takes pride in their many deformities and they like to have humans nearby them at all hours of the day to help the weaker members maintain their human disguises as best as possible."

"They have a hard time keeping them?" That was concerning. If the yokai took over, would they kill all humans or keep some as pets?

"Their shapes are tied to their souls in a way that makes it hard to maintain an outward form that isn't their normal one. The weakest among them can't take shape at all, but that's not important right now." She glanced at me and frowned, then added, "Oni are different. We're demons and a form like a human is almost as natural to us as our normal form, just smaller and more fragile looking."

"Ah." I jerked my head at someone whose aura looked strong, even from where we watched down the street. "Some-one's going in there."

"That one gets a pass, it's one of the Wardens on his rounds." She watched for a moment longer and pointed. "See the talismans on his hip? What looks like a key ring? Those are for his work."

"Do they work?"

"They're packed with mana and holy energy. Enough that most yokai would be expelled from it, but it would take several at once against a member of the Parade to make it a viable option for combat." She leaned back and hissed, "I'm hungry. I knew we should have eaten something."

"Sorry." I shrugged and checked my inventory. I had one of Cassia's favorite Mochi candies in there. I'd been saving it for her, but figured what the hell. "Here, can't work with a starving oni."

"I wouldn't eat you," she grumbled but took the candy with a soft smile. "I love these."

"So does your sister." I smiled at the thought and vowed to get more if we had time.

"What do you like about her?"

Her sudden question caught me off guard and I floundered for a second before answering, "She's strong, smart, loyal, and funny. She's awesome, kind, and caring. I mean, the list goes on."

"So you like that she can defend you?" She said that in such a way that was almost grating.

"I like that she's strong enough to defend herself and is willing to stand in for others when she cares for them." I checked the street again. "She makes it really easy to care about her when she comes into the relationship as an equal. I wasn't really sure what I was getting into with her and Galaxy, but I realized over the last few months that I was getting a partnership that I haven't had before."

I smiled at the thought of it, because Cassia had shown me that I was worthy of her and her of I plenty of times. She brought me gifts, and I did the same. She told me she cared, and then showed me by pushing me to strive to be better. To truly find myself. She supported me.

"After the relationship that I'd had before?" I shook my head and grimaced. "It's a welcome reprieve."

"So you're damaged goods, and she's fixing you." Her flat tone was just so blunt that I should've had a concussion.

I managed a strangled, "What the fuck was that about?"

"Shh." She held up a hand, peeked around the corner, and grimaced. I joined her after a calming breath and found four men in suits walking into the place as the little boy sweeping the street greeted them happily and loudly. "That was surely a warning, but they didn't look like elves to me, what about you?"

"No, though they did have dark, almost purple auras clouding around them." They'd been strong-looking auras too.

"Thick, dark auras, and they weren't elves?" She hissed and then growled low to herself before muttering, "Those are yokai, but they're joy riding."

I frowned at her and shook my head. "I'm sorry, they're what?"

"Joy riding." She looked back around the corner to make sure no one was nearby, but stopped and pointed to the doorway. "Look at them, what do they look like?"

I rolled my eyes and looked. Sure enough, they had the same thick auras as well. "Same."

She clenched her eyes and hissed, "*Shiiiiiiiiiit.*" I raised an eyebrow at her and she just grunted and said, "We're so fucked if we try to go in there without more people to fight."

"I thought oni were all about fighting against the odds," I teased lightheartedly. I knew we were going to be at a disadvantage but not *that* bad of one if what she said was true.

"We love a good fight, not a stupid fight, though there isn't much of a difference to us most times." She stood up from where she knelt and jerked a thumb over her shoulder toward the bath house. "That... is a nightmare. Those look like they could be Yakuza thugs with yokai riders."

I folded my arms and grunted, "Explain."

"I am, shut up." She closed her eyes and then looked at me, and spoke again, as if it took effort not to just beat me. "Riders, or joyriders, are yokai that have been summoned to Earth but aren't strong enough to make their own physical bodies appear. So they possess a body and bring out the latent abilities within. They're the true foot soldiers of the Parade, and not strong enough to be part of the one hundred members."

I shrugged. "So, what, they take over a little old lady, they can lift a car?"

"They take over a little old lady, they can lift a car and throw it at you." She sneered at me for something. "That's too simple. They don't care about their host at all and will happily destroy it so that they can just go and inhabit another one when the one they're in gets destroyed."

"Any way to kill them?"

"Killing the host before they leave, but once they know that the host is about to die, they typically flee." She actually leaned forward and bit her thumb in thought. "This is bad, and it confirms what we thought—they're going to actually try it."

Galaxy?

I've already let the others know, but Cassia's run into a bit of a situation with her friend and will be a bit.

I grimaced. *She need us?*

"What are you thinking about so hard?" Kimiko stared at me as if I had started to sprout horns. "We need to make sure we can confirm that this place will be used for the meeting."

"Okay, I have an idea for how we can do that, but we're going to be on our own for a bit."

She frowned. "What do you think we could do that will keep them from getting suspicious? I was just thinking of sneaking in the back, or fighting our way in."

"Why not lean on their predispositions toward you?" She stared at me pointedly and I added, "You're going to go over there and offer to take over the post as a guard so that the important people can be used elsewhere."

She looked like she was about to attack me where I stood as she seethed. "I will not."

"Then you risk them finding out that we know and our advantage is lost if this is the correct place." I shrugged and looked at the two of them. Honestly, from this distance, I might be able to kill both of them in a single go with Reaper, or a couple well-placed shots. But that was going to draw a lot of unwanted attention to us and then from there to the bathhouse.

Galaxy stepped from my shadow and stated, "We should observe and wait for the others to arrive before doing anything rash, but getting closer is not a bad idea." She took her cat form and padded down the street toward the two guards and prowled like she was hunting for bugs or mice.

The two guards saw her, then turned back to what they were doing, which looked to just be standing there and chatting on either side of the doorway.

We stood around for another half an hour as nothing more happened and Kimiko ignored me to the point that I may as well have been alone. Just as I was about to call it, a car pulled up and more figures that had the same kind of auras as the joyriders got out after a pair of oni. The oni took over at the door and the others lined up beside each other, obscuring our view completely.

Then another figure got out of the car, Kimiko perking up at the arrival. "That could be someone important."

"Yeah, but how can we confirm that this is the place with just that?"

"Do the joyriders and oni not give it away to you?" She was loud enough that I worried that she would give us away.

I almost told her as much before my phone began to buzz in my pocket, stealing the thought. I pulled out my phone and answered it without looking at it out of habit. "Hello."

"What was this about Seelie in Japan?" His voice was a bit irritated as he came over the line, and his speech was slightly slurred. I wasn't sure who I was speaking to, Chris or Zeke, but I assumed since they'd been asleep, it had to be Chris.

"Yeah, just that. We have Seelie in Japan trying to fuck with the natural order of things and they're going to help the Night Parade take over the place, then start tearing shit up all over the world."

He was quiet for a minute, then muttered something to someone else and came back. "You need a hand with the elves there then?" He waited for a second, then seemed to come to grips. "Oh! Shit, sorry man. I'm a little hungover at the moment so my brain is a little... lemme call you back in a moment."

He hung up abruptly and Kimiko stared at me disbelievingly, having obviously listened in on the conversation. "You put your faith in that?"

"He's a good person when he's not a threat. Besides, I thought you didn't like eavesdropping?" I shot back and waited. It wasn't long before my phone rang again and I answered, "Hey."

"Yeah, hey, sorry about that." He cleared his throat and coughed before speaking again. "Really haven't tied one on like that since I partied with the dwarves in Djurn Forge."

"Where?" I frowned at the mention of the place, having never heard of it.

He just laughed and said, "Not important. So is there anyone of any real importance there?"

"Like if they were to be killed it could possibly be a cataclysmic 'fuck you' to the Seelie?" I grinned and nodded. "One of the fuckers here claimed to be in line for the throne, but how accurate it is, is beyond me. Though his daddy will likely get mad if true."

I heard a harsh laugh on the other end of the line. "You got a problem with me killing him?"

"Only in that I have a debt to settle with him that will end in death, otherwise, you're welcome to party with us if you don't mind helping a bit."

He went quiet. "This is the one who took your kid, the one

you spoke about?" I grunted and he growled, "Where are you again? Japan? Anyone around?"

"Just Kimiko, but she's Cassia's sister and an oni, so…" I shrugged, unsure what he cared about that for.

"See you in a minute."

The line went dead and I put my phone back into my pocket only to have him appear next to me two minutes later out of nowhere. He just appeared as if he had been there this whole time, except he made a motion as if he landed from a slight drop or jump.

"Hey!" He grinned and looked at both of us. Kimiko moved to attack him, but he just frowned at her and swept her fist aside like she was trying to high five him and it had irritated him. "Attack first and ask questions later is slowly becoming the norm for oni with me."

I held up a hand to stop her from turning and attacking again. "Kimiko, this is the man that I had called earlier, he's here to help us out."

She turned to him and snarled, "He just appeared out of nowhere and you *aren't* concerned?" She stared at him and spoke low. "Even the stronger yokai will give a tell of mana or ki before they arrive somewhere. The same is true of the Touched. I felt nothing from this man. Why? What are you?"

"Still hungover slightly." Chris hushed her softly with a wave and she tilted her head at him. "Just someone interested in wiping out the Seelie infestation in this world and wherever I happen to find them."

"And how's that going for you?" Kimiko shot back with her hands at her sides like she was still ready to fight.

"Pretty good, actually," he answered and grinned as he looked at me. "Better now. I'd love to find where the rest of them are hiding. Maybe you and your friends can come hunting with me and mine soon, and root them out of their hidey holes?"

"You'll be helping us save the world in one way with this, so if you're willing to help us, I'll be willing to help you if I can." I scratched my head and then filled him in on our current situation and the situation back home. "Think you can be in?"

He nodded. "In for a penny, in for a pound, I suppose. I'll do a lot to rid myself of the Seelie here."

"Why?" Kimiko asked suddenly. "You aren't an elf, what does it matter to you?"

He turned his gaze to her and smiled. "You're an oni with a Seelie problem. Do you also ask an exterminator why they hate rats, bugs, and other insignificant creatures, or do you let them rid you of your infestation?"

Kimiko looked startled at his logic and frowned, then looked at me. "So long as you do not harm any of my people or this land, I will not fight you, but do not tempt me again, and announce yourself before you come here."

That made me think. Curiously, I asked, "How did you get here, by the way?"

He held up his hand and waggled his fingers. "*Magic.*"

"No shit." I rolled my eyes and he looked around the corner at the building in question, the joyriders that had lined the walkway gone and replaced with the oni guards. "Those are oni, they just got here, and there are yokai joyriders inside. Anything telling from them?"

"Nothing yet, but how about we go ahead and get a little closer to watch them?" He held up his hand and his aura flared white hot for just a flash and then it was gone. "There. Let's go."

"What are you doing?" I hissed softly as he strolled down the street like he owned it. As he closed in, Galaxy streaked out of her hiding spot toward us, and though the guards followed her with their eyes, they didn't see him as he moved closer.

He stopped across the street and situated himself on a set of milk crates near the entrance and waved us toward him.

We stared at him for a moment longer until he stood up and made a show of walking over to stand in front of one of the guards and waving a hand in his face. When the oni didn't react, he pointed to us and jerked his head as if to invite us toward him.

I was the first one to move, and then Galaxy began meowing loudly. *Marcus? Where did you go? I can't find you!*

I'm in front of the guards. Chris cast some sort of spell and now they can't see us. I stared at the man as he sat on the crates and watched them curiously. *What the hell is he?*

Strong. The fact that he can do this is insane. She paused for a moment and stared at the guards. *Can I eat him?*

I wish you could, to be truthful. If we could have his power, we would be unstoppable.

She nodded and we continued to watch them for a time as they just stood there. Kimiko grew bored and walked away for a time and then came back.

She motioned for me to follow her and I did, leaving Chris to watch them.

Once we were out of the immediate vicinity, she whispered, "Cassia and your friend Arden are still very busy, and we will need to handle this well to avoid too much danger if someone stronger than the top twenty is here." I raised my eyebrows at this, as it seemed she had a bit of a change of heart since she last mentioned her plan to get us in.

"Well, we have the big guns back there so we should be okay." I frowned at her and narrowed my gaze. "What's going on with Cass and Arden?"

"The kitsune have agreed to help, but they have offered your friends a trial in exchange." She crossed her arms and explained, "They track a nasty nogitsune in the city, and it is very elusive and clever."

She stared at me for a time and finally asked, "Are you certain we can trust this man?"

I laughed, the sound harsher than I meant for it to. "No, not in the slightest. But he had a chance to kill all of us and he could have, but didn't. He's tried to be fair where he could and though I don't understand him, I think he could be considered honorable. If it helps, I trust that his interests here align with ours and we can at least ensure that the Night Parade will have a hard time going through with their plans."

She didn't say any more than that and just nodded to me. We rejoined the watching man and he nodded to us upon our return.

It took another hour and a half with night truly down around us for anything of note to happen, and this time it was the elves who came. Their ears were hidden by magic, but I could see their auras. Who I couldn't see was Qin Moira.

I looked back at Chris to find the King standing in his place, his clothes having changed into something like sweats and a simple tank top that hung loosely on his frame, but there was no mistaking that this was his real self. Kimiko went to turn toward him, but I stopped her and shook my head. I didn't need her freaking out and attacking him again, so I pointed toward him and mouthed his name.

Her eyes widened and she mouthed, *Is that him?* I nodded and she mouthed, *What is he?*

I didn't answer as the man motioned toward the opening door and made a hand signal I knew. *Slow.*

As the doors opened and the elves went inside, we joined them.

CHAPTER TWELVE

The interior of the bathhouse was nice. The walls were a deep brown color with stone around the bottoms closest to the floor of the reception area behind the entrance.

The lobby was narrow, then opened up to a desk and a set of two doors, women's and men's from the pictures on each. Then there was a third door that was hidden with magic that the attendant opened. Their aura was whiskered and looked almost like a cat that bowed as the guests and their guides walked through. We joined them but as we stepped through, the light dimmed and we immediately came out into a small, mountain-like area that was completely different from the bathhouse we had been in.

The mound of stone on the opposite side of us looked to have been hollowed out and a stream of steaming water burbled and bubbled into it from above.

The night sky shimmered with stars, untouched by the light pollution of the city and I wondered where exactly we were. There were people lining the sides of the area, then I realized they were statues that looked like monks with prayer beads in their hands.

"Welcome, my guests, to my humble reception area." A voice spoke all around us, from nowhere in particular. "Unfortunately, I am busy making other arrangements and have to trust you to my left hand and second, Saizo. Please, feel welcome."

"We came to deal with the leader of the Night Parade, not some lackey." One of the elves sneered, his hands in front of him as if he were making a show of his disdain by shrugging with his whole arms rather than just his shoulders. "Looks like this meeting was all for nothing."

A man stood from the hot water and stone and rock molded itself from the ground to surround him, flowing around his body like a living robe that he tied with a band of water like it was no big deal. He was handsome, sure, and his hair was wet and long, dripping down his face and framing it like a painting of some kind. I sensed an aura emanating from him similar to that of the riders, but this was much more powerful.

This must be a yokai powerful enough to not need a host. His voice was cultured and contained as he spoke. "And yet here you are without your own leader. Funny how when someone is disrespected first, they return it kindly."

The elven speaker spat on the ground and stepped forward, jutting his chin out. "I speak on his behalf."

"As do I, on *my* leader's." Saizo merely smirked and raised a hand. The joyriding yokai brought tea and other drinks to a low table that Saizo made with a wave of his hand and set things down. "Either you can deal with me, and we can come to an agreement, or you can refuse to drink with me and we can kick you off our island and come for you when we see fit."

"You don't stand a chance without our help," one of the other elves said, but sounded uncertain about it.

Saizo lifted his gaze, his eyes narrowing so that the amber light in them darkened slightly and almost disappeared. "If that is the gamble you wish to make, I will not force you to stay."

Saizo sat on a mat of woven grass that sprang from the

ground as one of the yokai joyrider guards poured a drink for him and he nodded his head.

After a moment of staring and muttered conversation, the initial speaker for the elves sat with him and the yokai poured another drink. The Night Parade liaison bowed his head and stared down at his cup. "An excellent and wise choice."

The elf just grunted and lifted his cup. "To business."

The yokai stilled and then smiled. "Business it is." He lifted his own cup with both hands and took a sip of it as the other man's head slid from his neck and onto the ground with a sickening, squishy splat. He turned his gaze to the other elves. "The junior never lifts his cup to the senior, and no one makes me wait for a drink."

He turned back to his drink and took a whiff of it. "Get rid of the corpse, and one of you others can take his place."

The other elves looked like they wanted to fight but when he went still again, the youngest stepped over and bowed his head. "Forgive our ignorance and lack of decorum in this matter. We are merely concerned with so many of our kind having gone missing."

That made me glance over at the man standing not three feet from me with a massive grin on his face; he knew damn well he had something to do with that. He must have seen me looking at him out of the corner of his eye and rolled his head my way to give me a wink.

"That is why we are willing to work with you. Desperate people tend to seek more reasonable negotiation." Saizo smiled wolfishly and nodded to the fallen man's cup. One of the others came to fill it and the elven replacement lifted it. Saizo closed his eyes and muttered, "To *good* business and strong alliances."

The elf repeated the toast and drank with him, stopping as the other man did.

The yokai nodded with respect and set his cup down. "To put things bluntly, you will need to produce much in a short amount of time. Can you do this?"

"How short are we talking?" the elf returned, pulling out an honest-to-goodness pad of paper and a pen.

Saizo just grinned and stated, "Days." He cocked his head to the side and closed one eye. "Three by my count now. The storm is later than it should have been, which is good for us."

"How much?"

Saizo grinned wider. "Enough to make the gods themselves bow to our whims."

The elf's eyebrows raised in shock before he scribbled something down, saying, "We have a supply already, but I don't know that it is *quite* that large. I will say that we are working on a redesign of the drug that will increase the output a hundredfold. If we were to have an advance of mana and samples from stronger yokai, we could possibly synthesize something more potent and streamline it for you. I can't say our production would be enough to fully stock you for a long time outright, though."

"What could this more potent cocktail do for us?"

The elf shrugged and began to figure on his hands. "It's already designed around our own unique metabolisms to strengthen us immensely. If we were to have a strong yokai host to sample from and use as a starting point, who knows what we could achieve for you? As I said before, currently we have improved the efficiency for us a hundredfold. It's hard to have an exact idea of what we could achieve for you without a perfect specimen to work with first, yet it wouldn't be out of the question to see similar gains for your people."

"Would it kill the yokai in question?" Saizo tilted his head to the side.

"If they were strong enough? No." He frowned and thought about it. "Siphoning mana and genetic material from weaker yokai, though, is a bit more deadly."

"I see." A pensive look washed over him.

Chris waved a hand in front of my face and motioned me backward and closer to him, Kimiko as well. I wondered what was wrong until I saw him motioning to his wrist like he was tapping a watch.

His spell must be nearing its end. Galaxy's voice startled me slightly. I knew she was within me as soon as I thought about it, but I hadn't recalled seeing her do it.

He closed his eyes and made a motion like he was throwing something into the air and the world shimmered slightly before us as he mouthed, *Stay close to me. There's a harrier.*

Barrier, Marcus. Not everyone thinks of birds.

I rolled my eyes and noticed that it was suddenly a little tense across the room for a heartbeat. I thought our cover was blown, but Saizo just grunted to himself and bowed to the other man. "Allow me until morning to find you a specimen, but in the meantime—continue your base production and ramp up the amount. We will bring you what you require."

"Communication in the same means?" the elf asked as he scooted back on his mat, but didn't stand.

Saizo nodded once and stood to his feet. "That will be all, and yes. Travel swiftly." With that, he turned on his heel and strode from the meeting place and into the water, where he disappeared.

A hand on my wrist drew my attention from the ripples still spreading across the hot water and toward Chris, who had his other hand wrapped around Kimiko's wrist as well. He pulled us along gently, likely to keep us in his barrier's range of effect so that we could safely follow our quarry.

Once we were free of the space and back in the lobby, I noted that there was a heavier presence of joyriders in the area.

A squeeze on my wrist made me turn to look at the other man. He mouthed, *They're suspicious.*

Of what?

Galaxy interrupted. *He bent the light around all of you to mimic invisibility, but the change wasn't as fluid and smooth as his work with shadows. Saizo likely noticed you and, instead of risking himself or his mission, has done this.*

Makes sense, I retorted and rolled my eyes. This was likely going to mean that we didn't get to follow the Seelie back to their place. We would have to convince Kimiko's informant to get us to the warehouse that they used and, even then, that could be one of many places like the last time they were up to this shit. *Should have gone hunting for Qin Moira once I had Connell back safe and ended this shit.*

"Is there a reason for all of you being here?" the elven negotiator asked softly.

One of the riders shrugged and said in a voice that sounded both hollow and like an echo, "Precaution. We will see you to safety."

The elves just sniggered and shook their heads. "Not necessary."

One of the other riders grunted. "Pretty cocky for Seelie who seem to be dying by the drove lately." When the elves stiffened and looked his way, the man grinned, but it looked weird. "Pretty shit to say that you need the alliance, then snub the assistance we offer."

"Not like they have a choice," one of the other riders stated calmly, as if daring the elves to refuse. "Saizo said to see them to safety, one way or another."

"Fine." The negotiator sniffed and lifted his chin. "Let's just get on with it."

"We killing them?" One of the other riders chuckled and the others laughed before he turned to their wards and smiled. "Just teasing, meat bags."

The elves walked out and we waited to join them as the joyriding yokai stepped into a tight formation along with them. Chris reached into his pocket and pulled out a small object that he muttered to. It looked like a spider made of shadows that stood up in his palm and shook itself soundlessly.

The creature leapt from his hand and scuttled along the dark ground until it stepped into one of the elves' shadows under a streetlight and disappeared into it.

That made my blood run cold. Was there one of those

things in our shadows? Was that how he had been able to get to us so quickly?

He kept us from following them into the cars that they walked down the street toward and finally said, "You seem stiff, big guy, what's up?"

"Is that a way to track?" He nodded at my question and I lowered my voice in a growl. "Do you have one of those things in our shadows tracking us?"

He laughed, shaking his head. "No. No, I don't."

"Swear on your power?" I raised an eyebrow at him in challenge.

He sighed. "I swear on my power that I am not tracking you with one of my little spidery pets."

I got the notification and he just looked toward where they had driven off. "They're getting on to a freeway now."

"How did you get to us so quickly?"

"Talent and magic. You want to drive, or am I going to have to do everything?" He seemed irritated now and I couldn't blame him.

Well I could, but he was here because I had asked him for help.

"Sorry, man. I know you're here to help, but it's weirding me out after seeing that and know you can get to me in a way that I can't even fathom."

He grinned at me. "Now you know how I felt with my wife." He stopped and looked at me. "Not being dismissive, just nice to be on the other side of the power spectrum for once, you know?"

"I'll drive." Looking around us, I asked, "Can you make a messier barrier like you did? Make it hard to see us for a moment?"

"Sure." He threw a hand up, the light above us dying in an instant, shadows and lights dimming. "Done, what'cha got?"

"This." I willed Mako out of my shadow and the massive drake stared at the man hungrily. "Down, Mako."

The drake sat and stared around us as the shadows drifted

toward me and pieced the Huntsman's armor over my body with my will tugging them onto me. "Pretty sure you can both ride along with me." I turned to Mako. "Got room for another couple riders?"

He lifted his chin and grumbled, like, "Think I can't handle it?"

I patted his side as he laid down and I hopped onto his back. "Hop on and hold on tight."

"We running?" Chris snorted. "Could probably run faster than the old boy here."

I shot a glare over my shoulder at him and spoke clearly, "Hop on, or your ass is the gas."

"Nice, man." He just laughed and hopped on behind me. Kimiko hesitated and he called, "We can always just send a taxi if you're scared."

She scoffed and clambered up the side of the drake, using his leg to boost herself onto his back.

"Yip yip?" Chris muttered over my shoulder, laughing to himself.

I just shook my head and said, "Let's fly, Mako!"

"Fly?" Kimiko squealed as the beast wiggled his rump for show and leaped as hard as he possibly could into the sky.

The city faded below us for a moment before the shadows spread along his body and he began to run on the air like he always did.

"Well, I'll be damned!" Chris chortled behind me. "A flying drake, who would've come up with that? Can you relax the grip just a bit, kid? You're gonna make me fart."

"I hate heights!" Kimiko hollered, much to all of our delight. It was good to know she had a weakness.

With directions from Chris, we were able to accurately follow them into the city and to a location that we hadn't heard about. This one looked to be an abandoned school or something with a rather large compound available to it. It didn't look dilapidated or anything yet, just had caution signage all around it and the gates were closed.

"This looks like the kind of place Seelie would use to lay low." The man grumbled and I had to say, it didn't sit right with me. Qin Moira was the type of fucker to demand the finest things, and this wasn't that.

"This isn't right." I explained my thoughts to Chris and he shook his head as we touched down a block or so away.

"They've taken to hiding in places that we wouldn't go looking into, but since this screams 'off' to you, we can be cautious." He grunted and pulled out a small hand-held TV and tapped it twice on the side, a little of his aura going into it. The screen flickered and he smiled. "There we go."

"What's that?" Kimiko asked cautiously.

"My little spy can send a signal to me within a certain radius, and I can see what it sees." He pointed to the screen. "It's no ten-eighty-pee but it'll do for this."

He watched it for a moment and grunted. "Looks okay from his perspective, but trusting your gut was never wrong for us, and it should never be wrong for you." He looked over at me and said, "You want me to send in some troops, or can we handle this?"

Kimiko grabbed him and whipped him around, pointing a finger in his face. "You mean to tell me that you had the option of calling people in to help us this whole time? We could have attacked them then and foiled his plans *now*."

"I was called to hunt Seelie? Helping you on your end goals is a byproduct of that, at best." He jerked his head back at the neck incredulously, freeing himself from her grasp as well, then gave her a menacing grin. "By the way, keep your fingers out of my face—I bite."

"As do I!" she shot back, her teeth lengthening and her tusks leaving her mouth as her skin mottled blue. She reminded me so much of her sister.

"Goddamn, can we cool the pissing match bullshit?" I rolled my eyes and shook my head. "You're both pretty, now can we focus on the task at hand?"

Kimiko looked at me like I was only so much ass to kick, but

Chris just snorted. "Gonna have to make you buy me a drink for that." He stood up straighter and brushed his hand by his head like he was waving his non-existent hair aside. "No one calls me pretty and doesn't buy me a drink."

"Is it done?" A familiar voice drifted out of the speakers of the TV, making us all lean closer to the shorter man.

The screen was darker, but there looked to be some light coming up as the shadows lengthened around the elf that the thing tagged along with walked into some kind of stairwell. "I got as much information as I could. Why are we speaking this abominable language still?"

"The boss prefers it, since he spent the majority of his youth entrenched in their disgusting society." The other speaker sounded a bit like he was going to either retch and vomit or was just really good at faking, because there was nothing after that.

Echoing steps clacked from the speakers for a moment and then the light flooded our sight and suddenly there was a gym of sorts in view. All of the equipment was gone, but the bleachers were out like there had been an assembly. Another voice that was grating and infuriating all at once came across to us.

"You're back with more than one of you?" There was a laugh, and Qin Moira continued. "I thought they would kill all of you, but I'm glad they didn't."

Chris didn't look up, but I knew he spoke to me. "That your friend?"

"Yup."

He nodded. "Okay, you can kill him." He closed his eyes as they continued their chatting about what they were going to need to do to ramp up production. It wasn't helping me not want to kill the little bastard.

He pulled the device out of his pocket and actually shut it off and put it away before leaning forward and shaking himself out like an excited dog. He opened his eyes and they were blood red rather than the usually vivid blue that they were when he took his other form. He leaned back and his clothes fell away before he stood in front of us covered in fur.

I blinked at him as the creature he was now stared down at both of us, a guttural growl coming from him, a rumbling, "What?"

"You're a fucking lycanthrope too?"

He just rumbled at me, "You really haven't read my books, have you?"

I shook my head and he shrugged. "No harm, no foul." He grinned. "I'm not everyone's cup of tea, but I like my readers and they like me. But that's not why I'm here right now."

He rolled his shoulders and stretched his neck. "I'm here to kill Seelie."

"Chances are, you go near any of them, this kid bolts." I grumbled as Kimiko just stared in horror at him. "What?" I asked as she couldn't take her eyes from him.

"I do not understand how a Touched is a Lycanthrope, unless they were born this way?" She continued to stare at him for a time as he just scratched absently behind his left ear.

He finally deigned to look at her, but it was more of a droll glance. "I'm very different from a lot of the norms that supernatural folks would consider for this world, because this?"—he motioned down to his body and then back up—"Is a hundred percent Brindollan-made man meat."

Her eyes widened as I fought not to laugh, but Chris just turned toward the school and growled low. "And aside from that is rage. Rage at the Seelie for who they are and the threat they represent. I can't have them mucking shit up for the Unseelie here, like they are at home. They all have to die."

"Is that okay?" I wondered aloud and he turned those red eyes on me. "Isn't there a kind of balance in their stalemate with the Unseelie?"

He snarled, "*Fuck* the balance. The only balance they deserve is the weight of the scales they see when they receive their judgement by whatever gods they worship." He closed his eyes and his lips raised, as if he fought with something for a moment. "You coming, or not?"

"Can you tell where they are?" He nodded once and I didn't question it. "Let's go mow the lawn then."

"We should have more people just in case," Kimiko stated, crossing her arms. "We don't know if they have that drug, and there are many escape routes from schools like this."

Chris shrugged and muttered something that a growl from his chest easily covered and a snow-white creature appeared next to him.

Her name is Eve, if I recall correctly.

You've been pretty quiet, you alright?

Paying attention to all of you at once is taxing, and all of the emotions are as well, but I think I'm getting better at it. She opened her eyes inside me and looked out of me. *Kill as many of them as you can, because I don't know if he's still leveling up or not, but he's so much stronger than he was. Maybe you should see what he's doing to get that strong?*

Maybe. I watched him as he dished out orders, especially considering there was a small crowd of elves who had joined us now too. They carried weapons that ranged from swords and staves to spears and one of them even had an M249 squad automatic weapon on a sling over their shoulder, the rounds in a canister at their feet. That impressed the shit out of me.

"All of you are going to hold the exits and Eve is going to run interference and basically just create general chaos." He looked at his troops, then saw the elf holding the gun. "Dude, seriously?"

The elven woman shrugged. "You said come armed, and when it comes to Seelie, I'll carry enough rounds to piss them off and then kill them."

"That gives 'laying down the hate' a whole new meaning." I chuckled and so did she. "I'm Marcus."

"Aelir. I love modern weapons like the dwarves do, stingy fuckers." She walked over and shook my hand, firm grip and all. "Killing Seelie is a hobby I hope to make a job."

I shook my head. "Jesus Christ. Where did you find her, some kind of Marine Corps hobby shop?"

"Came with the gun." Chris grinned and shrugged back. "Won't tell me shit other than that she hates them and wants to kill them all. That got my vote."

"If you two are done chuckle fucking each other, we have Seelie to murder?" Aelir growled.

Both of us were taken aback for a moment, and I couldn't help myself. "You kiss your mother with that mouth?"

"Seelie killed her," she stated, then narrowed her eyes at me. "So no."

"Ouch." Chris groaned for me, then smacked Eve as she rushed forward with a hiss, something about insubordination and ripping out teeth. "Stop it. She's just excited."

"I am too, but she will be dead if she *ever* speaks that way to my king again." Eve did nothing to hide her fury at the other woman, but it looked to me like Aelir barely cared.

"What the hell are you?" Kimiko muttered to herself as the elves began to move into the school grounds ahead of us.

He grinned and muttered, "Hungry."

CHAPTER THIRTEEN

It was so hard to keep up with the werewolf equivalent of Usain Bolt as he crossed the yard, and I wanted to keep as much of my mana available as possible, so I just sprinted across as fast as my legs would carry me along behind him.

He made it look easy, and it kind of pissed me off when he just touched the building and closed his eyes. "There's a lot of them in there, at least twenty times our numbers here."

"How do you know that?" I frowned at him and he just winked at me. "You're going to need to tell me how you have all this shit, man. I could use the help getting stronger."

He snorted. "You are stronger, Marcus." He looked around the corner of the building we stood beside and came back scowling. "This is gonna be fun."

"What?" I looked around the corner and saw that there was a Seelie elf walking toward us with an AK-47 pointed in our direction. "Well, shit."

I turned to look back at him and all I caught was a tail or two in the air over my head as he crawled *along* the wall upward and then around the corner. The elf kept walking forward and the barrel just broke the plane of the corner, my fist grabbing it as a strangled gasp reached my ears and the weapon jerked upward before going slack.

I looked around the corner only to come face-to-shoe with the struggling elf as the monstrous creature above grasped him by the throat and kept stabbing his clawed fingers into him like they were a serrated knife. After the tenth stab that I saw, he pulled the body left, then jerked it quickly back to the right, snapping the elf's neck before dropping the corpse like a sack of ugly rocks.

He grinned down at me, sharp teeth glistening in the light of the stars, and I suddenly found that I had no idea who I was staring at. "Are you Chris, or Zeke, right now?"

He hopped down onto the ground and considered it for a moment before answering, "I suppose both. I don't try to hide that it's me when I tell my story, but I've always *been* Zeke. I guess there's no difference in either one, though I'd prefer my alias not be known?"

"So... Zeke, then?"

He shrugged. "Yeah, that works." He grinned wide and added, "Just don't call me late to a party. Come on."

Weapons fire opened around the area and it was almost deafening to me, so it had to be bad for him. *Galaxy, you take care of the corpses?*

With pleasure, though you won't be getting much if they kill them. Granted, we can still gain some from the leftovers. She slipped out of my shadow and began to pull the body into herself.

Zeke was up and into the closest window in a heartbeat, leaving me to find another entrance by myself, which turned out to be only about twelve feet up. I took a few steps back and ran forward, launching myself up toward the window. I grabbed it and yanked myself over and into a classroom that was either a fucking nightmare, or a psychopath's wet dream.

Blood and body parts lay strewn about in a shower of crimson and spent casings that would have made a Jackson Pollock painting seem tame.

"What the fuck...?" Blinking around at the carnage made

me almost feel like I was back in the Middle East and Galaxy's temple prison.

I took a deep, copper-scented breath in and pulled my Fae Frame from my hip before continuing forward toward the sound of shouts and chaos.

The thunderous fire of the SAW spewing hatred in the distance made a grim grin grace my lips as I spied each doorway outside the classroom I had come in from. Shouting came from the left hallway and I shot toward the voices without thinking, recognizing their chosen tongue from when we'd hidden from them in the sewers on the way back to the High Table.

The rounds didn't do much other than cause them to try to retreat with their hands up in front of their faces, trying to protect themselves from the barrage of what may as well have been thick pellets to them and their magical skin.

Which was what I wanted in order for me to cast Embodiment of Lightning to step forward and land behind them in the blink of an eye, my fist lashing out at the back of the nearest one's neck. Bones cracked and he dropped as I shot another in the ear, then summoned Reaper.

The blade fell into my left hand from the ring I wore and I let loose. There was no need to cover it with elemental magic because the elves were too busy trying to figure out how I got on them so fast to really fight back. The sword cut through bone and metal weapons like they were paper.

Behind you! Galaxy cried and I whipped around only to receive a boot to the chest that sent me flying into some of the elven warriors.

I couldn't even cry out or grunt in surprise as I watched a behemoth elven fighter launch himself forward like a freight train of muscle and rage.

I tried to get my sword up, but he swatted it aside like I was a child trying to attack an adult. He had to be on the drug, and I was about to get my shit kicked in.

"Galaxy, warn them!" I knew she heard me as the elf

reached forward and grabbed my shirt, arm, and hip in his meaty grippers.

She roared back, *Do it!*

"Commence the Hunt!" Spittle flew from my mouth as I snarled the words that siphoned the shadows from our surroundings into me as the elf threw me through the wall next to me. I hoped that the others were in a position to get somewhere out of sight when their armor sprang to life.

Plaster and wood splinters cracked as I flew, but thanks to my Mantle, it didn't hurt as much as it could have.

"What the hell are you?" The elf sneered as he grabbed both sides of the wall and shoved outward to make room for himself to walk through.

I chuckled darkly and grunted as I stood up. "Pissed off."

I raised my right fist as shadows coated my Fae Frame and made it much larger in my hand, squeezing the trigger with a sacrifice of mana each time. The mana-coated rounds pierced flesh and did what they would to a human, but with his muscle density, it didn't seem to do as much as it should have.

I rolled my eyes and put the gun back in its holster, now a shadowy leather object on my hip where the actual holster was.

"Bad idea." The elf guffawed as he tromped forward.

I just tossed Reaper into the air and let my magic do the rest. Shadows coalesced beneath it and shot upward, catching the hilt of the weapon only to remake it into the scythe I fought with at times as the Huntsman.

He frowned at my grin while I attacked from where I stood. The scythe sliced through the air. He tried to catch the shadow-made haft of it, but it slid through his grasp and cut him on the pass through.

His arm from the shoulder down sloughed off his torso and fell to the ground. Blood flecked the wall behind him and something faster than even my sight blurred forward to rear up behind him.

Claws speared through the elf's chest and spread wide,

Zeke's deep voice trickling over the brute's shoulder evilly. "Hard to keep up with a wall of muscle in the way, bud?"

I grinned at him and he just shook his head as his other hand shot through and pulled the elf apart in a shower of gore that would have made a horror movie seem tame.

He grinned at me, a chill running down my spine as his crimson-stained teeth caught a sliver of moonlight from a nearby window. "The bad guy's gaining ground as we speak, Marcus. Don't you want to be the hero of your story?"

My blood boiled at the thought of Ascal Qin Moira getting away *again*. "Where is the little bastard?"

Zeke cackled. "Attaboy." He jerked his head behind him and bellowed, "Don't kill him, Eve! Don't harm a hair on his pretty wittle head."

A yowling scream rent the air and voices raised in discordant shouts of fear and rage. Weapons fire rang out and the silence was further broken.

The noise made me uneasy. "Cops should be heading here soon en masse, if not with the Marines and MPs to assist with how much gunfire there was."

Zeke grunted, then called back to me, "Then we better hurry the hell up."

My heartbeat quickened as we raced through the corridor down the hall toward more weapons fire. One of the doors opened as he further distanced himself from me and I just swung my scythe for the fences, the elf coming through the doorway with a Glock raised straight across, getting one shot off right in front of my face before his head fell to the ground.

"Sorry!" Zeke called back at me and sprinted onward. The hallway ended in front of us and he bounded off the wall to the right toward the rear of the school and down a flight of stairs. "Gonna get cramped!"

His physical form began to shrink slightly until he was no taller than about six foot and still covered in fur. *This is his fox-man form, according to the books,* Galaxy explained. *Cassia and Arden are finishing up their work with Cassia's kitsune friend, and know where we are. They will be here as soon as they can.*

I nodded wordlessly and put Reaper back into my ring, opting to pull out my oni blade and readying myself for a closer fight. He leapt over the stairs and onto a figure standing behind the partially open double doors at the bottom with a bow in their hands firing at something as machine gun fire rang out outside.

His fist connected with their spine and their whole body went limp and slumped to the ground as he landed, then his form shifted into a large, rhinoceros-looking thing and he battered the doors open all the way with a toss of his head. One of the doors came off its hinges and flew away and someone screamed.

Outside, the air held an oppressive thickness that I hadn't noted before, but the scent of copper and other things wafting through the area moved my attention back to the elves fighting before me.

Aelir steadily bled onto the ground from a wound to her stomach, which forced her to kneel and fire her weapon at the Seelie who closed in on her.

Can you heal her with my bond to Cassia, Galaxy?

She thought for a moment, then answered, *I can try, but you're the Huntsman, Marcus. You have to touch her.*

I rushed toward her and touched her shoulder as the bond between Cassia and me flared wide.

Healing Fist – The oni with this ability can heal friend and foe alike with all the care in their body and fist. 50 Mana.

She gasped as the wounds stitched back together in the blink of an eye and I readied myself to battle with the elves.

I directed my will to channel Hoarfrost along my arms, the air coalescing around them as they were coated in ice from fingertip to elbow.

They would flit inward and try to stab at me with short swords, while I turned and fought them with my icy fists. Some of them took me lightly, but with my demonic appearance it was harder to get most of them to underestimate me and present an opening.

Use your abilities and weapons to your fullest, Marcus. Galaxy purred and stepped from my shadows to begin eating those who had fallen.

That in mind, I brought my hands inward toward myself, then flung them outward toward two Seelie who approached. The ice flew from my arms as I shot forward with my guns drawn, infusing them with mana to cause the most damage possible.

The ice impacted their bodies and tore through them, leaving gaping ice-encrusted holes where their chests used to be. Then I continued to move forward, blasting my way through the crowd of Seelie that had formed toward where I heard Zeke baying and howling. My guns were larger now as the shadows surrounded them, and that likely helped me cut an even more intimidating figure as I ran.

Bloodied elves dropped as others shot in, one of them managing to stab my arm with his blade, but Galaxy, in her larger cat form, pounced on him and tore into him.

His screams made me grin, her pleasure at a hot meal almost overwhelming me and my will to keep the Mantle intact.

Left! My eyes widened and I tipped backward in time to avoid an arrow to my shoulder from my left side.

I lifted the shadow-covered Silvaero in my left hand and returned fire, managing a hit to their thigh that made them flinch, but they found cover and stayed there.

"Get a move on, you leatherneck fuck!" Aelir snarled behind me. "I'll cover you, just get these bastards."

A white tiger burst from behind a shed where some of the Seelie hid and fired at us, blood covering its front paws and mouth and attacked savagely.

"Fly, Huntsman!" I recognized Eve's voice. "They gain distance."

The thought of Qin Moira getting away again brought my blood to a boil and red into my vision. "Mako!"

The massive black drake surged from my body, landing on four of the elves with a cracking crunch that meant Galaxy would eat more soon.

I hopped onto his back and rode forward with all his strength and rage clearing a path for us as shadows danced along his scales. We lifted off the ground slightly as he strode forward and about a hundred yards in front of us, I saw the largest gathering of bodies with Zeke in the middle of them.

The mass of bodies surged around him, trying to get a hold of him while he flowed from one form to another; his furred form to his dark-skinned human form to his fox form.

Then, as he stood in his fox form and they pressed closer to him, he grew larger until he was in his massive bear-like form. At this point, Seelie fell in droves as his claws sliced and pressed down on those around him, clearing a space once again.

No time to be awed, Marcus, you can be of use too.

Find the leader, Galaxy urged from behind me. *Cut the head off the serpent and the body can but only flail.*

I grimaced and replaced my pistols, opting instead for the M-16 that Jayvali had loaned me.

Shadows surged over it as I focused and looked through the scope. Mako had taken us outside of the building's grounds as I searched for my quarry.

Riding on Mako and trying to find my mark was vastly different from being sprawled out on the sand or riding turret in a Humvee.

I could find nothing of use right away, until something caught my eye closer to the roadway behind the school.

A small force had someone huddled in their center as they worked toward a running vehicle.

"That'll be him." I patted the drake on the shoulder and urged him on. "There they are, faster."

His bulk shifted and we ran faster, my rifle raised and pointed, I squeezed the trigger and the shot rang out like a bell.

Boom! Flames burst from the vehicle and I grinned with grim glee as the group of fleeing figures bowled backward due to the detonation.

I bellowed, "Ascal Qin Moira!"

The figure in the center of the puddle of people peeked out from under them and paled.

He tried to sound strong and like he wasn't worried, but I could see his fear from where I rode atop Mako. "I have no beef with the Hunt!"

I grimaced and spoke back, my voice raised to be heard over the din, "But I have beef with *you.*"

I hopped off of Mako, landing in front of the group with my pistols leveled at the guards over top of him.

One of them raised a weapon at me, a mini-crossbow attaché affixed to his wrist that shot a small bolt. It was easy enough to deflect with my armored forearm, but another bolt flew at me from one of the others and caught me in the shoulder.

It hurt, but it wasn't going to be something that would stop me from doing what was necessary.

Bang! Bang bang bang! The two attackers fell backward and the other two surged forward to take a guard stance between myself and their charge.

Eve, bloody and furious, pounced on one of them, then Zeke was there to grab the other in shadow and yank him away.

"So this is the one?" His chipper question caught me off guard.

I nodded my head and he tilted his gaze down at the elf, and grinned wider, eyes closing slightly in an almost-predatory delight. "I hear that you're somehow related to royalty, hmmmmm?"

Qin Moira stared up at him blankly and tried to sound more important than he was. "I am. And my father knows where I am." He turned his head toward me. "I don't know what I've done to piss off the Hunt, but I'm just trying to take care of my people, okay?"

"Oh, I know." I crossed my arms and willed the shadows away from my head so that my face would be visible. "Remember me?"

His eyes narrowed and he was up, nearly ready to punch me, shrieking, "You! You're the filthy Normy who stopped my operation in Columbus!"

"Yeah." I smiled coldly and stared back at him. "The one whose kid you took, and royally pissed off."

"I… Fuck you!" He spat at me and the shadows on my chest swirled and the flecks of spittle just rolled away.

Zeke poked his head between us, and though I couldn't see his face, I could hear the mocking, jovial tone his voice held as he said, "I don't care who you want inside you or who you wanna be in—call your dad here." He clapped and wagged his hand, then shook his head. "Better yet, summon the Seelie King's attention. I just wanna introduce myself."

"You don't rate." The entitled elf scoffed and shook his head, forgetting what had happened to his people.

"Kid." He motioned to himself, his body shifting to that of his humanoid self with the dark, star-covered skin. "I'm about the only motherfucker in existence he's going to care about."

He grinned and tilted his head, tossing his thumb casually over his shoulder. "Because all those folks we just killed are just a scratch in the dent we put into your people over the last few months." Ascal frowned and then realization dawned on his face and Zeke chuckled, in a sing-song tone as he said, "That's riiiight—I've been hunting and killing all of your Seelie friends and family."

He tossed his arms outward and raised his voice. "And I've just been *itchin'* to say hi to your king. You know, one monarch to another."

Ascal frowned, eyes narrowed but cautious now. "You're no king."

Zeke laughed and rubbed his eye like he was wiping away a tear, which really just smeared blood onto his cheek and eyebrow to make him look completely unhinged. "Yeah, yeah I am. I'm the *true* Unseelie King."

As he spoke, his aura flared and a simple three-pointed crown appeared above his head like it was some sort of emoticon. It flared brighter and brighter in a myriad of colors, green, blue, red, black, gold, and so on as he added, "And I'm taking it all for my people."

Ascal reached in his pocket, earning a glare and a growl from Eve, but he pulled out a phone and tossed it on the ground. "I won't call anyone for you. Let me go, and you can just use that."

Zeke snorted. "Nah, a call can be ignored. I know that if you say his name, his attention will come to you and he'll see me." He motioned to me. "The only reason I'm not getting what I want expeditiously is because *he* has the claim to your head and I gave my word he could have you."

"I won't do it." Ascal crossed his arms and raised his chin.

Zeke scratched his head, then snapped his fingers. "Tell you what." He clapped me on the shoulder. "Marcus here wants you dead, and you wanna leave alive. So, if you can kill Marcus, you win your life—I won't make you do anything that will get you in trouble, and you can run and tattle to your king about me and try to come for me. I'll welcome it."

"And what happens if I lose, how do we decide that?" The elf looked to be calculating his odds.

Zeke held up his hands and smiled. "I will, but, I swear on my power that I will only call a win for Marcus if he's about to kill you, and then you'll call for daddy and the cavalry anyway and we can get this shit show on the road, how's that?"

He snorted derisively and then paled, his eyes widening as they drifted from right to left looking at him. "It's true?" Zeke nodded, his predatory smile returning. "You really are the king of the Unseelie, but... but how?"

"Not important." The man spoke softly at first. "What is important is that you have an offer to keep your life now. You gonna capture it, or just let it slip?"

"Eight Mile, really?" Kimiko snorted, her arrival startling me.

"I get around," Zeke retorted with a glare, then turned back to the surviving Seelie. "Well?"

"I'll take it." Ascal lifted his chin. "It won't be fair. If a Normy is the Huntsman, how strong can he be?"

I laughed and let the shadows return to my face. "We will see, won't we?"

By this time, Zeke's forces had joined us with the elves forming a ring around us. Eve and Mako stood on opposite sides of each other, both cleaning themselves as if they were in sync with it. The only one missing looked to be Aelir. I briefly wondered where she went, but with no one to really ask, I was just left waiting for the fight to be called.

Ascal reached into his suit jacket and pulled out two vials, downing them in a smooth, practiced motion before I could get to him in time to try to stop him. I was already halfway to him when I ran into a barrier of flesh called Zeke.

He shook his head. "Nah. You're better than that."

"He's juicing." I growled and motioned behind him.

He shook his head and muttered to me, "So are you. Galaxy is still eating the evidence of our time here, and I know that you can do more than you've shown all of us. Call it gamer's intuition. Get back to your corner, or I really will have to start imposing rules."

I stared at him as he lifted his hand with three fingers held up. "Luci said that you were resourceful and had strong friends. You do." He lowered a finger. "Show me."

I turned on my heel with one finger left raised and walked back to 'my side' of the small circle and waited as a now growing and likely severely 'roided out Ascal panted on the other side. His suit was torn and shredded but he had clothes on under that stretched to cover the majority of his center and upper body.

He had tattoos that looked to cover all his upper body, mainly interlocking chains and things like that. If it had been on anyone else, I'd have been curious as to what they meant and the details, but with him, it was just a detail to disregard. He was just a walking corpse to me.

That was all he could be. Images, memories clouded by the fog of seething crimson hatred that I felt at hearing Connell calling out in pain when one of this guy's goons had hurt him. Taken him hostage. Put *my son* in harm's way, because he just couldn't concede that he'd failed in his endeavor.

All that rage flooded back through my veins and instead of making me sloppy like it would have for most, it felt cold. Calculated and comfortable. It was like slipping into a cool ice bath after a hard work out that should really fuck up the body.

"Fighters, ready?" Zeke called out, the others still standing around us beginning to make noise, but it all fell away. Galaxy's consciousness rubbed against mine, a warmth against the barren cold and I just shrugged her away. I needed to do this one myself. "Begin!"

Ascal raised his hands and muttered something in old Gaelic. I recognized the language now as flames spiraled between his outstretched fingers. I had been recovering some mana slowly as we stood here with Galaxy eating, but not a lot. I needed to conserve it if I could, at least for now.

Galaxy's voice echoed through the coldness within me. *No. Use our bonds to replenish. Merlin and Amabala insist.*

I grimaced and flung myself to the side, bonds opened wide and just avoiding the flames spearing toward my hide only to roll into something solid. I could see massive legs and just knew it was Qin Moira's hulking figure. I sighed and called upon our bonds and cast Embodiment of Lightning.

I stepped around him, the Bolt that fled from my body slapping against him, but when I went to lash out with my foot, the man was just gone. *The fuck?*

Pain cracked against my jawline from the right and he stepped from the light that filtered down from the moon and the street lights along the grounds where we stood.

Stumbling backward, Ascal pressed his advantage, shooting

in for another punch to my gut this time. With his bulk, it was a pretty solid attack.

But pain wasn't stopping me. I grabbed his wrist and spun my foot over it, kicking him with my other foot in a move I had learned from Kenshi.

Kimiko gasped somewhere nearby and I ignored her. I still had the larger man's arm in my grasp. Twisting back toward him, I punched him and slammed the heel of my palm into his eye socket.

He grunted, but just grit his teeth and shoved me away before stepping back and becoming hazy. "You should have just stayed in that shit city, Normy."

"Stop hiding and come get this ass beating your daddy should have given you." I growled and tried to focus. My head was still ringing slightly from that punch but even as I stared at him, his outline just grew fuzzier until he was gone from my sight.

"My dad showed me how to do this, unlike your Normy one." He sounded smug as hell as he spoke, but his voice wasn't coming from anywhere that would help me pin down his location.

A sudden flash of inspiration took me away from the fight and I smiled as I nodded to Mako and the drake stopped licking himself and focused on the fight instead. He took a deep breath and his eyes snapped to my left and he nodded once.

I cast Hoarfrost as my mana bar dwindled, then stilled with the influx from Merlin and Amabala, then began to climb once more as Merlin continued to push mana at me. The ice forming in my fist shot from my palm like a spear when I lashed out and sailed toward the spot that Mako had stared at.

I followed it, gliding along the ground as the blistering cold seeped from me and froze the earth around me. Crunching grass greeted me to my right, my leg raising and kicking instantly like a spooked mule.

"Guk!" His pain brought a smile to my lips as I kicked again, the ice behind him shattering as he fell.

Already, more ice formed around my fists, fingers becoming claws that I could use to grab and freeze him to the ground. His form shimmered as whatever invisibility he'd had dropped away and he punched at me.

It was a weak punch, but his aura solidified around it and flames lapped at the ice on my hands, steam forming around us as I grabbed his arm.

Flames spewed from his hand toward me, but I leaned back, then dropped my weight—all of it—onto his elbow as it was locked.

Snap! His cartilage and muscle helped keep the limb from completely deforming, but the flames stopped so I pressed the cold along his forearm as hard as I could, my mana depleting again. His skin started to freeze just before his foot caught me in my hip and shoved me backward and away from him.

I grimaced, then grinned as I held up his left wrist and hand. "Whoops!"

The frozen, bloody stump he stared at threw him into a panicked frenzy, but instead of making him just go berserk and lose his mind, he gathered himself and muttered a string of words I took for curses under his breath and thrust his one good hand in front of himself.

Thanks to my open bond with Amabala, the tear in the space in front of me was something I could pick up on and a head broke through the side facing me as Ascal clambered to his feet. The head was humanoid for a second. When it saw me, it snarled, "You!"

The features shifted and time seemed to slow down. I could see Ascal's feet churning to carry him toward the portal and the head poking out started to grow shoulders that sprouted scales of mercury and power flared from it.

Zeke snarled, "Not so fast, you!" His hand raised and suddenly the area grew so thick with power that it was all I could do to stand up straight.

That's it! Amabala's voice echoed by Galaxy shrieked, *That's the power that created the portal that creature came through!*

The portal shattered as Galaxy confirmed, *It's a Dominion, Marcus—Zeke is using one.*

The figure fleeing the portal toward me roared and then its eyes bulged as the portal flickered once and faded, leaving only half of it there falling to the ground, but it was slowly growing even as it failed to breathe, with a pool of blood puddling around it.

Kill it, Marcus! Galaxy bellowed in my mind. *Kill it while it's not focused on you, and we will get Qin Moira after!*

I stepped forward and shoved my fist into the creature's scaled head, the metallic wedges forming on it blocking the ice growing from my fist. It did nothing, so I pulled out Reaper and focused my mana into it, casting Mana Blade around it, hoping that it would just help empower the sword. The blade hummed dangerously, a sliver of silver searing the edge from hilt to tip just before I stabbed toward the creature's eye.

Slight resistance, then blood welled up on the outside of the blade as if something was coating it in see-through plastic. My mana bottomed out as the blade pressed further in and the creature continued to grow *around* the blade, but stopped struggling to breathe so much, eyes glazing over.

I cast a glare around, trying to figure out where Qin Moira went. When I found him, Zeke was holding his body off the ground by the shoulders currently in his kitsune form with his tails fanned out around him. His aura was massive now, and looked exactly like he did currently, only now the aura had things in it. They just sort of floated there with it. There was a silvery-gray cast to it around his head that almost formed a halo of sorts.

I had to know. *Are you sure that was a Dominion? Is that what I'm seeing now?*

Galaxy was quiet for a second before answering softly, *Yes.*

She seemed to be deciding on something, and in the silence, I muttered mentally at her, *He was the one who killed Janus, isn't he? The one who made the monsters all appear?*

And he has to be connected to the creature who took the god from the Vorna, and thrashed her so completely we could kill her.

My heart fell to the bottom of my throat, and for some reason, my hearing returned and all I could do was shiver as he spoke to Qin Moira.

"I gave you a chance to keep yourself alive, and you try to *run*?" He sounded surprised, then shook his head. "That wasn't a part of the deal."

Qin Moira grunted and spat. "Wasn't mentioned either, so you had no right to stop me."

"Escape is a form of forfeit," Zeke corrected with a grin. "I said that you had to *win* in order to escape with your life, and since you tried to run rather than kill him, Marcus wins by default."

There was a finality in what he said that dropped a weight onto my chest. He had the power to back that statement, and he had. I won. That meant that more Seelie would likely be coming and we couldn't afford that. Not right now with me having next to no mana and being injured as I was.

"Call them," Zeke ordered with a growl to his tone.

"No." Ascal sneered, and then froze, his body shaking slightly, which caused his still bleeding stump to spray blood in arcs around him.

I frowned, not knowing what was going on. "What's happening to him?"

"His body is trying to fight what's happening because he went and refused to do what was required by our deal." Zeke turned to face me, a small nod of his head before he spoke was all he gave me. "Good fight, Marcus. Never doubted you."

"Good to know," I said, softly, then added, "But we… need to talk."

He blinked. "What're you, my girlfriend? Talk to me, man."

Now it was my turn to stare at him in surprise. "You killed Janus."

"Who?" He stared at me, confused.

Galaxy stepped out of me in elven form and explained,

"The god, Janus. The one who can create doors to other places?"

"Oh, him?" He shrugged and turned back to stare at a now-convulsing and foaming-at-the-mouth Ascal with distaste. "Yeah, I killed him."

"Why?" Galaxy pushed and stepped closer to him. I stopped her from getting too close.

"He was in my territory first and decided that when I was awake, I was a threat." He frowned and raised an eyebrow at me, my hand still wrapped around Galaxy's bicep in a gentle restraint. "He came at me while I was trying to mow the fucking lawn, Marcus."

"How can we be sure?" I asked softly, just to try to keep him from thinking I was going to attack or anything.

"Do I really have to give my word over everything?" He frowned and stared at me, then motioned to the people around us. "Marcus, Galaxy, I came here to help you—sure, I get something out of it too, but if you had just asked me to help, I would have. I told you, I'll help you if I can."

"I know." Galaxy spoke in a soothing tone. "But a god is murdered, and then your new power allows someone to come and take an injured god that was later confirmed to have been killed. Can't you see how that may be a little worrisome?"

He froze, then blinked and asked, "How did you know that the powers were the same?"

"Because I can feel them," I lied, spreading my hands wide. "Look, we aren't your enemies, man. We just want to know what's going on with you. Gods are dead—our friends are scared, Zeke. They feared for their lives when they thought someone was out there hunting them down."

"We just want to be sure that everything is okay." Galaxy pulled her arm out of my hand and stepped closer to him. "Just let us know what we can do to help."

He sighed and let his head fall back as he stared up at the sky, then said, "My entourage can leave. Eve, I know you killed Aelir for her disrespect. You can expect a punishment later."

The massive white tiger stalked past with her tail in the air, her figure flashing before becoming the woman that we had seen before. She was serene, almost accepting of his resolute anger. "As you wish, my King."

He shook his head and let Ascal fall to the ground, then grabbed Eve by the back of her neck and pulled her back toward him. "I know you did what you thought was proper, but if you think for a second that killing someone useful to me was what I wanted because she had been *slightly* annoying to deal with, you had better return to my wife and send back your brother."

She looked scared then, her eyes wide. "I cannot leave you, my King. If I do, she will kill me now that she knows you are awake."

He stared at her for a second then squeezed his hand hard enough that I could hear his knuckles popping. "Then I suggest you think long and hard about how your service to me should be handled, and who makes the decisions around here. Go."

He let her go and she stumbled forward, turning and kneeling. "As you will it, my King."

He snarled, "Fuck *off, Eve!*" She faded from view and he stood there in silence, shaking for a moment before taking a deep breath and turning back to us. "You want to help?" He stared at us and as we both nodded, he sighed. "Stay out of my way."

"Zeke, you can't go around killing gods, they'll come for you." I was trying to implore him while maintaining my distance. If he was going to lash out, it wouldn't be pretty. Galaxy made it harder being closer to him.

I'm trying to use my apparent likeness to Maebe to get him to relax and open up. Maybe we can learn something from this. She muttered, *Maybe stop him from being a threat.*

"Let them come." He shook his head as he stared at the ground for a moment. "You know, when I first took these powers, I thought I could open a doorway to go home. I was so

145

excited that I poured *everything* into that one portal. You know what it did?"

He continued to stare at the ground, then growled, "It opened a *window*. Just the barest glimpse into the Fae Realm where Mae stood near my friends' bodies. She was crying near an empty crystal… *thing*. I could only see her for a second, and it…" He frowned and clenched his fists. "It drew attention that I didn't want. So, now, I'm making it so that anyone whose attention it drew, like the Seelie, can't come snooping anymore."

He turned and glared at me. "You going to stop me from killing them all, Marcus?"

"Could I?" My question caught him off guard and his eyebrows knit at me. "To me, it seems like the entire time you've been here, you've been showing me exactly how out of my depth I would be to try it. Every time I turn around, you have some new ability, or power. You tore through an army of Seelie with drugs to empower themselves and you *still* barely had to try."

"Caught on to that, eh?" His teeth flashed in a smirk. "I like you guys, man. I really don't want to have to kill you, but I want to go home."

He marched back over to Ascal, who had stilled and picked him up like a parent lifting a child under their armpits. "And I'm willing to do anything I have to, to get there."

Galaxy frowned, then her eyes widened and I could see the edges of them where I stood as she spoke, "It was you, wasn't it? In the video?"

Zeke turned to look at her and said simply, "No."

The hair on the back of my neck stood on end as Galaxy said, "But you know who it was."

He didn't speak to her, just stared for a long moment before turning to Ascal and saying, "Abide the terms of our contract and call for aid, Ascal Qin Moira."

I couldn't not know. "Zeke, what do you know about what's going on?"

Ascal opened his mouth and began to mumble gibberish in

the language his people spoke, the wind around us warming up until it was almost a light summer breeze. I shouted, "Zeke!"

The fox-man turned toward me, staring me directly in the eyes and said again, "Anything I have to, Marcus."

A portal opened behind him and he tossed Ascal at me, shouting over the wind as it whipped harder, "As agreed upon! Have fun saving Japan and the world from what you can, bud." With that and a sly, sad grin, he stepped backward into the portal and it closed.

CHAPTER FOURTEEN

The wind died down and while I stared at the place the portal had been, the elven juicer at my feet began to mutter and mumble incoherently. Looking down at him, his muscles began to deflate, like balloons that hung limply around the bones while his bloody stump now only dribbled blood.

He wept, and with the realization we had just come to, it was hard to see him as anything more than just a peon and wasted time. It didn't mean he couldn't be a threat, but he just wasn't the one that we really needed to concern ourselves with.

Not really.

Closing my eyes, rage coiling around every fiber of my being, I just lifted Reaper and stabbed it into Qin Moira's chest, not even bothering to look at him as he died. Then I thought about it some more and cut his head off before Galaxy began consuming him.

She finished and stared at the sky for a long moment.

"Zeke is the problem," Galaxy uttered softly, scowling as the words left her lips like they were venomous. "If he knows everything, he probably has partners keeping that video out there, but why?"

I frowned and thought about it, not liking the conclusion I came to. "Merlin said that the gods require blind faith to keep their power, right?" She nodded, her scowl only growing. "What if he found that out somehow, and is trying to weaken the gods?"

She stared at me for a long moment, but I could tell she was truly thinking hard on it. "But why would—"

"Because he knows that if he goes on a rampage and kills too many of them, they could come and take him if there are enough of them working together." I growled and shook my head. "The question is, how the hell is he doing it? Can someone just kill a god and take their Dominion like that?"

"The Vorna can—I probably could too."

"Okay, so he has one Dominion already." I frowned and tried to think of everything he'd said. "And someone connected to him likely has whatever came from that bear god. Right? He got to us so fast when we were at the bathhouse that it was like he knew *exactly* where we were, but he wasn't using one of his little spider things. So how could he have known?"

"We can trust it's not a little spider thing, because if it was, he would have been lying." She frowned and stared at me, then shrugged. "I can't think of it. He knew exactly where we were with the god too."

I closed my eyes, knowing that the answer had to be in how he was presenting what he could do and it had to be something that had been used, right?

My hand flew up and hit my forehead so hard that my head ached immediately.

Galaxy grunted. "Ouch, what?"

"Reaper," I muttered, then sighed. "All the shit he gave us, he enchanted."

"Okay, and?" She frowned, then her eyes widened. "He enchanted it!"

I rolled my eyes and nodded, then my own eyes widened. *Mentally! Speak like this. All the shit that he touched and enchanted can likely be used to know where we are, right? It may not even need to be out for him to know basically where it is, or where it's been used. It just has to be somewhere or something he's tied to somehow that can be used to spy on us.*

That makes a lot of sense, but he hasn't mentioned any kind of powers like that before. They're not in any of his books either.

Doesn't mean he has to be the one doing it, right? She thought about it for a minute, then shrugged so I continued the thought. *Someone else could be keeping tabs on us like he did with the TV, like a crystal ball or something like that. Think about it.*

I am, and it's not a pleasant thought. She grimaced and sighed. *How do we let the others know about it?*

Tell them to gather the items and put them all at Arden's house. We don't go near them when we plan, and we sure as fuck can't use them.

She complied, and there was more push back than I thought there would have been, especially from Arden, whose chair was a godsend to her ass. The jinn's response had even made Galaxy giggle despite the seriousness of the situation.

I rolled my eyes and grumbled, "I'll wait to see her to explain to her how I feel about her ass."

Galaxy raised an eyebrow and gasped, "Thinking of her ass, are we?"

I blinked. "Has my bond with Merlin been open this whole time for that to happen?"

She laughed and we moved on with Kimiko watching us cautiously, muttering, "I hate it when you talk in your heads like that."

Sirens blared in the distance, so we decided to get the hell out of there after Galaxy ate the man that had been cut in half and even Ascal. It was weird seeing her consume his body, but the results were nice.

Level up!

———

Cassia and Arden, clothes torn and dirty as hell, met us back at the room, the latter hopping into the shower almost immediately. She had really only stopped long enough to gripe about her chair and her ass while she grabbed a bottle of beer from the fridge before heading into the bathroom.

Galaxy perched on one of the chairs at the table across from Cassia, tiredly staring at the ceiling as I stood by the sink, still too wired to even consider relaxing. I glanced into the living room and saw Kimiko sprawled out on the small couch and rolled my eyes. She was still covered in blood and there she was on the furniture.

I checked over Cass, who honestly looked a lot better, and asked, "Search go well?"

She shook her head. "The nogitsune are a wily bunch, and it took us a while to find this one. He'd been killing for a while and Raisha was able to land the killing blow, but not before her people took a big hit."

"Will they be able to help protect Tsuki?"

She shrugged. "I made the request and she said that she would ask their elders." She scratched her head and sighed. "After that, we will see what they have to say about all of this."

"Should we at least reach out to Tsuki to make sure she's aware of all of this?" Galaxy's question caught me off guard, and she knew that she'd fucked up. "I thought she knew."

"You didn't actually *tell* her?" It was hard to keep the accusation in my tone from leaking in. "Do you want her to die?"

Cassia frowned, rolling her eyes and crossing her arms. "No. I just want her to be able to focus on what she's doing. I thought we were going to be able to take care of all this on our own without telling her." She kept looking away, then added softly, "Like a present or something."

I stared at her, gaze narrowing. "You've never lied to me before, why would you start now?"

Her eyes widened in shock, but she remained quiet, then stood and walked away. Galaxy cast a baleful glare my way from where she sat, so I knew that if I followed, there was a chance to actually come out of this unscathed. Or at least unscarred.

"Cass, wait." I wasn't dumb enough to grab her and try to turn her around, but I did step to the side so that she didn't think I was going to come at her back like a threat.

"I didn't lie." She seethed, then muttered, "Not on purpose anyway."

She turned to fully face me. "Tsuki was the first person to look at me and really see me for who I was, and not just as some terrifying muscle for the Night Parade. She was scared at first, sure, but when she saw that I was there to help, she knew I was okay. That I was Cassia and not just some monstrous muscle."

She scratched her head and gently thumped her knuckles on the doorframe to our room. "And it's hard to have someone you care about look at you differently, you know? She gave me the courage to be me when I doubted myself back in the States. She's always been looking out for me since we met and now this?"

"Trying to keep this from her is my way of thanking her for that, Marcus." She stared at me then, biting her lip in a way that I'd never seen before. "I want her to ascend and look down on this country—and me—and see that everything she went through was worth it. If she has to worry about anything, I want it to be about what she has to be focused on and not her own safety."

I shook my head, a soft smile spreading across my lips. "Listen, I get it. I really do. But hiding things from your friends like this can be detrimental too. *If* this is what you want, then okay. We can do it without letting her know, but I think getting her some extra guards would be good."

"Who can we call?" She sighed and began to pace in front of the door. "We can't trust Zeke to, he might get distracted or just decide not to if it suits his needs or plans, and then we can't ask the High Table because they're neutral."

"The Unseelie are currently in lockdown with what's happening to the Seelie, so they're out too." I rubbed my chin, thinking it over, then grinned. "Why not ask your sister and the Phantomu?"

I almost heard Kimiko's eyes snapping open as she sat up. "No. Tsuki is not oni."

"She's the Luck Dragon-in-waiting," I clarified for her and she just stared at me without care. "She's the only person in the world whose sole existence is to take over for Shin Bai to continue to fuck over the Night Parade and their schemes. You want to show them you're more than just muscle? Show them that they should truly see your people as a threat."

Kimiko's eyes widened and her jaw clenched. "And you would have me put my people in the way of danger for someone purely to spite the Parade?"

Cassia threw her hands into the air, shouting, "Isn't that what you're all about?"

My girlfriend's sister crossed her arms and muttered, "Well yes, but it's still dangerous."

"And you'll have the luck dragon's attention and favor," I added to the mix, then held up a finger. "Not to mention, the oni who work for the Parade will see that there is someone out there who stood against everything they were relegated to instead of just a group of oni fighting against them with no real purpose. This way they see you for the protector of your people you endeavor to be."

Oh, you're so fucking bad. Galaxy purred in my head. *Cassia is screaming 'scrap' in her head as we speak. It's quite loud.*

She stared at me for a long moment, gaze only briefly flickering with pride before she spoke again. "Go on," Kimiko encouraged.

"Just think about it," Cassia said, wrapping her arm around her sister's shoulders, waving a hand as if presenting the very idea of what she spoke of. "The look on Mom's face when they show up to try their luck and get fucking stomped. She would see how wrong she was, and how strong we are. I get to protect my friend, and then you get to ensure that our people are held in better regard."

"Fine." Kimiko shoved her sister away, but noticeably less

rough than she could have been. "I will do this. The Phantomu will protect Tsuki, but I will not lie to her."

"What do you mean?" Cassia stilled and stared at her sister intently.

"Meaning, if she has the chance to ask me what is going on, I will tell her everything." Kimiko lifted her chin. "I have begun to rebuild my respect for you, Sissy Cassia, but I will not sully my honor by lying to someone for you. So either you tell her yourself, or you take care of the problem before the need for her to know arises."

Cassia stared at her sister, to the point that I worried that she was going to attack her, then nodded. "Fine. You guard her from the shadows and I will let her know what's going on, how I choose."

Kimiko held out her hand and smiled, Cass took it, and they shook once. I could swear that I heard cartilage popping with how hard they carelessly gripped, then let go.

A shriek from the bathroom drove us to spring toward the door, opening it to find Arden on the ground, dirty and trying to cover herself. I looked away before I got my ass kicked and snarled, "What the hell happened?"

"The water was cold!" she whined and I could have strangled her for it.

Kimiko snorted. "You have to flip the switch and then *wait* for the water to heat!" She went into a tirade in Japanese that made Cassia stiffen, then chuckle as we left the room.

I had some calls I needed to make back home to try to get Merlin and Amabala the help they needed.

CHAPTER FIFTEEN

The phone rang for a moment, then went to voicemail. "Merlin's phone, leave a message please."

I growled and called three more times before he slurred a greeting. "Whadyuwant?"

"You to answer your damn phone."

"Marcus?" Some of the drowsiness cleared from his tone and he perked up. "What's going on?"

"Passing news to you guys, I need you and the gnomes on anyone who could be connected to Zeke."

"Listen, I know that he's been creepy and can stalk us somehow with magic, but now we're stalking him?" I rolled my eyes at this as he paused, realizing something. "Wait…"

"Yeah," I confirmed, then sighed. "We believe he's somehow connected to all the videos." I turned my head. "Galaxy, fill him in. I need them on this yesterday."

Her voice entered my mind. *As you wish.*

I raised an eyebrow at her but she just closed her eyes and related all of our memories of what happened.

"Holy shit…" Merlin whispered and a sleepy voice

muttered something on the other side. "Come on, we've got work to do."

There was a mewling complaint, then Merlin sighed. "We can get you another energy drink if we have to, but they make you hyper, you know that."

I snorted. "Amabala there with you?"

"Uh." His voice wavered for a heartbeat then came back mildly confident but still questioning. "I'm an adult?"

"Then you better be doing the adult thing and use protection." I tried not to sound too gruff, but I knew there was no way this kind of thing wouldn't happen for him some time.

"Oh God." Amabala gasped in the background.

Cassia and Arden bellowed, "*What?*"

I rolled my eyes and pulled the phone from my cheek. "Hush."

"Don't you tell me to hush, I'll kick your ass!" Arden snarled, forcing her way closer, still wearing only a towel. "Is my baby brother being risqué?"

"Merlin!" Cassia howled, fists clenched at her sides. "Don't you fight her, she's not strong enough yet!"

Merlin's groan was audible over the receiver from where it was. "Oh my God!"

"Enough, enough." Galaxy waved her hand and joined us. "They have enough to do that they don't need us badgering them about their own business."

"But…" Cassia looked distraught. "They're babies."

"With needs and desires like anyone else," Galaxy corrected her. "They're young by our standards, but by human standards they're adults and we should respect that."

"No." Cassia crossed her arms and stared obstinately at me. "You can think this way about Connell."

"I'm not Merlin's dad." I growled back and both she and Arden growled under their breath. "And when Connell is of age, I can only hope that he's careful when he decides to…"

My cheeks burned despite my own life choices. "Yeah."

"Can we *please* stop discussing our love lives?" Merlin tried to sound indignant but the embarrassment was evident. "So you think that someone close to him could be involved with this, if not him directly?"

"Yes." I smiled and offered him a sincere, "We care about you both, so please be safe."

"We are." His voice was more of a growl than anything else. "We haven't…"

I grinned. "Say no more." He started to speak again, so I reiterated, "Seriously. Just don't."

He laughed weakly. "I'm not the best at social media, but I think Cornelius and Kaz will be able to help a lot."

"Thank you for taking it on, on top of the video thing." I thought of how best to proceed, and just opted for caution. "Do not let anyone attached to us get even remotely close to them. If we interfere…"

"He may very well kill us all," Merlin finished the thought for me. "Got it. How's the situation over there?"

"We think we stopped the Seelie, but it's hard to tell how much of the new drug the Parade had access to before now." I shrugged despite him not being able to see me, then added, "Zeke went into a portal of some kind, likely hunting down the Qin Moira clan."

"Did you kill the guy?" Amabala asked over the phone; it sounded like I was on speaker now.

"Yeah. He's dead." It made me feel almost hollow to say it that way. Such a big pain in the ass taken care of like that, but it was the truth of it even if I felt like the victory was somehow… cheaper than it should have been? "My concern right now is that the drug is possibly still out there while Zeke is with the Seelie doing God knows what."

"Probably killing them as gruesomely as possible," Galaxy stated coldly as she stared out the window.

I nodded. "Probably, and there's no real way for us to get that video and possibly others taken down without resorting to shutting down the damn internet."

"If I lose my cloud of games, Marcus…" Arden closed her eyes and held up a shaking fist.

I shook my head and waved her off. "We need to get ahead of an almost literal war coming and the only people who can do that are at the top." I sighed and thought about it for a long moment. "We can't really leave here right now. Not without putting Tsuki in jeopardy. Merlin, how high up in the government can the Wardens reach?"

"The Ventricals have a way that they could—theoretically—reach out to the highest power in the nation if necessary, but that's if shit has well and truly hit the fan." He sounded worried about it as soon as he was explaining. "You can't seriously be thinking that this warrants that kind of action, though, can you?"

"If we want to keep a race and holy war off our doorstep, we may need to start learning how to play and make nice with the Normies." I scratched my head and took a deep breath. "This kind of shit is way above a sergeant's pay, man."

"I'll speak to Uncle Yen." Amabala's voice was uncertain yet some confidence leaked into it as she said, "He listens to me, and likes to talk about his friends a lot. If we can have the High Table Council assist us in this, we will be able to ensure that all parties are heard."

"Sounds like a plan. Talk later." I hung up thinking about what this could entail for all of us.

"This is going to be hard." Galaxy's voice was soft, but she didn't look scared. She seemed excited. "Think about it. If the whole world knows, that's a wealth of knowledge that we would be able to access for anything. No more hiding and pretending. No more need for everyone to live the lie that they've grown accustomed to."

"How many forums on conspiracies have you gone through?" Cassia asked and Galaxy just looked away without answering, dislodging a chuckle from the larger woman. "Right. Normies are going to be terrified and angry regardless of what it could mean for them at large. Imagine thinking you knew everything only for the president to come out and say, 'We knew nothing, and monsters are real. They want to live peacefully beside us. That's cool, right?'"

"He wouldn't say that." I scoffed but she just shrugged. "Okay they might, it's hard to really judge by that. But we need to try, because this is coming regardless of whether we want it or not."

"It's the end of the world and we know it," someone said behind us. We turned together to see a woman with fox ears and whiskers staring at us with a mischievous grin as she finished, "And I feel fine. Hey kids."

"Raisha!" Cassia grinned and ran to her, throwing her arms around her. The woman hugged her back, but her eyes flitted around to all the faces in the room. "When did you get here?"

"Been listening in on all of it." She grinned wider. "Gotta say, I think it's time we stopped pretending it wasn't always going to happen with all of the technology the world has today. The only safe place anymore is Grestal or in the mountains. Well, that, or one of our dens, but we take few there anymore."

Cassia's eyes widened. "Did you talk to your elders?"

Raisha's hair moved as she nodded. "They said that the luck dragon owing us a favor would be a great boon, so we will oversee Tsuki until the end." She thought about it for a moment then added with a twinkle in her eyes, "I was always going to help her; she fed me once as a baby fox and I never forgot."

My hand buzzed violently and I answered my phone. "Yeah?"

"Emergency meeting in one hour with the council." It was Uncle Yen's voice on the other end of the line; he gave me the address to the local branch of the High Table again, since I didn't recall where it was, and then it went dead.

"Looks like we have our answer on if the council will meet us." I looked down at myself and grumbled, "Should probably shower and decide what exactly we can tell them."

"I'll get the heat up for you since I shut it off." Arden

walked back into the bathroom and returned a moment later. "You're all set."

"We can save on water, come on." I motioned to Cass and she smiled brightly. "I'll grab Mister Quacks."

Cassia snorted. "I hope he doesn't fall asleep with all the guard duty he's working."

Quacks? I raised an eyebrow and snorted. "Not him. He's the perfect Marine. Silent, deadly."

"A fart?" Kimiko tilted her head innocently as ripples of laughter came from the various other women in the room as I just growled and walked off.

We peeled our clothes off and I wished that I'd thought to tell Seamus where we would be to get our laundry done. That brownie could pull blood out of anything and my laundry was always so well folded when he was done.

I tested the water and it was just this side of boiling, which was great for me and I doubted Cassia would mind it as she tried to find an appropriate post for our ducky friend to watch over us.

"Worried about Tsuki?" The question was unbidden, really. I was just wondering and it bubbled out. She nodded and stood with her back to me for a moment. "Kimiko too?"

"Yes." I checked and he was in one of the small nooks in the corner of the room on the stool. We stood in the small furo rinsing the blood from each other before we headed into the actual shower. "She's so hot headed, like me. I don't want her to fight Mother at all, but I know that if it comes down to it, they will kill each other if they must to ensure that their goals are achieved."

"Would Kenshi be willing to come back and help us?"

She shook her head. "Bubba Kenshi can't come back for a while yet." She frowned like she was trying to figure out what to say.

"It's okay, you don't have to tell me everything, Kenshi is a big boy and can always explain things himself if I need to know."

Her features relaxed and I took the shower sprayer and went over her back and shoulders with it. We took our time showering, not so long as to be late for our meeting, but long enough to try to wash some of the mounting stress away.

Despite using the furo first, pinkish puddles of pooling filth formed at our feet as we washed and showered. No matter how hot the water or the pressure from it was, I couldn't get the dread to come away from me. It clung like tar.

Would this change everything for not just me and the world, but Connell too? Would he be safe? Was this the right path?

There was no way we could go into a fight with that guy and come out of it alive, right?

Not for some time. I would highly suggest allocating your points from leveling up. Galaxy was trying to be gentle, but there was no sense in trying to mince words. We just weren't strong enough yet.

CHAPTER SIXTEEN

I tapped my fingers on my chin as I stared at my status page with Galaxy, Cass and Arden sitting nearby doing the same. "How's our balance?"

"Fuck balance," Cassia and Arden snarled together, making Galaxy laugh.

The dark-skinned woman stared at me. "You know what your strengths are, Marcus. Better than anyone here."

I nodded and just did what I knew I would need to if we were going to be heading into this shit show for real soon, and poured my five points for stats into Charisma, pumping it up to an even thirty.

A ding drew my attention and I frowned as a wavy message appeared in front of my vision.

Vornal Blood awakened and statistical needs met for growth. Choose your weapon.

"Uh, the fuck?" I blinked and suddenly I stood in the same place that the Vorna I'd fought before had taken me to. The Null, I thought it was called.

Correct. The Null is the cradle for all life superior

to the weaker and lesser creations of the created gods. Choose your weapon.

Something touched my hand and when I looked down, there was nothing there, likely the book that Merlin had made for the instances when my memory and mind weren't exactly my own.

"I don't know what weapons I have available to me." I wasn't sure who I was talking to, but this was getting a little creepy standing here in this dark place that reminded me of the moon for some reason.

To display your available weapons, state 'Personal Arsenal,' or, to see if there are weapons available to you, state 'Vornal Arsenal.'

"Personal Arsenal?"

The weapons I had available were simple at first. My guns, the Silvaero, Fae Frame and my rifle, then Reaper, despite all of them being in my inventory. Then there was something intangible that I couldn't really see fully. It flickered in and out against the vantablack backdrop of the void. I tried to touch it and the voice and message returned.

You have selected the Huntsman's Mantle, is this choice final?

"No," I stated. "What is this for? What will selecting a weapon do for me? Or to the weapon as it is?"

Vornal Weapons become greater than their origins. With practice, they can assist in the duties of their bearers. Choose your weapon.

"Vornal Arsenal."

A door opened in front of me that rushed forward and left me in a room with various shapes that didn't quite make sense, but they eventually began to resemble things that could be considered weapons. There were whips, axes, swords, even guns and rifles.

"Is that a laser of some kind?" I raised an eyebrow at a gun that looked more like a blaster a kid might play with than a soldier or Marine like me. "Voice, why can't I choose my magic or myself as the weapon?"

Vornal Blood affects an inanimate object. Your body does not fully meet the requirements for an outward physical change. Grow stronger, or steal a Dominion in order to reorganize and change your physical appearance and genetic makeup. Choose a weapon.

None of these were really up my alley, if I was being honest with myself. My guns were closer to what I would really use, but if I had the opportunity to improve anything, it would be a greater boon to have my Mantle grow stronger. If Galaxy and I could hijack a Vorna-enhanced version of it and make it better on top of everything else, what was there to stop us?

I closed my eyes and said, "Personal Arsenal—select Huntsman's Mantle. Confirm."

Weapon selected and confirmation given, please stand by.

The vision of both arsenals faded from my vision and brought me back into the Null itself. The energy here was so cool and nearly comforting to stand in.

The Mantle faded from view, then I felt a soft tearing below me. I looked down and found it being pulled from my shadow, but there was no pain, only calm acceptance. I should be panicking about it, but this was fine.

Once it was fully gone from my shadow, it stood in front of me, appearing the way I must look to everyone else. It was terrifying despite the calm that surged through my mind. Empty red eyes stared into mine, the shadows writhing all over it reaching out to form a clawed hand.

Seal the pact with your blood.

I blinked and held my hand out to the shadowy figure and as we clasped, clawed metallic nails drove through my wrist and held on. Rather than the blood dribbling down from the wounds and onto the gray ground at our feet, it swirled around me and my wrist before slithering down the Mantle's arm and into its mouth.

It fed on my life essence and even as it did, it was still difficult to get too worked up about it.

The horns on top of the helm shifted to the front and curled back, lending the visage a more threatening look as a mask of teeth replaced the faceless visor that almost reminded me of the oni depictions in ancient art, but I knew better. This was to be intimidating, and it was.

The armor thickened and solidified, spikes growing from the shoulders that were curved outward, as if to stop someone from grabbing me. Then the shoulders flexed and dark wings spread from the back, their span at least twelve feet, then they fell to the ground as a leather cape of sorts. It was a little cliché, but still cool.

The leather continued to harden and grow ever more solid, the black of the shadows accented by the crimson of my blood. The armor itself grew until it was larger than me by a good foot and a half, making me about eight feet tall in it and it was even broader than it had been. Everything was much more firm, even my damn boots.

Call the weapon to you, Vorna, and say your name.

"Mantle, come to me." The mantle stood and gave me a smart salute of a fist over its chest. Hell, even the claws that had been on it looked more wickedly curved and dangerous.

It stepped forward and fell into my shadow, then my vision flickered and the armor flowed over me. My vantage point grew and now I could see so much farther.

"Marcus Bola."

Not acceptable. Other Vorna have claimed better names. Your name must encompass a part of you and your weapon.

I frowned and searched within. I was called a lot of things by friend and foe alike. Hell, some of my friends called me worse than even my most hated enemies would and we would laugh over it.

All I seemed to be doing lately was killing and protecting people, but that meant that a lot of things had to die in some cases. The staff had called me Marcus Massacre for a reason, right? I fought to fucking win, and I seemed to have lost a bit of that edge by letting people tell me how I was supposed to move forward. Don't kill them, Marcus, this is my mother, Marcus. She'd almost killed me despite looking so old and slow.

My friendship with Zeke made me blind to the fact that he was as much a threat to our peace as the Seelie and the Night Parade. And I was afraid of him. But that fear stopped me from acting and protecting people who couldn't do the same for themselves.

"I am Marcus Bola, Huntsman of the Wild Hunt—I am the Massacre." As I said it, there was a click inside me and everything was different. I could see so much better and when I concentrated, despite being in the Null, I swear I could hear and taste better too. The feel of the armor on my skin was almost too comfortable.

Massacre. The voice changed slightly, sounding less androgynous and more male as it chuckled. *We look forward to seeing what you can do, little brother Massacre.*

I clenched my fist and waved my hand, leaving the Null as it was in my mind and blinked at the girls in the living room of the apartment.

Galaxy read at my fingertips as I took my hand from the page and the translation of my thoughts. She finished reading and turned her eyes up at me. "Are you okay?"

I grinned. "Never better." I flexed my will, summoning the armor of the Hunt to myself without having to first call the Hunt.

Kimiko and the others gasped but it was the younger oni who spoke. "What the hell happened to you?"

I stared at her and her sister stepped in front of my sight, clearly worried. "Marcus, your killing intent is off the charts. You need to calm down."

I laughed. "I am calm. We have a meeting to get to, though, and I hate being late."

On intuition, I snapped my fingers. Arden and Cassia's armor surged from their shadows to cover them.

Army system awakened—would you like to issue roles and ranks to your riders?

I smiled. "Show me."

A list of ranks appeared in front of me and I frowned. None of them made any fucking sense.

"Scratch those, remake them from my memories of rank structure and chain of command."

"Marcus, who are you talking to?" Galaxy asked, concern on her features as she stepped closer to me.

"Climb in, Galaxy, we need to do this on the move." I turned and walked toward the glass door that led to the street. Once I arrived there, I muttered, "Mako, come."

The drake surged from my body and stood in the middle of the street, invisible to everyone who happened to be walking in the area. I patted his scaled hide and the beast stiffened as the shadows around him gathered and slithered over him, covering him in spiked armor that resembled my own. I shook my head and hopped into the newly remade saddle, then took off into the air with the beast striding beneath me.

I knew both Arden and Cassia were behind me and that Amabala and Merlin were confused about the fact that they could feel me wearing the Mantle and they weren't in their own armor.

Relation complete—roles and ranks have been updated to Marine Corps standard with the use of a billet system to decide roles.

Ranks

Huntsman: Leader of the Wild Hunt and the highest rank.

Sgt. Major: Second in command to the Huntsman. Can call the Hunt into assembly if needed, and use Bonds under extreme conditions.

Master Sgt.: Third in command. Can command their own armor into existence and two others.

Staff Sgt.: Leader of the troops. No special command power.

Sergeant: Commands smaller units when away from the Hunt.

Private First Class: Rank and file of the units. This will be the most numerous rank in the Hunt if the power is spread to others.

I nodded at that; this was workable. Seemed a little too heavy, but it didn't need to mirror the Corps exactly. I mean, it wasn't the Marines, it was the Wild Hunt. "Show me the billets and roles."

Billets

Huntsman: Supreme leader of the Wild Hunt. Holds ultimate power.

Quartermaster: Can choose new members of the Hunt for the Huntsman.

Master at Arms: This warrior oversees the training of the others in the Hunt.

Master of the Hounds: This warrior can choose and create the hounds of the Hunt from other creatures in order to fill the ranks and assist in the fight.

No other billets available at this time.

I nodded even though my lips pursed in thought. Though knowing who I would give these titles to almost on instinct was nice, it was still something to consider. Finally, I decided and stated, "Award the rank of Sgt. Major to Cassia, and her billets will be the Quartermaster and Master at Arms."

I looked over my shoulder at the large woman as she rode on her shadow horse and her armor changed as she moved. Her helmet matched her oni inside, but it also developed a golden trim around the edges of the armor as well, and there was now a Sgt. Major's rank insignia that hovered above her right shoulder that would only be visible to those of the Hunt.

How do you know all this? Galaxy whispered in my mind and I shrugged. *This power feels weird, Marcus, are you okay?*

I think I am. It was the honest answer, but I needed to make sure that my unit was filled now. "Award the rank of Master Sergeant to Ardent Flame."

I turned to hear her mutter, "The fuck is this bullshit?" She looked down at herself as her armor became more ethereal and burned a deep blue at the edges of her metal plates, her helm freeing her hair a little more so that it could burn and leave a trail behind her. "Oh, that's cool as hell."

I snorted and stated, "Award Merlin the rank of Staff Sergeant and the billet of Master of Hounds. Award Amabala the rank of Sergeant."

They're uncertain as to how to feel about their promotions, Galaxy stated, and I just grinned, making her ask, *What?*

I shook my head, chuckling inwardly as I said, "Most people are. That's a good leader for you. When you don't know what you're doing, you can learn and take everything you knew before into account. It's the fuckers who think they know everything and let the power get to their head that end up ruining a good thing."

The grounds for the High Table came into sight after I followed my map since we had been here before. We landed and several of the people, likely either Touched or supernatural creatures themselves, gasped at our approach. I was grateful that they knew better than to scream and draw attention to themselves as we walked through the entrance to the dive-bar exterior, then the hidden one as well.

The staff stared at us upon approach, then I realized that we were still armored for battle and willed our armor to deactivate. The shadows grasped at our armored bodies and plucked each piece from our bodies like attendants as we moved, never breaking stride. At least I didn't. This felt natural to me, whereas if I looked back on previous uses of it, those felt clunky and unnatural.

Like the power had never truly been mine and I was only using it like a child would their first spoon. Sure, I could get things into my mouth, but it was hardly an easy process.

"What do you want?" The security guard who stood near

the bar stepped into our path. He was a thin man, but the sword in his hand, held by a skilled warrior, would be terrifying. "This is neutral ground."

Hanazuki stood behind the bar and called out, "They are High Table, Ryo. There's a meeting. The grand lady told us to let them into her office."

"The Hunt?" Ryo asked as if the thought alone were insane.

"Yes. We're here to help you." It was Cassia who spoke, staring at me from behind her sunglasses. She stepped up to me and when she looked at me, she gasped. "Marcus, your eyes. They're red and black."

She took her phone and showed me. Sure enough what were supposed to be the whites of my eyes were pitch black and my irises were glimmering crimson jewels. I focused on them, but even then, there was nothing like the Mantle's power to bleed away and they stayed the same.

Is this a Vorna thing? It was hard to keep the concern from my tone, especially with Galaxy.

I don't know, but I can't even feel a difference in them from inside you. She paused and I could feel her poking and prodding things inside me. *Nothing. I'm sorry. You might need to wear sunglasses like Cassia for a while.*

Okay. These eyes could be useful for now, though. I blinked and stared at Roy for a second before asking—politely, "Which way is it to the office? We have a very important—world-altering—meeting to get to."

"I will show you." Hanazuki stepped out from behind the counter and whistled once with a piercing, shrill blast that summoned another bartender out of thin air. "Please, follow me."

She bowed her head once respectfully, then stepped backward and turned to lead us toward the side of the room we hadn't really explored last we were here. This one had a set of stairs that led to a hallway just like the Branch in Columbus and when Hanazuki knocked and opened the door there was a brief pause before someone called, "Open, and close. Pause, and open again."

"Yes ma'am." Hanazuki bowed at the waist, then opened the door. The room was an almost exact replica to the others that I had seen except for some plants and artwork along the walls. She shut the door, paused for a moment then opened it once more to reveal the council chambers.

"Council greets Marcus Bola and the others of the Hunt." The fact that Council Member Amelia didn't use my title as Huntsman irritated me and even Galaxy was silent at that. I felt her shift and then agree with a slight nod. "Thank you, Hanazuki. If you would be so kind, I could use a gin and tonic?"

Amelia looked around the room and when no one else shared her desire for a drink, she added, "Make it twelve."

"As the lady wishes." Hanazuki bowed and stepped aside so that the rest of us could enter the room and recount what we learned to the Council.

Uncle Yen sat at the table with all of the others, a look of concern on his face as Merlin and Amabala stepped from the shadows behind him and moved to join us. In addition to his stern visage was a haggard tiredness. Suddenly, it was as if all of the strain from the last few months had finally caught up with him. With my enhanced sight, I could have sworn I caught a slight flicker while I studied him.

"This council has heard disconcerting things," the walrus of a man on the other side of the table from Uncle Yen stated coldly. "Things like the world being in danger. Why?"

"Because of scheming immortal monsters?" I sneered at him, his eyes widening and his mustache quivering. I turned to stare at Amelia, who remained quiet, but there was a small smirk on her face.

"The Wild Hunt was reinstated to take care of these things." One of the other council members spoke. I didn't recognize her from last time either, so there had been a shift in power? "What good is a Hunt that cannot quell the evil that resides in the world and in Grestal?"

"Good enough to stop one of your branches from being outed to the Normies," Arden muttered as she stared pointedly at the table they all sat around. She grew bolder when no one said anything and added louder, "How is Council Member Serpath, by the way?"

"In recovery," Amelia stated softly. "She reabsorbed her other half after killing her for her transgressions against the Cairo branch. She will take some time, but will return to full duties there with my personal blessing, I hope."

That was a relief, but what had it been like killing her other half? That had to have done something to her.

I sighed as one of the other council members I didn't know opened their mouth to speak, cutting them off. "Can we skip the finger-pointing bullshit and get to the business at hand?"

The council member looked stricken, then smiled. "My thoughts exactly, Huntsman." His grin widened. "Our lives are all in jeopardy, aren't they?"

I nodded once. "Yes. The Night Parade moves on the ascending Luck Dragon in order to be able to freely leave Japan. If they get free of their fetters there, they'll be able to summon all of their people. Stopping them will be impossible for us without the Normy world finding out about all of us."

"Not to mention the videos that now threaten to out us that spread through the internets," mustache blubbered, then pointed an accusatory finger toward us. "This is due to *your* failure, I am certain of it. You're weak and cannot instill fear in the monsters to keep them under heel."

My eyes narrowed at him and I asked, "So all of the patrons we have are to be kept fearful?"

He lifted his chins and nodded once. "Yes."

"Good to know." I let the power of the Wild Hunt rush through me, throwing open all of the bonds between me and the others. My armor slammed onto my body from the ether around us and his eyes only bulged as he tried to speak.

My steps carried me to the table and up onto it in a few strides, the only sound reaching my ears was the beat of his heart, wild and frantic. "Maybe we start with the cancerous masses at the head of their world for that, then?"

Someone barred my path. Looking down, it was Uncle Yen. He held a staff and no longer looked solely the part of the wizened old man. The visage I had always known was flickering in and out with that of a man in his early forties, handsome with wisps of gray at the edges of his goatee and his sideburns, but otherwise he was younger than I had ever seen him. I was shocked for a second as what I had questioned seeing earlier was now in my plain sight. Was this my own power, or was he just that tired right now?

He grimaced up at me. "Attacking the council isn't the way, my boy." He shook his head. "Let the power go, Marcus. Let us help you protect the worlds how we can."

I stared at him, shook myself, and nodded once before looking over his shoulder at the man wobbling in fear behind him. "I don't talk shit I can't back, councilman. If you speak out of turn to me and mine again, I will end our relationship that has been amicable and see how you keep the masses in check with the Normies declaring war. Am I clear?"

He nodded, but that wasn't good enough. "Speak!" The air around us swirled as my power flourished and cooled it. Someone around us shivered.

He shuddered and cried, "Yes!"

"Now that the pissing match is over," Council Member Amelia started and pointed at me, "get the fuck off my table."

Something about the way she spoke was concerning. The aura around her shifted and began to gather around her eyes as she continued to stare at me. I started to wonder if she too was going to be something other than what I thought I had been working with since I first met her. I decided deference was the prudent path today.

I hopped backward and landed on the ground easily enough with Galaxy there to guide me and my movements. The cold, biting air receded back toward me and stopped. The shivering member of the council stared at the group of us in horror. My armor fell back into the shadows, but I continued to stare at the guttering fool with disdain.

"One: don't ever do that again, or I will end you," Amelia drawled, her gaze on me unflinchingly. "Two: threaten my council again, and I will end you. Three: change the temperature in this room again, and I will skin you alive and feed you to fucking Shamu—I did not finally get control of the thermostat spell for this room only to have a man get pissy that it's warm. The *nerve!*"

It was difficult not to laugh at the last bit, but that was probably a fourth thing that could have gotten me killed. She stared a heartbeat longer, then asked, "What do you know about all this that is happening?"

"Enough to get us all killed if we interfere with the whole video thing any more than we already are." It was hard to keep my tone neutral as I thought about all the things I had seen Zeke do while fighting. I was brutal, sure, but that shit was just on a different scale.

"You know who it is?" I nodded and she frowned. "Tell us."

"We can't," Cassia stated and when someone was about to object, she added, "They're the ones who killed the Roman god and another god as well."

"If we tell you, they will know and come for all of us." Arden sighed and ran her hand through her hair. "Honestly, the only reason they haven't killed us is probably more because we're somewhat useful in keeping their other nuisances at bay than anything else."

"What else could there be?" Mustache asked with narrowed eyes.

"Misguided affection for the weak?" I shrugged, not bothering to rein in my sarcasm at his insinuation. "The only reason we found out about it is the fact that he didn't bother to keep it a secret any longer."

"So it's a he?" Amelia quirked her head and stared at me.

I realized what I'd accidentally let slip and fought not to show it, however it was Uncle Yen who blanched and looked like he was going to be sick. His form was settling in on that of the younger version I had 'glimpsed' earlier. It was almost disconcerting.

"Yenasi, do you know what's going on, or who this person could be?" Amelia stared at him, openly questioning him in front of everyone.

"I don't know for sure, but if it's the person I think, we need to steer clear of him." He looked panicked and I wondered why. "He gave Lucifer a run for his money in a game of fucking tag. Not only that, but he beat him in an arm wrestling competition so badly it broke the table, floor, and part of my bar."

"Out drank him too," Merlin muttered with his arms crossed. He looked exhausted, haggard and his eyes had dark circles under them, but he was holding on.

Amabala stood close to him and looked little better, her ears stood up but her tail and whiskers drooped, with her eyes tired and half-lidded and unfocused.

"So you cannot tell us who it is?" Amelia confirmed, all of us nodding. "Because they'll kill you, likely even more people if you, what? Just if you get in their way?"

Once more, we nodded while Merlin huffed.

She stared at him coldly until his Adam's apple bobbed with a swallow that was audible before she spoke again. "Then they aren't very good at hiding themselves, are they?" Amelia pulled out a tablet and began to tap on the screen before a large white sheet dropped behind her with an image projecting onto it. It was a series of videos with dates on each of them. "I take it the night in question is one of these?"

"Yeah, that one." Merlin pointed to the most recent one.

She clicked on it and the image enlarged to fill the entire twenty-by-fifteen-foot sheet. It was of three men drinking at the bar, then talking a bit. Lucifer, Zeke, and someone I didn't know. They went outside for a time; they fast forwarded through that.

When they returned, the men were sweaty and laughing. They drank some more and started to sing, boisterously, with some of the other patrons laughing at them.

Then the other man, lanky and almost average-looking with dark hair, glasses, and a patch of hair on his chin, grinned and put his arm up on the corner of the bar, but the bartender shooed them to one of the standing tables nearby with a good natured grin.

They clasped hands and when Luci tried to pin the other man's hand he let the devil get a little closer to pinning his hand before he fought back. Luci went over the table, shattering it and broke the floor on the way to the bar itself.

Upon impact, the bar cracked at the foundation up to the corner where he was at and started to fall over.

"Christ," I muttered. That had to be the guy who attacked the Vorna. He was way too strong not to be and he was having *fun* showing off.

Sure, he looked to be a little taken aback and was apologetic, but there had to be something that much more different about him.

"Find them, Daglebr, but do not engage—report back to this council." Amelia lifted a hand and the mustache man stood, moving away from the table with a nod, throwing a grimacing glare over his shoulder toward us. "Do not antagonize them, Daglebr. I will not stop them again if you keep openly disrespecting them."

As I watched him slink from the room, the man rolled his eyes and disappeared into the shadows on the other side.

"Marcus, Wild Hunt, we have many new things to discuss, apparently one of them being customs and courtesies, but for now, we have a problem." Amelia touched her forehead with the back of her hand. "We cannot chase down the videos as fast as they are reintroduced, and more are coming. We can try to disprove them, or debunk the things in them, but there is enough evidence of an underworld beneath the humans to spark serious investigation."

"Then why continue to hide?" I asked quietly, but I knew it was a pointed question. I also directed my gaze at Uncle Yen, trying to make it apparent I was asking him a similar question.

"Humanity comes closer and closer to learning about all of this every year," Merlin agreed, staring at them. "Do you honestly think that there's not going to be a time when they don't find us and attack us anyway?"

One of the council stood and blustered, "Our magic—"

"Will only stop so many fucking bullets," I stated coldly. "You can stop all the rounds you can see coming at you, but the second you think you're okay, a Seal Team comes in and just rocks your shit. And you think that the High Table's enemies won't help them? You have—had—Seelie in Japan giving the Night Parade drugs to make them stronger magically and physically so they can be free of their home."

"We've never let the Normies know of us." Uncle Yen sighed. He shook his head. "Even the Touched are under a gag order."

"There's a group out there in the world killing *literal gods*." Arden sneered, then threw up her hands in exasperation. "It's time to open up and have it be on *our* terms. We need to control the flow of information before the public can figure out that something is amiss, because this *will* happen."

The council erupted into bickering, some on our side, others more vocal against it, calling for the Hunt to be dismantled or given new leadership, as if it was their choice to begin with.

Fed up with it, I cleared my throat once, then louder before just rolling my eyes and looking at my group.

"We came here and told them what was coming as best as we could, and now they know and will do what they want to anyway." I shrugged and shook my head. "We can only advise on what's happened and speculate on how the change that's coming *may* happen. This isn't going to end well." I turned to the council after a snap of my fingers with some will behind it finally caught their attention. "Thank you all for coming and meeting with us, but the Hunt has business to take care of and the world to potentially save."

I looked over at Merlin. "Get Theo on the line if you can. We need to chat and see if the Wardens are more willing to help."

He nodded as we all turned and walked away, not waiting to be dismissed. I was more than sure that it would upset some of them, but they had to know that we were a partner, not a tool. No matter how well they tried to keep us locked under their leadership, that leadership wouldn't last if they didn't do something about the shit coming.

CHAPTER SEVENTEEN

Once we cleared the room and walked back downstairs into the High Table back in Akihabara, the air felt a little more settled. I called my armor to me once more while Merlin immediately walked away to speak with the young Ventricle from Ohio.

"Do you think they'll do anything about it all?" Amabala wondered aloud, making me glance back at her. "About what's coming?"

I shrugged. "No clue. I think they have a lot to worry about, but a big part of their whole existence and need for their services depends on the Normies remaining ignorant of our kind." I scratched my head and a gust of air left me as I huffed with frustration. "I can't blame them for that, but I can blame them for not wanting to put their people first. It just sucks."

"It's how they've always been." Uncle Yen's voice carried over my shoulder, prompting me to look back to see him standing there fully in his younger form as he looked me over. "You alright?"

I nodded. "I'm okay. You?"

"Concerned for you and what's coming, but I'm alright for

now." His hand went to the back of his neck, as his other hand motioned to himself. "I suppose you wonder about this."

"I've known you were hiding something since I started to be able to see auras around other creatures, but I figured you had a good reason not to show off before now." His eyebrows shot up at that, but he just sighed and shook his head. "Are you okay with people seeing it?"

"I have been for a while now, but I just didn't know what to do about it all when you first came into the picture. Besides, with all the stress I've been under lately, it's just been too much to keep the image up." He looked at the others who seemed nonplussed about his chatter. "This was a gift from my…"

He hesitated and I frowned at him, not really understanding what he was talking about, but it was Arden who grunted, "Tell him, Yenasi." So, everyone else knew all this time. Huh. I decided immediately it wasn't worth bringing up anytime soon, if ever.

He opened and closed his mouth, then cleared his throat. "This, my slow aging and youthful appearance, is from my boyfriend." My eyebrows raised and he sighed. "Listen, I know it's odd to hear that, but hear me out."

I put up a hand and he stopped, Arden looking at me strangely, almost disapprovingly, as I spoke. "I don't care." Uncle Yen looked shocked. "I'm dating a goddess and an oni at the same time, together. You can date and love who you want, Uncle Yen. It's not going to change how I feel about you, and you sure as fuck don't owe me an explanation. I only wish you had trusted me sooner with this."

He smiled at me softly, then muttered, "I knew you were different from the rest of the family, my boy. And I am sorry for not trusting you more sooner, but thank you."

I grinned at him. "Always have been." I pulled him into a hug and he squeezed me back. "Stay like this, it looks good on you."

He nodded, then frowned. "We're in some shit, aren't we?"

"Yeah. Yeah, we are." I sighed and nodded toward the hall.

"Let's go have a drink real quick while Merlin is on the phone with Theo."

"Yeah!" Cassia agreed excitedly. "Then you can tell him who the lucky guy is."

"Oooh. The tea." I snorted, since Galaxy had started using language she had picked up from the internet.

"Can I have tea?" Amelia stated, startling us all and making us look back at her. "Am I not invited?" It was obvious that she had no idea what Galaxy was actually referring to.

"Has the council come to some sort of conclusion to what was talked about?" My question led her to nod, but it was a tense one. "Fine, you can join us for now."

We walked down the hall to the bar where the staff watched us, each of them just as wary of us like bouncers watching a naughty regular with a nasty temper.

"We're not a threat to anyone here." Cassia growled at the security around us. "You can leave us."

Amelia raised a hand when they refused to listen to Cass and they begrudgingly cleared the area, far enough away from us to be considered 'gone' but close enough to act if things got bad. "Good staff," I muttered as I glanced around.

"Can we get a round?" Uncle Yen asked Hanazuki politely. "I would love the house specialty. All of you?"

"Can I get some tea?" Amelia brightened up a bit, then added, "Could I also get a shot of Blodka?"

I raised an eyebrow at the order but Hanazuki didn't pay it any mind so I added, "Two of those Mojitos we had the other night would be great. Those were awesome."

Cassia and Arden ordered the same, though Cass asked for tequila as well. Merlin ordered, putting a hand over his phone's bottom, "One large mead, and vodka and Red Bull for the lady."

Amabala grinned wildly and kissed him on the cheek before he kept speaking to who I assumed was Theo. Watching them, I couldn't help thinking how they were so cute. Too cute. I loved it and as much shit as I might give them, I was glad they had each other.

We found a booth in the quieter part of the bar and sat in silence for a moment as we waited for our drinks, then once they came we took a few sips before Merlin came back. "They'll meet with us."

"The Wardens?" Amelia set her tea cup back down and stared at him as he nodded. "When?"

Merlin reached down to grab his mug and took a sip of his drink and grimaced before speaking. "Soon. Theo has to take care of something, then will use a portal network to get here to speak to us personally."

"Good. Might I tag along?" The young warden stared down at her and she added, "I have word to share from the council that I believe will be beneficial."

"I'll text Theo." Merlin's thumbs tapped along the screen of his phone and he nodded to himself before he sat with us. "So, what's the Council's stance?"

"We are divided," Amelia stated in a matter of fact tone, ending in a grumbled, "Unsurprisingly. However, it is the firm belief of many of us that we can no longer cling to our thinning veil of ignorance to save ourselves from humanity."

"But you can't invalidate your neutrality by being more directly involved." She nodded at my observation. Which raised a concern. "So then why come to the meeting with the Wardens if you're worried about your neutral status?"

"Because if anyone can benefit from the fall of the Table, it would be them." She frowned and looked at Merlin. "I know your kind thinks little of us, but I also know that you have seen the ill that they are capable of."

He nodded. "I worry that they stand to gain too much from this as well." Merlin crossed his arms and shook his head. "I know that there are some amongst them who will fight the change, because we work better without someone overseeing us, but there will be more who want us to work in the open for other reasons entirely."

Amabala put her hand on his shoulder. "It's okay to feel torn."

He nodded at her and put one of his hands on hers from where it was and Arden grumbled, "Stop being so fucking cute."

"Masonai has been asking after you," Amabala stated brightly, to which Arden smiled. "He came by your place just the other day to see if you wanted to hang out and talk some more about the videos."

Her face fell a bit, but she said, "He knows I'm here, he could just message me himself."

"He knows, but he didn't want you to worry about him, the rates and fees of international texting and things while you were here on vacation." Merlin smiled a bit wider. "I like him more and more all the time."

Arden put her head in her hands. "Oh, I'm going to bring him back so many books."

"Do we even have the time to go to the con?" I raised an eyebrow at her and she nodded. "How?"

"The con is a great place for people to gather. Touched who may not be noticed if they are taken," Arden reasoned. "If the Seelie are truly gone, we have nothing to worry about, but if we aren't there to at least make sure they're not doing it, we can't know for sure."

"You just want your cake and to eat it too," Galaxy teased, but she was smiling too big not to want to go too.

Arden snorted and grinned. "I'm a sweet fiend, of course I do."

"That you are." Uncle Yen snorted and winked at her as she narrowed her gaze toward him. "I've seen you down a whole cake, girl. I know."

"So, who's this beau you're seeing?" Cassia came to the rescue for Arden with mischief in her gaze. "Galaxy is taking bets."

He raised a brow and quirked his lips oddly. "Can't she read minds?"

Galaxy smiled, winking. "Just the important ones."

"Is it Anubis?" Merlin wondered aloud and to all of our surprise Uncle Yen just took a drink from his cup. Merlin's eyes widened and his voice went low, almost to a hiss. "No fucking way!"

"Yes." Uncle Yen smiled. "This isn't a recent thing, and we would have been a little more forthcoming about it, but I was worried about perceptions and reactions."

That weighed on me. "I'm sorry, Uncle Yen. I wish I had thought about it more than that." I took a sip of my own drink, somehow the plum less sweet than before. Almost bitter, like medicine on my tongue with the sobering thoughts on my mind. "Was it Mom?"

He heaved a sigh and nodded. "My mother and father as well. They weren't satisfied with me being almost a cookie-cutter version of Dad himself. Strong, strong-willed, and talented. I was the star for a few years when I was on the foot-ball team in school, but when I went to college, they found out that I wasn't entirely straight and at this time I had already discovered that I was Touched."

"It was so nice getting to meet you then, though meeting your folks was shit." Amelia muttered the last part bitterly, then took a drink and made a sound with her throat and grinned, saying, "Remember the time that they wanted to try to send you to some kind of camp?"

He rolled his eyes. "Yeah, I was already learning what I needed to know, what I needed to take over a branch of the Table, so I was so not going to do that. It hurt to know that they couldn't accept me for who I was, but it was their loss."

Cassia raised her chin and held her drink up. "To their loss and our gain!"

We all cheered and lifted our glasses, joining together in a brief respite of humor and merriment. We listened to stories of a younger Uncle Yen from both him and Amelia who, despite being an ex of his, was caring and kind. I didn't know if him shouldering some of the responsibilities that she had were what made her back off him or if she had always been this way or not, but it was good to see.

———

We made it back to our room, Uncle Yen, Merlin, and Amabala taking a portal back to the house in Columbus, promising to come back in time for the meeting if we needed them. I did make the argument that if they would be coming back to just bring Theo, but Merlin shook his head. "Kaz and Corn are both kicking ass and taking names right now for us to be here, so we need to get back and make sure that they can get some rest. They've also been pointing others in our direction to assist us in this."

"If anyone needs any kind of contract or source of payment to help us out, let me know and we can see to it," Cassia stated confidently. "We need to start bolstering our numbers."

"What?" I blinked at her as the others nodded and left with hugs and kisses on the cheek. I continued to stare at Cassia. "We can't bring more people into this."

"We need to." She shrugged. "There are some things that sheer numbers can do that we can't even for all our individual power."

"Galaxy is having trouble with all of us as it is. We can't just add more people to the roster right now."

"She's talking about the Hunt itself, Marcus," Galaxy interjected and stared at me. *You didn't need to tell them all that, you know. I can manage myself.*

I'm sorry, I just worry about you.

She rebuffed me quietly. *I know.* Out loud, she said, "I agree, we should grow the Wild Hunt. We need hounds and hunters."

I blinked at her and wondered, *How are we going to manage all of them?*

We aren't, Cassia and the others will. She stared at me and said, "Marcus worries about how we will manage them all if we increase our numbers."

I narrowed my gaze at her and she just stuck her tongue out at me. Payback, I guessed, so I left it alone. *Smart idea.* Her smugness as she said that made me reconsider but the others were already speaking.

"…Right?" Cassia turned to Arden and asked and the other woman nodded agreement before Cass turned back to me and added, "You're the leader now. The big cheese. We can handle managing the masses so long as your intent is clear."

"And if it isn't, we improvise." Arden grinned, then tapped her finger on her chin. "I seem to recall that being a part of the mindset for Marines?"

"Improvise, adapt, and overcome." I nodded with a smirk. "But I hardly doubt that Chesty had to worry about whether the Wild Hunt would be able to ride and operate without a clear vision of how to operate. Or Clint Eastwood, for that matter."

"Is that where that came from?" Cassia asked and I nodded excitedly. "Nice."

"He's not the Duke or anything like that, but he's pretty cool." Arden snorted and crossed her arms to stare at me. "Regardless, you need to let us take some of the work off your plate. It's what real leadership needs."

I sighed. "Fine."

Both of them stared at me a little bit longer than I would have normally cared for, Cassia theatrically speaking out of the side of her mouth to Arden. "I really expected more of a fight on this. What do we do now?"

Arden, fake aghast, said, "I have no idea, I honestly expected to spend half the night going back and forth over this. With a gap in my schedule like this, we just might be able to get some sleep in order to get into the con at a decent hour tomorrow."

I closed my eyes. "You two piss me off to no goddamn end, you know that?"

They cackled and nodded.

"Come to the corner store with me?" Galaxy stared at them. "Maybe he deserves a treat for this?"

Arden and Cassia shrieked and nodded affirmation and left to go do what they would. Having the place to myself, I reached for my phone.

There was a text from Luca that was from about six hours earlier. I opened it up and read it out loud because I was having trouble wrapping my head around it. "Seelie portion of Grestal under attack. Others looking at us for the attack. Sympathizers saying they'll be coming for us."

My eyes widened and I read it again. "Fuck." I dialed Chris, not expecting any kind of answer whatsoever but someone picked up. "Chris? That better be you, man."

"It's Eve, Marcus." Her voice was cool over the other end of the line. "How can I assist you for my King?"

"My son and his family are probably under attack right now." It was so hard to keep the edge out of my voice. "He promised that he was keeping them safe."

"And he is." She put her hand over the receiver, the line dulling a bit as she spoke to someone on her end. "He says he's having some difficulty locating you?"

I could no longer keep myself contained. "Because we know about the fact that the things he gave us were how he was keeping tabs on us and our whereabouts."

"Clever," she cooed and I closed my eyes, trying to hold back my rage until she said, "Yes, my king."

There was a sound of the phone changing hands and suddenly Chris' voice came over the line. "We need to talk." He didn't sound angry or anything, just matter of fact.

"Yes, we do," I confirmed.

"Can you meet me at the place that we went to originally?"

I nodded. "I can." I checked my map and found the bathhouse. "I'll be there in a bit."

"Text me when you arrive and I'll meet you." He didn't wait for anything else, just hung up as I was on my way out the glass door. I closed it after a moment of wrestling with whether I should tell the others, but decided against it.

I know you can read my mind, Galaxy, and I want you to not tell anyone what's transpired. I frowned and added, *Stay away, and stay ready to come and get the Mantle if needed. We can't afford for this power to be his.*

Going on your own is foolish. Arden and Cassia already know what's going on, so we're coming back.

No, I ordered mentally, unable to keep bass from my voice as I did. *If you all show up too, you paint a target on yourselves. If I need you, I'll open the bonds and you can send aid to me. But we can't afford this fight, or to have all of us fall. If I go down, you get the Mantle and get Connell.*

There was no response and I took a deep breath, knowing that they would find him and try to keep him safe if they could. They would die getting to him if necessary, but they would do everything in their power and that was comforting.

For now, I just had to get to the meeting place.

"Mako, let's go." The massive drake burst from the ground beneath me, my body flung into the air only to land in his saddle with an ease that seemed different as well. We took off into the air as the shadows warped around us.

CHAPTER EIGHTEEN

I landed, the others still quiet, but I could almost feel Galaxy watching from where she was. Like she was just waiting for the sign to try to intervene.

I landed and sent a text to him that said simply, *Here.*

My phone buzzed to let me know I had a text back. *Walk through the portal, Marcus. Let's chat.*

I frowned and suddenly there was a gaping maw of a portal in front of me. It was larger than me and I sighed as Galaxy's mind raced, trying to convince me this was a bad idea. My only rebuttal being, *Connell needs me. Be safe.*

The portal was nothing like the ones we went through with Amabala or even to get into Grestal. This one felt like just walking through a doorway. There was no compression or suction at all. *Guess that's what it's like to have the power to create doors like a god.*

The world was dark, but for some reason I could see like it was daytime. Must be related to my new eye color. The hall I stood in was massive, made almost entirely of the void between the stars, and that was confusing. I blinked and continued to survey the area, until I looked to my right and saw what had to be a set of stairs of some kind that led to a raised platform where a nearly-neon throne stood against the night sky.

"Welcome to the new Unseelie Court, Marcus," Zeke greeted me from the throne. It was bright like the stars of the night sky behind him and refracted the light in a manner that gave the air around it different hues of color at varying densities. His voice was soft but there was something solid in it, like a threat.

"What did you want to talk about?" I called to him, my voice carrying further as if the void made it echo to him, rather than swallowing up the words like I felt it all should. "The Seelie and others were going to go after my family and friends. I thought they were taken care of."

He waved it away. "Not a problem for them or anyone else anymore." He held up a hand and a bubble of darkness domed up from the floor, popping to reveal a man standing in torn robes and armor, his face bloodied and one of his arms missing from mid-forearm. "See this guy? This guy was the king. What was your name again, little fella?"

The Fae man just stared at him in disdain, remaining silent until Zeke just grinned. "Yeah, you don't rate one anymore, do you?"

The former king spat onto the ground, a mixture of blood and saliva that made Zeke laugh more. He waved a hand and the man disappeared from sight. "What a character, lemme tell ya." He slipped a finger under his eye playfully and winked at me but it still felt like it was a soft threat. "I called you here to show you something, Marcus, and to make sure you knew that I'm not trying to be an asshole."

"You just mocked an injured royal in front of me," I said, deadpan. "Your war on the Seelie affected my family."

There was a whine in the air and then what sounded like someone knocking on a door that made Zeke grin. "Oh, pizza's here."

He clicked his fingers together and hole tore in space right next to him and the massive armored figure that had pummeled the Vorna walked through with a group of hooded people following behind him. At the end of the line was a thin man in a blood-red hoodie that had the hood up around his face, but in the darkness of the hood I could see cold, ruby eyes staring out.

"You guys aren't the pizza guy!" Zeke groaned and sat forward on his throne.

The large figure turned and stared at him, then asked in a surprisingly light and normal voice, "All I have is sausage. You want it, or are you just going to be a tease again?"

The hooded figure just snickered and smacked the larger one as Zeke snorted, then tossed his chin my way. Both of them turned around and stared at me.

"Who's this fool?" Hood asked, a slight Hispanic accent coming through in his voice. "Someone else we need to take care of?"

"Nah, man. This is Marcus, he's cool." He frowned, then grimaced and threw his hand out toward the rear of his throne and grunted. "C'mere!"

Scuffling and grunting could be heard until the big guy stepped up and joined his king in dragging whatever, or whoever, it was that was behind his throne. Zeke slapped something in his grasp and what had been clear as the air we breathed, became solid and visible.

It was Daglebr, quivering mustache and all. But how the fuck had he managed to get in here?

"Who are you?" The man in the hood's question surprised him as the apprehended man just stared at me in shocked disbelief. As if he couldn't believe I was here, or he couldn't believe his luck.

"I knew it! I knew you were in league with them!" he sputtered and pointed a thick finger at me, ignoring the other people in the room. "They'll hear about this!"

The two goons closest to Zeke turned together and stared at me as I did my best to try to appear like I wasn't panicking. Even with the enhanced Mantle, I had no idea if I could take either of them, and the new guy was my only chance at it if that was possible.

"What do you mean?" Zeke asked coldly, holding the large man up as if he weighed little at all. Zeke turned to me and his voice had the same timbre to it. "What does he mean?"

"He came to the High Table Council in order to tell us what was going on!" Daglebr's voice quivered as he continued to try to damn me. "He led us to you!"

Zeke's head shifted to me so fast I could have sworn I heard the bones in his neck adjusting from it. "Did he now?" He turned back to the large man and set him down gently, his voice taking on an almost-comically nice quality as he patted the other man. "And did he say anything about me specifically? Did he tell you who I was?"

Daglebr nodded his head violently, but Zeke shook his head. "No, no, I need to hear the words if I'm going to kill someone and all of the people they hold dear. Did he tell you about me? Did he say my name when he told you who I was?"

Daglebr hesitated, obviously trying to decide what was going to happen to him, but when the two that had been talking to the King grabbed me and moved me closer in unison, it emboldened him. "Yes."

Zeke just smiled and said, "Eve?"

The tigress lounging in shadows nearby stood and walked slowly forward until she stood on the podium near her master. "Can you not taste it, my king?" Her voice startled the councilman and Zeke just shook his head. "You will learn, that acrid taste at the back of your throat was the taste of a lie."

"What?" Daglebr swore beneath his breath and shook a fist at the creature nearest him. "I would not lie to anyone about that treacherous filth!"

"Yet another lie." Zeke grumbled and looked toward me. "And you?"

"I went to the council, but true to my word, I told them nothing except for how powerful you were and that you were a threat we needed to take seriously." I frowned and added,

"When asked to tell them who you were, we refused and told them the truth that you would kill us all if we got in your way."

"And dangerously close to my way do you tread, Marcus." He stared at me as he shoved Daglebr away from him. "So they sent a spy here to check the validity of the threat?"

I nodded and the shadows on the floor of the room seeped up his body and held him in place, his mouth opening to release a stream of curses so vile that the man on my right, the large armored one, whistled low. "Man. You kiss your mother with that mouth?"

"He kisses a sandwich with that mouth," the other one grumbled.

"Guys, come on." Zeke just shook his head. "We aren't going to shame a big guy. I mean, shit, I'm one myself."

"Yeah, but you can also turn into a feral werewolf and fucking eat people," the armored one retorted sarcastically.

"Muuuuu," Zeke warned as he dragged out the man's name, or the sound of a cow lowing. "Not kosher."

"Fine." The armored one let me go. "Since he's not the threat we thought he is, shouldn't we worry about our guests?"

"Nah," the other said. "They got shadows on their heads. They can breathe, but they can't see, hear, or be heard. They're pretty docile too, though the guards were dicks."

"Thanks for that, Yohsuke, but these ones are actually here for him." Zeke motioned to the figures that stood between me and his throne, their shadow hoods falling away to reveal the other Unseelie royals.

Connell was perfectly fine other than some mussed up hair. Aeslyn and Luca looked okay, and the king and queen were battered, but not truly injured.

"Where have you brought us, you monsters?" The king's voice was a roar and the echo was almost painful.

"He needs to work on that," Yohsuke muttered to himself as he walked around the group with a wide berth. He didn't glance at them, but as the one called Muu moved the other way, mirroring the hooded one, both Luca and the king readied themselves for an attack.

Connell saw me and whispered, "Dad?"

"Hey buddy." He looked torn, like he wanted to run toward me, but his mother clenched her hand on his shoulder tight enough that he didn't move. "Stay there, you're safe."

"Obviously we fucking aren't," Aeslyn's hissed words reached me and she continued, "Where are we? Why are you here?"

Zeke called over her as she spoke. "He's here as my guest, as are all of you." The group turned to see him sitting on the throne and the queen strode forward to the bottom of the steps.

My eyes widened. "Stop!" My call for her to not go any further made her hesitate and look back. "I don't know how strong you are, or how strong you think you are. If you are a threat to him, they will kill you. He controls things that are——"

I found I couldn't speak as Zeke merely held a finger to his lips and shushed me like I was a kid about to give away a big secret too soon. Though to his credit, he did say, "Listen to him. He knows more than he's been allowed to say."

Connell brushed his mom's hand off his shoulder and stepped forward, asking, "And why isn't he allowed to say it?"

Zeke raised an eyebrow and smiled, deeply so that all his teeth showed. "Because sometimes, little man, grownups can meddle in things that they shouldn't. Ever have someone come into your room and play with something that is meant for one specific thing, and if anyone touches it but you, it could break it?"

"No." He was honest, I thought.

"I have," Zeke said softly, sadness in his eyes. "I lost something a while ago that I didn't want to lose because of the selfishness of others. Someone was playing with someone else's toys, and they came and took them back, and didn't care what happened to the toys when they took them."

Muu crossed his arms and growled. "And then they shoved

them so far into the bottom of the toy box that they could have drowned under a sea of ass before they were ever found again."

"Hey." Zeke snapped, his eyes feral. "Language. I know I'm not a good example, but he's able to hear us now."

"Fool." Yohsuke shook his head at the other man and spoke on. "What he means to say, is that he couldn't say anything, because if he did, we would have had to hurt a lot of people to make sure that things were put to rights again. We don't want to do that."

"You sure?" I challenged them, all of them turning their gaze on me. With the witnesses in the room, there was no way to ensure their safety if things got dicey. "Maybe we should speak in private."

Zeke nodded. "Sure." He motioned to all of the people in front of him. "All of you are now free and given to Marcus. I upheld my promise that you would be safe from the enemies I made. Now, I see you into his care and consideration."

The king and queen turned and looked at him and he added, "Oh, and the Unseelie are probably going to want to ally with me, seeing as though I'm the one who killed the lion's share of the Seelie. I can protect them from the shit storm that's coming without going into hiding."

The queen looked ready to bluster and fight, but it was her son Luca who put a hand on her forearm and said, "Not now, Mother."

She slapped him hard enough that I flinched and even the other three men on the podium grunted and groaned, Muu muttering, "Shit, that sounded painful."

"I did not become queen to see my title usurped by some furry creature with a god complex!" The queen held herself a little more regally. "I challenge you to a duel."

"She called you a furry, man," Muu muttered. "I would wipe her off the map for that."

"She's also the kid's grandma, man," Yohsuke muttered over the other man, his tone a bit more forceful. "Think of the kid."

"No one said anything about anyone else having to die,

right?" Zeke just shook his head and looked at Connell. "I don't want you to get slapped too, because that would piss me and your old man off, so I'm not going to try to have you talk sense into her."

"Royalty can get to people." Muu snorted and got a smack in the back of the head from the king behind him. "See?"

"Enough!" The queen snarled and took yet another step forward. "Will you fight me, or lay down your claim to my people?"

Rolling his eyes, Zeke ignored her and looked to me. "Marcus, I did what I said, you can't fault me for this." I shook my head and he nodded. "Good man. The rest of you are free to leave. *Encouraged* to do so, really. I'll be dropping you off to my new good friend Lucifer at the High Table in Columbus. Tell him to put a few rounds on my tab, huh?"

Luca looked over his shoulder, his face already turning red where his mother had slapped him and I said, "Take your family and go where it's safe. I'll come to you when I can."

A flex of space drew my attention and a tear opened up behind him. Luca turned on his heel and ushered Aeslyn and Connell out, the boy looking back at me to see what was going on and I just gave him a terse nod. I needed to think about him and his getting home to the others now with everything that was still going on. If I could make it out of this alive and get back to all of my friends and family, I would.

I stared over at the king and queen now, both of them glaring at Zeke and his friends.

"Marcus, we still need to talk. Do you mind waiting for a moment while I take care of my other guests?" Zeke's question caught me off guard and I nodded. "Cool. Thanks, man."

I was worried, but he had said he wouldn't kill them, right? So that was at least something. I had no particular ties to Connell's grandmother, but her treatment of her son and me prior to this had been under extreme situations, hadn't they?

"Make some space then, boys, and let's let her have a go." Zeke stood from his throne and heaved a sigh as he shifted into his human, dark-skinned form. He stared at her as the rest of us moved aside except for the king and queen. "What, you both going to come at me?"

"No, I stand in support of my wife and queen," the king responded and turned toward his woman. "Fight well, my love."

The queen didn't look at him at all and instead continued to glare at Zeke, her dress shifting along her body until it was less ball gown and more nightclub appropriate.

"I wonder if Mae can do that." Muu wondered as he came over to stand next to me. He held out one of his large, clawed hands. "Name's Muu, by the way, in case you hadn't picked up on that."

I nodded. "I had. I'm Marcus." I shook his hand and he cold-fished me, like when someone's hand is just limp and they don't move. Which I was grateful for really. "So uh, what's going to happen? And how do you and Yohsuke fit into all this? Are you guys like Zeke?"

"Sure are!" He grinned down at me and from this close, I could see that the armor on his head wasn't armor, it was actually his head. He was some kind of lizard thing. "We were with him in Brindolla when shit got heavy with War. We kicked his ass, though."

"You beat War?" I asked incredulously, recalling the name from speaking to the Vorna when she was talking about the others who were out there in the cosmos.

"Sure did!" He grinned. "Yoh and me did a lot of the heavy lifting, so don't let Captain Whiskers over there blow too much smoke up your ass."

"So... he's a demi-god now?" I kept my voice and tone friendly and questioning. He seemed like the type to divulge if he knew something if it meant being friendly.

"Something like that." He nodded and tilted his head toward me. "Me too, honestly. Though I can't do the whole time-space-wormhole thing. I'm just a whole hell of a lot sturdier and stronger than I was. Which was strong to begin with."

"And Yoh?"

There was motion beside me and his voice made both of us jump as he said, "What about me?"

"Jesus Christ!" Muu patted his chest. "You fucking vampire, spooky-ass-fisheyed—"

"Finish that sentence, fucker," Yohsuke challenged and lifted his chin. "I don't need the powers of a god to make you look like a fucking wimp."

"You should really learn to keep your pets under control, *King* Zeke." The queen said that last bit with a sneer. "Or keep better company altogether."

He shrugged and just smiled. "I lost one already, ain't no way I'm going to hang out with anyone else because they can be goofballs. Right, boys?"

"Fuck that, she thinks I'm a lizard, don't you!" Muu glared at her reproachfully. "Well, this gecko ain't saving you shit on your car insurance lady, so fuck you!"

"Dude, come on. You're better than that." Yoh put a hand over my shoulder and tapped his friend on the shoulder. "Gecko, really?"

"It was all I could come up with. I'll think of something better soon."

I watched the two of them incredulously, knowing that if it had been under other circumstances, I could have been pals with these guys. But at least now I could guess that Yohsuke didn't have a Dominion like the other two. Which was better than if he did.

I watched as the queen finished preparing herself and Zeke asked, "What are the rules to the duel?"

"You die, and leave my people alone," she roared as she launched herself forward and struck out at her opponent with her foot.

Zeke caught it and let her fall to the ground. "So... this is, what, a fight to the death? Or we just go at it until the other can't really move anymore?"

"I'll kill you for what you've done!" the queen howled as she clambered to her feet. "You've stolen a crown you have no right to, and now my people will pay the price to those who supported the Seelie and their ends."

Zeke rolled his eyes again and huffed, "Want to know what right I have?" He raised his eyebrows and held his left hand up, the one with the ring on his finger. "I swear on all my accrued power that this ring was given to me by Queen Maebe, Lady Darkest and Queen of the Unseelie Fae of Brindolla, a gift to show her love for me. I am her knight and king and, as such, will protect our people no matter where they may be."

The queen raged. "My people are *not* yours!" She lowered her center of gravity and began to weave a complicated spell in front of her, her words lowered and muttered but feeding power into it as well.

Zeke just shook his head and waited with his arms crossed in front of him as the spell continued to build and warp the very air around us.

"Is he going to be okay?" I couldn't help my curiosity at this point.

"He'll be fine. Honestly, the lady's delusional if she thinks she can take him." Muu shrugged, then snapped his fingers and shouted, "You're how old? *Too fucking old!* They should have put your old ass in a home with how delusional you are!"

The queen paid no mind to the barb from the man, but her husband bellowed and attacked, pulling a sword from his hip.

"Didn't anyone pat him down?" Yohsuke shook his head and Muu just grinned, prompting Yohsuke to speak again, "What now?"

Muu retorted, "I did, but I'm not going to touch his hips, because what if they lie?" Muu's laughter rang out around us as he reached up and grabbed the falling sword rocketing toward his shoulder and wrenched it from the man's grasp. "This isn't the time to be attacking. Your wife is in danger."

The king turned and started to move but Muu just grabbed his shoulder and held him for the king to watch in shock as her spell finished and streaked toward Zeke. The king stepped backward as the blast hit him and he disappeared from sight.

I was about to be shocked but he stepped out of the shadows behind her and grabbed her by the back of the neck. "I win. If you struggle or try to move away from me, I'll be forced to kill you, then your husband. I don't know about your son, but he's important to a child, so I think I can let him live."

"I'll never give my people to you," she hissed, fierce to the end.

He shook his head. "You have no choice, ma'am." He turned to her husband. "Convince your wife to stand down."

The king shook his head and stated, "Never. I will die before I—" His statement was cut off by Muu shrugging and gripping the top of his head, yanking it to the side savagely with a snarl.

"No!" the queen shrieked, struggling to get to her now-dead husband.

Zeke grimaced and clenched his hand as his other fist crashed through her body. I had to look away to keep the spatter from coating one of my eyes and half my face.

Shadows coiled around my feet and worked toward the bodies as the others let their victims fall.

"That could have been a whole lot less brutal." Zeke sighed, his clean hand wiping from his hairline back as he stared at the bodies, then up at me. "Let's chat, shall we?"

He returned to his throne, stepping over the body at his feet. Daglebr still struggled off to the side of the throne, struggling to get a word out.

"So, what's the word, Marcus? Think you can take the Night Parade now?" He stared at me with obvious curiosity but there was something hard in his gaze, as if he was judging me. "The Seelie aren't around now. That helps, right?"

"I mean, yeah, it does, but my team is still split right now trying to ensure your mess doesn't start a war."

He raised an eyebrow and frowned. "Talking about the videos?" When I nodded, he chuckled to himself. "I see. Didn't I tell you to stay out of my way?"

"Your way is going to get some of my friends killed, Zeke." I knew I should have held my tongue, but it was the truth. If I lied, he would know, or make Eve tell him. "Lucifer and so many others have to have blind faith in order to keep their power."

"So do the gods who tore me from my friends and family." His statement was cold and factual. "I don't want to hurt anyone, by any means, but those ones have to fall."

"So this is what, some big plot for revenge?" I couldn't keep the anger and frustration out of my tone. "Thousands, hundreds of thousands at a bare minimum, are going to pay the price so you can take it to the fuckers who wronged you?"

He stared at me dispassionately and said, "Would you stop at that to find your son?" He didn't wait to hear what I said and added, "From what I understand, you had quite the bloodbath on your hands against the Seelie, and then the Wardens when they got in your way. Somehow, you managed to get away with all of it. Does that not mean you wouldn't also do what my friends and I are doing to ensure that you can return to the people you love?"

He watched me as I remained pointedly quiet, then moved his hand flippantly from himself to his friends. "Hell, if I didn't know any better, I'd say that you'd try and kill all of us if you thought that it would work out in your favor."

"He would," Yohsuke stated, crossing his arms.

"Totally would," Muu agreed as he flopped onto the ground to sit with his legs crossed. "You could at least summon us some chairs, asshole."

Yoh rolled his eyes. "You're strong enough to jump damn near to the stratosphere, and standing bothers you?"

"I hate standing like this, it's boring." Muu's complaining was just enough to force me to rethink just attacking them or trying to escape with Amabala's power.

Not that it would matter. Zeke could pull apart the portal with ease and keep me here or cut me in half like that other thing he'd done it to already.

"I didn't bring you here to grill you, Marcus." Zeke sighed, flipping his hand so the shadows formed chairs for all of us. "I wanted to apologize."

That was... alarming. "I knew you were trying to stop the videos, even without knowing it was me and I knew that it wouldn't be possible for you." He scratched his head and shrugged. "Knowing that, I withheld information and played you a bit. I called you a friend, and that was such a dick move from me, so I wanted to say that I'm sorry if you felt used."

He scratched his head again and sighed. "I did use you, and it worked out in my favor, but if I had been honest with you, you may have understood where I was coming from and could have even been helpful to me. And me to you."

I stayed quiet, watching him a bit. This was a surprising turn of events, to say the least.

"You don't have to forgive me—I don't expect you to—but please try to understand that, and all of this, is nothing personal." He frowned and then sat up straighter. "I want to let you know I'm not going to hurt anyone from the Hunt for interfering as they have been. I made a promise and so far you haven't really broken it."

"Even if there wasn't a loophole that you could exploit just like we could, why wouldn't you?" He blinked at me as I spoke, confused. "Me and my people are actively trying to control the damage that you're causing by doing what you are."

"Because I'm not a monster, and I know that what I'm doing is going to put a lot of folks in compromising positions." He rubbed his head with the heel of his palm against his forehead, as if he had a headache. "I just can't give up on what I have to do. So, I wanted to let you know, you have nothing to worry about in this instance of defiance."

"And?" Yohsuke offered his friend as a way of continuing after a longish pause.

Zeke stared at me and asked with his fingers steepled in front of his face, "I wanted to see if you would join us."

I blinked. "What?"

"I'm navigating a world without true knowledge of it,

Marcus." He stood and began to pace in front of his throne. "I'm an Earthling, for sure, but before I met you, I was under the impression—like almost all the normal-ass people I fucking know—that magic was just a myth. Something to write books about. But now? Now, I have to navigate this world and make something of it while trying to get what I want."

"And what *do* you want?"

Muu cackled and bellowed, "To take over the world!"

Zeke shoved his hand outward and a wave shadows swept over him as he yelled, "Fuck, man, come on!"

The man laid on the ground giggling to himself and sat up. "It was so perfect, though."

"He wants to go home," Yohsuke explained tiredly, a baleful gaze cast at the larger man on the ground. "His kids need him, all of them, and the gods here did us fucking dirty."

"Did you want to stay there too then?" I raised an eyebrow at him.

"Nah, man, my wife is here." He hitched a thumb into his hood and pulled it back to reveal his gray skin and elven features before jerking his head back to Zeke. "But I'll ride for my friends, and this fool back here is a good one. I'd do damn near anything I could to help him."

"Let me show you, Marcus." Zeke closed his eyes and spoke out loud, "Yoh, make sure our council guest doesn't take off."

"We aren't killing him?" Yoh asked, clearly baffled. "He got into your throne room, dude, guy's an issue."

"He's fine for now," Zeke muttered and pulled some items from his pocket, scattering them over the floor in front of him. They were metallic and covered in etchings and precious-looking gems.

The pressure of his Dominion flared around him, his aura lurching from within and his crown glowing white-hot as the space in front of us lightened to a deep gray, then slowly turned white. It was only the size of a window, but the view of the other side was visible and clear enough to see.

There were two teenagers running from something, what

looked like a bunch of massive green people hefting simple-looking weapons. "My son and daughter are in danger as long as I'm not on Brindolla. They're dealing with the fallout of the battles and enemies we made while we were there. And that could have been avoided if we were still there."

The vision cleared and the Dominion faded from my senses, his aura and the crown faint in my sight. "I need to get home, Marcus. My children, wife, and our girlfriend need me and there's a war coming with the Seelie there too."

I frowned. His reasons for doing what he'd been doing to try to get home were sound enough, but he was fucking over so many people.

"Look, man..." I hesitated, my right hand on the back of my head as I stared at the floor and tried to gather my thoughts.

Zeke waved his hands in front of his waist and shook his head, stating hurriedly, "I don't need an answer right now." As I looked up at him, he said, "I just brought you here to say I was sorry, explain what was going on and to give you my offer. If I had someone as driven as you on my side, I could go home so much faster. But I know that you have an entire group of friends and your own ladies to talk to about it all, so I can't fairly ask you to decide right now."

I nodded, then lifted my hands and motioned to myself and said, "So what do we do then?"

"Well, my offer stands, you join me and we kit you out to make sure you can fuck up the gods." He motioned to the clothes that the others wore. "You've seen what I can do with enchanting, and that was just the basic shit. But other than that, you're free to carry on. We aren't going to stop doing what we're doing, at all, but you don't have to worry about me coming after your people for whatever you do to try to keep the damage to a minimum."

"Dude, it's going to potentially start a war between humanity and the supernatural underground." He stared at me as if he knew. "There could be a holy war on top of it all. Innocent peoples' lives are at stake."

"So are lives on Brindolla, but I'm doing what I can to try to minimize the damage here as I can without stopping." He motioned to the two with him. "We've been running interference on supes stepping on humans for a bit, even helped rescue some of them from the Wardens too. We aren't heartless. Though Grestal is a bitch and a half, let me tell you."

I nodded with a wry smirk. "Oh, I know."

This left us a *lot* of wiggle room, and I would need to make sure we utilized it as much as we could. "You'll give me your word on that?"

"Do you need it?" I felt like this was a test of sorts as all three men stared at me as the still-captive Daglebr struggled fruitlessly nearby.

Opting to take the safer path and earn some good will, I said, "If you say it, as King of the Unseelie Fae and as a friend, I'll choose to take your word for it."

He blinked and stared, his eyes moving for a moment before he grunted, "Cool. Thanks for the trust." He considered me for a moment. "I know that you'll likely not use the weapons and things that I gave you for fear of me listening in and things like that, but I do want to say that I'm not spying on you anymore to the degree that I was. Mainly a friendly check in kind of thing, but if that makes you uncomfortable…"

He must have seen the look on my face because he just coughed politely and said, "Message received, got it. No more spying." He took a deep breath and smirked. "That's really it on my end, man. Anything for me?"

I nodded once. "I can't convince you to stop and try to find another way?"

"Sure you could. Do you know where to find power so immense that it could pull me and my buddies through the veil between worlds and get me home?" He was so sincere with the asking of this that I almost told him that we could work with Galaxy and achieve that.

But if things got dicey and he needed to kill for another

Dominion, there was no way that he might not consider her something that could be viable for more power swiftly.

"Not off the top of my head, but I would be willing to try to find some alternative." I heaved a sigh of my own. "I'll talk to the others and see what they say."

"That's all I ask," he said. "Be careful out there, man. And good luck with your work."

Looking at him, it felt to me as if he genuinely meant that. "What will you do with the quivering mustache over there?"

"Oh, I just want to know what he knows and then I'll likely send him crawling back where he crawled out of." Zeke glanced at me. "Speaking of, he was pretty quick to throw you under the bus if it meant killing you. You sure you want someone like this out there?"

He turned to look Daglebr in the eyes, leaning down so that he was close enough to stare in them from only inches away. "Someone like that tried to fuck with me and mine would *wish* death would come for them." He glanced my way and grinned. "Want to kill him yourself?"

I snorted at his boyish, homicidal excitement, weird as it was, and said, "No. I have a feeling he knows *exactly* what I'm capable of now, and I know who holds his leash. I think she and I are about to have a little tête-à-tête concerning his slanderous tongue."

"Mmm." Zeke's response was subdued, almost disappointed. "Very well. See you later, and let's have a drink some time, eh?" He held his hand up and a rent in the air made my skin crawl. "That'll get you to where we met. Later."

"Nice meeting you!" Muu called and Yoh just waved once as he turned and mounted the stairs toward the fearful watcher. Eve stared after me as I left the room and entered the street where I had been picked up only to immediately be swarmed by the ladies.

CHAPTER NINETEEN

"Where the fuck were you?" Cassia gripped me and looked me over. "Whose blood is this?"

My phone was going absolutely ape shit, vibrating as if I got a hundred texts all at once. "You know I went to see Zeke." I looked at Galaxy and said, "Just rifle through my memories if you need to, it'll help everyone get the gist of things faster. I could really use a good shower and some sleep."

Galaxy nodded once and disappeared into me as Mako burst from me, the others riding along behind me in silence as I felt Galaxy sifting through my memories and sharing the happenings of the meeting to them as they happened, my thoughts and everything.

I got a phone call immediately. "Is he serious?"

"I know we just saw each other, Merlin, but this is hardly a way to start a conversation."

"Oh, come off it." He sounded disgusted as he spoke and then asked again, "Is he serious?"

"Probably." I shrugged. It was a lot to think on, but I still didn't know how they would all feel.

"Because it means that he's not going to kill us, and we have a chance to head this thing off," Galaxy interjected, there was a pause as she relayed my thoughts. "If we can figure out a way to stop things from progressing as they have been, the videos and such, we can control this."

"We can try." I heaved a sigh and put the boy on speaker. "I honestly don't think that we can do much, considering he's probably going to have the entire Unseelie court uploading shit if he can help it. He doesn't plan to stop, just to allow us a chance."

"And you think he was serious about us joining him?" Amabala asked quietly.

I nodded, then said, "That I *am* sure of. If we fly under his banner, he has a way to move in the daylight and keep a potential enemy closer." I scratched my chin, thinking on it a bit more. "He would also have more opportunities to buy our loyalty and potentially sow just enough discord among us to keep us looking inward as he did whatever he thought necessary."

"Could this be a way to get into his good graces and take him down?" Cassia stood closer to me than the others, her arms crossed as she considered it. "From the inside?"

"No." Merlin's answer was so fast it startled me. I had considered it briefly as she had said it, but I waited to hear his explanation. "He would drown us in so many different oaths that we couldn't do much of anything, let alone be a threat. Joining him isn't the option we would want unless we were somehow able to convince him not to, or find loopholes within loopholes."

"Yeah, only one of us is really the brain trust that can do that." Arden snorted and shook her head. "What do we do?"

"Meet with the Wardens and see what they suggest." Merlin was quiet for a moment after that. "You do still plan on seeing Theo and the others, right?"

"Others?" Galaxy wondered aloud, then stared at the device. "Is this a Warden council meeting?"

"Do they have a council?" I raised a brow and the others all nodded. "Of course they do."

"I wonder if Zeke would find this all boring if he were to write it in a book?" We looked over to Galaxy as she grinned. "Sorry. I've read them. He acts much the same way as the books would say, but he's not that good at it, I don't think. I think he should read a book or two on the matter and go from there."

Cassia snorted. "You would lose in a fight to him and you want to criticize his books?"

Galaxy shrugged. "When do the Wardens meet?"

"No news from Theo yet, but it will be soon." Merlin yawned. "We should all probably get some sleep if we want to be of any use to anyone."

"Good idea, sleep well." I hung up the phone as I yawned a second time and looked to the others. "I'll go to the meeting with Galaxy and Merlin. You two go to the con and ensure no one gets kidnapped."

Arden snorted and raised a brow at me. "Bit rude hanging up on him like that."

"I wanted you to see my cosplay!" Cassia whined, pouting suspiciously well.

Galaxy joined her. "I do too, but Merlin going on his own would be a shit idea." I crossed my arms and let my head fall backward to rest on the cupboard behind me. "They already don't trust him because of who he's with. Imagine him *alone* in front of the most influential ones."

"Yeah, as confident as he's become—not a good idea." Cassia huffed, her gaze fallen. "Just try not to take all day?"

I smiled at her. "As long as I can get away to see you, I will."

I thought through Galaxy with an inward grin, *And if I can't, could you just let me see later, maybe in private?*

She winked at me and I grinned outwardly this time. "We should get what rest we can so we'll be ready for what tomorrow brings."

———

"You're sure this is where they want us to meet them?" I stared at the building while standing next to Merlin, and could not comprehend that this was the place they wanted us to go. "Merlin, this is a shack. Are we not going to some place that is more aligned with the local Wardens?"

It really was. It looked like it had been abandoned long ago and, as run down as it was, it should probably have been bulldozed for the safety of others. There were three—almost four—walls and a door, sure, but it was barely standing.

"Locals have gone a bit... feral." Merlin cleared his throat and looked around into the trees of the park. "This is the location they spelled to me, so this is likely where the portal is. Is Galaxy here with us or is she with the ladies?"

I grunted. "Yes, she is here."

Galaxy bristled. *I am not letting you go* anywhere *without me after what happened with Zeke.* She stared out of me and hissed, *I cannot believe you went with him like that without us.*

You were okay with it when I came back, I observed gently. It was true, but as time had gone on, she grew steadily more agitated. It was to the point that when I woke up from my nap, she stood guard over me by my head in cat form with the tip of her tail thrashing about as she glared at me and scanned the room hatefully.

You could have been killed, Marcus. It was all she said as she continued to stare out of me.

"I don't envy you as much anymore." Merlin snickered as he straightened himself out, obviously having picked up some of Galaxy's displeasure. He'd dressed up for this, which was much more than what I had done.

His usual style drifted from comfortable and frumpy to wizardly clothes when he felt he was on duty, but today he wore a pair of dark chinos with black slacks, a matching dark belt, a shirt that was light blue in color, and a deep-brown half cloak that covered his shoulders. He looked rather dapper, if I was being honest.

Even though I wore something that I thought equated to

business casual, a pair of dark—almost copper—khakis and a black polo shirt with a clean pair of tennis shoes, I felt under-dressed.

You could always just wear your Mantle. Galaxy's voice was clipped, but I could tell why she liked that idea so much more.

It was protection for both me and my identity. It was a sound idea, but if the Wardens were half as competent as Merlin was, they would already know who all of us were and would likely try to leverage that against us.

We can make it a bit more cosmetic. Though with the Vornal awakening that it went through, I don't have the control of it that I did.

I shrugged. *Guide me through it and let's see what we can do?*

She stared at me internally and that was what we did for a few minutes, tinkering with my will and the Mantle's capability. When I thought about customizing it, there was a statement similar to the last one that had come from it.

There is a customization section for the Hunts-man's Mantle that is available to you. Further options will become available upon introduction of materials to improve performance and function.

I could improve the armor by adding things to it? This was a game changer!

Where can we find you some rare ores? Galaxy's excited question made me smile.

We can see about some soon, but for now, let's see about changing things first. I opened my status and saw that there was a new tab that gave me the options for customizing the Mantle, both in appearance and in function. Some of the functions were grayed out and unreadable, but others looked like they only needed to be offered materials to achieve. Increased defense, power, and things of the like. And the materials weren't that rare, either, which was a massive boon.

I pressed customize aesthetics and there were options that presented themselves to me and I just grinned, pressing one that I liked. Suddenly, my power flared and I stood in a black suit, perfectly tailored with pin stripes of crimson that matched the shirt that I 'wore' beneath the jacket. The best part of all of it was that I had better range of motion and maneuvering than I might in an actual suit with the benefit of looking snazzy as hell.

Lucifer would appreciate the look, Marcus. Maybe we take a selfie and send it to him?

I pulled my phone out and snapped one of myself and sent it to Cassia and Arden, both of them texting back that I looked good and who bought this for me. *I'll fill them in later, we need to get in there.*

I raised a brow at the mage next to me and cleared my throat. "We clear to go in, Merlin?"

"Have been for a couple minutes, but I've learned not to stop people from preening." He shivered involuntarily. "Arden has bad habits and when you tell her about them, they become your problem."

"If I'm making us late, tell me to hurry the fuck up." I was kind as I issued the order. "I hate being late."

"We're still early by Warden standards." He smiled. "Which means we will only need to wait forever for them to all decide to hear us out."

I grimaced. "We'll see about that." I jerked my head toward the shack. "After you."

Merlin opened the rickety door, which screeched as if it had been unopened in hundreds of years and had gained a painful aversion to use after all this time. Once he was through, he disappeared from sight with me following closely behind.

The other side of the portal may as well have opened into the Senate building receiving area with as nice as it was. The marble was bright and well maintained, with wood trim around the area both intricate and ornate. There was even a set of murals on one of the walls that depicted an epic battle against dragons, and another with shadowy figures standing against a wave of monsters.

Seeing it made me worry. "Is that *the* Hunt?"

"No." Merlin shook his head. "This is one of the first battles against monsters *after* the fall of the Wild Hunt. Once the dragons fell, there was an uprising as the Wardens formed and began to carry out their duties. It wasn't pretty, and we almost didn't come through it."

"How did it happen?" I stared at it for a while and noted one of the figures standing with a staff at the forefront of the defending army.

"My namesake, Merlin the Great, stood with the original leaders of the other Orders and helped stem the waves of monsters." Merlin stared at the mural with an air of conflicted emotion, his voice lowering to an almost reverent whisper. "He, along with Arthur Pendragon and Starel the Just led the charge into the enemy and Merlin nuked them with his magic."

"So…"

I was trying to figure out how to say what I wanted to without coming off like a complete asshole, but he caught on and nodded. "Yes, Merlin and the Knights of the Round Table were real, and my people revere them and their sacrifices."

"Don't shit on legends, got it." I nodded more to myself than to him, but he just snorted and let me know it was okay with a wave.

I glanced around and all I found was a bench made of dark, heavy-looking wood. "Come on, let's have a sit."

"No time for that." Someone grunted, getting our attention. A doorway had appeared within the marble wall directly behind us across from the bench. There was a man in it, older and griz-zled-looking, giving off some serious Sam Elliot vibes with his thick mustache and deep voice. "Get on in here."

"Thank you, sir."

The old man just scowled and stepped back through the door he left open for us.

Merlin and I walked into a room that, again, could have passed for Senate chambers or the floor of Congress, and I just gasped at the size of the room. There were hundreds of Wardens in attendance, all of them staring down to the main floor where we were being ushered by the older man. "Go on down to the floor, introduce yourself to the speaker, and then wait to be addressed."

We nodded and moved down the stairs. I glanced at the watching Wardens with placards denoting where they came from and which Order they served, the majority of them Heart from what I saw, and received tentative stares in return.

Pass this along to Merlin. Galaxy nodded to me and I said, *You walk down these stairs like you own this motherfucker, and don't show the slightest sign of fear or intimidation. Shoulders squared, chin up, and you scowl like you just got a whiff of some nasty-ass stank in the area, good?*

Merlin nodded and walked like he did own it. Though there were times that the irregular steps tripped him up and he had to look down to keep from falling.

A few moments later we stood on the floor with an older gentleman in a simple robe, who called himself Speaker Dillman. "Soon, we will have the council address you, and then you can deliver your news."

"And then you'll deliberate over it all?" My question caught him unawares and he blinked at me. "This is a time-sensitive matter. We can't sit on it forever."

He nodded and patted my shoulder, grimacing after he touched me and pulled his hand away, wiping it off absentmindedly. "I'm certain that what you have to say is important, but these things must happen as they are meant to happen— how they always have." He shooed us to the side of the podium, while he stood closer to the side of the room and out of the light.

Someone close by tried getting our attention. "Psst!"

Merlin grabbed my jacket and motioned with his head, jerking it to our right away from the podium. I blinked and let my eyes adjust to the darkness, which was faster than normal, and saw Theodorous the Ventricle for Ohio waving at us.

"Gentlemen." There was a slim smile on his face, but it was more tense than I had ever seen on him. Though I was less used to seeing him than Merlin was. "Hearing the news of what's to come, it's hard to believe it. Even as young as I am compared to the other Ventricles, and knowing that this day would come—it still feels hard to believe that it has." I was amazed he could so effortlessly throw his voice to us as if he were standing next to us.

We both nodded, and he blew air out of his mouth in a gust at the ground. "Well, I hope you're both ready for a witch hunt, because these old fogies are going to really be on it for you."

I nodded, dread coiling in my stomach, but I just took a breath and let it all go. We needed to convince them of the importance of stepping up and being part of the solution.

———

Walking out of the room to a chorus of shouts from bitter old codgers and worthless protectors, I heaved a massive sigh of disgust. "What a fucking shit show."

They had questioned us to the point of near obsession on the Hunt, trying to gauge whether we were a threat. When Merlin had ignored that and presented the problem at hand, the Ventricle from Egypt shouted at him about Amabala and his association with mongrels and curs.

I had wanted to kill people before, but in that instance I would have happily gone toe to toe with all of them just to make Merlin relax.

You have to respect him, though. Galaxy purred as she watched the young man walk ahead of us with his back straight and arms swinging. *He did very well, and didn't rise to the bait that many of them laid before him. I am quite proud of the man he is becoming.*

I had to admit that I agreed. Our faith in him since his rebirth as Galaxy's had been paying dividends and seeing his poise and tactful grace in that room with a slobbering band of bureaucratic buffoons beating their bellies and chests to try and back the boy down from his convictions and claims of a coming shift in the status quo made it seem that much more worth it, even if it felt like we got nowhere.

And those old bastards fought tooth and nail to delay,

diminish, and derail us at every goddamn turn. I honestly felt bad for Amelia as she stared at them in loathing as she arrived, fashionably late, to the party. She was due to speak after us, but I doubted that they would give her the time of day.

Theo hung his head as we passed by and Merlin's pocket buzzed as we moved along, guided by two Wardens who stood guard at the podium.

"If we hurry, we can still make it to the con. it was only an hour or so in there for us." Merlin glanced over his shoulder. "Think you could make a cosplay of that?"

I shrugged, wondering what I would do, if anything, and just added the demonic horned helm to my head with my visor raised. "How's that?"

Merlin nodded his head. "Very anime, let's go."

We fled back through the portal where I mounted Mako and Merlin on his steed, taking to the sky and heading toward the center for the convention.

"I never properly thanked you, by the way," Merlin called, riding next to me, the wind no longer taking his words from me. I could hear him better than ever. "For the promotion and billet."

"You earned them."

True statement, that. And if he hadn't before, he would have by his actions in the company of those monsters today for damn sure.

"True as that may be, it's still a great show of faith that I appreciate." He was quiet for a short time, then said, "Are you worried?"

"About?"

"What's going to happen." He looked at the city below us. "There's not a whole lot that can be done about the videos for now, just short of going to the Normies ourselves and breaking the news. But here? The Night Parade is a whole different kind of beast."

I paused in my thinking, wondering if that *was* a viable option. I mean, we could go to the government and prove it to them, or to a local news station. We could show them and prove we aren't meant to be feared.

It's a liability, Marcus, Galaxy warned, her voice cautious because she was wondering if it would work too. *If the humans don't take it well, then we could be seriously screwing the pooch.*

I rolled my eyes, mentally grumbling at her. *You really hang out with Arden and Cassia too much.*

I learned that one from Keith, actually. She smiled within me and fell silent.

"Yeah, the Parade is a new kind of beast." It sucked confirming it, but we had no choice but to do our best to try to protect Tsuki without drawing unnecessary attention to her or ourselves. We also didn't know what the Parade was capable of without Seelie backing. Would that make them more dangerous now that they knew someone was meddling and interfering with their plans?

"We've gone against tough odds before, and usually we manage to muddle through." I scratched the back of my neck and stared at the horizon line of the world. The beauty of this world up here was unrivaled, untamed. There was something so chilling and exhilarating about the way the sky crashed against the earth over the top of Mako's massive crested head that just made me wonder how far we could fly.

Could we go to other worlds? If we could, couldn't we help Zeke and save Earth without there being a need for the Normies to know about all of this?

"I don't know that muddling through will cut it if Cassia's mom is that strong." Merlin scowled at the ground beneath us. "She was a monster of a higher tier than she should be. There are always some that are stronger like that, but not *that* strong. She alone could easily be tier seven, and if she's that strong alone, she has to be serving someone who could really fuck her up."

"Better get to creating those hounds then, bud." I glanced over at him and he frowned. "What's the matter?"

"We require either souls to forge them, or volunteers for it."

He scratched his head and frowned a little more, making it a grimace that could have put the corners of his lips onto his chin. "The volunteers would need to be Touched in order to be powerful, or creatures like the girls."

He thought for a moment, then added, "We could also stand to add to our numbers as well." He looked over to me and saw my displeasure. "Historically speaking, we're supposed to be a host of hunters—stories tell of the Wild Hunt blotting out the sun as they ran down their prey. We need to grow, not just be a party of those blessed by our goddess. We could all benefit from having more help."

"We probably could, but we can't exactly go head hunting, can we?" It was difficult to tell how much of this was his personal feelings, and how much of it could have been Galaxy's previous meddling with his mind to make him more pliable to our needs.

"Cassia has a plan." He seemed reluctant to tell me, biting his lip as we flew on. "She plans to offer positions to the security staff at the High Table."

After the initial shock of it, I snarled, "Absolutely not." I shook my head for good measure. "I know that they love us, but the Table needs them and if we start scouting from them, they're going to think they're entitled to us, or that we owe them something when we don't."

"We don't have the luxury of being picky, and I know for certain that the staff would choose to join us over the Table becoming cinders due to Zeke's rampage against the gods." Merlin's tone held a challenge to it that both irritated me and made me wonder how long all of them had been discussing all of this since they found out what they would be responsible for within the Hunt. "We have no way of standing against him, and if we won't be joining him to try to earn his trust to keep him safer for the world at large, we need the numbers to try to over-whelm him."

"Numbers don't mean shit to someone like him and his godkiller friends." As this conversation continued, I wasn't as against the numbers bit.

"No, but access to more bonds will strengthen *you*." Merlin glared over my way and pointed to me when I refused to acknowledge him. "You are the real weapon of the Wild Hunt. Your abilities make all of us stronger and, in turn, ours do the same for you. If we ever have to stand against him, we will end up boosting you up so that you can fight for us."

I shook my head once and corrected him. "So that *we* can fight against him. I can be a one-man wrecking ball with a penchant for guns and violence all damn day, but when the shit goes tits up, I have to rely on my friends and party." He acquiesced with a sigh and a nod. "Okay, we can bring in some other folks, but we can't go too crazy and it's going to be need to be kept a secret."

Galaxy's voice rang out throughout my mind as she spoke. *Cassia, he's agreed so long as they tell no one.* Her laughter rang out in my mind as a surge of activity rang through my being, tiny spikes of energy that tingled as they dissipated in me, causing me to lose focus.

Congratulations, Huntsman, you have increased the size of the Wild Hunt from five to thirty-seven.

My eyes flared and I bellowed, "Thirty-seven?" I grimaced and seethed. "That's not some, Merlin. What the fuck?"

"That *is* some, Marcus." He grinned at me, adding, "That's only a few select members of the security folks. The rest of the staff at the Table is chomping at the bit to be of use to us and to assist us further. Even your uncle would like to join."

"How do you know that?"

Merlin shrugged, snorting as if I should know. "He loves you and thinks that things need to change in order for us to remain safe, or at least be safer than we could be."

"I get that, but we don't even know how to move forward." I rubbed my temples and grunted as the budding headache I had began throbbing behind my eyes.

"We'll figure it out." He glowered at the ground. "That's a

lot of people down there for the con. Cassia, Arden, and Bala are together, I see."

"Bala?" I blinked at him and then it hit me, "Oh! Amabala. She has a nickname now?"

He nodded. "Yeah, her name is a mouthful at times and she's aware of that." He blushed a bit as I watched him, then tried to change the subject. "Where should we land?"

"Anywhere, probably." I shrugged, not worried about trying to find the ladies just yet. "So, you two are an item, and that's really cool, man. You two happy together?"

He nodded and a soft smirk grew on his face. "She was more interested in you for a while there, she told me that, and it didn't bother me at first, but now?" He grinned my way, teeth flashing in the light. "It's just us."

"As it should be." I chuckled with him. "My dance card is more than full."

You'll be dancing to my tune soon, if you don't shape up, buddy boy. Galaxy's voice was just this side of manic and threatening, at least enough to make sure that I couldn't tell if she was serious or not.

We chose a slim alleyway to jump down from our mounts out of view of the general population, waiting for a brief momentary pause in traffic to cross the street and enter the flow loading into the building.

The auras throughout the place were few and far between, but some of them were strong enough that I could tell that they were stronger than your average Touched, or they were probably supernatural creatures.

We spent an hour or so trying to make our way toward where my mini map showed Cassia, Arden, and Amabala.

When we arrived, there were cosplayers with costumes so elaborate and awesome that it was like the characters had come to life. So many different popular figures walking amongst normal people who called to them to take photos.

Someone grabbed my jacket sleeve and when I turned,

ready to throw my fist into someone's soul, an older man held up a camera questioningly and pointed to me.

Merlin began to try to explain, "He wants to—"

I cut him off and said, "I get it." I stepped back as he bowed a few times excitedly and began to snap photos as I tried to pose in a cool manner. I was not cool with it, at least not to myself.

Soon, others joined him and began to snap photos of me from several angles. Hell, one lady got ballsy and told me how I should pose by showing me since I couldn't understand her as well, and Merlin had just given up trying to translate for all of them.

Fifteen to twenty minutes after that, I managed to separate myself from them and we found the ladies. Amabala stood to the side, bashfully watching Arden and Cassia being photographed. Arden wore a torn and bloodied white t-shirt and jean shorts with shoulder holsters on for a classic Lara Croft cosplay.

Cassia stood close by in a maid outfit with a dragon tail sticking out of her skirt and horns on the sides of her head. This one I recognized from another anime, but I couldn't think of the name at the moment. Both of them looked fantastic.

They saw me, Cassia seeing me first and screaming, "Marcus!" She flounced her way toward me and several of her photographers made to follow her, still photographing her until she collided with me. They made faces, then stalked off. "How was everything? Did you see our numbers? What's with the cosplay? I didn't know you had anything packed!"

"This is my Mantle." Her eyes widened and she grabbed the material. "Power up was nice. Also, what the fuck is with *thirty-fucking-seven people being invited into the Hunt?*"

"Kaz and Corn, then some of the security staff had been requesting to help us more with everything." She grinned and smiled. "It was like creating a guild in an MMO, all I had to do was ask if they wanted to join and when they said yes, they came into view in my status screen for the Hunt."

"Yeah, but that many?" She shrugged and I just grimaced. "I don't even know all of their names."

"Does a general know all of his command's individual service members' names, or does he see the units they make up and learn their capabilities?"

Cassia's question caught me off guard. She was right. So long as I was leading, I didn't need to know everyone as I could ensure that the unit as a whole could function and carry out the mission. "That's... fair. Sorry I freaked out. I guess I kind of lost sight of the whole picture there."

"It's been hard to focus on it like it was the big picture in the first place." She put a hand on my chest and stared up into my eyes as she explained, "Our big picture for a while has just been to survive all this. Now? We have to survive and grow strong enough that the threat of us is enough to make someone think twice, at least for now."

"Not going to make Zeke think twice." Arden huffed as she joined us, staring at my threads. "Who are you supposed to be?"

"The devil?" I tried with a shrug. She snorted and took a photo of me, tapping away on her phone then I had to ask, "Luci?"

She nodded. "Yup. And he's already responding."

She frowned, then her phone buzzed and she answered, grinning. "Hey, Luci. Uh huh. Yeah. Okay. Yeah, we're at Comiket. Okay." She paused and grinned wider. "Sure. Bye."

I frowned at her smug face, but she just shrugged and turned, walking away from us until she was about twenty to twenty-five feet before shouting something in Japanese and pointing away from us.

The people around us all turned and stared, captivated as nothing happened.

Lucifer's voice drifted over my shoulder. "Now, I know that I'm handsome, but the horns are a *bit* much." I turned and found him wearing his real wings and a mask. "Though I have to admit I am quite taken with those eyes. Are these contacts?"

I shook my head. "New power." I pulled him into a hug, careful not to jostle his wings. "What're you doing here?"

"I realized I hadn't gotten your number to text you or get things directly from you, so here I am." He grinned at me and pulled his phone out. "Would you like to exchange numbers?"

"Yeah, man!" I smiled at him and put my number into his phone. "I'm really glad you asked. I've been wondering if we were friends or if it was just that we were friends of friends."

"Definitely friends." He saved the number and texted me so that I had his. "How have things been? You missed quite the party at the High Table with Chris and his friend Nick. They're very nice people."

"Strong too." I raised an eyebrow at him and he appeared confused.

Then it dawned on him that I knew. "Ah. I take it you heard about that?"

I nodded. "Merlin had been there, right?" He nodded in return and I added, "You said they were nice? They treated you well?"

"Very. And I feel like they had some issues of their own, but they treated everyone there with respect and kindness, so they earned my affection."

So then they're capable of being kind.

Lucifer crossed his arms and smiled to himself. "Had a very nice conversation about religion and even the gods." He chuckled, shaking his head. "They asked all kinds of questions."

That made my mouth dry out a little bit. "Did they ask you about faith?"

"Well, if I recall correctly, they asked if the gods were really gods, and I mentioned that their power was faith-based and that the humans might *believe* they exist in a more overseeing capacity, but that they're usually a little more involved in their religions." He laughed. "Father likes to sit back and watch his faithful run themselves ragged being good people and laugh. While others go out and serve the multitudes of faithful."

"Fuck." My reaction was a little more visceral than I meant

for it to be, but it was true. They had found out the tie in, and had places to start looking for the weakened gods.

"What's wrong?" There was genuine concern that fell over his features. "It was just a general discussion of theology, I thought."

Galaxy spoke into me and sounded worried. *You can tell him if you need to, Marcus. It may help keep him safe if he does have a Dominion.*

The crowd around us pressed closer to look at his wings and see how well done they were, but he didn't seem to mind, flaring them out to scare them, the beginnings of anger working over his features. "Sorry, everyone, the devil and I have a discussion that needs to happen."

He stared around him harshly and pointed to a wall near a rather large fern in a pot that was all alone. "Let's go and talk, demon."

He didn't pull me or anything, but I followed along dutifully until we stood alone, though some of the less caring folks took photos of us anyway. He opened with, "What's going on, Marcus?"

Closing my eyes, I had to try to rely on a little more wit than I would have liked to. "If I tell you everything, my life is forfeit and everyone I care about will be endangered. I also swore an oath that I wouldn't actively try to get in this person's way."

He squinted at me and blinked three times before saying, "You didn't tell me, but I've figured it out based on context— Zeke is holding something over your head and it *probably* has something to do with the gods, with how our conversation went and your reaction to that." He tapped his chin, frowning and clicking his tongue against the back of his teeth. "I would venture a guess that he's also responsible for the mess that's gone on lately?"

I just stared at him and he tsked, screwing up his mouth. "So, he and his friends are killing gods and they have their reasons to try and make sure that no one else interferes?" I blinked and he smirked. "Likely because they want to return to wherever it was that they gained their powers in the first place."

I was gobsmacked. All I could say was, "How?"

"I was my father's first, most perfect creation before he created humanity—his Morning Star." He was reflective for a moment, then his smirk shifted into a sly grin. "Intelligence was something he blessed me with before he gave me my beauty. For that, I will always be grateful."

He winked at me and added in a softer tone, "They also filled me in on the fact that they were from another place and that they missed it. Alcohol has a funny way of bringing out the desires of people." He scratched his shoulder where one of his feathers brushed against his shirt. "I don't think they're bad people."

"They're throwing the entire supernatural world into disarray just to try to go home." I tried to keep my voice down but it was just mind blowing to me that anyone could defend them. "I get they have their reasons and that to most they would be valid, I would do the same thing, but I couldn't condone this level of selfishness."

"He's weakening the gods, Marcus," Lucifer stated. "If he can bring turmoil to the world that will affect the faith given to the gods, then he can weaken them and remain safe while working toward his goals. I know you wouldn't do it that way, but a lot of people would fall to you if you thought they had to pay for doing something wrong."

I frowned.

Galaxy interjected, *He's not wrong, but we still need to mitigate some of the blow if we can. Somehow. I think the idea you had was a good idea, but there's no real way to accomplish it without major risk that I can see.*

"Tsuki?" Cassia's raised voice drew my and Lucifer's attention toward her as the taller woman bent down and scooped up her older friend. "What are you doing here?"

"I came to see you cosplay. Someone told me about it, and I wanted to go to one last convention." Tsuki was grinning ear to ear. "You look fantastic! All of this is so well done. Did you make it personally?"

Cassia blushed and nodded. "Yeah, I picked the hobby up a few years ago and have been working at it since then."

"You look good." Tsuki smiled and patted her hand. She looked around and found me, smiled and waved happily. "That's an interesting costume, Marcus. Did you make it?"

I shook my head. "Technically, Galaxy did." I smirked and added, "I just made some modifications." I scanned the crowd around her and there were several figures with her with thick auras surrounding them, and there were even a few in the crowd posted around the room.

I nodded toward her and brought Lucifer over with me. Once I was close enough I lowered my voice, "Pretty slim on the guard detail, aren't you?"

She considered me for a moment and Cassia's eyes widened just enough to let me know I was fucking up and potentially telling her what was going on. Tsuki shrugged with just one shoulder. "I only brought the guards who wanted to come."

Cassia senses other oni in the area. The Phantomu, most likely. Galaxy looked around the venue inside me and stared intensely for a few minutes. *There are more. They're close enough to act if something goes wrong, but not close enough to alert her chosen protectors.*

I nodded inwardly and smiled at Tsuki. "So what did you want to go and do?"

"I think we should see what the vendors have to offer!" She grinned and took Cassia's hand in hers. "Want to come?"

Cassia nodded. "Arden!" The flame jinn turned to look at her with eyebrows raised. "Let's go blow some cash!"

"Woo!" She smiled and whooped, bowing slightly to the photographers before joining Cassia and Tsuki. "Let's go get shit we don't need but *toootally* need."

CHAPTER TWENTY

"It's been four hours, I'm good." Merlin huffed and turned to Amabala. "Can we take off? There's some things that I need to do, and this is just too much for me."

"Yes, I agree." Amabala nodded and looked at me. "Do you need us?"

I shook my head and agreed with them. Despite our inventories and ability to hold a lot of shit, I was still lugging around a bunch of shit in bags. "If you wanna take off, take off. All I ask is that you get a hold of Theodorous and see what happened with their council."

He nodded and tilted his head toward the empty rooms where there were some panels being prepared or emptied out efficiently.

As they moved away, there was a wave of *something* that washed through the crowded room, most of the humans bending over as if they were about to be sick, but the supernatural creatures were fine.

That was when the magic 'shots' began to fly through the room toward anyone still standing.

I couldn't tell what sort of magic it was at first, until some of it splattered against my shoulder. My Mantle prevented it from doing any more than pushing my shoulder forward, but it put down the others it hit.

I glanced around and found that we were being targeted by joyriders in Yakuza members and even some who were in cosplay.

What's the play, Marcus? Galaxy's concern was trying to get rid of the riders, but mine was in reacting and protecting Tsuki.

"Merlin, Amabala—take Tsuki!" I shoved the older woman toward the two of them and bellowed loudly, "Commence the Hunt!"

My Mantle shifted into my armor, and I knew that we would be exposed to the Normies here, but there was nothing we could do about it other than just hope that the Japanese Wardens would be able to keep them all from talking.

"Cassia, go with them," Arden ordered, making the other woman frown and begin to protest. Arden just shook her head. "She needs you to protect all of them, *go!*"

Cassia roared and lumbered after the kids and Tsuki, grabbing one of the joyriders who had tried to cut them off from us by the throat to throw them.

"Arden, get the Normies out of here if you can." Rocky appeared at my side as I spoke and began to try to guide some of the nauseated humans near us away from the fighting. Some of them had been hit by the magic that hit me and it looked to be making them shudder and flail wildly. "Thanks, Rocky."

The fox golem dipped his stone head, lichen-covered ears flicking weirdly for stone that floated over the top of his head. He returned to doing what he had been, so I turned my attention to our attackers. With so many attackers and Normies here, I figured the rules about guns and Japanese supernatural creatures would be moot, so I summoned my rifle from my ring and I started firing mana-invested rounds at the first one.

I killed one of them, the aura around the falling man fading inward and disappearing as he dropped. The others attacked en masse, making it harder to focus my fire on any of them, and as soon as my muzzle flagged one, the aura faded and fled somewhere else, another human rising somewhere else to try to attack me.

Arden didn't look to be faring much better. Every time she carried someone out of the room, one of the Yakuza riders would flit to her to try to attack her as she carried them. One of the magic blasts hit her directly in the chest and burned away from her armor, pissing her off, but from that close it was hard to try to kill someone. Not to mention burning them to a crisp would harm an innocent person.

"Foolish not to kill someone straight away," a familiar voice stated next to my ear. I turned to find the yokai Saizo watching me with interest and a gentle smile. "I was wondering when I would see you again outside my personal domain, Huntsman."

My heart pounded in my chest as his lips spread wider. "Did you not know that I could see all of you?" I blinked at him and he laughed, closing his eyes to do so. "Oh, you had no idea."

I attacked. I couldn't afford for this guy to get the drop on me again, and if he could see invisible things like that, there was a massive problem I wasn't ready to deal with.

My fist met his and he flipped me over his shoulder with an ease that sent a chill down my spine as he stared down at me a moment, smiling coldly. "My master is not thrilled at what you've done to his business partners and, I have to admit, I am less than thrilled as well."

Wings spread wide behind him and a large hand wrapped around his throat from the back. "Then go find somewhere else to play and leave my friends alone." Lucifer yanked backward, sending me and Saizo both flying through the air toward a wall. Hands on my legs pulled me back, but Saizo didn't let go.

Instead of panicking and loosening his grip, he clenched tighter, causing the muscles in my wrist to scream. He smiled even wider than before. "How cute."

My left hand raised and I cast Wisp into his face, but there was only steam that greeted me, burning my arm slightly.

"Not nice." He twisted like some kind of crazy alligator and my arm went with him as we fell toward the ground, and the landing just gave him more purchase.

"Ah!" My pain brought my mind to a crawl and I could see that every time he twisted and moved, his skin looked like scales for just a heartbeat and then he would look normal again.

Some kind of fish person? Galaxy perked up and stared at him, then nodded. *Then we have a way to fight back!*

I grinned up at him and his eyebrows knit together before I cast Hoarfrost on the hand that touched me, then Bolt as well.

The ice had shocked him almost as much as the electricity itself, but what shocked me was the amount of mana it had taken to actually get his arm to freeze. The zap flung him backward far enough that I could start to stand once Luce let me go.

"You okay, Marcus?" Lucifer stepped over to me and helped me up. He stood in the full glory that I had seen only once before, angelic strength and all.

"Been better." My wrist was bloody where Saizo had grabbed me, the appearance of small, bite-like dents in my skin making me growl. "The hell is he?"

"Kappa." Saizo smiled and crouched a little bit. "But I'm a bit more than that as well."

His body shifted until he looked like a bird-beaked ninja turtle, and as he held his hands up, I could see that his palms had small mouths on them with the same kind of teeth that left the marks in my wrist.

"No room for the weak pure bloods in the master's new Parade." The kappa beak spread in a weird smile. "All that matters now is strength and results."

He pointed at me and I rolled my eyes, muttering the same thing he said aloud, "And I always get results." He frowned at me and quirked his head. "Are you mocking me?"

"No." I shrugged, pulling the Silvaero from my ring.

Lucifer chimed in with, "You're just painfully predictable."

"Then let's just dispense with the niceties and keep you from interfering again." Saizo bolted forward, only to be beset upon by three oni, red-skinned and raging.

Kimiko, voice raised and tinged with homicidal intentions, said, "You're not going to do a thing, *Saizo!*"

I glanced over my shoulder to find Kimiko and another four oni stood near the entrance to the aisle we stood in.

"Phantomu!" She pointed at the kappa in front of us and bellowed, "There lies one of your oppressors! The path to your freedom begins here—seize it!"

The other oni roared and attacked in unison, their fervor only outshined by their ability as they swarmed the kappa.

Kimiko joined Lucifer and I, the woman frowning. "Who is this?" One of the oni screamed and she shook her head. "Never mind. We need to get to Tsuki, she's in danger. The Night Parade is hunting them as we speak."

My heart nearly lurched out of my chest as one of the oni attacking Saizo flew through the air toward us. *Galaxy?*

They're waiting for us at the High Table. Her voice made her sound like she was concerned. *She should be safe there for now, but I'm not sure what they could have planned.*

Then we had better get going to be sure she's safe. I grabbed Lucifer and Kimiko close to me, pulling open my bond with Amabala, hoping that she would be able to help fuel my mana regeneration. It was helping a lot, putting me at least up to half full.

I pulled once more on her bond with me and her ability came to me.

Portal Creation –

I stopped letting the words shift through my conscious mind and cast the spell. My mana depleted dangerously, and a migraine began to form behind my eyes.

I grunted through the pain. "Let's go while they have him distracted." My eyes flicked to the other side of the room where Arden roasted some of the joyriders. "Arden, let's boogie!"

She glanced our way and clenched her fists before flaring her arms out. Flames wreathed her whole body and flashed outward, the heat creating a natural barrier that she shot through toward me and then into the portal.

"We should kill him!" Kimiko insisted while advancing that way. Lucifer grabbed her. "Release me!"

"Nope." He walked through the portal with a nod to me and I stepped through after, closing it as Saizo fought the oni savaging him.

Before it closed completely, Saizo turned and roared something in Japanese, but I just focused on seeing where we had managed to get to. We were close to the High Table's entrance, maybe down the street from it. Luckily, it didn't look like anyone had come to look here.

Cassia sprinted down the street toward us. "What happened?"

"You know, a weird kappa attacked us and told us the Night Parade was much stronger now." I tried for nonchalance but it was much more difficult with the building migraine. I looked down and noted I still wore the armor of my station and so did Cassia and Arden. We would be invisible to Normies, but that didn't mean Lucifer and Kimiko would be.

I chanced a quick glance their way and saw that they wore their human forms now. With a sigh of relief, I waved them forward. "Let's go."

The sound of sirens in the distance and people talking on the streets made me look around us a little more closely. People held their phones in their hands and stared at the screens intently, the flashes looking somewhat familiar.

Cassia frowned but it was Arden, still in her own armor, who confirmed it. "That fight was broadcast to the entirety of the region and is online now."

Galaxy's voice crept through my concern, adding more fuel to the fire. *Merlin says that the Wardens are issuing commands for the Hunt to stand down.*

My phone began to buzz in my pocket, dread clenching my innards as I pulled it out to see Uncle Yen's name on screen. Then another phone number flashed along to try to talk to me. This one I didn't recognize.

I answered Uncle Yen, the beeps of an incoming call annoying me. "I saw."

"That ain't half of it, kiddo." His voice was deeper now and it startled me until I remembered he wasn't hiding his real age. "The council is calling for you to turn yourself in over this, Marcus. They can't trust that the Hunt is able to take care of what's going on."

"They were just on our fucking side to try to get on the right side of all this!" It was hard to keep the anger and confusion out of my voice. "We were under attack, and protecting the ascendant luck dragon. What were we supposed to do, let them kill us all?"

"Keep that attitude in check, son; I'm not telling you to turn yourself in. I saw what was happening too." There was an edge to his voice that sounded close to losing it, but he cleared his throat and it was gone. "The other council members saw it and are trying to act like they're abreast of things by calling for you to come to them. They aren't truly trying to get you to come in and turn yourself in."

I rolled my eyes. "Daglebr would."

"His head was returned to us with a note, Marcus." His voice held more concern and even a trace of fear. "It just said, 'Stay in your fucking lane.'"

"That sounds like him," I grumbled more to myself than anyone else. "So what now?"

"Any investigation into the culprits has pretty much stopped." I listened as he turned and spoke to someone on the other side of the phone, then came back, saying, "If you can't figure out what's going on and you need somewhere to blow off the heat, come back to us. You'll be safe."

I had to fight not to laugh. They were calling for me to come back and 'turn' myself in. How was that safe?

"You going to do anything about this?" It was hard to keep the bass out of the question for this. If there was a threat out there, I would need to see to it head on that it was taken care of for the sake of my annoyingly-growing Hunt.

"Amelia and I are trying, but with the videos spreading like wildfire, there's not much we can do."

I nodded, expecting as much there but otherwise it was as much a non-answer as anything else. "Thanks for all your hard work."

He sighed, tired and sounding more his mental age. "I mean it, Marcus, please come to us if you need the help."

"Okay, Uncle Yen. Be safe."

He cursed softly. "You too, kiddo."

He means only to protect you, Marcus, Galaxy butted in, her voice gentle but firm. *You needn't be so hard on him for trying.*

It's not just that. We continued walking toward the entrance. *It's that no matter what we do, trying just isn't good enough right now.*

She remained quiet after that so I just stared around us to make sure nothing was amiss.

Kimiko found me looking around and nodded once, making me frown. "Good instincts. Some of the Phantomu are here in the area now to make sure nothing goes on."

I grimaced but nodded, glad she couldn't see my face thanks to the armor, and walked on into the front then into the bar proper, letting the Mantle drop.

Once again, the entire security staff was there to stare at us and make me feel like we were just a hair away from being tossed out on our asses.

I found Tsuki and some people around her in a booth, all of them holding various non-alcoholic drinks. The woman in the center stared at us, mild irritation on her face. "What was all of that?"

I glanced over at Cassia, uncertain as to if she wanted the old woman to know or not.

The oni heaved a sigh and slowly started to speak. "Me trying to keep my friend safe without a worry in the world as she prepares for her ultimate purpose?" She stared at the floor for a short time before raising her sunglasses-covered eyes to meet Tsuki's level gaze bashfully. "I just wanted to help."

"I know what it's like to want to do something for someone

quietly." The elder woman stared at Cassia, but her glare softened significantly. "But a friendship like ours can transcend worry, Cassia. I'm ascending, it's not death. I don't need to have peace or be free of worries in order to fulfill my role. I can transcend despite them."

She held her hand out so that the larger woman would reach across and take it, a soft grin spreading across her lips. "I would take comfort in knowing that my friend is out there spoiling the plans of those gross bastards trying to kill me." She chuckled and winked. "And no small amount of spiteful joy."

I held up a hand and grinned myself. "I like her."

"I like her too." Arden snickered and tossed the older-looking woman a wink. "Let's get some drinks and prepare for the shit show that's coming."

"Here, here!" Kimiko growled, smiling, which made me raise a brow at her. She ordered a round, and then another three.

I drank only lightly, concerned about Saizo. The amount of times Kimiko's phone lit up made me edgy, wondering if all was okay.

She caught my gaze and checked her phone. "Phantomu have taken to the rooftops around us to keep watch."

I nodded at her report and turned back to the other ladies drinking and smiling.

It was good to have these brief respites of calm and joy between the shitstorm of action in the world around us.

I had my phone out and surfed the net, looking at the videos. You could clearly see everything. It didn't matter what angles they were, there was footage from phones and cameras from above with the security tapes and all that. Some of them were executed almost like a movie scene.

There were comments that sounded almost angry, saying the CGI was shit. Or that the special effects needed considerable work—it helped us, but it went only so far toward discouraging believers. There was one that I liked saying shadow monsters were stupid.

You are such a narcissist. Galaxy's playful jab made me grin.

The term you mean is masochist, dear. My correction just made her and I both laugh.

Lucifer wished us farewell, as he had to go home to take care of the puppy, and while the others chatted happily, I opted to keep myself occupied differently.

CHAPTER TWENTY-ONE

My browsing and trying to keep abreast of the situation online was interrupted by a slight commotion at the front of the bar. The subtle music that played over the whole area where people drank sounded like the record had been cut and all was quiet as three figures stepped through the door.

The first I recognized was Cassia and Kimiko's mother Chiasa; Saizo, whose clothes looked a bit torn and disheveled; and then another, cloaked figure. The one in the cloak was shorter than the other two, but for some reason the power that glowed around them was just that much thicker than theirs.

"The Night Parade will not make a mockery out of High Table's neutrality by coming here to start a fight!" Hanazuki bristled behind the bar, her friend Goro the yokai standing beside her. "Be at peace here, or be gone."

"I have no willingness to fight the Grand Lady," Chiasa called and motioned to our table. "We came only to speak to the children and to make introductions."

I rolled my eyes and spoke before they could walk much closer to us. "Table's full, sorry about your luck."

The cloaked figure raised a hand as Saizo and Chiasa went

to cross around them, stopping both of them in their tracks. The voice that came from within was firm and bass. "We don't mean to join you or impose. I just wanted to meet my daughter for the first time."

The figure pulled the hood from the cloak back, and a man of nearly human features stood in front of us. He was handsome, sure, but other than that, no physical features really stood out about him. He looked as if he could have been any ordinary Touched, except the aura that crowded him was absolutely stifling. Could this be the leader of the Night Parade come to say hi?

"I was told my father was too weak to stay in my life." Cassia narrowed her gaze at the man, then cast her gaze at her mother.

"I was," the man admitted with the barest of nods. "But I am not now."

His aura reared and behind him was a ripple in reality that bent the light in the room, his body shifting to match the ripple as it entered his body. Now, there was a handsome young man with tattooed lines on his face that looked like whiskers and more tattoos that lined his arms and neck that reminded me of a rocker in the US.

"Nogitsune." Tsuki and Kimiko hissed at the same time. Tsuki was the one who continued speaking from there. "No wonder the Parade has decided to step out from the shadows to pursue me! A trickster fiend like you would never let them rest."

"Still your tongue, old one." Chiasa growled as her leader lifted a hand to calm her, but she shook her head. "No! She has no right to demean you."

He turned his gaze on her and spoke with barely contained ice in his tone. "You did." She lifted her chin and opened her mouth but his glare silenced her before he faced Cassia once again and tipped his head side to side in a mocking manner as he spoke on in a clipped tone. "I was young. Naïve and weak. No longer. No more. Never again."

A strange look passed over Cassia's features and she was

quiet as she said, "You can't seriously expect me to just welcome you with open arms. I don't even know your name. You didn't even give me mine." She sat back and crossed her arms. "You're no one."

The nogitsune crossed his arms. "You killed your uncle the other night, you know." He stared at her and grinned, leaning forward. "I was quite proud, as it was you who took the final blow to him and killed him so spectacularly. The kitsune with you, what was her name?"

"Don't tell him," I said before I realized it and all eyes were on me. I blinked. *Why did I say that?*

I glanced around, the staff behind the bar and the security paying more attention to us as things grew steadily more tense.

Because something is off with this one. Galaxy frowned and stared at him. *I sense something off.*

"Come now, it can't be too important to hide her name." He stared at them for a moment, but when no one said anything he just grinned wider. "Seems I'll need to find out myself, since you're too afraid of what I might do to her if I knew who she was."

"Her name is Raisha, and she's no coward." Tsuki stood up and glared at him with hatred in her gaze. "She's more of a warrior than scum like you could ever be."

If he could have smiled any wider there would have been no way for him to have any kind of face left. "*Excellent.*"

"You leave her out of this." Cassia stood and clenched her fists.

"No." The fox spread his arms. "I mean to find her and kill her for what she did, but seeing as though you're my daughter, I'll allow you the chance to join me and keep her safe for just a short time longer."

"You have to be joking, right?" Kimiko snorted and rolled her eyes at him. "As if a threat would make anyone want to join you."

Think we could get Cassia to take a look *at her would-be dad?*

Galaxy's yowl of frustration made me want to shake the big

woman as her answer streamed through my mind. *She says it's dishonorable to use it without the most extreme circumstances.*

"No threats here." He grinned and spread his arms. "All I want is an end to our peoples' suffering."

He pointed to Kimiko and winked. "And I'll do anything to get it." He raised his voice. "Goro!"

Automatic weapons fire shattered what little remained of the peace in the bar area as joyriders flooded into the building and Goro opened fire once more on the security staff present. The bullets did little to some of them, but the others' auras were soon tainted by the purple of yokai energy. I could only surmise that it meant that somehow those rounds carried a yokai spirit to attempt to latch onto the victim.

Hanazuki was one of the first to be hit, blood ruining the dress she wore, falling to her knees. Just as quickly, her body started to rise with a quickly shifting aura of color while the plants behind the bar went insane. The plum tree that had helped make our Mojitos speared the grotesque-looking gunman and slammed him into the ground as his shrieks rose in fervor.

Amabala and Merlin, go! My orders through Galaxy were crystal clear as I bellowed, "Commence the Hu—*ghk*!"

The evil fox had me by the throat almost instantly, clicking his tongue on his teeth. "Ah, ah. Can't have that."

The kids had already taken Tsuki in their arms and bolted as the joyriders tried to surround them. Merlin unleashed an earth-shaking spell that made the whole building feel like it was going to collapse. Cassia was looked like she was about to call the order for the Hunt to begin, but someone else stopped us all.

"Enough!" someone roared over the din. "High Table Order: All Calm!"

The strange magic of the High Table rocked through us as a familiar vacuum-like sound rumbled the floorboards and the bar itself glowed amber.

A beautiful woman in a kimono-like outfit that was

somehow both ancient and regal, but also new and fashionable with slits that traveled up to her hips, entered our field of vision. All heads in the vicinity that could move bowed save for those of the yokai.

Chiasa fell to her knees, her head pinned to the floor. "Grand Lady!"

"We had received word that you would be preoccupied..." The nogitsune grumbled with his head bowed slightly, keeping his gaze fixed to my eyes.

"Raves are never more preoccupying than my work, Flit." The woman's raven hair, tied in a bun at the back of her head, came undone slightly as she bent a bit to stare down at the evil fox. His eyes finally shifted from me to her.

"Flit is no longer who I am, Ame-no-Uzume, and you well know it." His seething was kept to a minimum as she continued to stare down at him. "If you must call me anything, call me Felix."

The woman smiled, brushing ivory fingers over her mask made of feathers and fur. "Closer to Flit than any other name, fox."

He growled, "Do not tempt me to strike a goddess. That in and of itself should be a sin on your part."

"I am the goddess here, vermin." She stared down at him, then lifted her head and stared at the happenings around her. She waved her arm and the yokai that had infested the security personnel, who I took were really her people, burst as her aura lashed out.

The fox's fingertips were still wrapped around my throat as I started to lose the edges of my vision.

She reached down and grasped his wrist. "Release him, Flit."

"I have a new name." The nogitsune's eyes flashed dangerously at her.

She lowered herself so that she almost crouched next to him and whispered, "And if you challenge me again, you'll have new *holes* and no heart. Release him."

Clawed fingertips flexed into my throat, cutting into my vision even more and that snapped something within me.

I was terrified of Zeke. I'd been afraid of Cassia's mother. Worried for my son. And now here was someone else who was somehow miraculously stronger than me and I had just gotten to start my growth as a Vorna. I was more powerful than I had ever been and here he was treating me like I was some kind of small fry. A little fish in his pond for him to devour on his way to getting out.

Fuck that. My blood boiled and rage spiraled through me, my heart rate quickening as I once again inwardly snarled, *Fuck that!*

Galaxy tried to throw her warmth against the blizzard of my rage, reasoning with me. *Marcus, she's handling it, just hang on.*

A cold snap in my right hand froze my fingertips to my knuckles in ice that I sent crashing into his jaw in an attempt to get free, but all it did was make him angrier.

And he turned that anger on me and for once I could finally see the gauge sprout over his shoulder. It went from **Annoyance** to full-blown **Hatred**.

I didn't know if it was from how he felt at being mistreated by the goddess or what, but I used Bond Thief on him and grinned as something came to me.

A look of malice shifted into his gaze and he swung at me, but the goddess stopped him and he couldn't continue on as I checked my prize.

Fox's Cunning – The next spell you cast with this effect activated will be twice as effective and cost half as much.

There was no timer on it either, this was just mine to use once. That wouldn't be enough to necessarily kill him right now, but it would be enough that I could make a serious turning point in a fight if used correctly.

"Begone. You are banned from the High Table for the next three hundred years." The goddess turned to Goro and snarled, "And you!" She shoved Felix backward with a grunt which caused his claws to rake their way along my throat as his grip finally left me. She stalked toward the bar. "I don't know what he offered you, but I hope it was worth it. You're banned for life, and will never be able to enter another bar or the area of any music *ever* again."

"I'll kill you later," Felix muttered toward me before he turned to leave the bar, calling, "Parade, to me. We will march again on these fools soon."

All of the yokai who could walk left the bar itself as the goddess watched them, then turned toward us.

"Thank you for the assistance, Grand Lady." Tsuki bowed her head next to me, I hadn't seen her join us. "They mean to—"

The goddess held a hand out to stop her. "I don't care." She stared down at the luck-dragon-to be and frowned. "You're supposed to ascend soon, and here you are talking shit inside the bar, and almost getting yourself kidnapped? How brazen."

She snapped her fingers and both Cassia and I stood in front of her. "You both fought as well."

"We were defending ourselves," Cassia tried to explain but the Grand Lady wasn't having it, shaking her head as she spoke. In frustration, Cassia growled, "I know the rules, goddess. I'm security head for the Columbus Branch in the United States."

"I don't care who or what you are, oni." Ame-no-Uzume sneered down at us both. "I will not have violence in my club other than what is necessary to showcase the warrior spirit. You fought back, and you will be banned from the High Table too."

"My lady, surely you cannot be serious." Tsuki stood up and stepped around Cass and I so that she stood in front of the massive woman.

"I am." She stared down hard at us. "Matter of fact? All of you are banned from the High Table for thirty years."

I frowned at her and so did Cassia. Arden spoke up. "That isn't right, ma'am, and you know it."

"You can always have the council overturn my decision."

She looked like she was having trouble fighting the urge not to grin.

"So that was the play?" It was hard to keep from being pissed off. "The council sent you here to do this?"

She grinned widely. "No, I just know what I want and know that this will be helpful. All of them are looking for you." She spread her hands wide. "I know they'll be out there waiting for you to leave. So I'll look the other way while Hanazuki lets you leave a different way. Good luck out there."

She turned to the bar and nodded to the woman, blood trickling down the side of her mouth as she grimaced watching the proceedings. She took her apron off and put it on the counter. "I'll be taking my lunch."

The goddess smiled and said, "That's fine."

"For the next thirty years."

Ame-no-Uzume went to respond to her but she frowned and pointed to the trees behind her. "They would have fought to protect us and you're using their misfortune to further your own goals? You're lucky I'm not taking them and quitting for this shit, Uzu. That's a really shitty thing for a party goddess to do."

"But think of all the parties that we could have if I was asked to be on the council!" Uzume tried to reason with her but she was just ignored as the woman took the plums that grew on the tree right then. "Hana, I'm sorry!"

Hanazuki just rolled her eyes. "Think of all the parties you could have had with the Wild Hunt, Uzu, but now you've lost their gratitude and have replaced it with suspicion and distrust. I cannot believe how selfish you're being."

"I said I was sorry!" Uzume just teared up and sniffled as Hana jerked her head for us to follow her. "Come back!"

"No!" Hana flipped the goddess off and kept walking with her head held high.

She has balls of steel and I want them. Galaxy's phrasing made me snort. Hana cast a baleful glance my way, forcing me to shut up.

She led us back behind the bar, around the dance floor, and then into a tunnel of sorts hidden behind a waterfall that I hadn't seen before. It had to have only been for aesthetics, but here it was.

The tunnel led toward a soft, glowing light that emptied into a sewer. There was nothing liquid or stinky about it, unlike the one that we had crawled through when I first started working for the High Table.

"I'm sorry about Uzume." Hana sounded tired as she rubbed her chest where she had been shot. Cassia grunted and clapped her on the shoulder, the woman wincing and then sighing with relief. "That was wonderful, what was it?"

"I can heal people a bit." Cass grinned at her and cleared her throat. "Uh, you know you didn't have to do that, right?"

"Uzu is a childhood friend of mine and we're rather close, I just don't like to put that out there, but what she did this evening was unacceptable." She shook her head and crossed her arms as she walked. "Making you leave? Warranted, I would have done that myself. But a ban? That's some petty shit, and she knows it."

"It's nice to hear you a little less formal," Arden offered with a friendly smile.

"It's nice to be a little less formal in times like this, though I am sorry if my formality made you uncomfortable." She smiled ruefully. "Some of our customers are a little more impatient when it comes to the niceties they were used to that require formality."

"I get that." Arden grumbled with a roll of her eyes. "Old ladies."

"Ha!" Hanazuki shook her head as she continued to laugh. "Yeah, they're the worst."

We walked on in amicable silence for a time before Hanazuki said, "She meant well." She shrugged to herself and sighed. "More for herself, but she didn't perma-ban you, at least. She would have been within her rights to."

"Technically, but we also would have the grounds to rule it

null if we objected and fought it," Cassia retorted gently. "We defended ourselves and other patrons."

"She'd issued the calm *before* Marcus attacked." She didn't look at me when she said it, but I could feel the judgement in her tone. "She wouldn't have let them hurt any of you any more than they had already. Attacking after the fact was petty and unnecessary."

I could feel Arden and Cassia getting ready to respond, Merlin likely following them up with reason and logic, but all I could do was say, "She's right. It was."

The others stopped walking, but I kept moving with Hanazuki. "I was enraged that he could just handle me like that and hadn't let go of me yet, so I struck back. I was always taught 'give as good as you get' and that was one of those moments where I just lost it. It was my fault and I'm sorry, guys."

"There's nothing we can do about it now," Amabala said, surprising all of us. She had been quiet for the whole walk, but now she looked like she found her purpose here. "We can beat ourselves up for it, or we can move on. I'm tired of being beaten for mistakes, so we should move forward, right?"

Cassia grinned at her and nodded once with authority. "Right."

Hanazuki surprised us with a loud, clanking, metallic grinding as she grunted. "Here we are." The door she had opened with a lever that looked rusted to hell and back opened to a large wash of signs and concrete. "They're building something here, but we will still have a way in and out for those who need it."

"What will you do now?" Arden stared at her for a moment then asked, "Do you game?"

Hanazuki smiled. "Not nearly as much as my friends, no, but I'll likely pick it up. I have a to-be-read pile as tall as my plum tree, so that will likely be where I start."

I nodded at that, knowing damn well I had books I needed to read. A spell book included. Which reminded me, I still had

Spell Points I could spend, and I had a feeling I would be needing them. Hanazuki took her leave of us at this point and walked down a side street, humming a little tune. I was left with the impression that this 'break' of hers was something she may have been looking forward to.

"Tsuki, where can we take you?" I looked over at the older woman and she smiled at me. "What?"

"I'm taking all of you with me." She sighed and frowned at the world around us. "They made a move on me tonight, and I cannot have that happen as the storm is still days away currently. All of you are going to come with me and train."

"Train?" Arden seemed puzzled for a second and then her eyes lit up. "Does that mean you're going to teach us luck dragon stuff? All kinds of Kung fu?"

Tsuki looked from Arden to Cassia, back, and then to Cassia again. "What kind of bullshit is she on?"

Arden's hair burst into flame. "You wanna fight, grandma!?"

Cassia howled with laughter as we began to travel with the older woman toward the roadway while she spoke on her phone. Cassia and Arden were too busy teasing and trading insults to really know what was going on until it was too late. I had to admit that I was caught flat-footed as well, having followed their antics instead of our surroundings.

We were surrounded by auras thick enough that it could have choked all of us. "Commence the Hunt!"

Our armor slammed into place as the figures danced around us out of the shadows and pointed katanas toward us.

"All of you stop it this instant!" Tsuki howled and pointed at one of the figures. "I thought you more mature than that, Raisha. Honestly."

"I smelled nogitsune." The woman lifted her chin as she pulled a wrap from her face that hid her features. "Any self-respecting kitsune would happily hunt down and kill one."

"Yeah, but the scent isn't that strong." Cassia crossed her

arms, but there was a grin on her face. "The one we hunted down was stinkier."

"Yeah, for some reason this one smells weird." Raisha grimaced, her beautiful features hidden behind the brown hair she let fall around her face. "Tsuki-chan, we'll be taking you back to the temple."

"And our friends," Tsuki asserted, then pointed at Raisha. "And you'll be helping to train them."

The warrior fox stilled and tilted her head. "Oh? In what?"

"Slaying yokai." Tsuki crossed her arms and stared up at her as if she were waiting for a retort of some kind.

"It's really hard to kill them though." The kitsune frowned and grimaced at all of us. "You don't have the skills to do it now, let alone in a few days if they decide to attack you. It would be better for them to just support us as we fight the Night Parade."

"Not going to happen." Cassia lifted her chin proudly, then proclaimed, "I guess you can call my stubbornness on this matter daddy issues, but I have someone I very much would like to kill and this will help me a lot."

Raisha blinked a few times and said, "We should probably discuss that, but fine. The key to it is magic, and that gets a whole lot freakier the stronger they are. But that can be taught later. For now, let's get the lady home and in bed." Raisha turned her eyes on Tsuki and grinned. "It's past her bedtime and she gets cranky if she's not up early for her soaps."

"Ahh!" Tsuki roared and stomped forward toward the giggling woman and off we went to who knew where.

CHAPTER TWENTY-TWO

Again! I snarled and tried to make the mana coalesce around my arm as I willed Hoarfrost to work faster. It just wasn't working the way I wanted to. It was a lot more difficult to get the ice to work as quickly as I needed it to.

The others were already training with Raisha, and even some of the gods who worked closely with the Luck Dragon, so they had someone to lean on to grow stronger. Kimiko refused to be here with us. "The Phantomu are of better use keeping the perimeter of this place secured, so we will patrol the mountainside and allow you all the comfort of having the other guards closer."

That had been annoying, but I guessed dealing with your mom's new boyfriend and figuring out just who was who had to be draining for her. Dealing with the expectations of her people and how to lead them had to be hard, as well.

It made me think of Zeke and how his magic just seemed to work so effortlessly for him.

"How the fuck does he do it?" It was hard to keep the anger and resentment from my voice as the others continued to train in the distance. My magic made it difficult to keep warm in the mountains here and they risked injury if I got too close with my ice. We couldn't risk that, so Raisha had relegated me to this little corner of the grounds.

"Who?" Galaxy asked as she padded closer and looked me over with a soft shiver, as the air around me had to be at least twenty times cooler than anywhere else.

"Zeke. The shadows respond to his will as if they were a part of him." I looked down at my arm, frost still melting slowly from my forearm as I let my mana still and fall away.

"He still owes you a lesson." Galaxy shrugged and lifted a hand as if to say that this was a solution of sorts, holding it up like it was a display. "Maybe see if there's a way to learn how to do that, but also learn more about him. You know..." She looked around and then winked. "Just in case?"

I shook my head and chuckled to myself. "Sure."

I pulled out my phone and dialed his number, the ringing stopping on the second ring, "Yo! You make a decision?"

I cleared my throat and muttered, "No, actually. I was calling you about the lesson you told me you would give me?"

He was silent for a moment, then lowered his voice, "Do you think it wise to be indebted to someone who actively wants to have you join them?"

He wasn't wrong, but with what Galaxy had mentioned, I had a valid rebuttal. "Do you think it wise to go back on your offer to train me after I got you the access to the Seelie Court by letting you know about the Seelie here in Japan, who happened to be led by someone who could call their king?"

That made him laugh. "No. No, I don't suppose it is." He shifted the phone from the sound of things and came back. "When did you want to train?"

"Funny thing, that." I tried to sound nonchalant as I said, "Now would be good?"

He snorted. "Not trying to be a bother at all, are you?" I heard an audible click of his fingers and a portal tore itself open next to me. "Step into my office." I raised my eyebrows at this development. Did I really want to know how he found me so easily this time? Nah, I decided to let it go as I had work to do.

Tell the others where we're going. My order surprised her, but Galaxy complied and stepped into my shadow before I stepped through the portal myself.

They don't like it, but Cassia and Arden agree that if you can develop your own magic a bit better, you'll be more effective against the yokai.

I nodded at that, having thought the same. Just knowing that Galaxy would be with me gave me an edge that I didn't know if Zeke really remembered.

The scenery around us changed and there was a discomfort of sorts before I stood in the same dark place that we had been before. Rather than being on the throne as I had expected, he stood in front of a few monitors hanging from the ceiling by rods. On the displays were various locations where there were people moving and getting into position for something.

"Gotta say, you picked either the worst time to do this, or the best—how we define that will be wholly up to you." He turned back to me, his sharp blue eyes cold for just a moment. "Get a chance to talk to the ladies?"

"Yeah, but the decision is still up in the air." It wasn't necessarily a lie, and I couldn't see if Eve was or wasn't here, so it was a gamble. Technically, I could decide we were joining him and it would be what would happen. Though adding a bit of truth would be helpful. "They're a bit apprehensive about it. Mainly thinking that allying ourselves with you could lead to you placing constraints on us through oaths that would make it impossible for us to do the things we can do now."

He raised an eyebrow at me, then shrugged. "Valid fear to have, honestly, and for the most part? They aren't wrong. There would be oaths and pledges to go through, but mainly ones that would make it less likely for you to actively betray me and turn me over to my enemies or those who would seek to do my people or me harm." He scratched his head and sighed. "Gotta love people who think ahead. I could use more free thinkers, man."

Opting to change the subject so he didn't press the issue, I asked, "What's going on here?"

"Sympathizers with the Seelie and Unseelie have decided to come for me and the remainder of those on both sides." He grinned and glanced at me. "Hey, Galaxy uses bodies and things to give you experience, right?"

Marcus! There was an edge of fear to her voice.

I kept my voice even as I responded to her, *I'll be cautious.* Aloud, I answered, "Yeah, it's something she can do. Helps keep the place clean too."

He grinned wider. "I'm all about recycling." He turned around completely and swaggered toward me. "How about this, then? I'll teach you what I can for a little bit, then we do some prac-app to help keep my people safe. That way, you can get some real-time experience in."

"And you get someone else capable of killing, taking some of the heat off your people."

He nodded, tapping the side of his head. "Free thinkers, man. Gotta love 'em." He let his hand fall back down to his waist and frowned. "But that's not all. Aside from the leftovers, I seem to recall you learning magic through experiencing it, right? What is some magic you are strong with?"

I frowned at him. "Ice as the main one, for now. Shadow is really just a byproduct of my power as the Huntsman." I shrugged. "I have some fire spells, and lightning as well."

He frowned. "Your power sounds a lot like mine and Maebe's. I wonder what the Huntsman in the Fae Realm would have been like to fight."

I grimaced. "Likely hard if you were afraid of him."

"I was a low level too, once." He shook his head and then twisted his neck to the side roughly, the adjustment crackling along his neck like a bag of chips that made me cringe. "If I could fight him as I am now, I think I could take him. But I guess we'll never know."

"Could you let me see him?" He raised an eyebrow at me,

then grimaced. "Like you did with your wife. Could you open a window to him?"

"We've been working on some things to help thin the veil a bit. Really, it was Xiphyre who did it first and best, but I've been trying." He scratched his head and shrugged. "I can try to get a look at him as an experiment, though it'll be a bit before I can really teach you anything after that. Why, though?"

Do I tell him what you want?

Galaxy considered it for a second, then stepped out of me and stood with her chin raised, answering for herself, "The Wild Hunt in all the worlds, iterations, and existence is mine. If you will open a window to this Hunt, I might be able to recall them to me. If I recall, they were a source of power to the Seelie in your Fae Realm, were they not?"

"They were, and from what I understand, they've been giving my friends a hard time with the Seelie acting up." He considered it for a moment, then nodded. "This one? On the house. *If* you can take care of it. If not, then no training, and you have to help me defend my lands anyway. Deal?"

"Is there really any reason for me to think on this?" I held my hand out to him and he shook his head. I lifted a brow at him. "What, too good to shake a poor weakling's hand?"

"No. I want this to be a gentleman's agreement and not something that forces you to act." He smiled at me and winked. "I just want to make sure that you're keeping your word because it's who you are and not what my power makes you do. Can't have people thinking that I don't allow for folks to at least try to be shitty. You know, free minds and all?"

That made Galaxy snort. "That's very magnanimous of you, King Zeke."

"Just Zeke, is fine, Galaxy." He blinked at her for a moment. "Can I ask you a favor? Could you take a human form or something?"

I frowned and glanced at her as she stood next to me in her elven form, dark skin nearly blending into the surrounding room. Then remembered what Servant had said, that she looked just like a blonde version of his wife Queen Maebe.

"If you've been working on thinning the veil some, why not use it to go home?"

He pulled something from his pocket and laid it on the ground, followed by several other pieces and laid them on the ground. "Can't test everything myself. If I did that and it failed, it could kill me. Then I would be useless."

"Then your wife would really kill you." Galaxy cracked the joke almost effortlessly as she shifted into her human form.

He smirked. "Exactly. And thank you." He stood up and clapped his hands together, muttering softly to himself, "Sorry, baby, but here it comes... pie!"

I raised a brow at him but the world around us shifted and took on technicolor hues for a brief moment before the window appeared in the circle of small stones that grew slightly larger as the focus shifted. Zeke, through gritted teeth, groaned, "Little harder for me to find someone I'm unfamiliar with. Little help here, Galaxy?"

Galaxy shut her eyes and approached the circle, humming to herself, then she said, "Left." The vision shifted again turning the way she had ordered. "Forward three hundred feet. Right. Straight down."

The drop was the most disorienting part of it but it was as if we stood in a grove of mushrooms that had a host of creatures milling about in the darkness at the edge of our vision, save for one. This one stood in the light and tended to the mushrooms that grew in a circle around it, almost like a tender caretaker. He wore only simple clothing and a single black bracer with green etched into it.

As we saw him, he stilled, raising his watering can. He was handsome for an elven figure, almost like Luca, but his hair was silver and spun all the way down his back to his feet. When he blinked, I could see a bow on a nearby mushroom, his eyes flicking to it.

"Huntsman!" Galaxy barked and the man turned to stare at

her. "I call you to me. I am your mistress."

He stared at us and hesitated, Galaxy asserting, "My will is your own—come!"

His back arched and he struggled for a moment as the others in the shadows grew dissonant, their worry making them venture toward the light. There were grotesque things there. Horrible fiends that slavered and bayed at the dawn keeping them at bay.

"Zeke, can you get us closer to him?"

He grunted and nodded once as he took his hands and spread them apart, the vision shifting and closing in on the other Huntsman as he did so.

I walked forward briskly, taking a deep breath and shoved my arm through the larger window. "Ah!" The pain traveling up my arm was manageable and as I wrapped my fingers through something, I yanked backward and through the opening again. Galaxy joined me, her hands grasping the arm that tried to fend me off and yanked with me.

Zeke roared and the window shrank slightly before read- justing and coming back to full size. "Hurry!"

I now had him by the hair and pulled one last time as he fought, then we were all the way back through and he was on this side as all hell broke loose on his end. The creatures in the darkness threw themselves into the light toward the portal, screaming at the light as it burned them, but they didn't care and kept rushing toward us.

One of the creatures managed to get an arm through as the sunlight on the other end seared it, the stink of the flesh singeing my nostrils from where I stood with the Huntsman in my grasp, confused.

The creature reached a little farther and managed to touch the other Huntsman and that broke him from his stupor. He spoke in a language that was so foreign to me that I couldn't even begin to describe the sounds of it, but Zeke and Galaxy understood him just fine.

As the creature fought to gain entry to our world, Zeke

stumbled forward and slammed his fingers into its head, spilling its blood onto the ground. In addition, the stones around the door were soaked in its blood just before the window slammed shut and split the creature in half like what had happened before. The body flailed a bit, which set the man in my grasp off.

He shouted something that made the shadows beneath his feet darken and crawl up his body to begin forming the Mantle and his armor, with my own flaring in resonance to it.

A look of shocked horror crossed his eyes as Galaxy snarled through my mind at the same time as the voice of the Vorna did. *Take him, Marcus.*

Compatible material found to absorb through your Huntsman's Mantle. Take it to grow stronger.

I blinked at him and grimaced, then remembered that this was for a reason and cast Hoarfrost around my fist—freezing his hair and head to my hand as the shadows continued to roil up his body, closing around his chest now. Mine had already finished forming, seeming to be much faster than his own. He started to grasp backward and his aura flared, magic beginning to sweep down his arm as he pounded his fist against my armored chest.

I felt each blow and I knew he was only warming up, so I grit my teeth and cast Mana Blade, shoving it into his throat before the Mantle could complete its march up to his head. I put my gloved hand to his chest and willed the Mantle to respond to my will.

"Let me have it first, Marcus." I turned to see Galaxy looking at the body hungrily, so I tossed the lifeless body onto the ground in front of her as she took on her large cat form.

Her jaw opened impossibly large as she came to the head and began to work the body into her maw.

"That's…" Zeke looked like he was trying to find a nice word for it, but just decided on, "Creepy. That's creepy as fuck. I've seen and done some weird shit, but choking a guy back like a five layer from Taco Bell after drinking for a bit, is a lot."

I couldn't help but say, "That's what she said."

He blinked and grinned up at me, pointing. "Dick."

I nodded. "Dick *joke*."

Galaxy wiped her mouth as she finished and stood next to us. "No you aren't, Marcus."

Both mine and Zeke's eyes widened as the other man went, "*Oooooooh!* Shit!"

I just shook my head and watched her for a moment. Without her telling me, I could see she was digesting everything and as she did, tears fell down her face. Her shoulders shook and there was a lull in the teasing and ribbing from both of us that allowed us to hear the quiet sobs.

"She's not someone who regrets eating, is she?" Zeke asked with apparent concern. "I'm not mad about not being offered anything. I had a few souls earlier and couldn't eat another bite."

"The gods on Brindolla." Galaxy sniffed, then wiped her nose, looking back at Zeke, her eyes wide. "Who were they?"

He blinked and looked as if he were trying to recall. "One of them was Radiance. She was the one who worked with us the most, honestly. Fainne, god of the Dwarves, and there were others that I don't really remember as well. I think there were, like, nine of them?"

"What about them, Galaxy?" She shook her head and continued to break down, to the point where she could no longer stand and crumpled into a heap on the floor. "What's going on?"

"They're my children, Marcus." She cried for a second more, then said, "They were my children, and I didn't know it."

Isn't all life thanks to you? I tried to keep my tone even, but I was concerned.

You don't understand, Marcus. She sobbed again and then we were both in my mana sea where I could see her. "They were my children and I know nothing of them. Other than hearsay and what he can remember, I have nothing of them."

"So then... what do you want to do?" I glanced upward,

likely toward where my head should have been. I knew that all of this was taking place in a matter of seconds from an outside perspective, but it was still weird to have someone so close when it happened like this. "If we help Zeke, we could get you there to see them, at least. You deserve that much, right?"

"But what he said..." She was uncertain, then frowned. "No. No. We need to do this right. If we join up with him, he's going to fuck over a lot of people. We do what we can, and keep him at bay, or at least until a lot of our people are safe."

I didn't care for that, if I was honest with myself. I wanted to help her.

She stared at me, raw pain in her eyes as she stepped over to me and let me pull her into a hug. "I know you would drown the world if it would help me, Cassia, or your son. But there are others who need us, and I am too weak to go to another world to try to meet children I know nothing of. It would be folly to expect much, especially if they allow their Huntsman this much reign."

She stepped away, her back facing me as she spread her hands wide in front of herself before turning and holding something out to me.

"Take it, and grow stronger." She pressed the heavy cloth into my hand and as soon as it touched me, I was back in the Null.

I rolled my eyes. "This has *got* to stop."

You have touched the Mantle of another Huntsman that can be absorbed and taken into your own—would you like to absorb it?

I closed my eyes and said, "Yes."

The Mantle burst into being around me and began to eat hungrily of the object in my hand. The cloth around me thickened and pulsed almost happily. And then the visions began.

Hunting things for the good of the realm as it came into its own from the time of the great dissonance that had split the realms from one another to ensure the safety of all.

The gods were coming into their own now that the great

one was gone, and in that comeuppance, the realms' coexistence was not feasible. There were too many chances of the gods' hordes coming together and doing... something. Whatever that something was eluded me, but I had my mission.

Centuries of protecting the realm and hunting the most depraved intruders to the realms and putting them back have led me to be jaded and unhinged at times. There is little rest for me and my legion. To the point where I must forcibly add to my numbers and draw on their confusion to feed myself and stay going.

There was another skip in time and suddenly the Huntsman was being berated by the Seelie royalty. The prissy, pristine-looking leech playing her games of power in the Fae Realm. All these pointless struggles. Over it.

I'm so over it. I stared at her, as beautiful as she was to look at thanks to the lies she cloaked herself in as a symbol of status.

She droned on and on to the point that my boredom became apparent enough that my lack of care gave way to opportunity. Hers. She slammed the bracer over my wrist and it bound my soul to her will.

Then it was centuries more hunting for her gain and sport. The saddest thing was—I'd been enjoying it for half as long and relished in the thrill of it all. Killing so freely was *freeing*.

That freedom was taken from me for a short time when my Hunt was interrupted by the conniving witch Maebe. Her darkness and ice magic swept my prey away from me, and then the queen was taken shortly after.

The new king made sweeping changes, but the one thing he let me do was hunt. But this time I was unleashed on the Prime Realm and now I had all the time in the world to hunt down those who displeased me or took my fancy. There were times I was pointed to prey on someone specifically for the Seelie's benefit, but it hadn't happened since the two children that managed to make it into the orc highlands.

I shook my head, the memories fading away rapidly. So they had turned him into their hound, had they?

Sending him and his minions after children and letting him run rampant over the world.

Assimilation complete. Additional strengths of Huntsman's Mantle converted and added.

Weapon proficiency with Bow added.

I rolled my eyes; I'd never need that one.

Latent abilities unlocked by Vornal Blood. Would you like to sacrifice this proficiency for a different effect or reward?

I turned my gaze slightly and frowned. "Uh, yes?"

Analyzing... analyzing... error—tied too close to external power. Rerouting. Realigning.

Alignment met. Please say, "Display."

"Display." My voice rang out in the Null and an array of stars similar to that of my spell tree appeared in front of me, with their names and abilities arranged on them.

Select a spell or ability to sacrifice the proficiency to.

Everything would be good, right? But I had the idea that this would only give me one thing to improve.

I still had eleven points to add to anything I wanted, so I could do that beforehand.

Think, Marcus. Your main strength right now is your ice magic. It's what makes you different from the others. I stared at that portion of my spell tree. "Can I improve an entire tree of magic?"

No. The sacrifice is not enough to improve all of an entire tree of magic.

"Shit." I'd figured, but had to ask anyway. I blinked at all of it and though there was a massive amount of the ice tree open to me, all of them were so weak compared to Hoarfrost. "Can I choose Hoarfrost?"

The voice was quiet for a short time. The star for the spell shimmered and pulsed brighter before the voice returned.

Yes. The sacrifice will be enough to modify the spell to allow continued growth. Select a spell to sacrifice proficiency to.

"So not enough to make it improved on its own, but enough to allow it to grow more." I shrugged, thinking, *I can work with that.* "Sacrifice the bow weapon proficiency for Hoarfrost."

Stand by.

The rest of the tree fell away, leaving the spell to be changed, then there was a suction around me. As if the very air I took into my body had decided it was no longer necessary for me to survive on, and all I knew was the frigid void of space.

Sacrifice accepted. Spell adapted to accept more input from an outside source. Natural affinity included in the accounting. One point already placed for previous completion.

I looked at the new spell and saw that it would take ten more points to get it to the point where it was full and able to be completed again. Thankfully, I had eleven points in the bank for it.

I flashed out of the Null and back to the present where Zeke still watched me curiously. It didn't feel like all that much time had passed.

He frowned at me. "You level up or something?" When I looked askance at him, he elaborated, "Just got that look on your face like you'd leveled up. I know that my friends and I get that way."

"You're leveling up too?" It was hard to keep the shock out of my voice.

He snorted. "Slowly. Not nearly as swiftly as I would like, but it's something." He pointed to me. "What'd you get?"

"Nothing yet." I thought of my status and opened it up, skipping directly to my spells list.

Hoarfrost had one of eleven points in it now.

I selected the spell and dumped the ten other needed points into it and tried to contain my excitement as the spell grew and message prompts came to me.

Congratulations on fully investing in a spell. Here is your fully upgraded and realized spell.

Void Frost – Your control over the cold encom-

passes you, and you can freeze things within one hundred and twenty feet of you. 2 mana per second with an added point of mana consumed per ten feet from your personage up to max distance.

Upgrades*

The chill of your will rivals that of the barren void in space—Void Frost is as intuitive and easy to manipulate as breathing or flicking a finger. The strength of your cold can be added to by increased levels of Mana and Charisma.

WARNING!

I blinked, as this was new.

The caster of this spell is immune to its effects, however, those around them may not be. This is not a skill to be used in close proximity to those the caster holds dear.

I whistled low and nodded my head, as that made sense.

How did you get through to the next level of a spell that I didn't even know existed, Marcus? Galaxy rifled through my thoughts as I swiftly related things to her and she frowned inwardly. *I can still feel that the Mantle is stronger than it was before, but there is an unfinished-ness to it that I find confusing. See if Zeke will take you somewhere cold and we can try an experiment.*

I shrugged and looked over at the man as he stood and inspected the creature that lay on the ground in front of where the portal had been. He held his phone to his face, muttering, "Looks like a stable enough window, but I need to be certain enough that going through it will be quick and possible for me to step through without risk." He looked down at the now-smoldering stones. "Stones are incompatible with the magic that was used, and will need to be either re-worked or enlarged to contain more mana. We also need to be certain that it wasn't outside forces like Galaxy calling to something that was originally part of her to come to her that played a role in the subjects being able to pass through."

He frowned and considered the creature. "I'll also be

sending what's left of the creature that came through the portal after the Huntsman to be studied. It looks like coming through it really hurt it, more so than the sunlight over there did."

True to form, it looked about as singed as the stones were, and its stinking carcass wasn't any more pleasing to smell than it was to look at.

Having ended his call, he pursed his lips and clicked his fingers, elves stepping from the shadows of the room. He pointed to the corpse. "Take this to our dude who does the autopsies of creatures for me and get him on it asap."

They both bowed their heads. "Yes, my King." They moved in unison to collect the corpse and then carted it out of the room by hand as the king continued to consider the previous entry from one realm to another.

"He remembered you." My statement made the man crane his neck my way, then tilt his head curiously. "The Huntsman from Brindolla remembered you and your friends. He's always resented you for being able to get away how you did." I frowned, curious. "How *did* you get away?" What I saw in the memories didn't make sense.

"The Fae have a weird thing about their names. If you say it, they become aware of you. This is especially true of the more powerful ones, like the royals whose true names become how they are referred to." He shrugged and stood up, dusting his hands off by clapping them together lightly. "Yohsuke called to Queen Maebe, Heir to the Deep Dark and Frigid Fortress, and the Unseelie Queen—my now wife. She summoned us because we dared speak her name, but it was more in curiosity than for retribution. That was when she realized I could see her with my True Sight."

"You have True Sight?" He nodded at Galaxy as she spoke and she added, "Does it work on everything?"

He smirked. "For the most part. There are some creatures that are pretty fucking good at hiding, but I can usually find them, or tell they're hiding something." He held his hand out to me for me to shake it. "Thank you for that. That guy was a real pain in the dick for my people."

"Well, I think I got something cool out of it, but there's something I need to do." He lifted an eyebrow at me. "Can you take me someplace with a lot of really cold ice? Like the tundra or something?"

He frowned. "Does it need to be natural or can it be magical?"

I glanced over at Galaxy just as she shrugged in return, but in my mind she said, *Natural is fine but magical would be best, because this is a magical weapon we're talking about.*

"It doesn't matter to me, whatever would be easiest really."

He just nodded and held a hand up to his lips, snapping his fingers in a way that caused the sound to grow louder as it went farther from us.

"Yes?" Eve's voice rang out behind me, she sauntered into view and stared at me and Galaxy. "My queen?"

"I forgot you haven't seen Galaxy in her humanoid form yet, even if it does only partially hide what she looks like in elven form. True Sight helps some, but it's shit when it's as strong as ours." Zeke scratched his head. "That's Galaxy, Eve. I need you to help me make some ice."

The woman actually rolled her eyes at the man and said, "Listen, I know it's nice to have cold drinks, but I'm not here for party tricks."

Zeke stared at her for a moment then sighed. "I was drunk —one time—and I swear I needed the ice. Can we move past that and just make with the ice?"

"How much?" She raised a brow at him.

I answered, "About a hundred pounds of it to start with."

Eve blinked, looking from me to the king who dipped his chin once and stared at her. She grimaced and held her hands up, spikes bursting from her body and along the floor toward us, forcing me to step back and pull Galaxy with me. Five spikes lifted from the ground, the girth of them growing as we watched.

Cover yourself in the armor and then touch the ice to pull it into yourself.

The ice from her was supposed to be cold, but it didn't feel that way to me. Not anymore.

I willed the Mantle to impart my armor to me and let it cover me as I held my hand aloft over the ice just barely beneath my fingertip. Once it covered me, I touched the ice and *willed* the Mantle to collect the offering before me.

The same sort of siphoning suction that I felt in the Null came over me and from my hand the ice pulled through to me and thus into the Mantle itself.

The cloth grew rigid, chilled against my flesh where the clothes didn't protect it, but it wasn't unpleasant. But it wasn't enough.

I kept my tone low. "More, please."

Both Eve and Zeke glanced at one another before turning to me, the king shrugging. "Let's do it."

Both of them raised their arms as I stepped forward and raised my own arms in a mirror of their movements.

As the stalagmites of ice formed and grew to rival my height, they met my palm and became food for the Mantle. This continued for a few minutes straight before the Mantle stopped accepting the materials and a notification flooded my view.

Assimilation of materials offered to the Huntsman's Mantle is complete.

Would you like to see the gains?

I rolled my eyes and said, "Duh. Yes."

While the Mantle is active, all castings of any ice-aspected magic will be ten percent more effective, more cost efficient. Also, while worn, resistance to ice and cold-based spells increases significantly.

I grinned at that and looked to Zeke. "I think I want to take the time to work on the prac-app as we train. Get the most bang for our buck, eh?"

He grinned right back at me. "I knew I liked you."

CHAPTER TWENTY-THREE

"There you go, feel the element all around you, and then interact with it." Zeke encouraged me as I stood in the center of a village maybe a half an hour walk from where the throne room was. It was a small one, and I wondered why it was so close to the throne until I realized that as we were walking toward it, we had *shifted* in some way to wherever here now was. Almost like going through a portal, but not. Was this a new aspect of being able to create portals? A thought for later.

I swirled the darkness around me and tried to pack it into a ball about the size of a beach ball and as soon as there was a lapse in my focus, it flew away in all directions as easily as it had come.

"You're still viewing the darkness as an object to be manipulated instead of as a part of you." He stood next to me and lifted his hands, the fighting around us ignored for a moment as the shadows bolted toward his hand and he made it form itself into a spike.

"How did you get like this, man?" It was hard to hide the frustration in my voice as I picked up a discarded spear and flung it into a shape next to one of the buildings by us.

Hit! Galaxy snarled with zeal as she flitted from my body to collect her prize.

"I'm beloved by the elements and have all kinds of elemental manipulation abilities." He smiled at me. "Though I've been here for a little while, and the elementals don't respond to me here. They're quiet for some reason."

"Maybe they worry you'll eat them?" That made him laugh but I was kind of serious. "How did you get that?"

"The gods in Brindolla wanted to give us every advantage they could, because their best weren't enough to stand up to War and his minions and generals." He scratched his head and shrugged, almost to himself before continuing. "When I picked Druid and kitsune as my class and race, I was trying to meta-game just a tad, thinking I was going to wake up. But I didn't. The more I worked with magic and tried to understand it, the better I learned. It was Elder Leo who taught me to reach out to the Elements themselves to augment my power, though looking back, I doubt that he ever imagined what would happen."

He laughed boisterously at my confused stare. "I had no idea that some of them would take a liking to me the way they did, but it worked out for the best, really." He considered me thoughtfully for a moment. "Maybe we try that with you."

The fighting going on around us was enough to make me glare at him, but he just waved my stare away and snapped his fingers at me before pointing to the ground. "Pop a squat, Marine."

"You know I outranked you, right, Corporal?" He grinned as wide as his mouth would stretch. "I don't give a shit if you *are* a king who could kick my ass. Good order and discipline demands I make you do pushups until I'm tired."

He raised an eyebrow at me and grumbled, "So you can eat all my purple crayons while I'm distracted? Fuck that." He pointed to the ground. "Sit down, Marcus. I'll guard you while you work."

I grimaced and did as he said, opting to just humor him. I sat on the ground as the fighting around us in the distance continued, Zeke leading me. "Close your eyes and envision an element. Choose the one you feel the most drawn to and just say what it is for me."

There was no hesitation in my tone as I stated, "Ice."

He grunted and I heard a splatter of liquid on the ground. "Ice, okay." I opened an eye and turned to look at him as a rather large lizard-like person tried to spear him with a stick. He slapped it away and chopped the creature in half with a large axe made of flames. "Hey—eyes closed, man, and imagine the element as I speak."

I rolled my eyes and complied as he said, "Ice. Death, or the symbol of it in many cultures, worlds, and realms. It forces the life from the blood, freezing all it touches warmer than itself, sapping strength, and killing the cells of the body. Winter kills the living world, and forces it to slumber until spring comes. But it also allows for life to carry on. Ice can keep infection at bay. The cold keeps food for those who wish to save it for later and when warmed, can even become water that is much needed for life and continued existence. Ice can kill and keep things beautiful forever, but it can also hold the fires of corruption at bay. There is a give and take. See the ice in your mind's eye, ponder it and think up how it can be used. How you can make it your own."

Weirdly, I'd been doing just that as he had been speaking, imagining ice keeping food and in the winter, freezing a lake and all the fish within barely surviving. The polar bears walking over vast swaths of it in the frozen north in order to hunt for food, but falling victim to it when they couldn't hunt enough. There was a balance, until it did what it wanted.

Ice melting and becoming raging rivers that split stone and then refreezing later. All of it was connected.

A blossoming chill pulled me from my rumination and a soft voice echoed through my mind, wispy and frigid all at once.

I do not know the claim you have, but your warmth insults me, creature. I can feel that you use my magic, and that it feels innate to you. Come to me and state your case, but tell no one.

I blinked inwardly and suddenly I stood in a hall of pristine walls of ice and snow banks that built chaise lounges along the walls. The place was smaller than the hall Zeke's throne sat in, but this somehow felt no less grand to me.

"Again, your warmth offends." The voice was behind me and I whipped around, ready to defend myself.

A being stood there, something between an ice sculpture of a woman, legs and arms visible with the body itself being made of packed snow that had a crust of rime along it that looked like a jacket of sorts. She stared at me for a short time. "Why did you think to summon my attention, warm-blooded creature?"

"It was a suggestion from someone more powerful than me." I stared at her, her features never fully deciding on what they wanted to be. "My name is Marcus."

"I am called many things." Her voice was still chilly and she continued to stare at me. "Must you call me anything?"

"I guess not?" I frowned at her. "The whole point of this exercise was to bring me closer to the element I have the most affinity to, I think? To be truthful, I don't fully expect that he knew anything would respond."

"That freak was the one who sent you to me?" Her vitriolic response caught me off guard hard enough that I just nodded. She growled low and the temperature in the room lowered dangerously, even to the point that I could feel it. "He's been trying to reach out to the elementals for months now, and we've left him alone because he has too many bonds already. Seriously, he's a freak of nature."

"He's a self-proclaimed Druid. I thought that was the point." Staring at her, it was easy to realize just how little I actually knew about what was going on around us at all times.

"No one should have so many bonds with natural elements." She sighed and stared over my shoulder. "I can sense fire, shadow, water, earth, wind, light, and lightning. That many elements should weaken the host as they degrade the others, but for some unknown reason—he's fine. It should be impossible. It should be killing him."

He had all that? I took a steadying breath and cleared my throat gently. "Well, as shitty as it is to realize I'm that far behind some imaginary power curve, I just came here to see if there was a way to get better at using ice magic. Sorry to have bothered you or stressed you out."

She considered me for a time, then spoke softly. "Did he really not tell you what you had to do?" I shook my head and she tilted hers to her right. "You're here to seek my blessing. My blessing would allow you to use my brand of magic better depending on how deeply I bless you."

"Then…" I paused as she continued to stare at me. "Do I have your blessing since I'm here?"

"No." Her statement was firm, but cruel. "I brought you here because I thought you were his way of trying to get to us, and I was going to fry your brain a bit to make you believe there was no way to meet us."

I blinked at her. "Thanks for not doing that."

She lowered her chin waiting for a time and finally said, "Make a deal with me."

That made my blood pump a bit faster. "What kind of deal?"

"Your magic is strong. Strong enough that I could bless you with my full might and allow you a great deal of my power, but I want three things in return."

Carefully, I said, "And those things are…?"

"First, I want you to tell him we won't work with him. His bonds are strong enough that it prevents us from being too close to him without worrying about being destroyed." She watched me but when I said nothing, she continued. "Next, I want you to summon an elemental when you're free of him so that I might be free of my prison for a short time."

I frowned. Those both seemed easy enough. Hell, it felt like a steal to me, but that had to mean something more. Especially since she called it a prison. "What else did you want?"

"Your fire magic." She stepped closer to me, the ice that made up her limbs refracting the light of the room flashing into my eyes. "It offends me greatly, and I do not like that it dwells within you. Relinquish it to me, and I will give you power you cannot dream of."

"I have a goddess who lives inside me who allows me to grow stronger all the time, I doubt that." I lifted my chin. "I worked hard for that magic and it allows me some differences in my fighting style. Do you really expect me to give that up just for you?"

"I don't care whether you give it up or not." She shrugged, turning her back on me. "You can leave here powerless, for all I care, but it's obvious that you have some reason to think you need my strength."

I frowned. *Could I even give it up like that?* If there was an option to, there would have to be a way. Besides, Merlin and Arden had more than adequate flame magic. *Don't suppose you can hear all this, can you, Galaxy?*

I was wondering when you would reach out to me. The goddess purred at me for a moment then said, *It is possible, and the blessing would give us an edge in combat certainly. I just wonder if it would be worth it in the long run.*

Being the jack of all trades isn't my thing. I stared ahead at her as she nodded in agreement. *I think I'm going to do it.*

I will stand with you, but if she touches my things, I will kick her ass.

I laughed to myself and the woman turned on me. "Do you find my threats funny, warm blood?"

"If we're going to work together, you should call me Marcus." I stepped closer to her and held out my hand. "I'm the Huntsman, leader of the Wild Hunt and chosen vessel of Galaxy, the first goddess. If I'm going to give you my fire magic, I'm going to need to know who I'm working with."

She cleared her throat and raised her chin. "I am the Primordial Elemental of Frost, and I am called Hollow." She stared at me and glared down her nose at me. "Will you form a bond with me under my conditions?"

"No." My answer clearly startled her. "I've been steamrolled too much recently by giving my word on things without something in return. Thanks."

"Then you refuse my power?"

I shook my head. "No, I want to offer my own conditions. I have no problem with any of yours, but I'll add in that while I'll tell him not to bother you anymore, I'm not denying your existence." I held up two fingers. "I'll summon a golem for you to take over if I have the ability to, but that means you won't be attacking anyone who doesn't attack you first, and not just for perceived or accidental threats."

Her head tilted further. "You think yourself strong enough to make demands?"

"I think I have a right to bargain when you're stuck here in this prison and I'm the safest means you have of escape." Thinking of it just then, I added, "There's not a damn thing stopping him from going out and finding someone to come and form a pact with you of some kind. And I'm not entirely certain that he couldn't figure out a way to force your hand either."

"He wouldn't dare." She lifted her chin to a level that made it look like she was staring at the roof and I just rolled my eyes.

"He's killed two gods, the entire Seelie Court, took over the Unseelie Court because he has a legit claim to the throne, and now he's probably going to send the world into a shit show if left unchecked—do you honestly think he couldn't figure out how to get an elemental to bless someone under his control?"

Her head lowered until she stared at me with cautious consideration. "You think he could?"

"He made it so that if I told anyone about him out there in a manner that interfered with his plans, that I feared he would kill me and my friends." I crossed my arms and stared straight back at her. "If it wasn't for the fact that I didn't think he really needed to add you to his massive fucking arsenal already, I'd be dead."

This was purely conjecture on my part, but it felt as if there was enough of a grain of truth to it that it would stand up to scrutiny.

She frowned. "I can defend myself, and with my blessing, you'll be able to summon me forth with ease. I will guide you myself. Just ensure that it is not where he is at first."

"And my fire magic?"

She shook her head. "Not a negotiation. If you want the full breadth of my power, your offensive magic must be gone."

"What about lightning?" She considered it, narrowing her gaze at me before I said, "I can't give that up. It's what I use the most, if I'm being honest."

"As it is not *directly* fire, it is not as big an issue or offender." She held her hand out. "If you do this, there is no going back. We will be bound together."

"I've already got some ladies in my life, so consider it platonic." I took a deep breath and grasped her hand. "I look forward to working with you."

She pulled me to her and embraced me, muttering, "As do I, Marcus. Go with my power, and entrust yourself to the blizzard."

The warmth within me fled from the cold that touched my flesh, everywhere she touched. Galaxy shivered within me, then acclimated quickly. A burning sensation gripped me, all of it traveling to a central location in me—my right hip just above my pelvis.

I frowned, wanting to look and see what burned there so fiercely, but she shoved me backward. "You have promises to keep, Marcus. When you are ready to summon me, freeze the ground and call my name. I will come."

I nodded once and said, "Thanks," before returning to myself and opening my eyes.

Zeke was still talking, all the things he mentioned were cold, his particular thoughts at the moment, "...Frosty. Oh my *God*, I'm fucking hungry and one of those sounds so fucking good. Eve!"

The tigress, covered in blood, stepped from the shadows near us and bowed her head. "Yes, my King?"

"Could you run and get me a Frosty? I don't know if

Marcus might want anything, but I'd reckon if he got anything, it would be a burger and a Frosty."

"I could go for that." I grunted as I stood up, my body stiff and achy for some reason. "How long was I gone?"

Zeke responded without turning around. "Few minutes." He pointed finger guns at Eve. "If you want a burger, get yourself some." He pulled out his wallet and handed her a card. "Just don't break the bank, okay?"

She snorted and disappeared, leaving us alone, so I had to ask, "Has she before?"

He laughed. "Oh yeah. She gets a bit peckish." He turned around to see me, eyes widening. "Uh."

He lifted a hand and warmth radiated over me in a wave, then faded, but his discomfort didn't change. "What?"

"You look like you had a run in with a glacier and it won?" He scratched his head and frowned. "You okay?"

A quick inventory showed that I felt fine. *You know what he could mean, Galaxy?*

No clue, but we waste time here that could be better spent hunting.

I nodded. "Yeah, I feel fine. Can we go hunting now?"

He looked surprised. "Uh, sure, man." He motioned behind me. "The others were told just to try to corral those who remained here so that you would have somewhere to go and play. Did you talk to anyone?"

"Yes." Which reminded me of what I needed to do. I turned around and faced him, speaking plainly. "The elementals here want you to stop trying to approach them."

His eyebrows shot straight up, so before he could speak, I lifted a hand. "Look, I don't know everything, but they do— your bonds with the other elements make them uncomfortable and you risk killing them when you encroach on them and their realms. Something about your existing bonds being stronger than theirs can be? I don't really know, but I was asked to pass it along."

He frowned. "I see. Thanks for that." He shook his head as if to clear it and pointed behind me. "We can go that way and find where the enemies have been pinned in, if you think you're ready?"

I grinned and shrugged. "I'll try to make it work." I turned to walk away and then looked back. "By the way—dick move using the items you enchanted to keep tabs on us."

He snorted. "Paid off, didn't it? I got to you in record time when you needed me—*and* they were badass. I know that Arden likes that chair, by the way. I couldn't make myself one of those because I couldn't get out of hers for a minute. Too comfy."

"They were badass, that's right. But now we can't use them for fear of you spying on us."

He sighed, joining me in walking toward where he had pointed. "Look, man, if you're fishing for an apology—stop. I've had some fucked up shit happen, and even though I like you, I don't entirely know who I can trust here anymore. I have my friends and those beholden to me through my power." He scratched his head and grimaced. "The gods on Brindolla would have let us stay if they could have, but the gods here forced their hands. As I didn't know the gods here were real, I have no clue who had the most direct hand in our being forced back."

"So that makes all of them potential enemies." He nodded at my statement and I frowned. "But the Hunt aren't gods."

"Galaxy is." He didn't look at me as I stared sidelong at him. "Like I said, Marcus, I don't know who is at fault and that makes almost all of them complicit."

Four paws alit onto my shoulder which stopped me from responding to him. I turned my head to see her opening her mouth, her voice coming from within weirdly. "I swear on my power and on that of those who I hold dear that I had nothing to do with you being pulled back from the realm of your choice, at least not consciously. There are creatures out there who have access to shards of my power that could have interfered."

He stopped where he was and looked to be reading her statement, nodded once to himself and then grunted. "Okay. I believe you." I was more than a little relieved until he added, "But one good goddess doesn't absolve the rest of them."

"Zeke…" I tried to think of what I would say and he just shook his head.

He stared straight ahead as he said, "Two of my kids grew up without me. I know they resent me for that, even if it isn't my fault. They didn't ask for that. And now they're stuck in a world on the brink of civil war and there's nothing their supposed 'hero' of a father can do." He grit his teeth and clenched his fists. "I've let a lot of shit go before because I like to help out and not bother folks—but I'm going to get mine for what was done to me and my friends."

"It's not like any of you died." It was hard to keep the bitterness out of my voice. "My brothers and sisters died in Galaxy's temple prison and you don't see me blaming her for it, though it would be convenient to."

Galaxy's voice echoed softly in my head. *Marcus, please…*

No! I was fuming now. "I had my son taken from me, and I'm just now getting to build a relationship with him. You think I'm not mad? But it's not like I'm out there killing the Unseelie for making it impossible for his mom to stay with me. For essentially using me. And no one on your side is dead for it. You have the power to get home again. And you're killing people who may not have been involved. That's not right, Zeke—you know it."

He moved so fast I didn't have the time to react as his fingers gripped my throat and lifted me into the air. "You're *wrong*, Marcus." He sneered hatefully as his eyes darkened. "*Dead wrong.*"

One of them flashed crimson before he shut them both, gritting his teeth as he let me go, dropping me from above his head. I landed roughly on my feet as he spoke. "We got back, and while our souls were still slumbering, Jake was in a car accident." He opened his eyes and started to walk again, but the rage was still in his tone. "He was brain dead, our paladin and probably the best of us, died because he caught the flu in transit to another place for treatment. If I had known who I was, and what I could have done, I could've saved him. If I had known your world existed, I could have sought out help."

It was hard to think past the crow I was having to swallow. "Come on, man, that could have happened to anyone."

He roared in anguish, "But it didn't!" Screams in the distance began and he shook himself out, snarling, "It fucking didn't. Now I have to live with the knowledge that there was nothing I could do, because I was kidnapped against my will and basically drugged to keep me complacent."

He turned to me and pointed a sharp claw into my chest. "You might not blame Galaxy for what happened, but I can damn sure guarantee you blame her guards for the death of your unit. How many gods knew of us and did nothing, hmm? Who pulled the trigger on hunting us down and taking us back, and why when there are so many souls here for the taking?"

It was hard to know what to say, and he wasn't wrong for feeling that way. All I could offer was simply, "I didn't know."

He snorted. "Of course you fucking didn't." He lifted his arm and just tossed his hand up in defeat. "No one ever stops to hold the gods accountable, because they're some nameless, face-less beings or ideals that govern society and make all the good little boys, girls, and other people behave in an attempt to gain some kind of fucking reward that they can yank away at a whim. That shit ain't me, anymore."

He turned and glared at me, the crimson returning to his gaze, his voice deepening with an almost beast-like edge of a growl to it as he said, "I'm out for blood, Marcus. Blood taken for the blood shed. If you can't be a part of that, fine. I can respect that. But you get in my way and you won't stay there for long."

"Hard to want to be friendly with someone constantly threatening to kill you." I grumbled as he turned away from me to stalk off in the direction of the shouting and screaming.

He glanced over his shoulder and raised an eyebrow at me. "Hard to want to be friends with someone who can't understand your point of view on religion, but there are people out there who do it all the time, Marcus." He faced forward again and called out, "I don't hate you for wanting something different from me, man. I don't hate you for having other ideals. I don't hate you at all, actually. I see a good man doing the best he can with what he was dealt and I would love to help you."

"So I can help you?" I smirked just a bit at him.

He laughed. "Maybe." He shook himself out, then sighed. "But it's not fully in me not to just want to help the people I like either. I'm not that jaded… yet."

We continued on in silence until we came across one of his subordinates, the man pointing to a larger building. Zeke heaved a sigh. "The warehouse, really?"

"Seems cliché, doesn't it?" The other man crossed his arms. "There are at least a dozen or more of them left over, and that's not to say that the Seelie side doesn't have more. Lords Muu and Yohsuke have been fighting the stronger foes as the guard takes the weaker ones."

"They outnumbered?" Zeke raised a brow at the other man. "Give it to me straight, Dal."

Dal sighed. "Yes, my King, they are." He tossed his chin at the warehouse. "Our forces are enough to keep them contained for now, but with you not allowing us to move on them en masse, they assume us weak."

"Let them make asses of themselves and we'll show them what for next time." Zeke gripped his shoulder amicably and jerked his thumb back at me. "Dal, this is Marcus. Marcus is going to go in there and take care of this for us while I go see to the others."

"He's going to go in there alone?" Dal seemed a bit taken aback.

I clenched my fists, cracking my knuckles in anticipation. "Yup. I need to see how strong I've gotten and work the kinks out."

"It's okay to like feet, big guy." Zeke grinned at me and winked as he disappeared without another word.

Dal grimaced with evident distaste. "Feet are gross, Marcus."

Galaxy cackled as I just ignored the man and headed into the building. Two stories high and made of simple enough materials that I worried I would destroy it if I worked too hard.

He could fix it if he really wanted to, he's just allowing them all to work instead. Galaxy observed openly, *He's got the power for sure. Go wild.*

I nodded and closed the door behind me, willing ice through Void Frost to seal it shut.

The spell spread so fast and completely that the entire door was covered with it. The cold was... comforting.

"Who the hell are you?" someone asked, then in a louder shout, "What'd you do to the door?"

"Wasn't raised in a barn, so I shut it." I turned around, willing my ice to cover my arm in an armor-like mass, my fingertips covered in dark ice that sank into the speaker's throat. "But none of you need worry about that now."

CHAPTER TWENTY-FOUR

Eat your fill, Galaxy.

She fled my shadow in her cat form and began to viciously devour the corpse at my feet.

The other creatures here hid. Some of them were unable to fully conceal their bulky figures, but with all the materials in the room, it was still difficult to try and pick out what was just an inanimate object and what wasn't. *Wait. Materials?*

There was stone and other things. Not a whole lot, but at least enough that it was hard to get through the place. *If this is his place, I wonder if he would mind me adding some of these materials to my Mantle?*

Galaxy's eyes shot to me and her voice echoed through my mind. *If you destroy the place, he might not know what's missing.*

That made me smile. I'd pay him if I needed to, putting the lair off for a little bit, but there was at least a good chance that I could gain a little more from this. Reaching out, my fingertips touched a pile of wood and a prompt flooded my vision.

Material component contacted. Absorb it?

I silently confirmed it and the wood was just gone, all of it.

The entire pile of roughly hewn logs for about ten feet by eight feet just gone as if it had never existed.

But it didn't seem like it was enough to get any benefit from, so I just moved my attention elsewhere.

A figure hopped out from behind a barrel with a spear that they shoved toward my heart, but I lifted my arm and formed a shield from ice using just an image of what I wanted, the blow glancing to the side. I thought, *Freeze!*

Void Frost screamed from my body and covered everything in a sixty foot radius in ice so thick it could have been there for thousands of years. The sound of the attack was almost enough to bring me to my knees, but it was the absolute desolation that it left in its wake that made me question whether it was safe for me to have this power.

The enemies here are all of tier nine and above, but the power you've received has brought you to at least tier eight, if what I remember from the others is to be believed. That was hard to believe at first, but the four frozen creatures close to attacking me led me to recognize that it was at least partially true if nothing else. *Do you not trust my judgement?*

Not so much that, as it's hard to cope with suddenly being this *strong, you know?* I touched the ice and it genuinely felt cool to my touch but nothing more. "Hollow."

My mana throbbed once and a massive chunk of my bar froze over, almost like it wasn't mine anymore, before it melted and the bar shrank by more than a hundred and fifty mana. It was a costly chunk, that was for certain.

"I was wondering when you would get away from him." Hollow's voice came from a small, slowly building snowy figure that looked vaguely like a smaller, stumpier version of her body. "This is… annoying, but a start."

"Will my mana recover?" She looked up at me as I spoke, her ice cube like eyes unblinking as she regarded me and nodded once. "How quickly?"

"As quickly as it does." She shrugged with emphasis, then paused. "This is going to take time to get used to."

"Is there a way to make you more comfortable?"

"Get stronger and grow the ability to summon me." She turned and wobbled over to a frozen monster. "This creature was killed nearly four seconds ago. Your ice is not cold enough to kill instantly."

"So I can get better than I am?" Her whole body leaned forward as if in a nod. *Galaxy, when she took my spells, did I get to keep the points from them?*

No. She stole those from you and your spells. That was enough to make me groan outwardly. That had been a *lot* of points. *She did, however, give you Golem Summoning and opened up the entirety of a new ice spell tree for you.*

Find the one that improves… whatever summons her and put the last point that I have available into it?

I received a notification and smiled.

Improved Golem Summons – As your power grows, so do the abilities and shapes of the golems that you can create and summon to you. Mana cost varies.

It was one of the ones that only had a max of six points that had to be in it for it to be completed and fully evolve into something else, if the branch it was on was to be believed.

"Status."

Level 16
Stats
Brawn: 20
Dexterity: 16
Physique: 19
Mana: 35
Charisma: 30
Points to spend: 0
Spell Points to spend: 0
Spells Known
Physical Buff 1/6
Bolt Havoc 1/8
Mana Blade*
Embodiment*

Void Frost*
Arcane Infusion
Golem Summoning (Ice)*
Passive Abilities
Improved Golem Summoning 1/6

I nodded once, glancing at Hollow, who grew larger as I watched her. She was a little more well put together and defined than when she first came to be.

Her head dropped down to look at herself. "That is much better." She looked up at me. "You have fulfilled all the requests I have had of you, and as such, I will impart the gift that I meant to give you to begin with."

She hobbled over to me, pointing at my right hip. "Please, pull down your... cloth thing."

What?! Galaxy was out of my shadow so fast that I was surprised she didn't make me spin. "What are you asking?"

"His marking of power." The golem Hollow just stared at her, emotionless as her voice was cold. "It is different and varies from place to place, but I can feel it." She turned her icy head and eyes toward my hip just below the line of my waistband. "I feel it here."

"So that wasn't all of the blessing you wanted to give me, just some of it?" She nodded and I looked at Galaxy. "Then that's fine."

She's not interested in a scrap, Galaxy, just giving me more power. We need this.

She glared at me, her arms crossed. "I'm going to eat."

I sighed, knowing this would likely come back to bite me in the ass.

You bet your sweet ass it will!

Galaxy's voice echoing through my head made me smile as I glanced over at her and shot back, *Promise?*

She turned her head back toward me and blushed. "I said it." She turned back to her meal and left me to be prodded by Hollow. "Oh! Sorry."

I pulled the edge of the cloth away from myself and saw

that a small snowflake was settled there against my skin. It was only slightly darker than the flesh around it.

Hollow reached out and touched it with her small, cool hand. Ice-cold waves of power seared my flesh and brought me to my knees. This was so much worse, but better than before at the same time. It was confusing.

Blizzard's Blessing – The Primordial Frost Elemental has imposed her blessing upon you, giving you access to more frost and ice elemental magic than previously available. Your bond with this element has given you a great deal more than intended thanks to the Vornal Blood in your veins.

The voice that I had begun to associate with the Vorna within me echoed into my mind.

The predatory blood within you roils at being given power so freely, please choose between the two following options available to you.

Frozen Form / Ice Breath

I raised an eyebrow at that and checked both of them. Frozen Form made my body more adaptable to the cold, and Ice Breath made it so I could breathe ice like a dragon. If I could freeze a room like this without trying my hardest, Frozen Form would be better, right?

I chose that one and dismissed the other off hand, the burning on my hip gaining my attention again. I stood and pulled my jeans away from my hip only to see the snowflake growing and being ringed in crimson that dripped like blood. The blue hue of the snowflake became purple near the middle, the crimson at the bottom.

Frozen Form will now overtake you. Stand by...

Goosebumps ran over my skin and suddenly I was warmer than I had been before. There was a lot of warmth. That flooded away from me instantly after that, and I was just the perfect temperature. Looking down at myself, I appeared normal but Galaxy gasped and drew my attention back to her.

"What the hell happened to you?" She flitted across the

room, not caring that there were prying eyes on us both to look me over.

"I accepted a bit more power thanks to my blood." I looked over to see that the golem Hollow stared at me and I could almost feel her ire rising. "I didn't know."

"I am angry, but I see that you had no choice." I blinked at that and she turned to walk away. "I can tell because it was at the same time I was blessing you, and I have heard of those kinds of creatures before. One of them ate my sibling, the Water Primordial Elemental."

Galaxy and I both bore down on her, to the point that she couldn't continue to walk away from us, Galaxy questioning her. "What creature was this? When? Where was it? Do you know where it is?"

"Why are you interested?"

She went to move around us, but I stopped her with a hand, her cool body comfortable in my grasp. "Those creatures have some of her power and are something we need to hunt down in order to get it back."

"So does that mean I can kill you and take mine back?" The golem didn't even glance my way as she spoke, just matter of fact words and a spear of pure ice growing from her left arm. "I can try that. I don't know how killing you will work if I want to stay here, but I can always find another useful summoner."

I grimaced and flung my hand out, to the right, not forgetting that we were being watched. Ice skipped the twenty feet and a jagged spear of it burst from the ground at the lizard person's feet, slipping into its scaled ribs with a sickening sound. "I don't think that would work the way that you hope, but if we can go and get their power back for the elemental, or save them from the creature, we would."

Hollow stared at me, the spear in her deformed hand forgotten. "You speak truly?"

I nodded. "Our plate's a bit full at the moment, but when we can get there, I don't see why we couldn't."

There's the whole supernatural world going tits up about any time now to worry about too. Galaxy peered at me over Hollow's head but I just mentally shrugged. *I know that it may not all boil over right* now, *but it will need dealing with.*

I know, but if we can reclaim more of your power, we can still get that taken care of too.

"Very well. Then I will do what I can to assist you in clearing this plate you speak of." She turned and waddled off in the other direction, this time toward a shivering and cowering pair of elves that could have been pale enough to blend in with the ice if it hadn't been for their clothes.

They lifted their hands and there was a writhing spark that burst from the two of them together that ignited and sent a wave of fire swirling toward the golem.

I grimaced and stomped my foot, sending Void Frost under the golem and forced it into the air to form a barrier as the flames raged. The golem touched the ice and reinforced it, my steps crunching on the ice at my feet loudly berating my ears over the *whoosh* of the flames eating at the barrier. Steam rose into the room and Hollow was suddenly gone.

I blinked and there was screaming from the other side of the barrier. I dropped it and found Hollow stabbing both elves through the thigh, blood soaking into her frozen weapons. Their feet were solidly encased in ice, preventing them from moving anywhere.

"They will die soon." Hollow ripped the spikes from their victims, splattering the ground with blood, and waddled toward us. "I will find the others if Ms. Galaxy would like to continue eating?" The blood flowed down their legs and froze in rivulets, similar to when wax ran down the side of a candle and solidified again.

Galaxy blinked at the retreating figure before staring at me. "Does that make me sound fat?"

I frowned and shook my head, scoffing. "Nooo!" I put my hand on her hip. "You're thick—with two Cs. And beautiful as hell."

Galaxy tilted her chin up. "Thank you." Her hips swayed a

little more than normal as she walked over to her newest meals, both of whom were in fact passing out from blood loss.

I searched for other threats but with there being a second story to the building, it didn't seem that there was anyone down here.

With that, I checked for a set of stairs and found some on the far side, near the entrance to the warehouse.

Up the stairs I clomped, trying to figure out where the other sympathizers could be hiding and found four of them glaring at me with gleaming teeth and hatred in their eyes. All of them looked like some kind of monkey or ape.

Their bodies were lean—sickly looking, even—while their limbs were large and muscular as they squatted, huddled together against the cold in the room.

I swore under my breath and summoned the Fae Frame from my ring, firing at the first one to jump from the rafter they sat on to try to attack me. The shot hit him in the shoulder, and his massive right forearm slammed into my jaw.

My bell thoroughly rung, it was more annoying trying to get another shot than anything else, the others joining their larger compatriot. I glanced at my mana, saw that I still had some, and growled, "Fuck *off!*"

I cast Embodiment of Lightning and appeared behind the other three with my random casting of Bolt striking the one nearest me and sending him plummeting to the ground, shattering some of the spikes below him and puddling the ground with blood which quickly froze. The other two attacked, trying to pin me down as the third one jumped back over toward me.

It missed me on the leap, slamming into the smallest of the remaining creatures, but they were agile enough to catch the rafter that I stood on, and swing themselves back up and over to re-engage with me. With a snarl, I stomped my foot on the rafter and shattered the wood, splinters shooting downward as we fell from it, one of them grabbing me as we did.

I didn't even have the time to roll my eyes before I had to

worry about the ground coming as we twisted through the air, but I did have one secret weapon. "Mako!"

The monstrous drake screeched from my body and I landed on him awkwardly as the creature clutched one of my legs. Mako's tail slapped the ice below him out of the way, making a place for us to land. The creatures I fought cared less about the growing chill around us than he did, his venomous breath searing the one that collapsed onto the ice just to his right.

The noxious fumes burned at my nose, so I just fought to hold my breath as I spun and shot once more into the creature attacking me. Three more shots rang out through the air and rounds caught it twice in the chest and once in the shoulder, forcing it to let go of my leg. I didn't think it was dead, but it was at least off of me for now.

I urged Mako to move and get out of the remnants of his breath weapon and he whipped around, his massive head lurching forward to snap up the morsel in front of him now. The shot creature shrieked as Mako's teeth tore it to shreds and tossed blood left and right as his tail wreaked havoc behind us.

Whistling made my hair stand on end as creeping cold sliced through the air and four pieces of ice shattered against the creature that was left. I glanced back, Hollow's voice sounding like footsteps crunching in the snow. "I'll be the one to kill you if it's anyone, thank you."

I rolled my eyes, my body bucking a bit as Mako dropped his head down to try and bite at one of the creatures' corpses. I let him have it; he'd earned this one and while I did feed him, there was only so much nutritional value to burgers and fries.

He likes the occasional sweet treat too, like a candy bar. Galaxy snickered at me as I stared at her in horror. *He's a drake, not a Great Dane. Chocolate won't affect him—shit!*

Watching him and how he glared at the cold, ruffling his scales, I figured I would have to be a little more careful with the cold and him in the future. Maybe have him fight a little further from me? We would have to cross that bridge later. For now, it was nice just to see him getting along with Galaxy.

She was up onto his back in a heartbeat. "Cassia and Arden are freaking out." She frowned and focused for a second. "Kimiko is missing and there's a report that the Night Parade is currently out hunting for a way to get to Tsuki."

"So we really don't have time to fuck around and continue trying out this new power." It wasn't a question. Honestly, if something like this didn't happen, it wouldn't be my damn life. I glanced around until I found the golem. "Hollow, I need to dismiss you if you don't want to meet him, since we're about to have to see him about sending us back to Earth."

She stared up at me. "Very well." She dissolved into the ice that crowded her feet and was gone.

"Make the call, Marcus. The ladies are freaking out because they can't find her or her people anywhere."

CHAPTER TWENTY-FIVE

My phone didn't work in Grestal, since this seemed to be where we were. Annoyingly enough, both of us forgot that, however talking to Zeke's people proved much easier to work through.

The man outside stared at us, scuffed up as I was and chewing on a granola bar from my inventory. "Can you just hurry up and call Zeke? There's a bit of an emergency going on and I kinda gotta go."

"He's in the middle of something and is working on getting a portal made for you, so stop your incessant whining, human."

That made me raise a brow at him and he just crossed his arms as he stared at me some more. He then had the gall to ask, "Did you make a mess inside?"

I nodded, grinning to spite him. "Just for you, big guy." He looked like he was about to say something, but I just kept grinning at him as the power kept building to my right.

"There's your portal, human. Get the fuck out."

I shook my head. "Must suck to kiss your mother with that mouth." I lifted my left hand and flipped him the bird as I walked through the exit from the Grestallan realm and then onto Earth into nearly the same spot that I had been training at beforehand.

The other members of the Wild Hunt stood huddled together with the kitsune and the other trainers, talking to one another softly. The only one aware of our arrival being a rather timid and scared-looking Amabala. I allowed my voice to carry a bit as we walked toward them. "What led up to her going missing?"

At the sound of my voice, all of them turned and their auras shifted into view faster than they ever had before, which was strange to me, but I was also stronger now with the additional Mantle's power.

"What the hell happened to you?" Cassia whispered as she bolted toward me, catching me into a hug and lifting me. "You've been gone for two days."

"Did someone call and say they needed a nega-Backstreet Boy?" Merlin's laughter caught me by surprise and made me frown at him until he waved at his head and said, "Your hair is silver but for the tips where it's brown. Even your eyebrows are."

"And with the Huntsman's eyes still out, it's hard to really not think it intimidating," Amabala whispered, then cleared her throat and added, in a forced cheerful tone, "Maybe we could get you some sunglasses to match Cassia's?"

I smirked. "Maybe. Now, fill me in."

"Kimiko and her people were supposed to do a changeover after a twenty-four hour shift, but some of them weren't responding by phone, so she went down the mountain to look for them." Merlin spoke quickly, pulling out a tablet to show me a map of the area where there were red Xs on the positions that the Phantomu went missing. "We've been waiting for twelve hours for her to come back, but there's no answer."

"Okay, and the Parade is on the move?" They nodded. "How?"

"They've been spotted in towns in the area and some of the stronger flyers have been soaring over the mountain at night looking for this temple." I frowned at that explanation, but Raisha just added quickly, "There's a barrier that stops them from being able to see in, but that doesn't mean that they can't get into it if they fly close enough."

"I doubt that they realize that, but at this point the storm will be here tonight, and they've been flying lower ever since the cloud cover started to get thicker." I grimaced at that, looking up at the darkened clouds that gathered overhead, but instead Arden pressed on, speaking softly. "Tsuki is preparing to ascend as we speak, and we're only a little ways from the altar where she will shed her mortal form. What do you think we should do?"

Considering everything that was going on, there was little reason to think we would get out of this without a fight, so I just took a deep breath and sighed.

Looking around at all of those gathered with us, maybe fifteen people total, there was no way we would be able to stand up to the full might of the one hundred strongest members of the yokai race, at least those stuck in Japan and active members of the Night Parade. There was really only one thing that we could feasibly do.

"We put up one hell of a fight." I stared at the others and then turned to Amabala. "You're going to be crucial for this part."

The sushi that we ate was honestly to die for, freshly made and absolutely delicious with the sauce that Raisha gave us for it. The food went a long way toward helping me recover my spent mana, and Galaxy having eaten as much as she did was a great boon too.

"You think this is going to work?" Cassia mumbled with sushi in her chopsticks.

"I can only hope it does," Arden whispered as she took a

bite and swallowed it. "God, I need to get her to teach me how to make this."

"Fresh ingredients, Arden." Raisha grinned as we looked up from our plates to see her standing over us. "And hundreds of years of practice."

"So what's the duty of a kitsune where Tsuki is concerned? Aren't you a part of the yokai?"

She smiled at my question and shook her head. "We can be considered that, yes." She scratched her shoulder and sniffed before shrugging. "We as kitsune find ourselves in harmony more with the kami and their will than with the other yokai. We serve Inari and, as such, assist the gods in their works. The luck dragon protects all of Japan, and then the world after that. Their sacrifices cannot be otherwise dishonored, and had we known that Tsuki-sama wished to ascend, we would have been with her from the beginning rather than coming late as we did."

Cassia growled low in her chest. "I told you it was for the luck dragon from the beginning."

Raisha sniffed and lifted her chin. "And I had a nogitsune to kill, so we added a little more priority to that."

"It was your uncle, after all," Arden added offhand and that made Cass pause. Arden looked shocked as she realized what she had said. "Shit, I am so, so sorry."

Cass shook her head. "It's okay. I didn't know before, and it kind of ate at me, but that's just what I have to deal with now."

"Oni blood outweighs all, Cassia." Raisha laid a gentle hand on her friend's shoulder. "The man may have been nogitsune, but you are not. And he is not your father, no matter what he says."

Cassia closed her eyes and tried to smile, patting the other woman's hand affectionately. "Thank you, Raisha. You're a good friend, for a furry."

Raisha gasped and started to try to tickle the larger woman, but Cassia was up and manhandling her in an instant. It was hilarious to watch as the rest of us ate.

We continued to wait for another hour or so before Tsuki,

led by four monks with traditional clothing and cleanly shaven heads, walked her from the main house to the raised altar on the top of the mountain, maybe four hundred yards from where we had been training.

She wore a simple silk robe over her shoulders that fell to just over her ankles, her hair piled on top of her head and a jade necklace over her heart that swayed as she walked to the altar.

"This is where she will take care of her final rites, and pray for the former luck dragon to come and take his place in the cycle once more," Raisha explained to us.

"How long does that typically take?" I asked as bird calls rang through the air, signaling the arrival of our unwanted guests.

"I can hope that it will not take long, considering what is coming." Wind whipped at us, the signal of the squall to come all too real as we turned toward the direction of the bird calls.

Are they ready? My simple question made Galaxy fidget nervously within me.

Her response was uncertain at best. *They will be, but many of them are not certain of their abilities.*

———

We stared at the mass of bodies milling about before us as the nogitsune and his entourage shoved their way to the front, having finally found where we were.

All they have to do is trust in me, and we can get through this.

I stepped forward, watching as the Night Parade's cream rose to the fore of the crowd, the rest of the crop just standing there, their purple auras letting me know that the vast majority of them were being used. All of them wore the traditional suits that we had seen, like they were gangsters of some sort.

"Surrender!" Felix called to us, flanked by Saizo and Chiasa. The large oni enforcer reached back and shoved two riders out of the way so that Kimiko could be shoved forward.

Cassia gasped then roared, "How dare you hurt her!"

Felix's eyebrows tilted up, shocked. "Hurt her?" He made a show of stepping around Chiasa to look the younger oni over. "She's untouched! Are you not, Kimiko?"

When she said nothing, hanging her head, her mother snarled something in Japanese so quiet I couldn't hear it but Kimiko did. Her voice rose. "I am untouched."

"See?" Felix spread his arms. "Her people aren't, though. And when I made her watch a few of them die, she agreed to turn you over."

Cassia frowned, then shook her head. "No. She didn't." She looked sick as she said, "Kimiko wouldn't have stopped for anything if she thought her people were in danger. They would have fought to the death."

"What are you saying?" Arden whispered back softly.

"That she knows that they're lying," Raisha grumbled. "Why a nogitsune would try to make someone look better, or like a victim is beyond my knowledge and experience."

Set up. I growled in my mind, Galaxy staring out of me curiously. *But why? The only reason I can think of is because they might think we would overlook her or try to protect her.*

"And in that moment, she can strike at Tsuki." Merlin sounded horrified as he stared at them.

Galaxy's voice rang out through my head, and made me grimace deeper, since I knew the others could hear her too. *Play into it.*

I raised an eyebrow and she spoke on. *Make them think she's our goal, or at least have Cassia go for her as Arden takes care of the riders, and then when she's out of the way, we strike all of them at once.*

I muttered softly, "Very well." I glanced over at Cassia as the wind began to pick up around us, small droplets peppering our bodies. "Get your sister."

"And mother?" She looked genuinely concerned, likely for the rest of us.

"We can only hope to contain her long enough for the right things to happen." Amabala cleared her throat and nodded toward the other side of the clearing where the Night Parade watched us. "If you want, I think I have an idea that we could use as a hail Harry."

"Hail *Mary*," Merlin corrected gently, patting her hand with his. "Pass it on to Galaxy and she and Marcus can approve of it at their leisure."

I snorted at that, knowing damn well leisure was off the menu for a bit. "You should leave!" My voice echoed through the distance and Felix frowned. "We won't let you get to her. The ascension goes as planned."

He tilted his head at me and grinned, motioning toward the yokai at his back. "There are so many more of us than all of you, and we have a little surprise on our side."

Several larger figures tromped into the area, massive oni that stood more than twelve or thirteen feet tall that could have very well been fucking mountains of their own.

"Yes, see, these ones were a little bit easier to control with this new drug gushing through them." He smiled wider, his face becoming steadily more wicked and beastly as he spoke. "Might have killed the original supplier, but there's always someone smarter out there, mortal."

The running train of fucks through my head and Galaxy's only stopped when he was fully transformed. He had three tails of midnight and crimson trailing behind him, his well-tailored suit ripping as his real figure came to the fore. He stared glee-fully at us with glowing amber eyes as he snarled, "Gotta love the good doctor's improvements!"

Though I wasn't sure what the hell he was talking about, it did beg the question as to what they were capable of.

Our group facing the horde that was the Night Parade consisted of myself, Arden, Cassia, Merlin, Amabala, Mako, Raisha and her four friends, along with two warrior monks who actually stood with us. Rounding out our group were the four protecting Tsuki. We were outmatched and outgunned if this was all he had up his sleeve.

You forgot about me, Marcus. Galaxy's gentle chiding was full of apprehension.

Are we sure we're ready for this? I asked, but the only answer was the obvious rhetorical silence.

I shrugged, shaking my head and adjusting my neck just a bit before spitting. "Fuck it." I stared hard at Felix and his gang and bellowed, "Tsuki! You just focus on your ascension—we got you."

"Are we ready, Marcus?" Merlin asked excitedly.

I smirked before bolting forward in a sprint straight at the Night Parade, then shouted, "Commence the Hunt!"

The armor washed over us all, but it was the momentary look of fear and trepidation in the eyes of the joyriders, even in Kimiko's and Chiasa's gazes as our own secret weapon came flying out of the tree line off to our left up the mountains toward their line of fighters.

Six snarling, shadow-covered Hounds the size of horses with their own Hunt handlers chasing after them bounded into combat, weapons soaring through the competition. It was our first time really going into a fight together, but with Arden and Cassia calling the shots and Merlin controlling the Hounds, it was easier to coordinate now.

I slammed into a few joyriders, my momentum carrying me forward, and mentally urged Mako out of my body and into the crowd where he would cause the most mayhem. Arrows tinged in an aura I barely recognized streaked into joyriders around me and I glanced back to find Raisha and her fellow kitsune warriors in their furred forms firing furiously into the fray.

Heat radiated from the center of the fight and above us as Arden lifted both her hands into the air. A massive ball of fire roiled over her head, sizzling with the rain hitting it and, for just a heartbeat, I could have sworn I saw a gigantic dragon-like cloud structure in the sky that looked like it could have been staring down at all of this as lightning crackled through the clouds around it.

The building intensity of the fireball prompted me to get

the hell out of Dodge, using Galaxy to tell the others to get the out of the area as Arden launched the flaming bomb down into the crowd of riders.

Dozens of them went down, their auras fading as their hosts disintegrated before they could flee. One of the warrior monks had been caught in the crossfire as well, which sucked, but there was no time to dwell on it as two of the larger oni bore down on me together.

Their eyes were sunken in, and they looked just as confused as they did enraged, but their intent was to crush me, so I had to move. Ducking under the first that tried to grab me, I called to the others through Galaxy. *Stay away from me, and if you can corral some of them my way safely, do it.*

Lighting seared the sky as my Void Frost leaked into the area around me as I focused on the oni. *"Freeze!"*

The oni about to pummel me with his gigantic fist roared and reared back with ice climbing up his legs and torso so fast that it cracked and splintered under the shifting weight of the oni's upper half. It was his friend trying to shove through him that fully parted my initial attacker from his lower half.

I twisted and slid to the right, casting Mana Blade and slid it into the nearest enemy, one of the joyriders falling as a wave of energy made the hair on the back of my neck stand on end.

Galaxy, how many of these creatures do you think you could drain?

She considered it. *Safely? Not many, unless they were either injured or unconscious. Why?*

I turned to where the energy gathered, seeing Saizo, Chiasa, and Felix fighting their way through Raisha and some of my Hunt while Cassia and Arden 'tried' to get to Kimiko as she was dragged behind them by her mother. *Them. We need to cut their numbers basically in half if we want to stand a chance of keeping them from Tsuki.*

I think it's time to put Amabala's plan into action. That or you spend a lot of mana to flash freeze a massive area.

Very well, let her know when it's time. She nodded and I took just a second to orient myself.

Focusing inward, it was easier to see what needed doing, so I inwardly issued the order for the newer members of the Hunt to primarily focus on the joyriders while two of the Hounds and their riders joined me as I sprinted toward them from behind.

Kimiko turned and saw me running toward her and gasped, making her mother turn toward the sound. *Is she even trying at this point?*

Chiasa whipped around, throwing her youngest toward the other two Parade members with her and took a stance in my path. She stomped her foot once and waved her arms in a wide circle as she prepared to take my assault head on, only to be attacked by the two Hounds that had flanked her.

They bit deeply enough that I could see her blood, but she barely registered them until one of the riders bore down on her with a lance made of shadows. She snapped the weapon away from her, breaking it in a fluid motion that reminded me of Kenshi's level of skills as she pulled the rider from his mount and dumped him onto the ground behind her. Then she twisted and flailed her arms out to try to rid herself of the four-legged fiends on her forearms.

There it was! *Now, Amabala!*

I cast Embodiment of Lightning as the cheetah-woman opened a portal right behind Chiasa. I kicked her as hard as I could while the momentum of my spell carried me forward. She didn't budge as much as I thought she would, but between me, the Hounds, and the discarded Hunt rider she had thrown behind her, we were able to shove her backward just enough to push her through it.

It was too soon to celebrate, though, as her red hand came back through. "Drop the portal!"

I cast Bolt at the portal and just as her head popped through, the spell hit her square in the nose and her face went back in. The hand was still there and I worried she would lose it, but one of the Hounds attacked, grabbing a knuckle in its mouth and savaging it. Chiasa's fingers flexed and gripped the

Hound by the muzzle, dragging it into the portal with her as it shut.

"No!" Felix and I both snarled in unison. As the portal was gone, we had a clear view of each other and there was no way that he wasn't going to attack me. I muttered to Galaxy, *Time to start eating as fast as you can. We'll need the mana if this is going to work.*

She fled my shadow as Felix made to rush me, his claws out and fingers clenched to strike at me. My arm arced, the dense mana of my spectral sword whirling toward him but he stepped aside and sneered as if he didn't think I was that capable. He whipped his arm out and a dark, flaming circlet shot toward me, splitting and growing larger as it sliced through the air.

Don't wanna let that touch me. I dodged it, ducking beneath it and someone else yelled something, prompting me to dodge again. Sure enough, whatever spell he had cast was tracking me.

Eat fast, Galaxy! She mentally nodded to me and I did my best to keep ahead of the circlet, circling back and sprinting toward the mass that was the still-standing and fighting joyriders.

A burning sensation seared at my neck and I kicked it up just a bit more as the spell threatened to catch up to me.

I grabbed onto one of the riders and twisted, falling with him above me in front of the spell. The circlet slid over his head and neck, singeing my thumb and heating my face as a black ring was left behind, his whole body going slack. Even the aura around him that was the spirit was bound.

"Fuck!" I tossed him to the side as Galaxy surged through the crowd, nibbling here and there. We couldn't fuck around anymore, and that thing wasn't going to get to me and catch me either, because if it did, I was pretty sure I was going to be bound. My magic too.

Amabala stood on the edge of the altar platform, striking at the yokai joyriders that came close to her. Merlin was doing the same, but with magic and his sword flashing. As impressive as they both were, there just wasn't a way to keep up with the

Parade, even with all of our new members. We just didn't have the numbers to really match them man for man.

One of Raisha's warrior friends, her sword covered in a vibrant light, slashed at Felix from behind as he was distracted and managed to hit him. He roared, swinging behind himself and slitting her throat with a lucky strike that made Raisha and her friends scream in fury.

Saizo had Cassia and Arden pretty well matched with the occasional purple blast of energy from a random joyrider trying to assist him, but they couldn't get too much closer thanks to the two of them keeping him at bay. I wished she would just put her honor aside and turn his punk ass to stone, but she wouldn't and Arden was too close.

I pulled myself together and grit my teeth. Raisha and her friends were fighting well enough against the nogitsune for the moment, so I turned and tried to figure out where I was needed the most. Then decided to just say fuck it and get a little payback, seeing as though the Hounds looked to have pulled the last towering oni from their feet and savaged it viciously.

Muttering, "Mako," I reached out to my left and stuck out my hand as I flexed my will. The now-full and happy drake sprang to me, my grip settling on the reins as his momentum pulled me up and onto the saddle. I again flexed my will, this time drawing upon Void Frost to grow a massive icicle long and thick enough to act as a lance and rode for all I was worth as I took aim.

He must have heard Mako's thunderous approach as we bore down on him, because Saizo turned and threw his hands up, the rain water shifting and beginning to whirl like it would make a shield.

I was only about twenty feet from him now. The distance was made up of Mako's nose from his shield and him a couple feet behind that. With me inserting myself to the fight, there was a lot more leeway and now both Arden and Cassia had the opportunity to help me and themselves.

Cassia took her massive mace and slapped the ground,

spikes launching from the ground and into his feet, Saizo's eyes widening as he yelled in pain, lightning streaking through the air.

The storm was upon us fully now, and though I shoved the solidified lance through the water shield with more ease than I expected, it only sliced his cheek open, the kappa having the mental prowess to dodge.

I growled in frustration as the bleeding yokai slumped to the ground while I held out my hand, the thicker water droplets turning into hail as I cast Void Frost. The ice shattered against Saizo like thousands of tiny spikes, but it was Arden's now-frozen whip that cut his head off as it wrapped around his throat.

Two down! Galaxy bellowed excitedly as the wind carried the thunder around us. It boomed and rolled so violently it could have been a fucking guttural roar for all I knew.

Glancing up at it, I knew that it *had* been a roar. The dragon was no longer just a bunch of clouds that could have been the thing—it was the actual thing. And it looked like it was judging with a harshly glaring gaze on all of us as the long, flowing whiskers on the side of its great nostrils shook with terrible rage as it roared once more.

Felix killed yet another kitsune warrior, using his black wispy flames that wrapped around their necks and made them fall to the ground unmoving, as if they were just so much meat.

He stared up at the dragon in the sky. "Your cycle will not end soon enough to keep us in this wretched place once I kill her, old friend!" He pointed to Tsuki, his finger glowing amber and black. "She will be the final stepping stone to our race's ascension from the shadows—humanity will fear us finally as they were always meant to."

The dragon watched as Tsuki lifted her arms and continued to pray on as she was meant to.

We need to end him, or his people—our riders can't keep this up as long as we can. You have grown far beyond where you started compared to everyone else. Galaxy's urging spurred me on as she leapt from my shadow to devour Saizo.

Once she was done with him, I sighed. The returns on mana had been pitiful, all considered. I wasn't sure if the joyriders' souls dissipated or not, but there was so little magic from them that there was no mana to gain. And Saizo had only given me back enough to cast Embodiment once more. I hadn't used a *ton* of mana so far or anything, but it wasn't going to give me a lot to go on so far as options in fighting a crazed nogitsune. Not at just about *190/350* after all the ice that I had affected, distance taken into account and all.

Cassia wants to try to attack him on her own, to see if she can whittle him down.

I shook my head. "We can move together, but we really need to focus on thinning their ranks and keeping the joyriders busy. Their potshots aren't getting any better."

Cassia clearly wasn't happy about that, but she was a team player for sure and as she lifted her mace, the flashing lightning gave me an idea.

Galaxy, how much of your Dominion would it take to affect nature?

She thought about it for a heartbeat then responded, *Enough that we would be vulnerable if a Vorna were to attack us, but I could try to save some if we had the right circumstances for it.* She paused, reading my mind. *That's devious. I love it.*

I nodded. *Tell Cassia to get rid of Kimiko because I can guarantee that she will interfere with this if she's not actually a victim.*

Cassia took her full oni form and disappeared from sight, grabbing her sister around the waist and springing away with her and from the fighting. Arden was currently battling additional nogitsune and casting way too much fire.

Felix was fast, for certain, and it took everything I had not to spring after him when he closed in on the altar and the people there, but the warrior monks weren't fucking around and cast a protective ward with the talismans on their staffs.

We need to get some cool shit like that, I muttered to myself mentally before I hopped off Mako. "Go create some havoc, buddy."

His scaled lips lifted and showed off the scraps of cloth and flesh in his gums before bounding off and leaving me alone.

The object of this, if it worked, was going to be to limit his movement.

I took a deep breath and slowed my heartbeat as much as I could before casting Void Frost and freezing the ground in front of me so that it was solid ice. Felix didn't notice and took a step. He skittered along the ground as Cassia came back and slammed her fist into the side of his head before bounding away again.

Arden came in and used the rainwater much like she had earlier and splashed him where he stood, the proximity of the liquid to my ice freezing it along his skin and fur.

His eyes widened as he focused on me, his teeth bared in hatred. "I knew I should have just murdered you in that filthy bar!"

I shrugged. "A lot of people probably feel that way."

He threw his head back and roared, enraged. Crackling energy raged down his arms into his hands as he clenched his fingers into fists and then flung them outward despite the coating of ice on him.

Figures grew from the ground at his feet and then came crawling out of the ice and broken dirt. They were foxes, misshapen and rotting, that moved jerkily and settled into a position to run.

Even with the rain pounding the icy ground, the scent of rotten flesh and moldy earth were pungent. "What the fuck are those?"

"Don't let them touch you!" Cassia called, her massive mace in her grip as she glared at the man and his new guardians. "They're his rotten past lives. When the nogitsune die, they grow a new body so that they can use their old bodies as minions."

Felix grinned, adding, "And if they touch you, you get all my past poor luck, plus interest." He stood a little straighter, calling to Cassia, "Join me, daughter. If you stand down and stop fighting, we can forget all this. Travel the world and become what our people were always meant to be—emperors!"

Tell Cassia to do it now, we can't afford for this to happen. Galaxy nodded and did so. *Arden and Merlin are ready to keep him distracted, but you'll have to do it quickly.*

Cassia scowled. "If I fight with you, what will I get?"

The fox grinned widely. *"Everything!"*

She stepped over to the ice on the ground, her footsteps crunching but also melting the ice beneath her feet. Her form shifted from her leaner and more agile form to that of a monstrous yang form, her Huntsman's armor falling away from her as she glared past him toward me.

"Cassia, don't do this!" I called loudly. This hadn't been what we had talked about doing while we were resting. She was going off script here.

"Will you keep my friends alive?" She spoke with uncertainty and tilted her head toward the rest of us.

"You can have pets, certainly." Felix tried to sound like the accommodating and doting father that he'd never been before. "Some of them need to be taught to fear the hand that feeds, but we can do that together. And your sister as well."

"Fine." She was right next to him and his grin, victorious and infuriating, made my skin crawl as he touched her lower back like a proud father showing off his baby. "All of you stand down."

"Get away from him, Cass!" Arden spat, her hands roiling with flames that matched her hair. "I'll burn him for you."

"No, Arden." Cassia pointed down to the kitsune laying on the ground just a few yards away. "It's time to recognize that this fight is pointless."

She looked up at me and there was something in the way her glasses shook on her face as she smiled, softly. "This whole trip was a massive bust. I just wanted to read some new manga and cosplay, but someone ruined that and I'm mad."

Felix's grin faltered for just a heartbeat. "You can have your own mangaka, if you like." He rubbed her back and offered a hand to her. "And a convention? Please, you'll have all the attention of our subjects that you could ever dream of."

"What about tapioca?" I recognized the safe word that Connell had used, making me pause. Felix was about to open his mouth, confused, but it was too late, her mace slammed into the ground and spikes ran up and around him, trapping him and his undead minions inside. "Now, Marcus!"

Galaxy stepped from my shadow in her elven form and held out her hands. "Don't move!"

At the same time I activated my stolen ability, Fox's Cunning, and added as much ice around him to bury him inside as I could. The mound of ice was thicker than an SUV on every side and lifted just above his head.

His body shook, but didn't move as we worked, his snarls and cries of, "No! You don't know who you're dealing with! I'll kill you all!"

The dramatic threats just made me smile as Cassia stuck the head of her mace into the top of my ice prison. "Merlin, Marcus—light him up!"

He and I did just that. I cast Bolt Havoc and the weapon conducted it into the spikes around him, causing the creature to scream. Merlin held up a hand and bellowed, long and deep, his hands grabbing the sky and *yanking* lighting down from the heavens into the weapon, further frying Felix in his fetters with his festering, fiendish fellows.

Amabala whooped and clapped. "That was amazing!"

There was no more motion or movement inside the trap, and we assumed we had him dead to rights. There was no way he could have survived that, his still body in the now-melting ice that had been pretty much nuked.

As his body fell onto the broken and gravelly dirt, it shifted and Felix was no longer there—it was Kimiko.

"What?" Cassia rushed to her, healing her as much as she could with shakes, all the while muttering her name.

"What bad luck!" Kimiko's voice rang out over the rain and din of the thunder with a whipping wind. She stood there next to Tsuki as the woman continued to pray to whomever, her words lost to me from this distance.

She reached down and lifted her up into the air, the dragon above roaring loudly as the wind continued to whirl around us.

The whole motion of it broke through whatever magic he had been using. "Perfect possession is such a great technique, but being able to switch souls and then morph the body?" He laughed and shook his head. "It takes a lot out of you, but tricking a trickster is hardly something that someone so new to the world of foxes and festering rage can handle. You'll learn, little one. Someday."

He turned his head to look down at Tsuki. "Always have a contingency plan, children."

Amabala appeared beside him and slashed, his shoulder bleeding with that one stroke of her blade, but he lifted his arm and swatted her aside as if she were a gnat.

Marcus, she's still praying, we can do something about this. I grimaced and remembered what Cassia said about guns in Japan. This had to be the circumstance that would be okay, right?

I pulled out my rifle and took aim down the sights, safety off, and squeezed the trigger. The retort of the rifle firing was enough to bring Felix's attention to me.

Cassia's cry of anguish and rage made me pause and look over at her out of the corner of my eye. She beat her chest and roared, the depth of her loss finally hitting me—we'd just killed her sister.

She bellowed into the air as she continued to beat her chest, "Raijin-sama!"

"Chiasa, no!" Felix snarled and turned to Tsuki as Arden attacked him. He didn't seem to care about the flames in the slightest, but he did lift a finger and hit her with a purple energy blast like the joyriders used.

The thunder boomed around us as the lightning looked to

have moved away at this point striking elsewhere. Thunder crashed again and a shimmering figure appeared, a massive, twelve foot tall man with drums fastened to his hips on each side of him and one carried in his left hand against his belly. He had a long, flowing scarf that wrapped around his shoulders and floated there, a large tambourine-like circle of drums floating behind him as well.

He looked like an oni himself, his skin red and his teeth coming out of his mouth on the sides, both from the top and bottom lip. His face was surreal, terrifying as he regarded the lot of us, the markings on his face pulsing with the beat of my heart, weirdly enough.

He continued to survey the scene. "Who calls my name amidst the storm of their turmoil?"

Cassia put her sister down gently and stood, her fury evident. "Me, Kami-sama."

"Speak, oni."

"I wish for the power to take my revenge against my own blood for the murder of my sister." I couldn't move, but at the same time, it didn't seem like any of us could. His Dominion flooded the mountaintop and touched everything. Was the storm making him more powerful?

It could be, Galaxy answered me, then paused and whispered, *There's no moving at all. Even the yokai, Felix, and the world within a mile are frozen. The normies won't notice it, but this is... power.*

He looked down at the corpse that lay on the ground. "You assisted in the killing blow."

"Yes." She clenched her fist hard enough that blood leaked from where her nails pierced the skin. "I was tricked by a fox."

The god considered this for a moment, then nodded. "They do that to you." He scratched his head, then his ear. "What will you sacrifice to me in return?"

Cassia clenched her teeth. "What will you take?"

"What is most important to you that you never knew you had?"

She considered it for a moment, then frowned. "Figuring out who I was, not knowing my father."

"You are wrong." He came over and pointed at her chest, then her stomach. "You are with child. And that child will belong to me."

My eyes widened and her eyes did too, as her hand fell to her stomach. "I cannot give you my child."

"I do not want to take the creature." Raijin stood, looking over at me. "It will be powerful, and I want to add my mark to that strength. Because these are such... uncertain times. Can you do this?"

Cassia looked to me, I blinked once and just told Galaxy to tell her, *If you have to. We will stand with you.*

"Yes." She lifted her chin. "I will raise my child to honor the Storm, to strike quickly like Lightning, and with the sound of Thunder in their cries."

"Very well." He reached out and touched her stomach, then touched the drum on his right hip once, the crashing sound of rumbling thunder in the distance shaking us, then the lightning danced against the clouds. "Strength of the Storms."

He beat both drums on his hips, then put his fist through the drum in his arm and pulled out something that he gave to Cassia, her eyes lighting up, then he nodded and was gone. Cassia's muscles bulged and she bounded toward the nogitsune whose fist had just plunged into Tsuki's stomach. The shockwave the blow released was enough to knock all of us to our knees.

"I *win*." He sneered and lifted his other arm, pointing at the dragon in the sky. "Enjoy your new lives, old friend. I will enjoy hunting you and your line into oblivion."

Tsuki's old hand lifted and grabbed the fox, a smile on her face as she muttered something that only he could hear. "No. No, you can't be serious!"

Cassia said to get Tsuki, as she's going to kill her father before she can get to him. Galaxy's interruption was enough to get me to move. *Move, Marcus!*

I grunted and clambered to my feet, growling as I sprinted headlong at the two figures. It was nowhere near fast enough to get to Tsuki before Cassia got to Felix. She hit him so hard that it tore the arm that held the smaller woman aloft off as she bit and clawed, throwing his evil ass against the altar and then back toward the majority of the joyriders still stunned from what they just witnessed.

I made it to Tsuki as she fell to the ground and landed, grabbing her hand. "Hey, it's going to be okay, we'll make sure you can ascend."

She just coughed and shook her head. "I am." She touched my forehead and I could hear the echoing words she had spoken to Felix. "You may have been more clever, fox, but your bad luck cannot exceed the luck of those who know how to prepare for the worst, and with the foresight to let go where they can. You *failed*."

The dragon in the sky was so close that I could have sworn I could feel his breath. Tsuki coughed. "I know, I know. I'm coming."

Her body faded into cherry blossoms and fluttered into the air, the dragon above us rearing back as a new one began to form, her figure a bit more shiny and robust than his. To look at him, he looked older compared to her. And now here she was, the baby.

The luck dragon's ascension had completed. The other dragon bowed his head and closed his eyes, falling out of the sky and turning into rain so that it could fall into the air. With one final deluge, the storm broke. The thunder and lightning were forgotten and receding as the clouds separated and the sun shone on the land.

Joyriding yokai screamed in agony as they burned, their hosts knocked out from the fighting and the host of the Wild Hunt cheered.

I looked around, finding Cassia still leaning over Felix, her fists pummeling him. His dying looked to be taking a little while as she was healing him and beating him to death slowly. Likely beating the lesson into his very soul.

I spotted Kimiko's katana and picked it up, limping over to bring it to her, all that sprinting having done a hell of a number on my body and with my stomach empty, my regeneration wasn't going to help me anytime soon.

"Here." I offered her the weapon and she ignored me. "Cass, the longer he's alive, the more of a threat he can become again. Kill him now, and then we can find a way to dishonor his memory."

She seethed silently for a moment, then took the offered weapon. She stared at it as tears for her sister flooded from her eyes before nodding to herself. She raised it and stabbed him in the gut, then in his right lung. Then she pierced his heart.

Though he was probably dead, she stabbed him several more times, his whole chest a mass of bloodied flesh with holes and lacerations.

She stood, her chest heaving as she lifted her head and palms to the sky. "It is done; my revenge is claimed, and I no longer deserve the strength I carry that is not mine. Raijin-sama, reclaim your might from me, so that the storm continues to wash the sins from the world."

A thundering boom echoed over us one last time and his voice carried in the echo. "It will pass on to your child."

She nodded and turned to stare at me, a look of profound loss warring with uncertainty and joy. "Marcus."

I just went to her. Whatever she was feeling, she'd just lost her father, her sister because of him, and then found out she was pregnant. The amount of shit on her plate was unimaginable.

Soon, Arden and the others joined us, the power of the Hunt waning as I muttered, "Hunt complete."

Merlin grabbed me and pulled me aside, a somber expression affixed to his face. "Congratulations, first of all, and uhm..." He rubbed his head and lowered his voice and head.

"The Hound who helped push Chiasa through the portal to the desert outside Cairo was Keith. He…"

I closed my eyes and just let the news wash over me. Keith had died trying to make sure that I didn't get someone else killed, or kill her and take Cassia's mother away.

"Fuck," I mumbled and rubbed my forehead as doubt and desolation raged through me.

"Yeah." Merlin huffed, putting a hand on my shoulder. "I didn't want to have to go get him either, but he's pretty insistent on coming back home now that he's managed to lose his irritable shadow."

I blinked twice, then lifted my chin to stare at him. "He's alive?"

Merlin raised both his eyebrows at me and said, "Well, yeah. That was the point of letting you know who it was that went through the portal so we could go and get him." He shrugged, a contrite but mischievous smile on his face. "Or let him sweat it out in the heat and humidity for all the pranks and bad jokes he likes to play on us."

I grabbed Merlin by the back of the head and pulled him into a hug, laughter helping cut through the morose dread running through my veins. "Thanks, little brother."

"Any time, man."

CHAPTER TWENTY-SIX

"Can't believe it's been three days already since then," Cassia muttered to me as she stared at her sister's photo in the main area of the temple that Tsuki had been using as a place to ascend.

Incense burned around us, pungent and stinging, as the remaining monks said their prayers and bowed their heads. The Wild Hunt had stayed by Cassia's side as she grieved and mourned, some of them going out to try to find gifts and things to celebrate her sister as offerings, others bringing back things they thought Cass might like.

One of the younger security guards brought her Pocky, and Cassia gave her a kiss on the cheek in thanks. When she walked away, the oni woman just stared blankly at the box. "Kimiko loved these."

My heart broke for her; it was so hard to know that we had been responsible for her death, but how were we to know? Felix, the sonofabitch he was, made it impossible for us to know.

Cassia clenched the hand that didn't hold the Pocky. "I need to get stronger, so nothing like this ever happens again, and so that if the Night Parade ever rises again, they can be crushed swiftly."

I nodded. "And so our baby has a strong mother to guide them."

Cassia blinked and glanced down at her stomach, her fist unclenching so that she could hold it softly. "Yes. I will not be like my mother, and they will be the strongest."

"Yes, they will," I assured her. I found myself wondering what it would be like for Connell to see this child. Would he like them? Would he care? Would they be friends?

"Has Galaxy come back yet?" she asked absently.

Our partner had taken some time to herself for her own reasons, vowing she wasn't upset about the child, just that she needed space to look within herself for a time.

"No." I frowned, picking up voices outside. I turned and stalked out, about to yell at them for causing a ruckus as Cassia paid her respects. When I saw who it was, all I could do was growl low in my throat and take a fighting stance.

Somehow Chiasa had come home, and though she looked completely fine physically, outwardly she appeared emotional.

"You have *no right*." I tried not to let the Huntsman's authority leak too much into my tone, but it was nearly impossible. The air around me turned crisp, the scent of snow and fresh ice taking over.

She regarded me coldly. "Mine is the *only* right."

"Let her in, Marcus." Cass's voice rang out from inside. "She has a right to mourn too. She's no longer a threat, we made sure of that."

It took me a moment to work through everything, but finally, I stepped aside and let the woman through to where her daughter and the memorial of her late daughter were.

They cried for a time, and it was so awkward that I had no choice but to move away, asking the others to keep an ear out for anything so I could come running.

I stood at the base of a large tree, the blossoms of it falling down around me as I pulled out my phone. There were the usual suspects online, the news reporting an uptick in vigilantes taking to the streets to war against crime and things. What caught my eye was that the majority of them stated that these people were super strong. Or very fast.

Was it Zeke doing more again? The videos were still out there, but there were people like Cornelius the Bigdealius who commented and called it a fake video that someone made just to fuck with people for a movie or something.

Then there was Prisoner of Kazkaban who stated, "These vigilantes ain't nothing but hoodlums and varmints! They'll be sorted out soon, but y'all stay safe out there."

I had to laugh. How many online personas did the phone gnomes have access to?

There was supposed to be an address from the president on this, which made me roll my eyes.

The man stood at the podium with his security team around him as he addressed the crowd, "My fellow Americans. I come to you today with strange news in these troubling times, and I swear to you, until recently I thought all of it a hoax too."

My heart beat wildly as I watched the scene unfolding. Theodorous the Ventricle of Ohio stood behind him as the president motioned back toward him. "This young man, Theodorous, claims to be a part of a secret watcher society called the Wardens, and says that the supernatural world is real."

The crowd gasped as something blotted out the sun above them, a massive creature that reminded me of a dragon but the arms were replaced with great wings. This thing was easily the size of an F-22 and looked mean as shit.

Screaming began and Theo stepped up to the mic. "Ladies and gentlemen, do not be alarmed! This is my partner in all this, the man who will show you that this world is just as real as you and I. For he has been to another world and when he speaks to you, you'll know the truth!"

Trepidation made my mouth go dry, almost like I'd tried to eat sand.

The beast landed and shifted its shape so that it stood there in a dark-skinned human form that reminded me of the night sky and I *knew* that this was Zeke.

"Monsters and myths are real, folks." His voice was soft, but there was no doubt about what he was saying as he stared out into the crowd of people too frightened to speak. "The gods watch over you, and play games with your souls, and it's time to decide if you want to play that way or not."

He stared into the camera as he said this next part. "I didn't. And I'll make sure that no one else ever has to worry about that again." As if he knew I would see this, he added, "Everyone deserves a chance to do the right thing."

"Marcus!" Galaxy's voice called excitedly. I looked up to find her running toward me with a piece of paper in her hand.

"Where have you been?" I cried, glad she was okay, but I held my phone up and said, "We have a fucking problem."

"Not important." She huffed and patted the paper. "I found it. I found the next sliver that Hollow had spoken about."

I was having trouble wrapping my head around what she was saying over the replay of what was on my phone. "What?"

She smiled and shoved the paper into my face, forcing me to look at it. It was a map of the ocean with a large slit in the middle of it, a term written in a language I couldn't make out on it.

"This is cool and all, but we've been publicly outed, Galaxy."

"We knew that would happen." She huffed and stomped her foot.

"Not this fast!" I shot back and she just glared at me. "Fine! What... what're you trying to tell me?"

"Atlantis, Marcus." My heart stopped as she tapped the paper and said again, "The next sliver of my Dominion and memories is in Atlantis."

I fell into the grass at the foot of the tree and leaned back as all of this swirled in my mind and said the only thing that came to me in that instance that wasn't a scream of near psychotic break, "Fuck."

ABOUT CHRISTOPHER JOHNS

Christopher Johns is a former photojournalist for the United States Marine Corps with published works telling hundreds of other peoples' stories through word, photo, and even video. But throughout that time, his editors and superiors had always said that his love of reading fantasy and about worlds of fantastic beauty and horrible power bled into his work. That meant he should write a book.

Well, ta-da!

Chris has been an avid devourer of fantasy and science fiction for more than twenty years and looks forward to sharing that love with his son, his loving fiancée and almost anyone he could ever hope to meet.

Connect with Chris:
Facebook.com/AxeDruidAuthor
Twitter.com/JonsyJohns

ABOUT MOUNTAINDALE PRESS

Dakota and Danielle Krout, a husband and wife team, strive to create as well as publish excellent fantasy and science fiction novels. Self-publishing *The Divine Dungeon: Dungeon Born* in 2016 transformed their careers from Dakota's military and programming background and Danielle's Ph.D. in pharmacology to President and CEO, respectively, of a small press. Their goal is to share their success with other authors and provide captivating fiction to readers with the purpose of solidifying Mountaindale Press as the place 'Where Fantasy Transforms Reality.'

Connect with Mountaindale Press:
MountaindalePress.com
Facebook.com/MountaindalePress
Twitter.com/_Mountaindale
Instagram.com/MountaindalePress

MOUNTAINDALE PRESS TITLES

GameLit and LitRPG

The Completionist Chronicles,
The Divine Dungeon,
Full Murderhobo, and
Year of the Sword by Dakota Krout

Arcana Unlocked by Gregory Blackburn

A Touch of Power by Jay Boyce

Red Mage and
Farming Livia by Xander Boyce

Space Seasons by Dawn Chapman

Ether Collapse and
Ether Flows by Ryan DeBruyn

Dr. Druid by Maxwell Farmer

Bloodgames by Christian J. Gilliland

Threads of Fate by Michael Head

Lion's Lineage by Rohan Hublikar and Dakota Krout

Wolfman Warlock by James Hunter and Dakota Krout

Axe Druid,
Mephisto's Magic Online, and
High Table Hijinks by Christopher Johns

Skeleton in Space by Andries Louws

Chronicles of Ethan by John L. Monk

Pixel Dust and
Necrotic Apocalypse by David Petrie

Viceroy's Pride by Cale Plamann

Henchman by Carl Stubblefield

Artorian's Archives by Dennis Vanderkerken and Dakota Krout